DARK LEGACY

by

SAMANTHA LEIGH

AmErica House
Baltimore

First printing

ISBN: 1–58851–891–4
PUBLISHED BY AMERICA HOUSE BOOK PUBLISHERS
www.publishamerica.com
Baltimore

Printed in the United States of America

Acknowledgements

First to my husband, whose steadfast support has opened doors for me I never knew were there.

And to my children, who exhibited patience beyond their years for their mother's hours of endless typing.

To my friends—Mary for helping me through the process, and Ab for giving me the kick I needed to begin.

To Andy and Lois who were brave enough to read the first draft. And to my mother, who always said I could do whatever I put my mind to.

Finally, to my father, who shares with me a kindred spirit and a writer's soul.

Thanks dad, you'll never know....

Dedication

To my dear sister, Sarina,
for all those dark nights we shared.
You know better than anyone how
much this book means to both of us.
Love always, your sister Sam.

Prologue

It was a place she'd stood many times before, on this crumbling stone wall, but never had the scene before her stole her breath away, as it did now. So many...my God...there were so many. She'd known, yes...though the sun was warm on her neck and the wildlife at her feet denied the existence of a winter, cold and harsh, she had known. For weeks she'd walked streets of desolate destruction and it was in the silence that she had known, the raw and aching silence that sharpened the air with a constant reminder of things past. But to see...to count...ripped open wounds she thought had begun to heal.

Fresh graves dotted the uneven terrain of the cemetery, stretching as far back as the creek that bordered the church property. Like the work of an army of overzealous ants, the mounds each peaked to a perfect rise. A few lay alone among the older graves, fit in wherever there'd been room, but most were grouped together in fours and fives, two large mounds were alongside two or three smaller ones. And some were so small, so terribly small...their little rises were barely visible amidst the others. Three yellow daffodils held by a white ribbon lay atop every site, the tedious efforts of a town still in shock.

The bodies had been transported as soon as the ground thawed and for nearly a month she listened to the bulldozers as they went about their grim task. Wherever she was during the day, whatever she was doing, she heard them, though no one in town dared speak of it. Those who were left, that was. They went about their business of clearing streets and hastily rebuilding and turned a deaf ear to the constant hum of trucks on the hill...turned a blind eye to the emptiness that greeted them every way they looked. But she heard them and when she closed her eyes at night, the hum of the trucks followed her into her dreams.

The heart and soul of her town now lay beneath six feet of

dirt and as her eyes scanned the cemetery, she felt the pain that rose from this earth. The fear, the confusion. *How...how had this happened...*It was the same question she'd asked for weeks now.

The small hand in hers tightened, bringing her back to the stone wall, to the bright summer day around her. She squeezed back.

It was time.

They walked slow, hampered by foliage that had taken advantage of the preoccupied cemetery workers. The small hand was hot and slippery against her palm and the shorter legs took two steps for each of hers, but she could wait. There was no rush.

When at last they reached the newest sites, she read the writing on each cold slab of rock. Names she'd heard since childhood paraded by, each with a face and a voice that echoed in her mind. Again and again, she stopped to clear her eyes and calm her pounding heart, until she moved faster down the rows, no longer reading each name, but scanning quickly for just one.

She found it by the weeping willow tree at the west end of the lot. Three slate–gray stones, side by side. Only two were covered with fresh earth. The third lay closest to the tree, surrounded by grass that was almost obscene in its brightness. This stone had faded with age and though the writing was still clear, there was no need to read the familiar words today.

She came upon a shady area under the tree and stopped by the first stone. Dropping to her knees, she closed her eyes and breathed in the warm air, trying to drive out the drafty places where winter cold still lingered. She could hear the creek from here, the rushing torrent of water that flowed endlessly from the peaks above the town. She smiled. It was good that the sound reached this place, good that the silence was filled with the hopeful noises of life, regenerated.

Her fingers ran over the writing in the stone, tracing each letter and feeling the gentle cut of granite on her skin. Whispered words flowed from her lips, words she'd said before, but not at this place, not with the sound of the creek in her ears and the reassuring touch of summer brushing her face.

Slowly, painfully, she stood. The second stone beckoned her, but she hesitated, wanting to listen to the water and let its cleansing noise wash away the clutter around her heart. Finally, with her head down, she moved away.

A mound, identical to the rest, rose from the base of this second stone, though its yellow flower had fallen from its perch. Now it lay at her feet and she stared at it for a moment, watching its brilliant petals flutter in the wind. Then, with a grunt, she crushed it beneath her shoe.

She stared at the stone…at the words and found herself reading them over and over again. They offended her, with their assuming tone and sickly sweet intention. They were lying, deceitful words that only wanted the appearance of what they said. She kicked soil from the mound, onto the slab and felt better to see some of the words disappear. But one remained and it stared back at her. She knocked down more of the soil, then ground the dirt into the chiseled markings with her shoe, until only the M was left of the offensive word.

The wind picked up and on its gust rode a voice, old and scratchy with time. It rang true in her mind though and she shuddered to hear it.

Get back here you little bitches…

She stepped away quickly, feeling the old fear race through her veins. No, there would be no tears today for the woman that lay beneath the earth. No forgiveness for things done long ago. Never would she forget, though the strength it took to keep it alive was taking its toll, still…she would not forget. Not now, not ever.

The small hand was pulling at hers and when the words finally came, they reached her ears only on a brief gust of wind.

"Is he really gone?"

So tiny were the sounds she wasn't sure at first she'd heard them. She looked into those eyes, those narrow, dark eyes that had seen far too much for their short years. Fear, bright and shining jumped from behind them, as if just saying the words could bring it all back.

She squeezed the hand again, searching for something that could take away all she saw in those dark eyes...something that would bring joy back to all the dark places for both of them.

The wind shifted, blowing her hair from her cheeks and rustling her clothes. A familiar scent wafted by her nose and it took her a moment to identify it, but when she did, a smile eased her face. It was the smell of summer. The smell of new beginnings and promises for the future. The sweet smell of honeysuckle that tickled her senses brought her back to a time when she'd known joy and the hope for a future. A time when only the creek rose above the sound of childish laughter.

But it was one summer in particular that rose above all the others. Their last summer. The summer that began with all the wondrous celebration of youth and ended with the harsh realities of betrayal and death. And from that summer was born an evil that followed her throughout the years, always hiding beneath the surface...whispering to her...calling to her. An evil she only had come to fully understand a few weeks ago.

PART ONE

Chapter One
The End of the Beginning

Kate smiled as she skipped across the thirteen stones that enabled her to cross the creek. She liked to take them fast, challenging herself to reach the other side quicker each time. Her steps landed securely and Kate made the final leap to shore with an exhilarated little yelp.

It had been a good day. Miss Trimble had pulled her aside after class and told her how impressed she'd been with her paper on the Statue of Liberty. Kate could still see her eyes glowing as she spoke. Miss Trimble had wanted to hang it on the bulletin board at the front of the school, but Kate shook her head, snatched the paper and ran from the classroom. She folded it into a tiny square and jammed it deep in her pocket until she could get home to put it with the others under her bed.

She continued along the creek, humming to herself and kicking pebbles into the water as she made her way to the cut in the earth that would lead her back into the woods. Getting a firmer grip on her books, she climbed the ridge and was circling around the tree at the top when a rabbit skittered across her path. She jumped, almost falling back down. The rabbit darted into a nook at the base of the tree, then turned to stare up at her. Kate moved slowly, careful not to make any noises that might scare it away, and then crouched down so they were eye to eye. The rabbit didn't move and as she inched closer, she saw this was just a baby. Its brown fur was still thin and shiny and its ears seemed too big for its tiny head.

"Hey little guy, where's your Mamma?"

The rabbit twitched his nose.

Kate crept closer and closer, scraping her knees in the pine needles and holding her books with one hand. She wanted to see its eyes. Wanted to see if what she'd heard about rabbits was true.

That they were special and if you looked long enough and were quiet enough, they could tell you secrets. What secrets, she didn't know, it was something her Daddy had told her. They read a bed-time book about rabbits one night and in the story, the rabbit had been very special indeed. Be careful of the rabbits Katie, her Daddy had said, they are the forest's special creatures and carry secrets as old as the world itself. Kate had been impressed and had turned it over in her mind, long after he kissed her goodnight. What secrets could they be?

But now she would never know, because Daddy was gone. He had been gone so long now that Kate had trouble seeing his face anymore, but she could still hear his voice. It was deep and smooth and when he wasn't laughing, his voice had always sounded like he was about to. She wished she had asked him.

Growing more determined, Kate moved closer, snapping a twig beneath her palm. The rabbit jumped at the sound and disappeared around the tree, splashing through the puddle on the other side.

Leaping to her feet, she ran around the base of the tree, but the rabbit was gone. Only a bobbing honeysuckle bush showed it had been there at all.

"Hey kitty, kitty," said a harsh voice from behind.

Spinning around, she smacked into the broad chest of Ben Easley, the biggest kid in the fifth grade. He was smiling.

"I don't know why you call me that," Kate said, letting her anger boil over before Ben realized he'd scared her. She hitched her books higher on her hip, wishing she hadn't forgotten her book bag this morning. "It's stupid."

"Don't call me stupid, *Kat*lyn" he said, pronouncing it like the feline. He advanced a few steps and took a swing at her books. Kate was expecting this though and moved away.

"Just want to play, kitty cat. Hey, check this out." He turned his pants pockets inside out, holding the insides toward her. "Ever kiss a rabbit between the ears?"

Ben broke up laughing at his joke and Ricky Kerrisk,

standing a few feet behind him, let out a nasally snort through the greasy mop of hair that covered his face. Ricky was only slightly smaller than Ben and the two of them made a formidable team at Newclare Elementary. Even though Kate was a grade behind the boys, she had run into them more times than she could count, but never alone, or in the woods.

She wrinkled her nose at Ben and hopped over a dead tree trunk. "You're gross."

"Hey, where are you going?" Ben rolled on his belly over the trunk and followed. "We just want to talk to you. How come you're always so quiet, cat got your tongue?"

More snorting laughter erupted from Ricky.

"Not anyone worth talking to, just a bunch of *stupid* fat boys," Kate said, backing out of range and behind the tree.

"What did you say?" Ben was moving around the side of the tree, angry, red patches emerging on his cheeks that matched the color of his hair.

"You heard me," she said, continuing around the other side.

"She called us stupid, Ben." Ricky closed in on the left, an ugly sneer twisting his face.

Called you fat too. Kate would have laughed, but for the mean glint she saw in Ben's gray eyes.

"Well at least my mom ain't no whore," Ben said, breathing hard. "My mom says your mom sleeps with anything in pants."

"She's just jealous and besides," Kate said, standing on her tiptoes to stand eye to eye with Ben. "So does your *dad*."

The words were barely out of her mouth before Ben was on her. His hand reached out and snatched the ends of her hair, pulling her down and into the puddle at the base of the tree. Her books flew to the ground, as she threw her hands out to catch her fall. He held her face in the mud and she choked. Thick goop traveled up her nose and down the back of her throat.

"You shut up! Shut up!"

He let go for an instant to get a better grip and Kate took her chance. She shot out her foot and felt the gratifying thud of heel connecting with bone. Ben let out a strangled cry, falling on top of her and knocking her back into the puddle. They wrestled for a moment, until they were both covered, head to foot. She slithered out from under him, gave him a hard kick in the back and scrambled to her feet.

Ricky stood looking on, his eyes dumb with disbelief as Kate took off for the woods, her mud–soaked hair flying out behind her.

"That bitch, come on we gotta get her!"

Breaking into a full run, she soared over the scattered branches and brush. Ben and Ricky were huffing and puffing only a few feet behind her, so she put out a little extra effort to lengthen the distance. They entered an area of thick trees and Kate managed to pull far enough ahead to chance a look back.

Ben was still coming, his red face pouring sweat through a layer of mud, his stained football jersey heaving with effort. Ricky was several paces behind him and losing ground fast.

She turned, just in time to dodge a low–hanging tree branch before it smacked her in the head. Instead of running on though, she stopped, the branch still in her hand and a smile widening on her face. The smile spread into a grin, as the boys careened toward her. She waited until Ben was three paces away, and let go. He took it flat across the face. "Fuckin' bitch!" She giggled, avoiding his groping hands and backtracked toward the creek.

Jumping off the shoreline and flying over the first two rocks, her foot landed firmly on the third. She crossed the creek and made the final leap to the shore, scraping her bare knees before scrambling up the embankment. She paused at the top to crouch behind a bush and watch.

Ben and Ricky burst from the trees a few moments later, lumbered down the slight incline and splashed into the water. Hands outstretched like ugly, overgrown ballerinas, they tiptoed across the stones, their feet slipping on the wet surface. Ben spotted her hiding behind the bush and he shook his fist, yelling more obscenities. The gesture threw him off balance though and as he turned to grab Ricky's t–shirt, Ricky shoved him away. Together, they fell on their backsides into the icy water.

"You asshole," Ben sputtered, "what'cha do that for?" He sat up and hit Ricky in the back.

"Me? You're the one who fell!" Shaking the water from his hair, Ricky stood, waist–deep and glared down at his friend. "Jeez, my mom's gonna kill me now."

"Not if I kill you first," and with that, Ben lunged at him, dragging him back into the water.

Kate stifled another giggle, as she got to her feet and headed for the darkness of the trees. She heard them splashing and yelling for a while until their voices faded behind her.

Heading south, she followed the creek downstream until the ground rose and the water widened into something that could pass for a river. Kate skirted the cliff's edge, enjoying the thrill. It was a fifty foot drop to the bottom and the rock she kicked over the side bounced several times before making a splash far below.

She watched the rushing current for a moment and then glanced at the sky. Dustings of pink were beginning to etch the tree line, fading gently into blue. Kate backed away from the creek and headed for the trees. She would have to hurry now; Joey was waiting.

It was the project. It had to be. Every summer Joey came up with an idea that kept them busy for most of the warm months until school came again. The year before last, they built a dam down by Lady's Elbow, named that for the way the creek narrowed and turned, before widening again. They had underestimated the depth of the elbow though and only succeeded in getting soaked to the bone for three weeks straight. The freezing water had kept Kate at home with a cold for the rest of the summer.

Last summer, Joey had wanted to build a fort in the forest. For weeks, she and Joey had scavenged the town for scrap wood and when Joey thought they had enough, she'd talked Uncle Dave into loaning them some supplies from his store. The fort had turned out well and the girls spent most of the summer beneath its sloping ceiling. Those idiot boys had found it though and with great joy, Bed and Ricky trampled it down until it was just broken boards scattered over the ground.

Kate continued until she came upon a clearing and stopped, always in awe of the giant house, no matter how many times she saw it.

Its three stories were painted a wretched green that had peeled over the years, leaving naked areas of white. The roof came to a point in the middle and a rusted weather vane creaked lazily at the top. Thick vines and brush taller than Kate surrounded the house, like a moat. And as she stood at the edge of the clearing she realized for the first time that it was, overall, a rather ugly house.

But it was theirs. She and Joey had spent countless hours playing on the crumbling front porch and in the jungle maze that was the backyard. Last summer was the first time they'd gotten up the nerve to go inside and it had been disappointing. For years, Kate had imagined ghosts and goblins and monsters locked in the cellar, but there was none of that. Just some broken furniture, animal nests burrowed in the corners and mountains upon mountains of dust.

The only way in was through the backdoor, since the years had settled over the house, jamming the front door closed. Kate started toward the door.

"There you are, I've been waiting forever."

Joey was standing in one of the third floor windows, her feet planted apart as she grasped the frame above with both hands. Smiling, she leaned out over the three–story drop. She caught Kate's anxious look and leaned even further, dangling one foot over the backyard.

Kate looked away. "What are you doing up there?"

"What do you mean, me? How about you?" She pulled back in and put her hands on her hips. "Been playing in the mud again?"

Kate grinned and shrugged her shoulders.

"Well are you coming up, or what?"

She didn't need to be asked twice. Burrowing into the maze, she found the path easily and followed it until she reached the backdoor. She slammed through the kitchen, up the stairs, careful to avoid the broken boards on the second floor and reached the attic in record time.

"It's about time," Joey said as Kate joined her by the window. "So what do you think?"

Kate looked around the room and for a moment, couldn't speak. The trash and clutter had all been moved to a far corner and all that remained was a table, Kate recognized from downstairs and several cans of paint in the center of the room.

"We can get chairs too, I saw them in the living room and we'll bring in some games from home," Joey was saying, but Kate wasn't listening. She was staring at the paint cans that read, 'Dave's Supply' in black letters on top.

She turned to Joey. "What color?"

"What do you think?"

Oh, what color…only one color had held Kate's interest for a year, or more. The same one that colored the front of every one of her notebooks and was on every piece of clothing she wore.

Skipping over to the cans, Kate bent to read the label on the side and grinned. Turquoise.

"So?" Joey stood beside her, eyes twinkling. "What do you think?"

Kate smiled up at her and then threw her arms around Joey's neck, not caring if she called her baby.

* * * * *

"Step on a line," Joey sang, jumping on the break in the sidewalk with both feet. "Break your mother's spine. Step on a crack, give her a whack." She giggled and threw her book bag over one shoulder.

17

Kate trudged behind, head down, hands shoved in her pockets. Hot early summer sun beat down on the back of her neck and her high–collared shirt was chafing her throat.

"What's your problem?" Joey waited for her under the shelter of the apple trees that grew in Mrs. Culloty's yard. They were the only apple trees in town as far as Kate knew, and she and Joey helped themselves every chance they got.

"You've been a mope all day," Joey said when Kate didn't answer. She bit into an apple and let the juice dribble down her chin. "Your face is gonna stay like that if you're not careful you know."

"Bull," Kate said, her frown lessening a little.

"It's true. Remember Clefty Chloe? Why do you think she had to have that surgery?"

"It was like that when she was born, she told me."

"Nah–uh, Rosie Parker told me it was because she got in trouble for not taking out the garbage and stuck her lip out at her dad and when she woke up the next day it was frozen like that."

"Bull."

Joey laughed and handed her an apple. "Guess we'll see," she said, looking over Kate's shoulder. "Come on, she's looking at us."

Mrs. Culloty's puffy face parted the curtains and she wagged a finger at them. Joey waved back and skipped away.

"It's the last day of school, how can you be mopey?"

Kate shrugged her shoulders and let her chin drop to her chest. "I got yelled at in class," she mumbled.

"For what?"

"What do you think?"

Joey laughed. "You need to learn to keep your big mouth shut, Kate."

"She gave me a note." She crumpled the paper into a ball inside her pocket. It seemed to be carrying a heat of its own, warming her even more.

"You got a note on the last day of school?"

18

"Yeah."

Blowing her bangs from her forehead, Joey scowled. "They can't do that, its gotta to be against the law."

"You think?"

"And besides, it's not like you won't lose it over the summer or something, right?"

Kate's frown was completely gone now. "And I won't even have Miss Trimble next year."

"See, now cheer up." She paused as her eyes landed on something down the street. A grin spread across her face. "I know just the thing…"

Kate followed her gaze and saw Ben and Ricky coming out of Kelly's Kandy. They each held a candy bar in one hand and probably two or three more in their pockets.

"Put your book bag on, Katie," Joey said, her steely gaze never wavering from the boys. She jumped off the sidewalk and sunk her teeth into the apple.

Kate slipped the straps over her shoulders. "What are you doing?"

Joey shot her a dangerously innocent grin. "I'm your sister," she said, taking another bite. "And as your sister, I consider it my duty to cheer you up."

Kate shook her head, but followed.

They came within half a block of the boys when Joey shouted out. "Hey, lard ass!" And with an unfortunate, but dead–on aim, she pelted Ben's round rear with the core of her apple.

Like a clown on a top, he spun around, a chunk of chocolate falling out of his stunned mouth and leaving a smear across his chin. The tree branch welt that spread across his face from left jaw to right eyebrow, reddened when he saw what had hit him and who had done the hitting.

"Heard my little sister *kicked your ass*," Joey yelled insanely.

The chocolate bar twisted and fell to the ground as Ben broke out of his shock and took a few dazed steps toward them.

19

Joey's yanked on Kate's book bag. "Quit laughing and run, you idiot."

Kate ran.

Like the wind, she flew over the sizzling pavement, her sneakers barely making contact. Her bag thumped against her back in time to her steps and her pencil box rattled out a joyous tune. The rushing air lifted the sticky strands of hair from the back of her neck and cooled her sweat. *I can fly*. With her arms outstretched, she let out a whooping howl and lengthened her stride to race full tilt to the bottom of Shannon Street.

Joey glanced behind them and put her hand out to stop Kate. Ben and Ricky were just rounding the corner at the top of the hill and Joey waited for a moment before taking off again.

"This way," she yelled, taking a right onto Galway.

Kate ran after her, confused, but willing. Home was back the other way.

Again, Joey stopped and waited for the boys. They came, huffing and blowing, but no less eager for revenge. It shone in their dark eyes...their bared teeth...their clenched fists...

"You ready?" Joey crouched behind the tall fence that enclosed Mr. O'Neil back yard.

Now Kate understood. "Yeah," she said in a thick, hungry voice she'd never used before.

Ben and Ricky drew closer. Only a block away now...just three houses. Closer...closer...as Kate's stomach jumped and jived to its own private concert. She sucked her in lip and bit down, hard.

"Almost...almost," Joey whispered, timing out their arrival and slowly rising. Not a trace of doubt shadowed her face. Not a sliver of fear weakened her mouth. She was ready.

"Go, go, go!"

They bolted through the little alley and around to the front of Mr. O'Neil's house. The curtains opened like a whip and Mr. O'Neil thrust his face in the window. He saw the girls and without skipping a beat, threw the curtains closed and flung open the door.

"Get off my grass!" He bellowed, while hobbling on his bad leg to the side of the house for his garden hose.

Through the perfectly square bushes, across the small stoned walkway, around the parade of violets and soaring over the fenced in army of rainbow colored roses, the girls were well within the safety of the opposite sidewalk, before Mr. O'Neil emerged with the hose.

"Goddamn it, I said get outta my yard!" The faucet squeaked three times and then a stream of water burst through the trigger as Mr. O'Neil took aim. A flicker of familiar pleasure lit up his face as he steadied his arm, like a pro and pulled the handle.

Kate and Joey skidded to a halt, well out of range of the garden hose. They turned to watch the show.

Ben and Ricky came barreling out of the alley and headlong into the yard. So intent on their mission, they never saw Mr. O'Neil, standing by the house, a gleeful smile on his face and the nozzle of his hose now aligned with the backs of their sweaty heads. Ricky, who tagged several paces behind Ben, took it first. His shaggy hair blew out like a halo for an instant and then covered his face in a wet mop. Ben turned to see why his friend had shouted and the full force of the water pressure hit him in the chest, driving him backward. He flailed his arms in a desperate attempt to keep his balance and then fell with a squish on his backside. Ricky, with long, wet hair stuck to his face, didn't see Ben writhing on the ground and promptly tripped over him.

Mr. O'Neil moved in for the kill. Opening his grip on the handle, the stream widened and he was able to soak both boys without moving an inch.

"That'll teach your little punk–asses to come on *my* grass. Ra–ta–ta–ta–ta–ta–ta." On and on, like a machine–gun he shouted as Ben and Ricky took turns falling over each other in the wet grass, trying to flee the relentless torrent of water that now soaked the boys so thoroughly, Kate could see the outline of Ben's un-

21

derwear through his brown pants.

"Time to go, little sister." Joey took one last look and started away. Kate followed with her head lifted toward the brilliant sky; all gloomy thoughts of that morning wiped clean by the triumph of the glorious afternoon.

* * * * *

"Please hear our plea, oh ye most powerful and merciful ones. Take pity on our young sister and show her the error of her wretched ways." Joey sprinkled a handful of pine needles on the fire. It flared up and both girls scooted back.

"Where'd you get the matches?" Kate sat opposite, holding her knees and picking a burr from her sock.

"Shhhh," Joey hissed and lifted her face to the trees swaying above. "Keep watchful guard over her bewitched and unruly *tongue* and let it not create any more undoing. Let her thoughts reach her brain before they spill from her lips. This we ask of you, in your oh so infinite mercy." She opened her eyes and nodded to Kate. "Give it."

Kate rolled her eyes, but pulled the note out of her pocket and gave it to Joey. Unfolding it carefully, Joey waved it over the flames and started again.

"Great gods of the Teacher's Note, we call upon you, hear our cry and forgive little Katie all her iniquities—"

"That's not even a word—"

"And bless her with the gift of *silence*," Joey glared at Kate before continuing. "We offer this small sacrifice as a symbol of her atonement and pray you see fit to forgive her pathetic little soul."

Holding her hand high over the flames, Joey crumpled the note and tossed it in the air. A gust of wind carried it up, up and far above the fire. It rode on the freak gust, spinning and twirling and rising ever higher in its journey to the sky. Just as Kate started to rise, the wind slipped out from underneath it and the note crashed into the fire, like a meteor. Ashes flew out from the little pit Joey had dug and stung Kate's leg.

"Time to go," Joey said.

"Can we stop by the house? I want to get started."

Joey glanced at the sky. "No, it's already too late," she said in a voice Kate knew well. "We never should have stayed this long."

"Yeah, okay."

Joey gave her a little smile and thumped her on the head. "We'll go tomorrow, I promise, as soon as she leaves, okay?"

"Okay."

Kate stood and helped her sister stamp out the fire. A few minutes later, all that remained was a faint smoky smell in their clothes.

The girls said little on the way home. The gentle breeze picked up and rocked the towering spruces until a strange whining echoed through the canyon. Kate's hair slapped wildly at her face and ticked her nose. The wind continued to rise and call through the trees, sending a shiver down Kate's spine and moving her to fall in step beside Joey. Joey, her face pinched into a tight mask, glanced at her and instinctively slipped a hand into Kate's.

They stopped, as they always did, at the end of the rocky dirt lot. Their pastel–yellow trailer sat in the middle, stained and sagging. The roof buckled in the middle, frowning at the girls. Rocks poked out of the hard ground around the trailer, making it impossible for anything, but weeds to grow in the yard.

Joey's hand twitched inside hers and Kate looked up. A familiar anger burned in Joey's eyes as they darted from the trailer to Kate, to the slowly clouding sky and back to the trailer. Her legs bent as if to run and the grip on Kate's hand tightened as they locked eyes. Kate held her breath, waiting…hoping…

But Joey broke the spell and looked back at the trailer. "Come on."

Kate put her head down and followed.

CHAPTER TWO
FALLING AWAY

Summer came as it does in the mountains with startling flashes of rain that blow away before doing much more than dampening the ground. Wind that stirred the trees throughout the year, turned warm and heavy with the scent of the few flowers that dared to show their blossoms for the brief growing season. And everywhere was the sound of the creek, overfed to the point of bursting from the melting snow on the highest peaks above town. Its waters were an icy shade of freezing, having no regard for the calendar month.

In the attic though, only the heat reached the girls. The heat that made Kate's shirt cling to her back and caused sweat to sting her eyes. A deliberate and strangling heat, laden with the toxic fumes of turquoise paint. A dull headache hung in the back of Kate's head, as she dipped her brush again.

Joey worked on the other side of the room. She'd tied a scarf around her head and knotted her shirt, revealing a deeply tanned stomach. Splatters of turquoise covered her clothes, her bare legs and grubby sneakers. She was oblivious to this however, as she balanced precariously on the overturned bucket and worked on the ceiling. Her strokes were quick and precise, leaving long thick lines across the ghastly gray.

Kate's brush clattered across the floor and she sat with a sigh. "Let's take a break."

Flicking Kate a glance over her shoulder, Joey smirked and turned back to the ceiling. "You're such a weakling."

"It's hot and I'm tired," Kate said, hearing the whine, but not caring.

"A *gutless* weakling, there's a word for that."

"Shut up."

"Lame–ass, yeah that's it." Joey jumped off the bucket and

25

tossed her brush beside the can.

Kate glared at her until Joey's hard smile softened.

"It is hot," she conceded, glancing at the window. It was the only one on the east side, where the wind came from, not closed completely. But it too was painted shut. "Come on, let's it try again."

Kate pushed herself off the floor and shuffled across the floor to the window.

"On the count of three," Joey said, getting in position.

"One."

"Two."

"Three," they said together and pulled, baring teeth and grunting.

The window didn't budge.

Kate stepped back and rubbed her throbbing fingers. "We need some leverage."

Joey nodded, looking around the room. She spotted the broken rocking chair in the far corner and after ripping a board from it, shoved it into the crack. The board splintered like a twig under Joey's weight.

"Well shit," she said.

Kate sighed, watching the trees blow back and forth in the wind. She could almost smell the evergreen. "I'm going downstairs, you coming?" She asked, popping the lid back onto the can. The edges were filled with paint and Kate pounded on the lid a few times to force it closed.

"Hold on a sec, Katie."

Kate turned to see Joey, holding the metal bucket over her head. The weight of it caused her to stumble back before she regained her balance and swung it toward the window.

"Joey no!"

The glass shattered, sending shards onto the porch roof below. Joey let the bucket roll to the floor.

"Who cares?" She shoved the bucket to the next window. "Not like there's anybody to see."

Picking it up by the twisted metal handle, she swung around in a half circle and blew the second window to bits.

"You just going to stand there?"

Kate skipped to the bucket and pulled it to the windows on the other side of the room. The ragged edges of the handle cut into her palm and the metal made an awful noise as she dragged it over the floor.

It was much heavier than it looked and Kate swung around with it once and then again to lift it high enough to reach the window. As it crashed through the glass, she let out a piercing shriek and broke into giggles. Deliciously cool air rushed through the gaping hole and Kate dropped the bucket to inhale the sweet scents.

"One more should do it," Joey said as she knocked out the remaining glass with the end of her paintbrush.

"Yes ma'am." Kate kicked–shoved the bucket down a couple of windows.

This time she dragged it around on the floor for several spins before letting it take off into the air. Faster and faster as her hair fanned out around her, until it seemed the bucket was pulling her instead of she pulling it. She caught a glimpse of Joey on one of the rotations. Her hands were on her hips and the smirk was back on her face. Just as it felt like the handle would tear from her hands, she leaned toward the window and scrunched her eyes shut. A much louder crash sounded through the air as the bucket broke through the glass…and kept going.

Kate stared dumbly at the broken handle in her hands and then out the window. The silver bucket made several graceful spins against the bright blue sky before it fell out of sight into the back yard.

"Good job." Joey joined her at the window and the girls leaned over the shards of glass to look into the yard. The bucket was nowhere to be seen in the tall weeds.

"It wasn't my fault," Kate said, holding up the handle.

"Well I'm not getting it."

"Me either."

She and Joey stared silently down at the yard for a few more moments before Joey spoke in a solemn voice. "And so the jungle has claimed yet another victim."

The girls giggled uncontrollably, leaning on each other for support and then picked up their brushes and returned to work.

* * * * *

The light from the western windows was turning a salmon pink and the shadows rose high on the freshly painted wall as Kate wiped her hands on a piece of old sweatshirt.

"You ready?" Joey swung the backpack over her shoulder.

Kate closed the paint can. Over the last few days, they'd finished the east wall, most of the ceiling and the area around the bookcases. Joey's determination was contagious, as it was about all things and they were finishing much faster than Kate had thought. Now, while she stood, marveling at their hard work, she wondered if there was anything Joey couldn't do, but then quickly put the thought out of her head before the admiration spread to her face where Joey would see it.

"Plenty more to do tomorrow," Joey said as she waited by the stairs. "So stop staring and let's get out of here."

The rest of the house was already lost in deep shadows and Kate let out a breath she didn't know she was holding when they finally reached the backdoor. She ducked and followed Joey into the path through the backyard. The fading afternoon sun greeted them on the other side.

Joey took in the coming twilight and called back to Kate. "Shortcut, come on." She pulled ahead, as she liked to do, leaving Kate to trail behind.

The sun was dipping below the tree line and Kate's nervous eyes darkened with the sky. Joey's pace hastened as she led them north, toward home. The cover of the trees thinned as the ground turned hard with eroded dirt. Bird calls and squirrel chatter died off behind them.

They had entered the Badlands.

It was a place Kate liked to avoid. Nothing grew here. Nothing. The charred, naked remains of pine trees stood against the gray earth, the only testament that it had once been a healthy and thriving part of the forest. Like crippled giants, the trees hung over Kate, their bare branches hunched and drooping, their spindly fingers grasping at the wind. Bony legs dug out from the base of the giants, as if frozen in half step. Some had collapsed over the ageless years and lay like fallen soldiers awaiting a mass burial. Not a sparrow made its nest in the many hollowed nooks, no possum or skunk burrowed under the exposed roots. A smoky breath wafted through the trunks, dirtied by the scent of ashes. Ashes that should have blown away long, long ago.

Joey cut a straight path through the dead trees, never wavering her step or glancing to either side. Her eyes were focused ahead, to the line of green that beckoned beyond. Kate jogged alongside and together they were soon out of the Badlands and back under the dark canopy of the evergreens.

Lower and lower the sun sank, racing them home...and winning. By the time the girls stopped at the end of the rocky dirt lot, the deep blue of night spread above them. The trailer sat in the wispy shadows, looking slightly out of focus in the tricky light. But Kate could see well enough that the lamp was on in the living room.

And the shades were down.

Panic washed over Joey's face and she fell back behind a tree. "Oh no," she moaned.

Kate crowded in beside her. "What are we going to do?"

"I don't know, how should I know?" Joey peeked around the tree as if expecting the door to the trailer to fly open at any moment. She glanced back at the way they had come, a rare moment of indecision clouding her eyes. A chipmunk scampered down the tree and Joey stared at, glassy eyed. It paused, sizing up the humans for an instant, then tittered harshly at them and hurried away.

Stupid tears filled Kate's eyes and she ground them away with her knuckle.

"Stop blubbering and let me think," Joey hissed, looking back at the trailer.

Kate bit her lip and turned away. Joey would get them out of this and tomorrow…tomorrow they would spend the morning at the creek before going to the house. The smell of the water before the sun rose completely was like candy to Kate. It was so different from the wet plant scent that hung in the air by mid–morning. There was a boulder about a half–mile downstream and when she stood on top of it, she had a spectacular view of the peaks at one end and the southern tip of the valley at the other. Miles and miles she could see, while the water rushed along below. It felt…powerful in some way, as if the whole world were within her reach.

Joey tugged her arm, giving her a nasty look when Kate didn't immediately follow. They skirted the trailer and picked their way through the trees until coming up to the rear, by their bedroom window. The pile of rocks was still stacked underneath.

Joey untied the knot in her shirt and tucked it into her shorts. "You stay here," she whispered. "Wait for me, okay? I mean it Kate, you wait and I'll come get you, okay?"

Kate was looking over Joey's shoulder at the trailer as she nodded. The sun was gone, so the light from the windows seemed to glare at the quiet blanket of night.

"Kate!" Joey grabbed her, tearing her fixed stare from the trailer. "Did you hear me? You stay here and don't move until I come get you."

"Okay."

"Katie…"

"Okay, I said okay." Kate's voice sounded strange in her ears, but not nearly at strange as the sheen in Joey's eyes. They sparkled magically, changing colors and brightening with each new hue. Only on one other occasion had Kate seen the colored lights in her sister's eyes. On a vague, dark night when the smoke had gagged her until she could no longer breathe. The night her daddy had—The night they moved to Newclare. Those lights had been in her sister's eyes all the way up the mountain, had glowed in the darkness of the car with a strange kind of energy that made Kate want to start crying again. It had been more like a dream by the next day and Kate hadn't thought about it since.

Now though, darkness swam through the colorful sparkles and it was this darkness that sent a wave of cold nausea to Kate's stomach.

Satisfied that Kate would do as she was told, Joey turned toward the trailer. Her feet carried her away…farther and out of Kate's reach. Her sister stopped at the edge of the clearing around the trailer and turned again. Kate could make out only a hazy image against the white lights of the trailer, but the colors in her eyes sparkled, nonetheless. A moment passed as the wind disappeared and the night faded in the distance.

"Joey—"

Kate took a step, but Joey turned away, crossing the dirt yard and hopping up on their stack of rocks. In a flash, she hauled herself through the open window the girls had climbed out of that morning. And she was gone.

Silence.

Kate strained to hear anything, but only the quiet chirping of the evening crickets could be heard. She saw a shadow move across the living room, but there was no way to tell if it was Joey or her mother. The shadow moved away and Kate sat back.

She could wait. Wait for Joey and then go to bed. She wouldn't even eat; she would just snuggle under her cool, pink sheets and when she woke up, the sun would be back and Joey would be packing for the day. Kate's head rested against the tree and little by little, tilted to the side, as her eyes slipped closed…

* * * * *

Something was coming at her through the woods. Something that moved stealthily, trying not to be heard. Twigs snapped and the faint rustle of leaves reached her suddenly alert ears. Kate jerked to face whatever was coming, knowing whatever it was, would be on her by the time she rose to her feet.

"Kate, it's me," came the voice that sounded like Joey's, but wasn't. It was deeper than Joey's and had strange scratches in it.

Kate shied away, confused to see her sister running toward her from behind, instead of from the trailer.

"Joey?"

"Shhhh." She dropped to her knees and peered through the darkness at the trailer.

Kate saw the lights had been turned off. The trailer sat in the blue light of the moon that now hung high above the trees.

"What happened?" Kate asked, trying desperately to push away the sleep in her mind.

Joey didn't answer, only continued to stare at the trailer, looking for something she didn't find. As if that helped her make up her mind, she nodded slightly and turned to Kate. There was something wrong with her face and again Kate shied away, not recognizing her sister. But then she moved closer and Kate relaxed. It was Joey. Joey with a fearful, animalistic look, but Joey all the same.

"What happened," Kate asked again.

"What?" Joey's eyes darted all around, not stopping on any one thing, looking for something in the trees.

"What happened!"

"Be quiet, jeez. She was pissed, what do you think?" Joey said this in her usual, condescending tone, but it came out forced and fake. She studied her hands, rubbing her fingers and then her bare arms. She didn't look at Kate.

"So can we go?"

"No, not yet."

"Why not? It's cold out here."

Joey sighed. "We gotta wait for her to go to sleep."

"Why—"

"Stop arguing with me Kate. I'm cold too."

"So why can't we go?"

"We just can't, okay? Shut up about it, we can wait out here a little while longer."

"But I want to go to bed, I'm tired, come on," Kate said, dropping her head back to the tree.

Joey finally looked up at her. "We are going to wait a while longer and *you* are going to shut up about it."

The angry words cut through Kate's fatigue and she felt tears sting the backs of her eyes. Would this night ever end? She turned and tucked her head under her arms, so Joey wouldn't see and get even more upset because she was blubbering again.

A small hot hand rubbed her back in a circular pattern. Joey waited patiently until Kate could fight back the tears and then pulled her away from the tree.

"Katie," Joey said. "We'll go soon, I promise. I just want to make sure it's okay."

Kate sniffed and wiped her nose with the back of her hand. "But why, what's going on?"

"There's something," Joey paused, trying to find the word. "Wrong...with mom, I don't know..." She trailed off, lost in an image that played behind her eyes.

"What do you mean? You said she was pissed, right?"

"Yeah, but that isn't it. Something's happened to her, I think." Joey looked down again.

"Is she hurt?"

"No."

"Then—"

Joey looked back up and stopped Kate cold. This was not her sister. Her sister didn't have those sunken, fearful eyes. Her sister didn't wring her hands as the person sitting in front of her did now. This person had a slump in her shoulders, a slump that made her look small and...and childlike. And there was more, so much more that threatened behind those dark eyes.

"When I got in there," she choked out, "she was waiting for me." She paused again and a bitter smile turned her lips. "It was like, she was *happy* to see me."

Kate stared at her, not understanding.

"She was happy, did you hear me Kate? She was *glad* we got caught, but not for the reason you're thinking." Once she finished, she let out her breath and it blew Kate's bangs back.

"But that's—"

"Yeah, I know," Joey said.

A limp breeze pushed a strand of Kate's hair by her lips and then stopped, as the silence of early morning settled around them. Even during summer, nights in the mountains were chilly at best and the cold seeped into Kate's limbs with a throbbing ache. Joey crawled to sit beside her and the girls huddled close, finding warmth between their bodies.

As the moon set behind the trees, the night entered its black hours. Hours which were meant only for sleeping. To be awake and alone were bleak hours filled with flimsy hope and minutes that crawled with fear. The night wore on and on for the two girls who laid in each other's arms at the base of the tree.

* * * * *

The next morning, she and Joey moved around cautiously, getting their breakfast and preparing for the day. Neither of them spoke, afraid to break the silence that had enveloped the trailer. Their mother was not home and when Kate had dared to peek into her room, the bed hadn't been slept in. She didn't know if Joey knew this, but if she did, she gave no indication.

Joey stood at the counter, packing their lunch. She stood at an awkward angle, favoring her left side. Her hands slapped the sandwiches together at breakneck speed and then threw them into her book bag.

"You ready?"

Kate nodded. No need to climb through their window this morning. The padlock on the front door had been left unlocked from the inside and Joey waited there for her. Her face was much more puffy and discolored today and Kate felt some relief that school was over so there would be no one to see.

Morning dew wet the grass and a thin fog hovered above the ground. The mist swirled around the base of the trees, drawing the forest closer together.

At the bottom of the steps, Kate spotted her mother walking slowly up the dirt path to their house. She wore a white, button up shirt that hung around her jeans. It was dirty and wrinkled, as if she too had slept outside last night. Her waist–length hair was tangled, but still laid down her back in soft waves and shone almost red in the early light. Kate had a faint memory of resting her head on her mother's silky hair and watching it change colors in the afternoon sun. A hand had stroked her head as she watched how her own short, dark hair blended with her mother's to form a deeper, richer color.

Kate's lips trembled as she watched her mother push a lock of hair behind her ear and draw nearer. Joey stiffened beside her and Kate caught a wave of her fear. Their mother said nothing, however, only stared through the girls with empty eyes, as she passed and climbed the steps to the trailer.

"Let's get out of here." Joey pulled Kate by the arm and they started for the forest.

They worked at the house all day. Not talking, not laughing, only painting and stirring and painting again. Kate's arm shook with exhaustion and she was forced to hold her wrist with her other hand just to keep it steady, but she never stopped. The attic became stiflingly hot by midday and the girls were soaked in paint and sweat. Kate never noticed.

Almost there, almost there.

Like a little beat drumming in her head, it pounded out its message.

We're almost there, it's almost done.

Something pushing her, telling her there wasn't much time. Get it finished now, or it won't ever be finished. Hurry, hurry, faster, faster... Louder and more urgent as the day wore on, it built to a crescendo that became almost unbearable. She caught Joey's eye from time to time and saw the same need mirrored in her sister's fearful face.

And then it was done and they sat against the wall, surveying their work, Joey's arm around Kate's shoulder. The sun cast a red light on the walls and turquoise paint surrounded them on every square inch of the room. It reflected the sunset in a magnificent array of colors and they stared in awe of the beauty they had created.

After a while, Kate stood and went to the window. A radiant spectrum of orange and red warmth lit the pines in a blaze of color. The blue sky seemed set on fire by the embers, smoldering on the treetops.

"Look at this, Joey. It's amazing," she said, turning toward her sister.

Joey looked up, her eyes filled with a peaceful glow. The light circled her in an aura of brilliance and Kate lost her breath for a moment to look at her. An incandescent glow etched her face and hair, engulfing her in its blaze, and Kate felt her sister slipping further away, even as Joey rose and joined her at the window. Panic filled her stomach and Kate struggled against the urge to reach out and grab Joey before she was gone.

"It is amazing, Kate." Joey gazed out at the setting sun and smiled to herself, but Kate wasn't looking anymore. She was staring into her sister's eyes and watching as they shone brighter than the sun itself.

* * * * *

The street was quiet and Kate was grateful for this as they followed the sidewalk to their uncle's store. A hot July sun stung her already burned shoulders as she picked at her flaking skin and rolled a piece into a squishy ball. Joey walked a pace in front with her head down, letting her bangs shield her eyes against the white sun.

The bell tinkled merrily as Joey swung the door open and held it for Kate. It was cool inside the store and goose bumps sprung up on her arms, sending a shiver down her back.

Their uncle stood behind the counter. He rested on his elbows, as he leaned in close to Mrs. Whitmore. She ran the Wood n'More shop across the street with Mr. Bowing, her assistant. Her belly swelled large in front of her and it pressed against the counter. Kate knew about the birds and the bees, but the sight of Mrs. Whitmore's ever–expanding stomach gave her a little chill. There was a baby in there. One with arms, legs, and fingers. And after the baby came out it would grow up as big as Kate. It was amazing.

Uncle Dave looked up and his dark eyes brightened when he saw the girls.

"Hey, what's going on, girls?"

"Just wanted to return your stuff, Uncle Dave." Joey smiled, digging the pan with the roller and paintbrushes out of her bag and setting them on the counter.

Mrs. Whitmore patted Uncle Dave's hand and picked up her brown paper bag. "I'll see you later David," she said, smiling briefly with her pink–rimmed eyes. Mrs. Whitmore's eyes had been pink every time Kate had seen her since last winter. That's when Mr. Whitmore had had his accident on the way back from Quarryville. It was the first funeral she and Joey had been to. Well, they hadn't actually gone to the funeral, they'd found a hidden spot on the wall around the cemetery and watched. She had never seen so many people dressed in black in all her life and poor Mrs. Whitmore, she fell down at the end of it. The woman was standing by the casket with her head close to the flowers and all of a sudden it was as if she didn't have legs anymore. They had to carry her back to the black limousine.

Uncle Dave stepped away from the counter and frowned.

"Soon, I hope."

Mrs. Whitmore nodded, giving him a small smile in return. As she passed, she stroked Kate's face. "Bye sweetie."

"Bye."

Uncle Dave watched Mrs. Whitmore as she pulled the door open with both hands and disappeared up the street. He turned to Joey. "So, all done with your project, are you?"

"Yup, we sure are."

"Still not going to tell me what you two were up to?" He asked, the dimples under his almond–shaped eyes deepening. He was only a few years younger than their mother, but Kate always found it hard to believe they were even related. He had none of their mother's sharp facial features, the deep–set eyes, and the high cheekbones. Soft features blended into each other under his dark blonde hair, giving him a round, jovial face.

"Nope."

"You sure?"

"Yup."

"Not even a hint? Come on." He slapped his hand down on the counter. It was a game they'd played since Kate could remember. She and Joey would try to slap his hand before he could take it away. It was simple really, but usually ended with them screaming in laughter.

"Nope." Joey repeated, ignoring his hand as she smiled and wandered toward the magazine section. The store was filled with all kind of odds and ends, but mostly tools and hardware supplies. One side of the three aisles in the store held canned goods and boxed cereals.

"That's ok, I'm sure I can pry it out of your little sister, here." Kate jumped as he tousled her hair. "Hey, you were a million miles away. What's going on?"

"Nothing." She tried to meet his eyes and then looked down at her sneakers. "Just tired, I guess."

"Sure about that?" He asked, his frown deepening. "I'd say you look a little sick."

She crouched, pretending to tie her shoelace. She knew how she looked. It scared her to look in the mirror and barely recognize the girl staring back at her. Her eyes were as flat and lively as the stones at the bottom of the creek. Dark shadows lurked beneath them, contrasted against her skin, which had turned pasty, despite her tan. She had no appetite and it showed on her bony arms and legs. She tried to snap out of the gloom that had wrapped itself around her heart, but with no luck. It clung to her, leaving her spirit dampened and her body weary. She couldn't shake it and over the last couple of days, had decided to stop trying.

"What's wrong with my Katie girl?" He squatted beside her to look her full in the face. Kate's eyes welled up with tears and she wiped at them with the back of her hand. "Hey, hey, nothing's ever all that bad," he said, patting her back.

She looked over his shoulder and saw Joey glaring at her above the magazine. She needn't have worried. Kate knew enough to keep her mouth shut this time. Joey's bruises may have healed, but the horror of that night hadn't ended. There was silence in the trailer now. Their mother hadn't said a word to them in weeks. Not one word. The door was left open every day, leaving she and Joey free to come and go as they pleased, but...but as the days went by, the feeling of being locked in was growing.

Kate dropped her gaze and stared back at her sneakers. "Nothing's wrong, Uncle Dave." She picked at her shoelace, hoping he would go away.

He stood and walked to the front of the store where he flipped the 'open' sign that hung in the window, to 'closed, sorry we missed you'. Joey went back to her magazine, sitting on the floor with her legs crossed in the square of sunlight that came through the display window. It was a Tuesday afternoon and the store was comfortably quiet.

"Come here, I want to show you something." He stood over her and spoke in a gruff voice Kate didn't hear him use very often. In fact, she'd only heard it one other time. She and Joey were playing hopscotch out front and Joey was going out of turn, again. Uncle Dave had burst through the door and said in that tone, "Kate, don't move." The tone had frozen her and she stood, stock–still as Uncle Dave came around behind her. He scooped the wasp off her shoulder, wincing as it stung him and threw it to the ground. She was allergic, a fact they learned from a red–faced doctor in the Quarryville hospital. Only her mother had been there then and Kate hadn't been scared at all. She kept her eyes on her mother's while they put the tube down her throat and pumped her full of shots. Her mother's soft brown eyes never showed a glimmer of fear, telling her silently that she would be okay. And she had been.

Kate rose and followed Uncle Dave through the store and upstairs to the living quarters above. There where two rooms up-stairs, one Uncle Dave used as his bedroom and one Kate had seen only a few times in all the years she and Joey had been hanging out in his shop. As far as she knew, he used it for stor-age. Boxes were stacked neatly against the walls and books lined the shelves of the two bookcases. It was into this room Uncle Dave led Kate. He shut the door behind them and had her sit on the small couch under the window.

"I know it's in here somewhere," he said as he dug through a box behind the door. "Never fails, as soon as you're looking for something…"

Kate laid her head on the couch and listened to the shouts of laughter from the kids playing in the street below. A warm breeze brushed the top of her head and she closed her eyes.

"Here it is," he said, pulling out a small box. It was old and faded, but it looked like it had been red at one time. Decorative gold designs covered the top. He brought it to the couch and sat beside her. She sat up, wrapping her arms around her knees.

"It was my grandmother's." He lifted the lid and Kate peered inside.

Lying on a pile of yellowed tissue paper was a crudely shaped metal object the size of a silver dollar. Two crossed tree branches were impressed on one side. It hung from a thick brown rope. Uncle Dave turned it over and read the writing on the back.

"*Tine Croi Cosain.* In Gaelic it means, 'to protect the heart's fire.' " He placed it in Kate's open palm and she closed her fingers around it. It warmed instantly in her hand and she jerked to drop it back into the box. Uncle Dave closed his own hand over hers and spoke softly. "Close your eyes Katie."

The heat traveled up her arms and spread to her face and then down her body, completely absorbing into the top layer of her skin. It then sank deeper, until it reached her bones. She realized that it was not uncomfortable, much like taking a hot shower after coming in from the cold. The amulet shifted in her hand and began to hum soothingly against her fingers. The heat reached her chest and warmed the hollow place that had been growing there for weeks. It worked into the barren regions of her heart and filled it with a peaceful heat.

She opened her eyes and was surprised to find her face wet with tears. Uncle Dave was smiling, still holding her hand and waiting. A family of birds chattered noisily outside the window, bickering back and forth and competing with the shouts of the children below. She watched them a moment and then turned back to Uncle Dave. He took the amulet and placed it around her neck, lifting her hair out of the rope. She buried her face in his chest and he rocked her, slowly, as the birds chirped on outside.

Chapter Three
The Eyes of the Rabbit

He closed the door behind them and then peered between the slots of the blinds. The girls walked, side by side, holding hands with their heads down. There was no hurry to get home. He sighed and let the blind slide shut.

It was getting dark and judging from the deserted street, it was a good day to close early. Ignoring the candy display that needed restocking, he shuffled to the register. He would just count the drawer and sit in front of the tube until he fell asleep. It was trick he used more and more these days. As the nights grew longer, he found comfort in the flickering light and constant voices. One night about a week ago though, he'd been startled awake by the cracked cackle of Joan Rivers. Some poor sap had invited her on his late show and said something to make her laugh. If it could be called a laugh. The cackle stayed with him long after he changed the channel, inspiring several dream–filled hours. Witches circled the store, laughing and cackling, then hopped off their brooms and broke into the Chim–chimney routine from 'Mary Poppins' on the roof. It had been a long night.

After two tries, he slammed the drawer shut and leaned over the counter, his head in his hands. It was no use. The dullness in Kate's eyes wouldn't go away. He'd spent so many years trying to forget those hollow, unexpecting eyes and to see them again in the face of his little Katie....

But what made it worse was her voice. It was once like music in his ears. To hear her laughing and talking with Joey on the sidewalk outside was like listening to pure joy. He could sit across the counter for hours as she wove her tales, his eyes half closed as the lilting power of her voice took him away from the store and to places too imaginable for words. The girl could tell a story, could talk forever if you let her, but it was her voice that held him. The pitch that rose and fell with a rhythm of which Kate seemed to be unaware. It created a beautiful symphony of notes and beats that captured his heart and sent it soaring.

But today… He shook his head and sat back. Something had broken in it. The strong, confident thread of innocence had been cut and now it hedged and shifted in uneven tones, like someone batting softly at piano keys. There was a wary quality behind it, one that matched the look in her eyes. Amulet or no, he knew she'd never regain what had been lost, now that it was gone.

The amulet. Yes, that had been good. It had done what he had hoped, something he hoped would never be necessary, but was thankful for it all the same. And now it was hers. It was all he could give her, all he could do and he hated himself that it was so pitifully little. But it had been time to give it to her and he'd known it, just as his grandmother had known to give it to Maureen.

She had been older than Kate by five years and at fourteen, Maureen had reached the statuesque height at which she stood now. Her long legs were folded under her, as she sat on the porch swing in the yard that day. She didn't swing, only rested her chin on the wooden back and stared into the trees. Dave was making the trek home after a long, lazy day of fishing and when he caught sight of her, he dropped his gear and headed for the swing.

He loved the time spent doing nothing with his sister in the backyard, the time before their father came home and put an end to it. They'd spent an entire week one summer, years ago, digging a hole in the backyard. Maureen had learned in school that China was directly below them and she promised Dave she would buy him a sword if he helped her dig there. Dave wanted that sword. In a Saturday afternoon movie he had seen a man who had a sword and moved so fast and was so strong and Dave knew that if he had the sword with the funny writing on the side, he would be able to fight just as well. Eagerly he'd scraped the dirt out with his hands, letting Maureen use the plastic shovel and the hole was about three feet deep when they both thought they felt heat rising from it. Realizing they'd reached the ceiling of Hell, they hurriedly filled it up again before washing for dinner. The next day, Maureen made him a cardboard sword and he played with it until his evil nemesis hid behind the living room lamp and made him knock it over. His father had been standing in the doorway at the time and well...that had been the end of the Chinese sword.

As they both grew older there was less digging and more talking. His sister was fascinating to listen to. She had a way of looking at the world that made him feel as if what he saw was merely the black outlines of things, while she saw the colors, textures and subtle hues. It was this that drew him back, time after time and this that put speed in his step as he approached the swing.

She turned and he waved, but she didn't see him. His hand dropped and his feet stuttered to a halt.

It was good she hadn't seen him, because all he wanted to do then was run, run in the other direction and as fast as he could. What he had seen in her eyes had been...had been...

Twelve was a hard age for a boy, full of conflicting signs of adulthood and moments of sheer boyish panic. He wanted to be a man, maybe not like his father, but strong and confident and not the chicken–boy who was spying on his sister from behind a tree in the backyard. He wanted to go to her, and say something that would take that look from her eyes, he did, really. But he couldn't get his stubborn feet to move. They grew roots and secured themselves to the needled–covered ground, happy to stay all day and all night if it meant not having to see the dull sheen in Maureen's eyes again.

She hadn't looked like that yesterday, he was sure of that. Wasn't he? He couldn't remember and now there was something telling him that maybe she had, at least a little. Something was changing inside his sister. Had been for a while. It glowed in her eyes when she glared at the back of their father's head. It twisted her mouth and made her cry out in the night with moans that invaded Dave's dreams. And when she spoke, the words were harsh, brittle and not like his sister's at all.

But this was not anger, not what he just saw. This was worse. Her eyes told of things not expected, things undeserved and things gone, never to return. The marrow of sorrow had crept into the chocolaty pools of her eyes and made itself comfortable. But that wasn't what made his feet one with the ground. It was the death that hid behind them. It was like looking into the eyes of a corpse, though he'd never had the misfortune to do so. A corpse that breathed and blinked and even tucked a piece of hair behind its ear. It was the dead eyes that made Dave wish he'd taken the long way around and gone straight inside the house.

Time ticked away with Maureen staring sightlessly into the trees and Dave hiding behind one, not sure what to do. Just when he thought he'd be spending a cool night outside, their grand-mother came through the backdoor. She lived on the other side of town, but managed to visit almost every day. Her face wrinkled even more, (if that was possible) whenever Dave was around. Boys were trouble, that's what her face told him, even if her mouth said different. She had a hard time with their father, or so she told them every chance she had. Maureen was her favorite, but Dave felt no ill will toward her for that. It kept the grouchy old lady away from him.

The grandmother sat beside Maureen and they exchanged a few words Dave couldn't hear. So, like the chicken–boy he was, he crawled to a closer tree and knelt behind it.

"It is yours now," the grandmother was saying. She lifted the amulet out of the box.

Maureen took it, wondering in the magic of it for a moment and then strung it around her neck.

"I give it to you as it has been given to generations of O'Connor women. It will keep you and protect you," she said in her gravelly old lady voice. "Women live close to the surface, they keep their feelings and emotions near at hand, always turning them over, always striving to be true to them, but most importantly, always *living* them."

Maureen nodded, transfixed by the woman's words.

"That is why," she continued, "it strikes us harder and brings us farther away. It sees our strength as a weakness and it plays on that, uses it. But, you must remember that it is *your* strength and with strength must come knowledge, do you understand?"

Again, Maureen nodded.

"Good, I knew you would," she said and patted her knee. They were silent for a moment as they rocked together in the swing.

Dave jerked his head off the counter as the lights of a passing car made their way across the ceiling. Rising slowly, he flipped on the overhead light and closed the rest of the blinds. After counting the cash drawer, he made a light supper and settled in front of the television set. Show ran into show until it was the wee hours of the morning, but the sweet amnesia of sleep did not come. Frustrated, he turned off the set.

Again he glanced at his truck keys on top of the television and considered taking a ride out there. It was late, but he knew Maureen would be up. If she was there. He'd heard the rumors about his sister. She'd picked up some strange habits. Roaming through the woods in the middle of night. Hitching rides down to Quarryville and picking up strangers in the bar. Eddy had told him about it a few months ago. He thought it was pretty funny when he recognized her as Dave's sister and couldn't wait to tell him. The idiot got a big laugh out of it and Dave resisted the urge to knock him to the floor, in order to get the story out of him. She was all over the men at the bar, he said, promising them things to get them to buy her drinks. He detailed what she said to him and Dave *did* shove him out of the store then, before he could hear any more.

He ran a hand through his hair. Something was wrong with Maureen. Had been for a long time, she just knew how to hide it. And he had an idea as to what was wrong, but no idea how to help. Chicken–boy to the rescue, again. He sighed. He felt the urges as well, the impulses that raged through him at times. Saw the images, the shocking things that made him sick with fear and loathing. He felt as if he was holding on with only his fingernails sometimes, but he never let go. Not once.

He was beginning to think maybe Maureen had.

Anxiety trembled through his body as he climbed the steps to his bedroom and laid down, clothes and all.

How he remembered that summer day, when he'd hidden behind the tree being attacked by the ants on which he'd accidentally sat. The grandmother's voice went on and on in a story that had both enthralled and horrified him. Maureen had listened, patiently at first and then becoming more and more frightened and upset. She struck out at the grandmother toward the end, in an attempt to stop the devastating flow of words that never seemed to end. Dave had been crying with her by that time, crying and wishing more than ever he'd just gone into the house.

When the grandmother was finished the sun was low on the horizon and Maureen had dried her tears.

He had never seen her cry again after that day. She came around, slowly and with much prodding and the amulet seemed to help. They never discussed the reason it never left her neck. And they never discussed what the grandmother had told her, though he figured she must have guessed he knew. There wasn't much he could keep from Maureen.

There was another day. On this day their grandmother was gone, along with their parents. Their father had died not long after that summer, keeled over at the kitchen table after one too many whiskeys and their mother died just a few years later from a series of strokes. It was this summer day while the two of them stood in the living room, that haunted him more than the other.

Maureen had blurted out in a nervous rush of words that she was pregnant and Dave had been shocked. Before she left, she took the amulet off and handed it to him.

"You keep it, okay?"

He could only stare at it so she had been forced to take his hand and close his fingers around it. "But why, I don't—"

"I know and it's okay." She smiled, but the harsh brightness in her eyes did nothing to comfort him. "It's just, I don't want it around the baby and I don't care what she said," she said stubbornly, as he tried to interrupt again. "It doesn't have to be the way she said. It doesn't. She didn't know everything; she couldn't possibly have known everything. And I'm not going to let that crazy old biddy ruin my baby's future, I just, I can't..."

Her voice broke and Dave crossed quickly to hold her. She leaned her head against his chest and her words were muffled. "This is my baby, *mine*. I can protect her and I will, I just don't want any of this...this dirty garbage to touch her." She took a deep breath and looked up at Dave. "I know how it sounds and I know what you're thinking, but I *am* thinking clearly. I'm better now and there's no reason to keep it."

"But—"

"Don't argue with me David. You should know better by now. You keep it for me and if something happens, which it won't, but, well...I trust you to do what's right." Her voice trailed off and she leaned back into his chest.

And that had been the last he'd seen of his sister for five, long years. Years spent wondering and worrying, until one rainy night when she showed up on the back porch with two tiny girls, still in their nightgowns and smelling of smoke and ash. But it was the sight of Maureen, standing strangely calm behind them that started his epidemic of sleepless nights.

Her nightshirt had been covered in blood.

Closing his eyes, Dave let the rhythmic ticking of the clock lull him to sleep, but Kate's dull eyes floated behind his lids and followed him into his dreams.

I trust you.

I trust you...

* * * * *

49

Summer heat soaked the air, making her instantly sticky, as she shaded her eyes against the light and looked for Joey.

"Hey, over here," Joey shouted, seeing her first and waving.

Kate hurried over and flopped down in the grass. "Jeez, it's hot," Kate said, fanning herself with a book.

"Tell me about it, what took you so long?"

"You could have come with me. I don't know why you wanted to wait out here."

"Inside some stuffy library, looking at books? I don't think so."

Kate never understood Joey's disinterest in books. She was a better reader than Kate, could scan a page in seconds and was done with a book in a day sometimes. But usually Joey would sit for only a few minutes before she was up and around...and complaining. So sure that she was missing out on something vital. "How can you just sit there for hours Kate, doesn't your butt fall asleep? And besides," she would say, "there's more to life than what's inside a book." And then she was off, in search of something better to do.

Joey sighed, plucking a book from Kate's hand. "What did you get anyway, not more of the headless queen?"

"So," Kate said, grabbing it back and shoving the book inside her bag. She had read about every hanging or beheading in England from the seventeen hundreds, on back. It was thrilling to read about impossibly rich and famous people who dressed in the best of clothes and ate the finest of foods, but had such horrid problems. "Oh, and here's one for you."

The cover of Joey's paperback pictured a man in a battle with another man whose face was painted in bright colors. A woman was in the corner, holding a baby wrapped in a blanket. Fear filled her face. Westerns held Joey's attention, when it could be held. Cowboys and Indians, and women braving the frontier. The Cowboys and Indians killing each other and occasionally killing the women. Joey was fascinated with the whole scalping aspect of it and subjected Kate to hours of speculation on how it was done.

"We had better get going." Joey slammed the book shut and tossed it in her backpack.

"Yeah."

"It's your turn to clean the bathroom," Joey said in a firm voice.

"It is not, you know I did it last time."

"You owed me that time, 'cause I did the dishes two nights in a row. Remember?" Joey started for the street, not waiting for Kate.

"But, I made dinner."

"That wasn't the deal," Joey sang.

They were still arguing a mile down the road, their voices echoing through the canyon. The sun lowered behind the trees and a refreshing breeze blew Kate's hair away from her face. The road carved out the side of a small mountain and dead–ended at their trailer. She heard other people had lived on their road at one time, but they either moved, or had found another summer place to visit. Tall pines grew on either side and Kate could hear the creek gurgling alongside, about a hundred feet, straight down.

"Fine, I'll do it, but you owe me," Kate said. She never knew how Joey did it, but she always got her way.

"Owe you what? I don't owe you anything, in fact—"

"Shh!" Kate stopped and listened.

"What?"

"Don't you hear that?"

"I don't hear any—" Joey stopped and her eyes widened as the rumbling became louder.

Kate whirled around, trying to find where it came from. It sounded like an eighteen–wheeler crashing through the forest, maybe a mile or two away. She closed her eyes, concentrating on the sound, but it seemed to be coming from all around them.

Joey took Kate's hand and squeezed it. "What is that?"

The gravel began to jump around on the dirt and Kate felt

51

the earth vibrate through her sneakers. The rumbling was getting louder and Kate realized it was coming from below them.

She ran to the side of the road and looked over the edge. Her breath caught, preventing her from venting the scream that slammed against her throat.

The forest was collapsing into itself. As if a giant lawn-mower was plowing the trees down, one by one. Flocks of birds flew from the branches, voices raised in screeching disbelief. Squirrels, deer, skunks, all ran for the safety of the creek only to turn in terror on the other side, realizing there was no place else to go. Some of the animals scattered to either side, but a few deer tried to make the steep climb to the road and tumbled back down to lay broken at the bottom.

A giant cloud of dust blew through the trees, likes ashes from a volcano, turning everything brown and hazy. The haze rolled up the cliff, over her legs and into her nose and mouth, choking her with its strange, honeysuckle scent. The rumbling was close now. Her lungs rattled against her rib cage and even the dusty air seemed to shudder around her. Something was coming, through the trees and toward the creek. Her mind screamed at her to run, *run*! But her feet inched forward, perversely fascinated by what was coming.

The last line of trees fell into the creek, as the earth crumpled beneath them, but the bone splintering crack of their trunks was stifled by the thunder of what came behind.

A voice whispered in her head as the world ground to a halt and her breath solidified in her chest. And the voice sounded sus-piciously like that of her teacher, just last year. "And beyond, lay monsters and demons and other such terrors which waited for any unsuspecting seamen who dared venture so far." The monsters and demons were missing, but the rest was straight from the pages of her third grade textbook. She could hear the monsters though, howling and laughing above the ear–splitting roar of the earth breaking away from itself. And, as she lifted her dazed eyes to the horizon, she saw nothing, but for the dusty haze of a churning, murky sunset. She was standing on the edge of the world.

"Kate, come back!" Joey was screaming, but her voice was small and insignificant behind her. Slow, but steady the edge came nearer, swallowing everything in it path. Trees dropped off into the brown haze, dragging roots and rocks with them. The rift approached the creek and as it ate away the bank, a great waterfall was born, if only for a moment. Its thirst filled, it began ripping away at the base of the cliff.

A tiny, brown rabbit was racing up the side, trying to outrun the hungry mouth that followed him. His black eyes looked straight into hers and his nose twitched in panic before he was swallowed up and gone.

"Kate!"

The urgency in Joey's voice finally broke through Kate's daze and she turned to see her sister scurrying up the side of the mountain. It was time to go. It was *way* past time to go.

She took three slow, oh so slow, steps away from the side. But her feet sank into the pavement, sank lower and lower into the quicksand that was suddenly the road. It sucked her down, tripping and drawing her into its depths. The trapped scream rose again in her throat and she opened her mouth, desperate to get it out, because it threatened to choke her if she couldn't. But it was like a bubble that wouldn't pop and she wasn't getting any closer to Joey, not any closer at all and the trees, the few that had found roots on the rocky cliff side, were breaking apart and crashing into each other. She could feel the breeze of their fall on her neck and thought she felt a branch brush down her back. She made a painful gurgling noise in the back of her throat and lunged forward. And then she was free.

With nothing holding her legs, she flew to the opposite side of the road and began to scramble up to where Joey waited with an outstretched hand. Movement in the corner of her eye took her eyes away from Joey and down to the bend in the road.

It was a boy. A boy, laying on his stomach with a mouthful

of gravel and looking back at her. His face was full of fear and his mouth worked as he shouted. But she couldn't hear him, couldn't hear anything but the roaring behind her. The roaring softened though, as she continued to hold his eyes. He'd come for her, risked himself for her and she recognized the strength in his face, his jaw, his eyes, oh his eyes… *I know you.* She had, for a long time, she had only to come to this place to find him and now…now she couldn't look away.

The world blackened around her as she gazed at him and heaven was in the swirling sea of colors that were his eyes. Nothing penetrated the colors; they were pure, true. It was, it was…she almost had it and then they changed.

The colors turned dark and were gone. He broke the gaze, as his mouth moved in warning and he pointed, not behind her at the rift, but toward Joey.

"Katie take my hand!" Joey leaned over and held her hand out for Kate.

Kate turned from the boy, feeling a tear in her heart as she did. She reached for Joey's hand, brushed the tips of her fingers, but couldn't grab hold. She had to get closer, but her feet kept slipping out from under her. She reached again, just as a figure emerged from behind Joey.

He was dressed completely in black and a round object with inexplicable writing hung on a chain around his neck. He bled dry whatever had been left of the sunlight and the air was suddenly bitten with cold. His coat actually brushed the ground as he drifted closer to Joey and the strange scent of honeysuckle was suddenly overpowered by the gassy stench of rotting apples.

He stopped, just behind her and smiled the smile of a madman. His eyes turned down, without moving his head and he gazed at Joey. She still reached out for Kate, not seeing this man behind her. He held one gnarled hand over Joey's sunny blonde head and raised an eyebrow at Kate.

Nooo…

But again, her voice was an elusive creature, bound by her

own crazed mind, crazed now from the horror of what she found in his eyes. They were filled with black, like two pools of night and had no whites at all. Evil, wretched things that smiled even more as he saw the rift was just behind her now.

And as he backed away, Joey went with him. Rising, she stepped away from the edge and followed him into the trees. Her eyes never left Kate's though and they were sad, so sad to be leaving, but filled with love and hope.

Joey...

But she was gone and Kate was alone and dangling above the road. The rumbling became deafening in her ears, as the ground gave way beneath her and she finally found her voice and screamed. Screamed over and over again, but there was no one to hear, as it rose up out of the rift and she was falling down and down and down...

CHAPTER FOUR
INTO THE DARK

"Kate, *Kate*! You have to get up." Joey's voice broke through the dream and Kate opened her eyes.

Joey was kneeling on the floor by her bed. The only light in the room came from the moon, which shone through the window.

"Wha–what's wrong?"

"You gotta get up, now." Joey's voice was quiet, but it carried a note of authority Kate couldn't ignore.

She sat up and tried to shake the sleep from her body, but it clung to her, making her feel oddly disconnected and fuzzy. The dream was still thundering through her head, the rabbit, the man...Joey. And then there was the voice on the other side of their bedroom door that made her think maybe she hadn't woken up yet.

"Joey?"

She turned, hiding the fear Kate had already seen. "It's mom."

Kate nodded and the last remnants of sleep blew away.

"We have to go. She's been talking to herself for hours out there, saying things. Bad things."

Sliding out of bed, Kate pulled her sneakers from under the bed.

"Come on, just put them on outside," Joey said tiptoeing to the window and flipping the latch open. She yanked on it and let out a startled little grunt when it didn't move.

Kate joined her and they pulled on the window again. When it didn't open, Kate whined and battered the glass with her fists. Joey grabbed her hands.

"Shhh, she'll hear," Joey said and turned back to the room.

Kate stifled her sobs and leaned against the glass. This was their way out. Their only way out. What was going on? She ran her fingers stupidly over the open latch and that's when it hit her, like a hundred lights exploding in her head.

The window had been painted shut.

"Nooo," Kate groaned.

Frantic now, she shook the window until the glass rattled in its frame, but Joey stepped back.

"We're not getting out that way," she said.

Kate spun around and pulled clumps of sweaty hair from her neck. "How then?"

"I don't know, just wait I guess." Joey's face was drawn with resignation, but the fear flickered behind it. "We'll wait."

Back in bed and sitting beside Joey, Kate hugged her knees to her chest and bit down on her lip. They sat in Kate's bed because it faced the door, the door Kate stared at with an ever–growing feeling of dread. She couldn't understand her mother's words as they rose and fell on the other side of the door, but she caught their meanings. And she really didn't want to be in this room one...more...minute.

Tighter, tighter, she hugged her knees, trying to feel anything that wasn't the hard pit in her stomach. She tore her eyes from the door and watched her fingernails digging into her legs.

Joey put a hand over hers and squeezed. "It's okay, Katie. I promise. We'll go tomorrow and—"

But Joey never told her what they would do as the door swung open and light poured into the room.

"Well, isn't this cozy, we're all up." Her mother stood in the doorway, the hall light shining behind her, making her face indistinguishable. She wore the red, terry cloth bathrobe she and Joey had bought for her last birthday. The matching slippers poked out from the bottom folds.

"And just what are my *darlings* doing up past their bedtime? Huh?"

Kate and Joey remained silent. It was her voice that held Kate's tongue more than anything. It was hard and raspy and nothing like her mother's voice at all.

She came into the room, waltzing really and certainly enjoying herself. She circled the bed, watching them and smiling as if this were a game. There was a spark in her mother's eye, one that would ignite if either of them spoke.

She stopped and bent down to Kate's level. Fierce, black eyes peered into hers. "Are going to answer me, or are you just going to sit there, like some stupid...little...idiot?" Spit sprayed across Kate's face and she flinched. She couldn't speak, couldn't move, even though she knew the longer she remained silent, the angrier her mother was becoming.

"Leave her alone," Joey said, leaning to block Kate, her voice strong and even. "We haven't done anything wrong,"

"You didn't do anything?" She turned those hateful eyes on Joey. "You didn't do anything? YOU DIDN'T DO ANYTHING!" The last words sounded like thunder as they vibrated off the flimsy trailer walls. She could smell the rage steaming from her mother's body as she grabbed Joey by the arm, her long red nails sinking into Joey's skin. "It's you! It's always been you! From the very beginning, all of this has been your fault!"

Joey ripped away from her grasp and backed up against the wall. Her eyes were shiny with tears, but she wasn't crying, yet. "What are you talking about Mamma, I don't—"

Their mother screamed, the cry of an enraged animal. She tore at the sheets and pulled them out from under Joey, throwing them to the floor. "Don't you call me Mamma! I was never your mother. Never! All you've ever been to me is a curse."

She laughed suddenly and Kate shrank further away. "A curse! My whole life you've been nothing but a curse and I could never escape, never run far enough or fast enough, you followed me wherever I went and you never let up, not once!" Running her hands through her wild waves of hair, she looked up at the ceiling and Kate saw her face was wet with tears, even as she screamed out the hateful words. "Everything's been taken from me, everything good, it's all gone, Mitchell's gone, Mitchell's gone," her words broke up as choking cries overcame her. "He's gone and

59

it's your fault, everything, everything, your fault—"

"Stop!"

Joey's shout rose above her mother's ramblings and for a moment, Kate thought she saw her mother's eyes clear.

"Stop it right now!" Joey was screaming. "Don't talk about Daddy, don't you *ever* talk about my Daddy!"

"Don't you talk back to me you little—"

Her mother raised a fist, but Joey didn't flinch, instead, she seemed calm. Her eyes narrowed. "I know about you Mamma, I saw you that night. You *know* I saw you."

Her fist hesitated in mid–air as their mother let out a burst of wind that sounded like she'd been hit in the gut. "Wh–what did you say?"

Joey's eyes let loose the tears that had been trapped for so long and her face opened to show the burden she had carried, a burden that had crushed her over the years and when she spoke, she sounded like a small frightened child.

"That night, with the fire," she sobbed. "I couldn't sleep and I came downstairs, but you guys were fighting so I waited. And I *saw* you Mamma, I saw what you did and I know how you pretended it was something else." Her eyes hardened, as she brought the memory to the front of her mind. "But *I* know the truth, I always have, so you can't tell me it's all my fault, because I know about you, I know about your lies and I know what you did to my *Daddy*!"

It one startling motion, her mother leapt to the bed and dragged Joey down to the mattress by her throat. "Shut up! Shut your filthy lying mouth!" She screamed, bouncing Joey's head off the headboard with each word.

Joey cried and flailed her arms, trying to break free. The words she screamed were garbled and choked.

Kate ripped at her mother's arm, trying to unlock the hold she had on Joey's neck. "Momma stop please, please!"

In a flash of movement, she let go of Joey and threw Kate to the floor. She brought her slippered foot back and slammed it into

Kate's side, the force throwing her across the floor where her head ricocheted off the dresser. She could still hear her screaming, despite the thunderous ringing in her head.

"A curse, a curse, a curse," her mother repeated and laughed in a cracked, shrill way. She brought her foot back again and Kate cringed.

But she never felt the impact because her mother was suddenly on the floor beside her. They locked eyes for an instant and now Kate knew...nothing remained of the woman she'd loved in the shiny black eyes of this deadly stranger.

Joey jumped off her mother's back and pulled Kate to her feet. "Come on," she screamed, dragging her from the room.

Down the hallway, through the kitchen and to the door. It was closed, and locked and it stuck like a leech as she and Joey pounded and pulled on it. They got it open and Joey yanked, but it held fast by the chain at the top. There was movement behind them now and heavy breathing. A vase, full of the wildflowers Kate brought home yesterday, exploded in the air just above their heads and Kate screamed as a shard of glass sliced into her cheek. Joey's hair was dripping with the oily water as she slammed the door shut and tore the chain off.

"Go, go, go!"

Kate flew down the steps and into the cool, honeysuckle sweetened night air. Joey followed two steps behind her and the girls caught hands at the bottom, as they ran for the woods. Rocks cut into Kate's feet, unfelt as she struggled to keep up with Joey. They hit the edge of the trees and ran on at full speed. Branches smacked her in the face and she stumbled several times, tripping over the tangled brush at her legs.

"Kate, come on!" Joey paused to help her up again and then looked past Kate, eyes wide. Kate followed Joey's gaze and saw their mother, barreling down behind them, only a few yards away. Her hair flew out behind her, her mouth was pulled back in an ugly grin and her skin was ghastly illuminated in the light of the moon. She raised her arm and the moonlight bounced off of something shinning in her hand.

Yanking her arm with a tremendous force, Joey pulled Kate to her feet and held fast to her hand as they ran deeper and deeper into the forest. Joey's eyes focused straight ahead as she maneuvered them around the trees and rocks.

"Get back here you little *bitches!*"

Kate heard her only a few feet behind them, thrashing through the bushes and cursing. A dog–like quality had ravaged her voice, sending chills up Kate's back and driving her feet faster.

She squeezed Joey's hand as they ran side by side, into a small clearing. The night was suddenly filled with the brilliant glow of a thousand lightening bugs, jostled from their home by two sets of pounding feet. Thorns, hidden in the waist–high grass, ripped at Kate's legs and tore holes in her thin pajama bottoms. A searing pain shot down her side and she bent over, gripping her stomach as she ran on. Sweat poured down her face, blurring her vision and causing her to stumble again.

They reached the end of the clearing and almost skidded off the edge and into the creek. Joey went first, scooting on her backside and starting an avalanche of pebbles along the way.

Dropping on her butt, Kate pushed her way down. She landed at the bottom with a thud and scrambled to her feet.

"Come on Kate, we're almost there." Joey waded into the water.

A high–pitched wail rose from the top of the hill. It shot through Kate's head and she put her hands to her ears as she turned to look up the hill. Silhouetted against the night sky, her mother stood with her mouth open wide. Her hair blew out at the sides and her body was shaking with rage. On and on she screamed until she ran out of breath.

"Joey!"

"I know, I know, come on."

Kate splashed into the creek to join Joey and gasped at the icy water that swirled around her legs. She could hear her mother stumbling down the slope behind her, but didn't look back as she fought her way to shore. Her bare feet slipped on the smooth stones and she fell, choking on a face–full of water.

Joey lifted Kate from under the arm and helped her out of the creek. The other side of the embankment was much steeper and the girls paused a moment to find the best way to climb it. Kate shivered in her wet clothing. She searched for her mother, but for the moment, she was gone.

"There," Joey said, pointing to a crevice on the right that ran the length of the cliff.

Kate went first, crawling on her hands and knees, digging her fingernails into the dirt. She grabbed at weeds that sprouted from the opening, but her wet fingers and feet slipped, slowing her progress. She paused to catch her breath on a rock that jutted out about halfway up and turned to wait for Joey.

"No, no just go," Joey said climbing much faster then Kate. Kate turned and scrambled up the rest of the way.

At the top, she took hold of a sturdy sapling and used it to pull herself up. Joey was still about ten feet away and Kate laid on her stomach to reach down and hold a hand out to her.

"Here, take my hand," she grunted, stretching as far as she could. The creek was farther away than she'd thought and the height made her dizzy. She tightened her grip on the sapling as Joey came within arms length. Kate snatched her wrist. Joey held on with both hands and began to walk up. Her foot slipped and she fell on her stomach with a tiny shriek, as her breath was forced from her lungs. She scrambled for Kate's hand.

"Joey!"

Kate let go of the sapling and reached out with both hands for Joey, who was already gaining speed and sliding down the cliff, her pink pajama top riding up her stomach and bunching up under her arms. She looked up and their eyes met, Kate's wide with disbelief and Joey's flashing lightning with horror. Her blonde hair shined in the moonlight as she hit the big rock in the middle and spun, head over foot, to land with a bounce in the shallow water, seventy feet below.

"No! Joey!"

Joey had landed on her back, her pajama top stained with mud and her hair twisting like seaweed in the water. One bare foot rested on a dead branch and her eyes were open, staring sightlessly up at the starry night. A dark trickle flowed from her nose and spread down her cheek.

No, no, oh God please, no.

Tears streamed down her face as she began to make her way down the embankment.

A rustle in the trees made Kate turn.

Her mother stood to her left, still in her red bathrobe and slippers, which were now soaked with creek water and covered in mud. She stared at Kate, her chest heaving.

"So there you are you little whore."

* * * * *

Will was lost.

He knew he made the right turn at the end of the road leading out of town, but that should have left him only a few minutes from his house. It had been much longer than just a few minutes. Stepping out from under the shade of the tall pines, he winced as the sunlight glared in his eyes, giving him an instant headache.

New town, new people, new school and now he was lost. Great. There was nothing remotely exciting or intriguing about it all, even though his mom would try to convince him otherwise, *every* time they moved. Just the same old school in a different neighborhood. Same old house, in a different color.

His dad had worked construction all of his life and he explained to Will why they had to go to where the jobs were. Will understood all right, he just hated it. Hated being the new kid who never knew where to sit at lunch or what was going on after school. It wore on him. The eyes that dissected him the moment he walked through the door and had him pegged by the time he sat down. Loner. Loser. Punk. Dork. It never mattered. He would take his seat at the back of the classroom and try to seem as if he didn't care. After a while, they forgot about him and moved on to something else. Even the teachers passed over him. They took little interest in a quiet kid who caused no problems and made decent grades. Will moved around the schools like a ghost. Never talking to anyone, never putting down any roots, because he knew it was only a matter of months before they moved on.

He was twelve now and for the few days they had been in Newclare, he actually felt at home. He liked this town. Liked the mountain that seemed to watch over him, liked the smell of the creek he could hear just about any place he went. His dad told him this would be it for a while and for the first time, Will let himself hope it was true. The new freeway they were building in Quarryville, twenty miles south of town, might keep his dad busy for years. That, coupled with the fact that new traffic would require several new stores, burger joints and such, his dad said they could be here until he graduated from school. Will had trouble believing it, though. Being in one place never sat well with his dad, who had an overused saying about the grass growing under his feet.

This time was different in another way, since they were living with grandma. The last job had gone sour for dad and his grandmother had invited them to stay. She said she'd been lonely now that Grandpa was gone.

Will missed his grandpa. Missed the smell of his pipe, and the strange, greasy scent of his hair. He had a habit of slipping homemade Kahlua into his milk and letting Will try out his pipe on the back porch. And he had the best bedtime stories, even if Will did lay awake all night, his eyes glued to the door, waiting for the swamp monster to burst it open and gobble him whole. They only visited Will and his parents twice a year, but it didn't seem to matter. Being the only grandchild, Will knew he was the shining spot of grandfather's life.

The night they got the news, Will had sat at the top of the

stairs, his head in his hands as he listened to his mom and dad talking in the den. Grandpa had been sitting in his rocking chair, smoking his pipe when his heart had seized up. The pipe fell out of his hand, burning a hole through his pants and well into his leg by the time grandma had found him. That shook Will up more than anything. He couldn't get that burned pant leg out of his head, no matter how hard he tried.

The sun finally dropped behind the trees and Will looked around, trying to find something familiar. The trees swayed in a wind that blew dust up around his face and he slowed, listening to the soft rustling. The countryside was great, perfect for high adventures through the forest. He loved the isolation of it, no cars, no people, quite a contrast from the smell and noise of Philadelphia.

The road now led uphill as it cut into the side of the mountain. He knew he was nowhere near home, but went on anyway. There was no hurry. His dad didn't get home until well after dark and his mom was so busy unpacking, she would never miss him until then.

A rabbit skirted across his path and Will stopped short to avoid stepping on it. He smiled, as he watched it cross to the other side. The rabbit ran to the edge of the trees and looked back at Will.

The smile died on his face.

The rabbit's black eyes were terrified. A human–type horror lurked behind them and Will felt a chill rattle his spine.

Turning abruptly, the rabbit dashed into the woods and disappeared.

Still a little shaken up, Will started walking again. He tried to laugh at himself for getting so spooked, but it was a weak laugh. The mood of the forest had changed and suddenly he very much wanted to be home.

Just as he decided to backtrack into town and start again, he heard a rumbling noise from up the road. It was a low, powerful sound and Will knew then, that going back to town was the best idea he had all day.

Two steps in that direction and Will stopped again.

Wrong way.

What? He jerked around and searched the woods. The voice had come from inside his head, but he looked anyway.

Hurry, hurry.

This is crazy, he thought, but didn't move. The rumbling was closer now and Will could hear crashing noises below it. He began to run, but not toward town. Dropping his bag, he jogged farther uphill and toward the bend. He took the corner too fast and his feet slid out from under him, sending him to the ground. The palms of his hands stung and he ate a bitter mouthful of gravel. Looking up, he saw there were people on the road up ahead.

A girl stood, staring at him, her beautiful face crumpled in confusion. Their eyes met and Will, still a city block away, was drawn into the kaleidoscope of color that swirled in her eyes. The rumbling was replaced by a gentle rustle that murmured in his ear, telling him of other times he had been in the presence of her incredible eyes. The mountain, the creek, the songs of the wind, all told of her power, her simple virtue.

It's you. Relief too great to be held, flowed through his body and moistened his eyes. How long had he waited for her, not knowing he did? It didn't matter. She was here and he could go to her now, could—

But someone else wanted her as well. Had waited for her as long, maybe longer than Will. And this person, this presence was near and came nearer, even as Will tore himself away from the ecstasy he'd found in her eyes.

There was a man emerging from the forest above the road and in a wave of explosion, the roaring was back in his ears, louder than before, because it was just on the other side of the road now. The ground pitched and rolled beneath him, but he kept his eyes on the man who advanced from the trees. The angle prevented Will from seeing his face, but he knew in a blinding flash of insight, that this man, dressed in black, was a much bigger threat than whatever was making its way up to the road.

"Watch out!" He yelled, or at least he tried to. No sound came from his throat, so he pointed to the man, trying to get the girl to look away. She turned, slowly and started to take the hand of the other girl who was hanging onto the side of the steep slope.

Now she saw the man in black. And she began to shake.

Will leaped to his feet and raced down the road toward them. The trees on his left leaned crazily and fell into each other in succeeding bursts of thunderclaps. The ground crumbled away at the edge of the road and Will lengthened his stride, knowing he wouldn't make it. A gulch formed directly in front of him, splitting the road in two. He skidded to the edge, as his arms pinwheeled, trying to catch his balance. Taking several steps back, he watched as the split widened and reached the girl. She clung to the side of the slope, staring transfixed at the man above her. Then the ground caved in under her sneakers and her hands flew up, before she disappeared. Her scream rose out of the gulch, again and again…

"No!"

Will reached out for her and fell out of bed.

Rubbing his head, he took a deep breath and snapped on the light. He had broken a sweat and his flannel nightshirt stuck to his chest. He couldn't remember ever having such a vivid dream. Nightmares had plagued him most of his life, but they were always vague, dark impressions, which were seldom remembered by the time the sun rose. With a sigh, he dropped his head back on the bed.

Boxes towered around him and he groaned, thinking about how he promised his mom he would unpack today. He wasn't going back to sleep any time soon, so he opened the one next to him and began to pull out the model planes he'd been building since he was eight. The wing on his nineteen–forty–two Japanese Zero had broken down the middle and he held it in his hand, bending it back and forth, thinking about stopping by that Dave's Supply place he'd seen earlier that day. He reached to set it on his nightstand. They would have some model glue and probably the wire he needed to hang them.

His hand stopped, still holding the plane, as he glanced out the window.

A tiny cry had echoed through the woods, not much more than a whisper, but Will heard the fear in it. He stood and went to the window. Some fool had painted it closed and it wouldn't budge no matter how hard he yanked on it.

Turning off his light, he tiptoed out of his bedroom and made his way through the dark house to the backdoor. Cool night air chilled his sweat–covered body. The crickets were quiet in this early morning hour and Will felt the silence weigh around him. He stood on the porch and cocked his head, listening.

"Joey..."

This time he knew he'd heard it. The girl's voice sounded broken and terrified and a familiar feeling washed over him as his heart began to beat loudly in his ears. He had to find her.

Returning to the house, he searched behind the backdoor for his sneakers. They were gone. Back to his room, he threw open his closet door, but they weren't in there either.

"Damn." Hurrying back to the kitchen, he was about to leave without them when he spotted something peeping out from under the couch. Will strode across the kitchen to the living room and pulled them out. The door slammed shut behind him, as he jumped off the porch and ran into the night.

* * * * *

Kate froze, staring back at her mother. Panic crushed her chest, making the air too thick to breathe. Her tears stopped as the world spun around her and she almost pitched over the side. Blinking against the dizzying fog, she managed to rise to her feet and face her mother.

The butcher knife that usually hung by the sink in their kitchen now glittered dangerously in her mother's right hand. She flipped it over with her fingers and ran one red thumbnail down the handle.

"My sweet Katie girl," she said in her dog–voice. Kate saw death shine beneath the light that danced in her eyes.

Spinning on her heel, Kate darted for the trees, but only ran three steps before the weight of a sand bag, slammed her from behind.

Landing on her chest, hot pain sliced through her side. She screamed and thrashed, kicking her feet and flailing her arms. Flipping on her back, Kate brought up both feet and shoved her mother in the stomach with all her strength. The force sent her mother into a tree and she sat down abruptly, stunned for a moment.

Kate scrambled to her feet and slipped in the loose gravel, landing on her hip. Springing to her feet again, she ran blindly into the forest. Her side throbbed. Her head throbbed. Only her heart was still, lost in the lightening flash of her sister's eyes.

Oh God, Joey, no.

Joey's pale face flashed between the trees as Kate tripped and stumbled her way through the forest. Each step sent raging flames down her side, slowing her feet and making her cry out. One more hard fall brought her face to the dirt and she laid there for a few breaths.

No further. No more. She was too tired. But the thrashing noises behind her forced Kate to rise to her feet and run on.

Out of the mist of the trees the house came into view, like a beacon in the night. Thick clouds blocked out the last of the moon's light and the house stood in a dark silhouette against the sky. A violent shiver rattled her body and her teeth chattered.

She glanced back into the trees and heard her mother, breathing hard, but catching up fast. Kate rounded the side of the house and dove into the jungle at the rear.

Using the path she and Joey had learned by heart, Kate had

no trouble reaching the backdoor in the dark. Each stride opened the gash in her side and her sobs were weak, as she limped up the steps. She pushed the door open and fell against the wall, fighting to catch her breath.

Blood flowed freely down her side and it warmed her leg as it soaked into her pajama bottoms. She closed her eyes and took another deep breath. Stars twinkled beneath her lids and they gradually became brighter and brighter. Her body seemed to float up to a glowing light that came from the ceiling and she succumbed to the drifting peace it brought her.

A rough hand clamped down on her mouth and another grabbed her at the waist. Shards of panic pierced her heart and the last of her breath came out in a small puff of wind. Her muffled scream darkened the room again and she fell back down, as she battered the body behind her with both fists.

"Stop it, stop it! She's coming, we gotta get out of here."

He spun her around and away from him, but still held her tight at the shoulders. Kate tried to focus on his face, but only caught a glimpse of blonde hair and sparkling blue eyes. His hands warmed her where they gripped her skin. They seemed to melt into her and for a long moment she thought she could feel his heart beat in time with hers. Electricity raced through the air in pulsating bursts that also exploded with every beat. He was only an inch or two taller then she, but he seemed to grow larger as Kate stared up at him. She shook her head, trying to think straight, but not wanting to trust her eyes.

"Snap out of it, where can we go?" His voice trembled with panic, but his eyes had filled with shocked wonder and she realized, he felt it as well. She finally decided he was real.

"Come on." She whispered and headed for the stairs.

A shadow fell across the room behind them and Kate turned to see her mother climbing the last step of the stairs, outside.

She threw herself at the open door, but a second too late. Shoving her weight against the door, her mother forced it open, slamming Kate into the wall. A burst of light exploded in Kate's head as she fell. Moaning, she opened her eyes to see the boy lift a dinning chair over his head and bring it down on her mother's head. She collapsed on top of Kate and Kate shoved her aside as she pulled herself up. Her mother rolled to the side and bumped the door closed with her arm.

The boy snatched the sleeve of Maureen's nightshirt and led her into the kitchen, to the living room.

"No, there's no way out here." Her words came out in a whisper as she pointed to the boarded windows.

"There." He nodded at the jammed door.

Kate shook her head and started to explain, when a scraping noise tore through the air and she jumped. She dropped to her knees and crawled behind the couch. The boy followed. They squeezed together as tight as they could and waited.

The footsteps in the kitchen were uneven as her mother staggered through the room.

"Come out, come out wherever you are…"

The voice was raspy and Kate's head hurt to hear it. She was in the living room now and Kate heard her panting as she stood there, listening. Kate held her breath and she felt the boy tighten. She looked up and saw his face, frozen with fear, sweat droplets glistening on his pale cheek.

She looked down at his feet. An insane giggle erupted from her stomach and she barely stopped herself from collapsing in a burst of suicidal laughter. He was wearing pink fuzzy slippers. They were ruined with mud and grime, but the crocheted hearts on the side of them were still visible. He elbowed her hard in the side, trying to quiet her and another wave of dizziness seized her as her wound opened and fresh blood flowed down her side.

The top of her mother's head passed by, as she walked back to the kitchen.

Kate sagged against the boy and let out her breath. Silence for a long while made her wonder if maybe her mother thought they'd run out the backdoor while she had been unconscious.

"I think she's gone." He poked his head above the couch

and looked around. "Let's go."

He pulled her to her feet and the two walked into the kitchen. The house was quiet and Kate held onto the doorway as relief flooded through her.

The boy was looking around, his face growing more and more confused. He ran a hand through his hair as he peered out the window over the sink. Kate saw now, he wore red flannel pajamas above his pink fuzzy slippers. She sighed, closing her eyes and trying to calm her shaking body.

I'm going to wake up any second now.

Joey's face floated behind her lids. Kate saw her sliding down the hill, her eyes blazing in the moonlight.

She opened them quickly.

The boy had been watching her and rubbed his head, trying to get the words out. "You want to tell me—"

"Watch out!" Kate screamed and reached for him, as her mother came up behind him and raised the knife with both hands.

He whirled around and managed to block the knife with his arm, but she shoved him in the side with her knee and he went sprawling into the shelves on the wall. Glasses and dishes shattered down on top of him and he let out a groan before falling over.

Kate made a running leap at her, knocking the knife out of her hand and pushing her into the dinning room. Kate ran at her again, screaming. Her mother clasped her hands together in a big fist and brought them down at Kate's open side. Fire radiated through her body but she shrieked more from anger than pain. Balling her own hand into a fist, she struck her mother as hard as she could across the face. The force of the blow shoved her into the open doorway, but she caught the doorjamb with her hand and steadied herself.

Kate ran for the kitchen and grabbed the back of the boy's shirt. "Come on, come on!" She screamed, leading him to the stairs.

He ran beside her, still dazed, but rapidly coming out of it.

At the landing, she glanced behind them and saw her mother sweeping up the stairs at a frightening pace.

Kate hooked right at the landing, tangled her feet under her and fell. The boy grabbed her hand and began to pull her up. She was only three steps from the top, when Kate felt claws digging into her ankle. She shrieked and yanked her foot hard as she tried to break free but her mother's grip only tightened. The boards of the stairs began to buckle and Kate grasped the boy's hand with both of hers. Her foot came loose as she heard the crashing of the stairs breaking apart and falling onto the floor below.

Scrambling up the remaining stairs, Kate looked back and saw her mother. Her body had fallen through the open hole and she was scraping the walls and stairs around her for something to hold onto. Her legs dangled uselessly below.

"Katie!" The blackness had cleared from her eyes, leaving them wide and frightened. And her voice…it was Mamma. "Katie, help me!"

Kate let go of the boy's hand and threw herself down the steps. He wrapped his arms around her leg to keep her from falling in as well.

"Take my hand!"

With a jerk, her mother grasped her around the wrist, but instead of pulling herself out of it, she yanked back with a brutal force and began dragging Kate into the hole with her. Her eyes narrowed as her lips widened into a broad grin. She gave another yank. The boy kept his grip on her and she managed to pull free just as the step gave way and her mother plummeted to the level below.

"Momma, no!"

Kate screamed with her mother each time her body broke through another floor. Then there was silence.

"No, no, no," The words tore at her throat. She let the boy pull her to her feet and she slumped against the wall. A weakness that started in her belly, spread throughout her body. It was over. All she wanted to do was get away from the black hole that now engulfed the stairs.

"Oh my God." His voice quivered and he stumbled a little and caught himself on the wall, still staring down the stairs.

Her legs would no longer hold her, so she crawled to the open window. The moon had come out for one last look and she lay in its soft pool of light, the amulet clutched in her hands.

The boy was beside her. Kneeling, he turned her over and gasped. "You're hurt," he said, pulling up her shirt for a closer look.

She saw his face floating, high above through her slitted eyes. And she saw his eyes, his wondrous eyes that cared so much for a girl he didn't even know.

"Ah, jeez, you're bleeding all over the place." He ripped off his shirt and wadded it up to put at her side. His bare chest shone with sweat, but then he grew fuzzy and started to fade away.

"Kate, Kate, can you hear me?"

Her heart beat softer and she could barely feel him shaking her. There was darkness up ahead. One that could make this night go away and in its embrace she would never hear the ravaged voice of her mother again. Never see Joey's pale, still face.

"Wake up, come on, don't do this." His voice cracked and she felt droplets splattering her face and then that was all.

The wind picked up and she listened to it sing to her as she drifted into the darkness.

PART TWO

Chapter Five
Home again, home again...

"You all packed?"

"What? Oh, yeah, I think so."

"We'll be waiting downstairs." Carl gave her a small smile and shut the door behind him.

Kate stood in the middle of the room, trying to see anything she'd missed. Her poster bed stood in the corner, its blue blanket folded neatly under the pillow. The white walls were bare, except for the gold–framed mirror that hung over the matching dresser. The Gates had done their best to make a nice room for her, but in the six years she had been with them, there was scarcely a trace that she even lived here. Just some clothes, books and a few mementos from trips they'd taken. A tiny replica of the Empire State Building, a bag of shells from the Jersey shore.

Sighing, she sat on the bed and let her bag drop to the floor between her feet. She was tired...so tired, though her restless night had little to do with it.

Kate hefted the bag over her shoulder and went to the door. It was strange how she felt no sense of loss, leaving a place she'd lived in for so long. Only a slight tug at her heart, one she barely noticed.

Carl was standing by the front door, when she emerged from the stairs and sitting in a far corner of the couch was Anita, holding her leather purse with both hands in her lap. Her eyes flicked toward Kate and then quickly moved away. It was the first time they had made eye contact all week and Kate noticed the nervous rash that had appeared a few days ago, had spread even further up Anita's neck, now reaching her jawbone.

Kate stared at the floor, wishing she had words for the woman. Anita had tried so hard over the years, done everything she could to make Kate her own, but Kate just didn't seem to have anything left to give. It had worn on her over time, that constant pressure to feel something she didn't, couldn't even, but now that pressure was gone. Last week had changed everything.

"I'm ready," Kate said, lifting the strap to her bag over one shoulder.

"Well let's get this show on the road," said Carl, using one of his more tired expressions. He had a phrase for every situation, which had often annoyed Anita, but Kate had found it endearing. Today there was a forced quality to his voice though. One she'd heard several times over this past week, when the tension in the house had been thick enough to be choked on.

He took her bag in one of his chubby hands and put it in the trunk, then slid into the driver's seat beside Anita. She sat in front of Kate, her head stiffly erect. Kate saw the red prickles of her rash were even brighter on the back of her neck. Sighing, Kate rolled her window down to let the cool air wash over her face.

She woke, some time later, when the car slowed and made a series of turns that led them off the interstate. Rubbing the sleep from her eyes, she sat up and looked out the window. The sun was high in the sky, stinging her eyes. They passed under a green sign with white letters.

Welcome to Quarryville.

The rational, even plains of the northeastern Pennsylvania countryside disappeared as they neared the lower, haphazardly placed summits that had formed at the base of the mountain. The highest of the three peaks was still dusted with snow, though summer had begun last week. Short, fat bushes of shrub, gave way to tall pines that darkened the road, as it converged into two lanes and zigzagged up the steep incline. Kate rolled up her window, shivering.

They passed over a long bridge and she leaned her head against the glass, looking down. Swirling rapids rushed beneath and Kate was impressed by the high water, so late in the season. The trees blocked most of her view, but she could see dots of color wading in the creek below. Summer people, who would be gone in another few weeks.

Stop it Kate, you're splashing me.

Slamming her eyes shut, she sat back in her seat. After a moment, she took a deep breath and leaned forward again. The palms of her hands stung as she dug her nails further into the skin.

Her fingers touched the amulet that rested between her breasts. She hadn't taken it off since they gave it back to her at the hospital. The cut in her side had become infected and Kate spent several days in near delirium, tossing around in a hospital bed, sick with fever. Voices faded in and out, all low in tone and laden with fear. Uncle Dave came many times, his face stricken with sorrow. He would sit by her bed and cry, begging her to stay and fight. When Kate would try to come out of it though, Joey's face would rush to the surface and Kate would sink down again, preferring the black numbness sleep could give her.

The boy from the house came one night and sat in the chair beside her bed. She could feel him there, even with her eyes closed and before he left, he stood by the bed, watching her a while. Kate struggled to see him through the fog that surrounded her. His eyes burned and his mouth moved as he spoke to her, but when she finally opened her eyes the room was bright with sunlight. And the boy was gone.

They came for her a few days later. The social worker, the foster parents and Uncle Dave. In quiet words and heavy tone, she was informed of her situation, while Uncle Dave stood by the door, staring at his shoes. The foster parents lived three hundred miles away and Kate would leave that very afternoon. A new home with both a mother and father was thought to be what was best for her right now and she felt her heart sink, as hopes of living with Uncle Dave were dashed. The words, fresh start and moving on, were repeated over and over again, until Kate thought she might scream.

At the car, Uncle Dave had hugged her fiercely and made her promise to write. He searched her face, tears streaming down his own. She smiled, gave him a peck on the cheek and assured him she would. Sitting in the back seat as the car pulled away, she'd settled back for the long ride. Yes, far from here was good. The farther, the better. Her eyes were dry as she left the town behind her.

But now she was back, and as that thought hardened in her stomach, another, smaller green sign appeared around the next bend. Newclare, pop. 987. The green had faded, making the sign hard to read.

Carl swung the car off of Kerry County Road and onto Main Street, slowing it to a crawl. The road was empty except for a few cars parked on the side. He stopped at a light and Kate saw Olan's Automotive still stood on the corner. Its charred remains had deteriorated at bit more over the years, but the frame held.

Beyond the light was Chainberlin's Pharmacy. Two boys sat on the curb, holding cigarettes behind their backs while they waited to identify the people in the car. The one with the dirty–blonde hair took a drag as they passed and let it out in a spiraling gray cloud. He gave Kate a knowing smile that made her shrink in her seat. She stared down at her twisting fingers.

"Place looks exactly the same," Carl piped up from the front seat. "Who says you can't go home again?"

Anita shot him a look that made Carl raise his eyebrows. Muttering, he went back to concentrating on the street.

The last building on the left was Uncle Dave's and Carl parked in front, shutting the engine off with a hefty sigh. The windows were dark, but the sign read 'Open'. The same green and white awning hung above the sidewalk, although the sign, which stood on top, was new with huge red lettering. Someone had drawn hopscotch in front of the door and the bright colored chalk showed up clearly on the gray sidewalk.

Come on, Joey, just one more game and then we'll go.

"Are you all right, dear?" Anita asked Kate, concern for herself clearly overshadowing any for Kate. *Don't do it again,* her eyes told Kate *please, please don't.* "You look a little pale."

Kate felt a little pale, but nodded anyway.

Carl went around back to get her bag out of the trunk and Anita followed, eager to help him be done with this messy business.

Kate rose from the car and stood on the street, staring at the store. Then slowly, slowly her gaze shifted down the street.

There were kids playing in the road. Well, lying in the road and playing a game she knew well. Chicken. Whoever laid in the street the longest while a car was coming was the winner, or not a chicken...or, something like that. She always had been the first to run. Never did she trust her ears or her feet to stay as long as Joey. It was a rush though. Those moments before she ran. Nothing since had given her that mixture of thrilling fear and adrenaline.

It was only the fear she remembered now and suddenly she could hear a car as it rounded the corner and bared down on her. And she wanted to run. Just run and run and be some place else. Anywhere else.

"Are you coming?" Anita asked, her frown deepening as she waited for Kate. Carl stood on the sidewalk, holding her bag.

Kate opened her mouth to say, why yes, of course she was coming, but no sound came out. She swallowed and tried again, but still...nothing. A stinging sensation started in her legs and traveled to her stomach. She clutched the roof of the car and the stinging worsened before it disappeared, leaving her numb. There was no air in her lungs. No...air... She felt the car sliding out from under her grasp.

Carl dropped the bag on the sidewalk and had made two running steps toward her, when the door opened and Uncle Dave stepped out.

"Katie? It that you?"

He squinted his eyes, looking her over. His hairline had slipped a little farther up his forehead and some gray sprinkled the sides, but the same spark lit his eyes as he took her in.

"I can't believe it." The door banged shut behind him as he

ran to pick her up and swing her around. His familiar smell wrapped around her like a blanket. "I'm so glad you're home," he whispered in her ear.

And she was, she guessed.

Home.

* * * * *

Kate rubbed her head, trying to towel dry it since she'd left her hairdryer at the Gates. She stopped outside her bedroom door when she heard her name mentioned downstairs.

"—anything else we can do for Kate." It was Carl's hushed voice.

"Well, I appreciate all you've done." Uncle Dave was standing by the sink and Carl and Anita were sitting at the kitchen table.

Balling up her towel, she tossed it in the hamper outside the bathroom and sat at the top of the stairs to listen.

"We've spoken with the school counselors and they say it's only a matter of time but you know, it *has* been six years. We should have seen something by now." Carl continued. "She's just so unreachable. Doesn't laugh, doesn't cry, hardly even speaks unless she has to. We've tried everything, the school, the church, and even a psychologist. This...bringing her back here, well we couldn't think of anything else."

Uncle Dave ran his fingers through his hair as he glanced up the stairs. Kate jumped back, but he didn't see her. "Well it was the right decision." He disappeared to the other side of the room to get more coffee.

Kate held herself, trying to warm her suddenly shaking body. It was so strange to hear them talking about her like that. The girl they were describing was a stranger to Kate though, she admitted, she seldom knew herself anymore. Or cared to. It felt comfortable and more importantly it didn't feel as...as...raw anymore. It seemed she watched life through a big glass window now. It went on around her, but she couldn't touch, or smell, or *feel*, any of it.

At the beginning it hadn't been like that. Everything had been too real. Too vivid. Her first few nights at the Gates were something she never wanted to go through again. It had been a long time since she'd had any nightmares though, or any of the flashes. At first that's all she thought about. She replayed it over and over in slow motion, as she sat at the desk in her room staring out the window, open schoolbooks in front of her. Or she would be sitting in class, sweating over her math and a scream, a familiar scream, would burst through her head and make her to jump in her seat. On more than one occasion she was sent home, trembling and sick. Anita would put her to bed, a million questions in her eyes, but questions she never asked.

That wasn't the only reason she'd been sent home. About three months after she came to live at the Gate's, a nasty girl named Greta Birmstein decided that the new girl was an easy target. Her plump feet slapped the floor behind her as she followed Kate mercilessly through the school, taking every opportunity to humiliate and torture her. She knocked her trays of food onto the floor, threw her books in the trash and banged into her in the hall, pushing her against the lockers. Kate endured this with the minimal of complaining. She tried to avoid her when possible, and even went so far as to not go in the girl's room all day just in case she was there.

One day though, the hall was empty and Kate was on her way to see the guidance counselor they insisted she talk to twice a week. She hated every second of it. The piercing eyes, the prodding questions. 'How do you feel Kate?' How did he think she felt? There wasn't much to talk about when Kate refused to answer and it usually ended in a staring contest, which Kate always won. She spotted Greta coming out of the girl's room and snuck into the stairway, but Greta followed and confronted her on the landing.

"Where do you think you're going?" She spun Kate around

by the shoulder. She put her hands on her thick hips and glowered down at Kate. Since she was easily a foot taller then Kate, she loved to get close and breathe her foul breath in Kate's face.

"None of your business." Kate tried to push past her, but Greta shoved her back.

"Don't get smart with me, I'll tell Miss Kirk you're cutting class and she'll give you detention." Her piggy face screwed up in a stupid grin. "Tell me where you're going and *maybe* I won't." She crossed her arms and waited.

Kate stared back. A simmering pot of hate began to boil deep within her, as Greta's bloated face grew larger and larger, until it completely engulfed her line of sight. This stupid, stupid girl who had nothing better to do than make Kate even more miserable than she already was. This stupid girl who knew no sadness other than what she gave others. This stupid girl whose mother must spend an hour fixing her hair every morning into those ugly braids.

The pot boiled over and her hate flowed out and all over Greta. Kate sprung at her. Her fists raised and teeth bared and the last thing she saw was Greta's squinty eyes widen with surprise. She didn't have time to raise her hands to block Kate, as she landed on her back with Kate on top of her. She remembered grinning at Greta and laughing as she begged Kate to stop. It was the best feeling she'd had in a long while and she was still laughing when Miss Kirk and the gym teacher pulled her off.

By then though, Greta was unconscious. Her nose was bleeding all over the floor and Kate had a flying thought about her bleeding like a stuck pig. Once the thought hit her she started laughing again and couldn't stop. She sat in the corner, on the cold cement floor and held her stomach as the tears rolled down her face. She didn't stop until Miss Kirk slapped her several times across the face.

The paramedics came and took Greta away on a stretcher. She heard that her nose was broken in two places. And her jaw. And her right cheekbone. Greta didn't come back to school for three weeks and when she did; her eyes were still purple and swollen. She never looked at Kate again.

Kate had spent a few days in detention and some sick days at home. She used the time trying to take control again and trying, actually, to feel some kind of guilt over what she had done. The churning, smoldering blackness had begun in the deepest regions of her mind and had exploded all over Greta, gushing forth in an eruption of rage. Having both terrified and pleased Kate, she tried to make sense of it. But all she came up with was the feeling she had at the time. It had felt good.

So incredibly good.

"Did you want me to call her down?" Uncle Dave was saying.

Carl slipped his coat over his shoulders and held the chair out for Anita.

Anita cast a quick glance up the stairs. "Oh no, we've already said our good–byes," she lied.

Get me away from here. It was so plain, the woman might as well have shouted it out, but Kate felt only sympathy for her. And a sense of relief. A week of circling around each other was finally over and now Anita could go back to her bridge club and Tuesday mornings breakfasts and not have to think about the strange girl who used to live in the upstairs room.

It had been sunset when Anita came upon Kate in her bedroom last week. Kate was sitting in the windowsill, watching the brilliant colors of the trees as they blazed in the reddening light, thoughts of other sunsets heavy on her mind. Sunsets that turned everything it touched to a luminescent gold. It had been so long since she watched a sunset and allowed herself to think of anything that might bring her more pain. But that day, the fading light stroked the trees in a way Kate hadn't seen in a long while and she was brought back to one particular sunset. One she watched from a third floor attic as smells of paint invaded the sweet scents of the forest. And suddenly, her sister was close, so achingly close she could almost feel Joey's fingers intertwined with hers.

"Thought you might like some soda honey," Anita had said as she walked into Kate's room. "I know I can't think if—"

Kate turned and Anita's next words died before they ever reached her lips. The glass fell to the floor.

"Anita?" Kate made a move to go to her and Anita let out a little shriek. A moment later, she was running out the door.

Anita sequestered herself in her bedroom for the rest of the day, as Kate sat on her bed and listened to the woman's terrible sobs. When Carl came home from work, he tried to comfort her, and Anita's choked reply reached Kate easily through the thin walls. "Her eyes! So evil Carl, you don't understand, her eyes…" Carl appeared in her doorway an hour later, and informed Kate that they wouldn't be going to dinner because Anita was ill. His eyes never left the powder blue carpet and he slipped out as soon as he'd delivered the message.

Uncle Dave shut the door behind the Gates and stood for a moment, watching them drive away.

Kate rose and went to her room. Closing the door softly, she surveyed her new living quarters. Uncle Dave had cleared out the storage room and put a twin bed against the wall in one corner and a brand new dresser in the other. The carpet felt soft under her feet and she curled her toes in its deep threads. A low light shone through the window from the last of the setting sun. She shoved her bag and some unpacked clothes off of her mattress, switched off the light and crawled under the covers. She was tired, and no sooner did she close her eyes, than the morning light opened them.

* * * * *

The next few weeks sailed by. Kate spent her days reading in her room, or taking long walks that always ended by the creek. The sound of the water rushing along seemed to drown out the onslaught of thoughts that stayed with her, day and night. She would spend hours by the creek, losing track of time and coming home well after dark. Uncle Dave never asked her about these trips, only greeted her with his easy smile and offered some dinner.

Thoughts of school loomed, like a black cloud on the horizon. Seeing her old schoolmates worried Kate more than she was willing to admit. She was aware that everyone in town knew what had happened to Joey and her mother, and the kids at her school, or anywhere she guessed, were not known for their sensitivity or tact. Unsure of how to handle the whole mess Kate sat up late at night, letting the prickly fear overcome her with dread. Uncle Dave tried to reassure her, telling her that it was old news by now. That it would be strange for a while, but then they would move on to more interesting gossip. Kate hoped he was right. Just being back was bad enough. Everywhere she went voices and faces rose up to haunt her. They followed her through her days and chased her at night in her dreams.

About two weeks later, she sat in her room, reading a book she'd gone though twice already. She wanted to get some fresh books from the library, but had come up with excuse after another, not to venture into town. A knock on her door made her look up.

"Can I come in?" It was Uncle Dave and he sounded excited.

"Sure."

He pushed the door open, but didn't come in. His eyes twinkled. "What are you up to?"

She glanced down at the book and back at him. "Nothing." She was wondering what *he* was up to. Like a happy little boy with a secret, he shifted from one foot to the other. Her curiosity peaked; she smiled at him and said, "what's going on?"

"Oh, nothing much. The store's kind of slow for a Saturday, so I was restocking the shelves and I realized that it's the eleventh. Time to put my order in for next month." He waited, crossing his arms triumphantly across his chest.

She stared at him. "Yeah?"

"The eleventh."

"Yeah?"

A tiny bell jingled in the hall, followed by an impatient scratching. She craned her neck, trying to look past him.

"What is—"

"Kate, don't tell me you don't know what day it is," he said, moving to block her view.

"I know, it's the eleventh, you keep saying—" Then a light went on in her head. How could she have forgotten? Dropping her chin to her chest, she smiled.

"Did you really think I'd forget?" He asked, crossing the room to give her a hug. "What kind of uncle would I be?"

Her smile widened and she brought her arms around his neck. He gave her a tight squeeze and pecked the tip of her nose.

"Be right back, birthday girl." Standing, he left the room, only to return a few seconds later with a large white box, which he placed on Kate's lap.

"Now if you don't like it, I can't take it back, so you have to like it."

She lifted the lid by the red silk bow, and a flurry of fur jumped out, landing clumsily on the bed beside her.

"She's an Australian Shepherd, about eight weeks old," Uncle Dave said, watching her intently.

Kate scooped her up and cuddled the dog in her lap. Playful black eyes peered through the mound of cream–colored fur. Kate ran her fingers through it, as the puppy covered her face and arms with sloppy wet kisses. She giggled.

"What do you think?" He stood back, watching them.

"Oh, I love her. Thank you so much." She held the puppy in one arm and stood to give Uncle Dave another hug. "She's so cute."

"What are you going to name her?"

Kate thought a moment. "Winnie, I think."

"Winnie, I like that. How'd you come up with that?"

"From 'Tuck Everlasting.' " She'd borrowed the book from the library many times when she was a younger and never tired of reading the fascinating story.

"Well, it's a good name for the little rascal," Uncle Dave said, patting Winnie on the head. "Guess I'll let you get ready now."

"Ready for what?"

"Oh, well I just thought, now that you're almost an adult, it's time you experience some fine dining."

"Sixteen is hardly an adult," she scoffed. "Where are we going?"

"You'll see," he said closing the door behind him.

She laid the puppy back on her bed and went to work making a bed for her out the box she had come in. When she was finished, she placed Winnie inside and dishes with food and water on the floor beside her.

"First chance I get, I'll buy you a real puppy bed, I promise."

Winnie blinked at her and then closed her eyes. A few minutes later she was snoring.

Kate sifted through her clothes, trying to find something appropriate to wear. She decided on the black dress she'd worn to Carl's Christmas party last year. The hem barely brushed her knees now, but it was the best outfit she had.

When she was ready, she stood in front of the full–length mirror. The difference was unsettling. She tightened the bow at the small of her back and saw her waist had narrowed, emphasizing her burgeoning breasts. Her cheekbones had lost most of their baby fat, which brought out the green in her eyes, but didn't make her look severe, as with her mother. The tomboy figure was gone, transformed into shapely curves and swells.

But she wasn't fooled. Under the dress and the young woman in it, was grubby little Kate, with dirt under her nails and scabs on her knees. Joey would have laughed to see her, all dressed up and trying to impress. Joey was the pretty one. Always

91

had been. She could have pulled this outfit off, without even try-ing. Could have had people look at her and not feel foolish, be-cause Joey had never known how to cower.

God. Sixteen is old.

"Wow, what a lady." Uncle Dave stood by her open door. "Hope you won't be ashamed to be seen with me," he joked, winking at her.

"Never, not even when you're old and gray and dribbling food down your face." She winked back at him.

"Now would that be the mashed peas, or the mashed car-rots?"

"Carrots, of course, I know how you hate peas."

He laughed. "Well let's get to it. Your chariot awaits, madam."

She slipped her shoes on, gave Winnie a pat on the head, and hurried out to the truck.

The restaurant was fantastic. The food, even better and when the lights dimmed and the waiters stood around their table, singing, Kate beamed her first honest smile in a long time.

Uncle Dave held up his glass in a toast. Ever conscious of the long ride home, it was filled with soda. "To Kate and many, many more song–filled birthday nights, but hopefully not too many more with only her crotchety old uncle for company."

"Why, thank you Uncle Dave."

She touched glasses and looked down at the bowl of deep fried ice cream. A single candle burned on top.

"Make a wish Kate."

Make a wish Kate.

The noisy chatter in the restaurant faded away and was re-placed by the swishing songs of pine trees. She knelt on the ground, her hair damp with rain and plastered to her face. A muf-fin lay in front of her. A match stuck out of the top.

"Hurry up, it's going to go out," Joey said, covering the flame with her hand.

Kate grinned and closed her eyes.

"Make it good, two–digit birthday wishes are stronger than one. But none of them are stronger than your first."

Kate opened her eyes. "How do you know that?"

"Because."

"Because why?"

"Trust me okay? And blow it out already."

Kate smiled, lifting her nose up ever so slightly. "Why should I trust you? You're not even older than me anymore."

"For three weeks," Joey said, not impressed by this old joke. "And besides, I'm still bigger than you, so you better blow it out."

Closing her eyes again, Kate conjured up the drink and wet baby she'd seen on television the week before. The baby actually wet her diapers and came with a crib and a high chair. She was halfway through the wish when the cry of a wolf rose from the mountain behind them.

Kate met Joey's eyes.

Wolves were scarce in this part of the country, preferring the less populated areas north of them, into Canada. Kate had heard more than a few tales about wolves carrying off small children to feed to their young. Not to mention the bad luck. Wolves were worse than a gallon of spilled salt, a thousand broken mirrors and a herd of coloredly challenged cats combined.

Kate held Joey's gaze as the wolf cried again, this time a little closer, or so it seemed. She could see the wolf in Joey's eyes and in a startling flash of insight, caught a glimpse into the unknown future in front of them. For the first time Kate understood that childhood would soon be over. And she didn't need a candle, stuck inside a pathetic little muffin to tell her. There was a stranger creeping into her thoughts, worming into her subconscious and with it came the stifling doubts of her pressing maturity. And as the wolf's cry rose again, she knew. Knew that their days of romping through the creek were rapidly coming to an end.

Her eyes were wet when she closed them one last time.

Please, oh please, let me and Joey always be together. Let

93

us be sisters forever…

   …forever…

   "Katie. Katie?"

   Kate opened her eyes and looked back at the candle. It danced and flickered in the breeze of a passing waiter. Uncle Dave sat across the table, the pleasure of the evening sliding off his face, like the ice cream that melted at the bottom of her dish. She stared at the candle. Stared at it and could find nothing in her heart to wish for, nor could she find breath in her lungs to blow it out. Long, uncomfortable moments passed as Kate stared at the candle. Uncle Dave leaned forward and she watched him try to put the concern she saw in his eyes, to his words. But before he could say anything, another waiter rushed by and this time, the breeze blew out the flame.

   On the way home Uncle Dave was quiet. She stared out the window and saw only blackness and the occasional lights of on-coming cars. The lid to the lock box rattled in the back of the truck.

   "You know Kate, you're growing up." He spoke haltingly, forcing each word out with painful precision. "And I know you've had a tough time. Grown men would have a hard time coming to terms with what you've seen and experienced." He coughed into his hand. "What I'm trying to say, but I won't say well I'm afraid, is that you have a choice. We all have choices in life. Unfortunately, there are too many people who don't realize that and believe that life happens to them. Or, there are people who know they have a choice and the decision scares them so badly; they never do…never make the decision. Instead they whittle away their lives, waiting for the next catastrophe."

   He jerked the wheel to the right to avoid hitting the skunk waddling across the road. It stared at the truck indignantly as they drove by.

   "The sad ones collapse under the hardships of life and make a decision to hide. And in the hiding, lose themselves. Lose who they were and what they wanted. They become empty shells without any hope or expectations."

He snuck a glance at her out of the corner of his eye. She was listening intently.

"But there are a scarce few who take the kicks and blows and stand strong, even thrive. They know that the good, as well as the bad, can help to shape and mold them into a better, more powerful person. Those are the people, Katie, who live life to the fullest. They taste life, feel it and don't shy away. They're not afraid of what may come; they welcome it, knowing that each new experience prepares them for another, no matter how painful it might be.

"But in the end, it's up to you. Nobody can tell you how to handle it, but you have to, handle it I mean, because life goes on no matter what."

Now he ventured a look her way, but Kate didn't trust herself to speak. Unshed tears stung the backs of her eyes and her throat felt too thick to swallow. She nodded and looked back out the window.

Chapter 6
Just a Girl on a Rock

He packed his bag, throwing the canteen, empty wrappers and bait inside with much less care than he had this morning. The sun was still high in the sky, but he'd been at it since the break of dawn and thought a walk might be more relaxing at this point. He would be back tomorrow though. Summers were short in the mountains and he knew his lazy days of fishing would be over sooner than he would like.

Not that the fish would breathe any sigh of relief. He glanced down at the scrawny trout, which panted and twitched at the end of his line. An entire morning of patience had brought about nothing more significant than this pathetic creature that stared up at him with one hopeful eye.

He stared back.

"Oh fine," he said, cutting the line. The fish disappeared into the rapids.

He threw the bag over one shoulder and took off downstream. It was hot out from under the shade of the oak tree where he'd spent the morning and sweat prickled the back of his neck. He stopped to splash some water on his face and take a drink from his canteen before going on.

It had been an uneventful summer so far, with the usual amount of sleeping in and watching reruns on television. He was beginning to think maybe he should have taken his parents' offer and gone to that soccer camp. He liked soccer. He was second captain of the team at school and most of his friends had gone. But for some reason the idea of camp food and eight weeks of male bonding hadn't set well with him. So he opted for a predictable summer of hanging out by the creek.

As he stood and watched the sunlight bounce off the ripples in the water though, he thought maybe this wasn't all that bad.

After all, in a few more weeks he would make sure the fish came to know him as, 'William the Terrible'. He would be their worst nightmare.

Smiling, he climbed up one of the boulders that sat by the edge of the creek, deep in a fantasy about fish slaughter and the heads that would line his walls. At the top, his breath caught and he ducked down.

There was a girl, sitting on a rock in the middle of the creek. Will waited to see if she would call out to him, but he heard nothing. Now what?

What do you mean, now what? She's just a girl, Slappy. Ever seen a girl before? You just walk out there, nod your 'howdy' and be on your way. No great feat.

But Will didn't move. He waited for his heart to catch up with his breath and then peeked through the crack between the boulders. She was still there, but he could only see a part of her leg. He glanced up to the cover of the trees above and made a break for it.

After settling behind a thick trunk, he peered around it, his heart picking up again. She hadn't seen his sprint up the embankment because her back was to him and the roar of the water had drowned out his frantic steps. He found he could watch her easily if he stayed behind the shrubs. The bright glare of the sun would make it almost impossible for her to see anything shadowed in the trees.

He inched closer, feeling all the time the foolishness of what he was doing. He had made it to seventeen without a Peeping Tom charge on his record, but hey, there's always a first time. Or worse yet, she's a karate expert and after beating the crap out of him, she douses his eyes with pepper spray and *then* calls the cops.

Closer and closer he came and then stopped at the edge of the embankment. He could see her fully now and all thought ended as he gazed at the vision she made.

She sat on the large rock in the middle of the creek, head

lowered, one leg tucked beneath her and the other dangling in the water. The hem of her flowing black skirt was pulled up to her thighs to avoid getting it wet. Her toe circled slowly, just skimming the water...around and around and then changing direction, in an easy little rhythm. His gaze lingered on the braided rope tied at her ankle, before climbing up...up...up to the creamy white flesh of her thigh. The skirt began to fall and she hiked it up again as he fell back a little, feeling the blood pound his head.

Go home Will.

But he found he couldn't bear to look away. She pulled him, beckoned him, like nothing he had felt before. He wanted to shout out to her, but had a childish thought that if he did, she would vanish. He glanced upstream and thankfully saw nothing, except for her sandals, cast by the shore. Moving farther downstream, he now crouched straight across from her, but still could not see her face.

She reached into the creek to dip her hand and sprinkle water over her leg. Beads gathered on her skin and the sun lit them ablaze with color. Now she leaned over and splashed water on her face, using her hand to rub it onto her neck and chest. As she sat up, she shook out her thick dark hair, letting it flow over her shoulders and down to her waist. She leaned back on the palms of her hands, arching her back and closing her eyes at the sun. Her profile was clear to Will and again, he felt the heat burn through in his body. Her lips were full and shockingly red against the white of her cheeks. A tiny pool of water puddled at the base of her neck. She jerked suddenly, swatting away a mosquito and as he watched, a line of water broke free from the nook of her throat and traveled down her chest, disappearing into the darkness between her breasts. She settled again, this time on her elbows, letting the loose collar of her shirt slip off of her shoulder. A thin strip of her stomach was bared to the sun and Will caught just a brief glimpse of her sunken belly button.

He dared to move forward even more and she would have been sure to see him if a noise from upstream hadn't distracted her. Will heard it too and backed away.

The trees swayed in the wind that was coming toward them and she stood, sure–footed on the wet surface of the rock to face it. The space of three seconds ticked by and then it was upon them, rushing through her hair and lifting the folds of her skirt. She raised her hands and…oh, heaven was the sound of her voice as she giggled at the dandelion seeds that spun wildly in the air and tickled her face. Like little white ghosts, they danced in a circle around her, getting stuck in her hair and falling into the creek. Then the wind passed and the dandelion seeds were gone.

She stared up the stream, an odd look shadowing her face. Darkness veiled her eyes, but he saw the tears that suddenly streamed down her face. Her mouth didn't move and she never sobbed, but soon her entire cheek was wet with tears and Will felt his own eyes sting as he watched her. The air was heavy and still around them as she continued to stare, transfixed by the water.

Will moved forward a little to follow her gaze, but all he saw were the trees that hung over the creek and the few clouds gathered just above the peaks. The lower clouds were dark and full of rain.

He turned back to the girl.

She was staring at him, her mouth parted, her eyes dry now and sparkling with fear.

Will put his hand out and moved toward the edge, but his foot slipped on the loose gravel and suddenly he was—

—was sliding down the slope and gathering more and more speed until the boy landed at the bottom and was still. Oh god, he was still and Kate thought she heard a scream in the back of her head that made her knees jell and her head swim. No, oh please, please…

But he was getting up, shakily, as his face turned a deep color. He brushed the dirt from his clothes and picked up his bag before turning to her.

"I'm sorry, I—"

She didn't give him a chance to finish. Spinning on one foot, she hopped off the rock and over the stones until she landed on shore. She heard him follow, sloshing through the water and when she turned, she saw him step up on her rock and hold his hands out again.

"Please, I'm sorry, wait," he said and thrust his arms out to keep his balance. He leapt off just before he fell.

Kate ran downstream, leading him through the roughest path, between boulders and over rotting tree trunks to a place where the embankment sloped to meet the creek.

She skidded around the corner and into the trees. Back-tracking along the creek, she slipped behind a bush and waited, high above.

The boy came a few moments later, not winded at all, but stumbling over the loose rocks and struggling to hold onto his bag.

"Hello?" Stopping, he shaded his eyes against the sun. "Hello? Are you there?"

His gaze landed on the bush where she hid and she slunk away on her hands and knees. Then he looked across the creek and called again. "I'm really sorry, I didn't mean to scare you."

She inched forward and saw he was holding her sandals. Puzzled, she leaned even farther out and watched as he continued calling to the wrong side of the creek.

"I know you're there, just come out," he said, running a hand through his hair and taking a few steps into the water.

She stood slowly, as if in a dream. His hand. She had seen him do that before, that nervous gesture which held so much in its simple action. It was his stubborn attempt to take control of a situation he knew to be out of his control. She had admired him that. And had known he would fight to the end for what he knew to be right. It was beyond him to do anything else. It was all in the steadiness of his fingers, the purposeful tilt of his head.

She didn't know this boy. But as she studied the back of his broad shoulders and the firm line of his stance, she felt something stir within her that whispered the relief of having found him again. And as if he heard her call to him, he turned and met her gaze from the top of the embankment. And his eyes...his eyes were so familiar. It was as if she not only knew this boy, but also remembered the feel of his touch. His scent. She was no longer afraid of him, but the fear remained, regardless.

His face brightened in an instant of recognition, but then clouded as he lost it. Not breaking the gaze, he began to climb up the embankment, toward her.

Something was surfacing in her mind, shaking off years of dust and groaning from being crouched in a corner, waiting for this moment. And as much as she was drawn to this stranger, the fear was suddenly too great. She sprang from her hiding place and into the forest.

"No! Wait!"

Into the safety of the trees, she ran. Through the paths she had known since she was small. But always, when she pulled too far away from the boy, she waited, even as the whisper turned into an ugly scream and told her to run, run far away from whoever he was and what he'd bring with him.

She entered a shady glen where the trees formed a circle around a patch of grass that felt like carpet under her bare feet. Moss covered the trunks of the trees in a blanket that muffled the noisy forest wildlife and a wet smell hung in the air like steamed vegetables. She listened for a moment and heard him not far behind, then took cover behind a tree and waited.

Just a few seconds later, the boy broke through the trees and skidded to a halt.

He looked quickly in every direction and again ran his hand through his hair. "Where did you go?" He called, the disappointment ringing in his voice.

She watched him. Watched the easy swing of his walk and the way streaks of sunlight lit the gold in his hair. He circled the glen, looking on the grass for any clue as to which direction she had gone. Then he sat with his head between his knees and sighed. He sat that way for a long, long time, but Kate never tired of watching him. Every move he made was graceful, but powerful. Even the way he retied his shoelace displayed an undercurrent of strength that was simply and wholly, male.

And as she watched, the fear subsided and was replaced by something that was almost as uncomfortable. But she found she enjoyed it, this rising tide of anxiousness that welled up from her stomach. It carried her in its current, lifting her away and to a place where she could feel it rushing through her without being afraid.

She started to move from behind the tree, had taken a few steps toward the boy before she realized what she was doing. Dashing back, she threw herself against the tree and held her breath, but he didn't call out and she closed her eyes in relief.

Minutes later she inched around the trunk and dared a peek. He was gone. Only the impression of his body remained on the soft forest floor. He had given up and went home. She had waited too long.

She walked to where he'd been sitting and felt his warmth beneath her feet. Well good. It was good that he had gone. He had been just a boy. Just a boy and not anything so special that she should be feeling this way. Just a boy who had stolen her shoes.

Really?

Yes really. What had she been thinking? There was no reason for it, in fact—

"There you are."

She spun around and into the arms of the boy who stood just inches behind her.

"Oh!" She stumbled but he caught her easily and brought her to him. Her face was close enough to feel his quickened breath on her cheek and darkness came as his scent washed over her. They stood in a frozen moment, trembling, until the shrill call of a blue jay broke the spell. She pushed out of his arms and backed away.

"Please don't go," he said stepping toward her, being careful not to get too close.

Her heel bumped the base of a tree and she put her hands behind her to hold onto its trunk as she circled it, keeping her eyes on the boy.

"I don't mean you any harm," he said and winced as he realized how stupid it sounded.

Something softened inside her to see his embarrassment and she almost smiled.

"I mean, you don't have to be afraid, I was just walking home and well," he faltered and came a little closer. "What's your name?"

"Why would you want to know my name?"

"Well, it's just, I don't know, I think I might already know."

"You think you know my name?"

"Why do you keep answering with more questions?"

"Sometimes questions are more important than answers."

He smiled. "Well my name's Will."

"How nice for you."

She moved further into the forest, using the trees as a barrier between them. Further and further, as the sound of the creek died away and the sun became hidden behind the dense branches above. Will followed her, shadowing her movements and always keeping her in his sight.

"Stop following me."

He climbed to the top of a fallen tree and stood above her. "Tell me your name."

"No."

"Why?"

"Why?" She asked, lifting an eyebrow. "Because I don't usually talk to people who make a habit out of spying on people and then stalking them through the woods."

"I wasn't, spying I mean, I was just walking home and," he stopped, his cheeks ablaze with color. "I don't spy on people."

She ducked behind another tree. "Yeah, you just steal their shoes."

He glanced at the sandals in his hand and grinned. "Tell me your name and I'll give you the shoes."

"I'd rather go barefoot."

His grin widened. "Since you have such pretty feet—"

"Stop it," she said, tucking her toes under the folds of her skirt.

"Then tell me your name. And tell me why I know you."

"How should I know."

He jumped off the trunk and strode to where she stood, half hiding behind a tree. She turned away, but not quick enough, as he grabbed her shoulders and forced her to look at him.

"Because you do know," he said, the teasing light in his eyes gone and replaced by an urgency that scared her. "Stop dancing around it. You know, I can see it in your eyes. Though, God help me, I see more than that in your eyes. It's almost like," he stopped and blew out his breath as he ran out of words.

"What?" The answer that had been eluding her was so close to the surface on his confused face.

"I don't know, but it's driving me nuts. How do I know you?"

"I don't—"

A rushing noise was building in the back of her head, like the sound of a wave rising up from behind and you turn, just in time to realize it's too late.

She *did* know him.

"What? What's wrong?"

Oh, but there were so many things wrong with meeting him out here, like this and for him to be looking at her with all that she found in his eyes was just more proof of how wrong things were.

The wave was directly over her now and a voice shot out from the depths of the dark water.

Kate, Kate can you hear me?

The wave crashed over her head.

"Oh–oh my God," she gasped, backing away.

He let her go, looking at his hands for a moment and then back at her. "No, don't go, I'm sorry," he said, realization breaking in his eyes. "I didn't mean, I–I'm so sorry."

But she was going. Backing away from him and stumbling over the twigs and rocks and turning to run from him, faster and faster away from those familiar eyes and all she'd known to be peaceful until now, as the wave continued to crash down on her, crumpling her under its pressure. Drowning...sinking into the darkness that had no exit but to run and run and hope to escape before it crushed her.

And as she ran, she heard him call. His voice reached her like a bolt of lightening in a storm, but she ran from it, knowing the pain in doing so was nothing compared to the anguish of meeting his eyes again. He raced after her, but she soon lost him as she zigzagged through the trees. Only his shouts remained, bouncing off the trees and raw with sorrow.

"Please wait...Kate...Kate..."

Chapter Seven
Dancing Round the Fire

The backdoor was slamming in the wind again and though she jumped with each bang, she made no move to leave the stool.

The store was empty, as it always was on Tuesdays and the silence was more distracting than anything else. The chatter of a passing couple reached her through the door and she briefly considered opening it, if only to have the noise from the street, not to mention cooling it off in here. The air was heavy with mid–summer heat and even the fly that swooped by her head every few minutes, buzzed slow and tired. An open door would probably stir up some business as well. She grimaced at the possibility and the door stayed closed.

She glanced at the clock again. Uncle Dave should have been back by now. He made a run down into Quarryville to pick up some lumber for the back porch. The guy on the phone had quoted a ridiculous price for delivery, so he had gone to get it in the truck. He'd been muttering when he left and Kate had felt a twinge sympathy for whoever had the misfortune of helping him when he got there.

Sighing, she looked down at Winnie, who snuggled by her feet. A soggy dog biscuit lay between her paws and she gnawed on the end of it with serious concern. The biscuit slipped from her grip and Winnie looked up at Kate with hopeful black eyes.

"Get it, lazy," she said.

But Winnie whined, not wanting to leave her box. She had bought Winnie a padded puppy bed from Chamberlain's, but the dog wanted no part of it and so it sat in the corner of the store, collecting dust.

Kate pushed the biscuit with her foot to where Winnie could reach it. She bit into it eagerly and resumed her gnawing.

The bell above the door jangled as it was opened and she sat up, arranging her face into what she hoped was a passable smile.

"Jesus, it's hot in here," said the girl who came in and shoved the door so it would stay open.

Kate felt her smile falter. "Can I help you?"

The girl turned to Kate, flashing a bright smile of her own. "So here you are," she said, widening her lips to show all her teeth. "I heard you were back, but I had to come and see for myself."

Kate's smile was completely gone now. "Hi Rosie."

"You remember me, that is so sweet. And it's just Rose now, Rosie's so 'little girl', don't you think, Katie?"

"Whatever."

She pranced over to the counter and lifted herself to sit on top. "Well my god, you really are here, we all just about shit when we heard you were back."

"Just about?"

"I mean," she went on, "when Lisa told me how her mom saw you last week, I was like, no way. I thought she was full of it you know, 'cause Lisa's always full of something. But well, you remember Lisa don't you?" She fluffed some of her fiery red hair over one shoulder and leaned closer to Kate on her palm. "I just didn't believe her so I had to come for myself and now I just can't believe it anyway. Why in hell would you want to come back here?"

Kate stood and drifted toward the end of the counter, away from Rosie. "Well my uncle is here, you know."

"Well yeah, of course, but what everybody wants to know is, where you've been girl?"

"I've been staying with my foster parents until now," she said, restacking the sunglass case and wishing she had locked the front door.

"Shit! Foster parents. I was sure you'd run off to California or something." She dug into her purse and pulled out a pack of cigarettes.

"Why would I be in California?" And why was she asking

such a stupid question?

Rosie lit the cigarette and inhaled deeply. "I dunno," she said through a puff of smoke. "Selling drugs or whoring maybe. Course most people just figured you'd be in the loony bin down in Quarryville."

"Nope, just foster parents, no drugs, no whoring," she said, narrowing her eyes. "And I haven't even killed anybody, yet."

Rosie hopped off the counter, sauntered over to where Kate stood and began fingering the sunglasses. "Touchy, touchy, some things never change. I just wanted to come by and welcome you back, you don't have to get like that."

Kate raised her eyebrows and stared at Rosie.

"Really, I wanted to be friendly–like 'cause I knew you'd probably be freaking out about being back here and all. I mean you are, right?"

"I am what?"

"Freaking out. I know you must be, it's got to be horrible being back here after what happened. I couldn't do it. I know that. I couldn't face everybody in this town knowing they knew what'd happened. I'd just want to die from—"

"Did you need something?" Kate's voice instantly cooled the hot room.

Rosie took another drag of her cigarette as her smile drooped into more of a growl. "Yeah, I'll take these," she said, plucking a pair of sunglass out of the case at random. "They'll have to do until I can get to the mall."

"Well if you're ready," Kate said, motioning to the register. Rosie stormed away and slammed the glasses on the counter.

Kate followed, the knot in her stomach going away, now that the stupid grin was gone from Rosie's face.

After taking her change, Rosie hurried toward the door, but stopped before leaving. "Guess I'll be seeing you at school, Katie," she said and breezed out to the street.

"Yeah," Kate said, sighing. "I'm sure."

The sun rose to hang directly above the street and wash everything in its blinding light and foot traffic thinned as the heat of the day weighed on the town. Even the occasional drafts that blew through the open door were stuffy and only made Kate hotter.

She tipped the stool to lean against the wall and prop her feet up on the counter. A magazine lay on her lap, opened to the re–subscription page. Kate stared at the shelves of canned goods on the opposite wall, thoughts of beauty tips and men–catching ideas lost in the rambling images from the day before.

He's real.

She said it to herself over and over again, but it didn't gain the grounded belief she was looking for. She'd seen him, touched him, and talked to him. That should make him real, right?

The fact was the boy from the house had grown in mythical proportions in her mind. She had considered him to be an angel, sent from God, to guide her through that hellish night. A tutelary spirit, which she most likely made up within her own damaged psyche.

But he *is* real. And probably thinking she really was a raving lunatic. She shook her head, thinking about her dramatically embarrassing exit. Why had she run? Would it have been so hard to simply meet him, make polite conversation, even *thank* him, for obvious reasons? What the hell was wrong with her?

She knew what was wrong. So much more than just the shame of seeing him again. And there was shame, oh yes. How could he look at her, let alone want to be around her after seeing what he had? He should have run the second he realized who she was. But he hadn't...and that's what was wrong.

The fly buzzed lazily by her ear and she swished it away with the magazine. She hit it, amazingly enough and it landed just outside Winnie's box. Winnie perked up her ears and sniffed at it before closing her eyes again.

Kate stared at the fly, noticing its one twitching leg. "Won't have the guts to do that again, will you?" She said, stealing one of Carl's worn out phrases. The leg twitched once more.

Tossing the magazine on the counter, she went to get the broom from behind the door. After sweeping up the fly, she made her way out to the aisles, taking her time and shoving most of the debris under the shelves. She pushed the broom around the corner, starting up the center aisle and her eyes were on the ceiling when the broom nicked the edge of the glass display.

Thirty shot glasses with 'Top of the Day from Newclare, PA' written across the front, came crashing down around her feet.

Groaning she crouched on her hands and knees to begin picking up the biggest pieces.

"Top of the day to you to," she muttered and threw a handful of glass into the trashcan. Winnie emerged from behind the counter and settled a few feet away. She pawed at the floor and growled softly, telling Kate she was ready to play, but Kate ignored her as she continued cleaning up the mess.

A shadow fell across the floor beside her and she sighed.

"We're closed," she said, without turning.

The shadow moved as if it were leaving, but then stopped, hedging in the doorway.

Kate picked up the bottom of another glass, shivering in the sudden cool breeze. "I'm sorry, but we're—" Her hand hesitated above the trashcan. She glanced at the shape of the shadow on the cement floor and felt goose bumps down her back.

He was watching her.

She turned and landed on her rear in the pile of glass, but didn't feel the shards cut her skin as she stared at the figure in the entryway. All she could make out was a large, dark man–shape. The sunlight filtered in between his arms and legs, haloing him in an unearthly glow.

He's here...oh God he's here, he's come for me now...

She skittered on her hands and feet, backing away from the figure and sending glass skating across the floor. The cool breeze turned into icy knives, hitting her bared skin as her eyes darted around the room, finding nothing more substantial to defend herself with than the rolls of toilet paper that fell off the shelf when she banged into it. She grabbed a roll.

The figure rushed into the store and bent beside her.

"I keep doing that, jeez I'm sorry," he said, taking the roll from her and setting it back on the shelf.

It was Will. Only Will. She closed her eyes and fought against the nausea rising in her throat. Who had she thought it would be?

"Are you okay? I didn't mean—"

"I'm fine," she said, feeling heat spread from her neck and into her face. Was there no end of making a fool out of herself in front of him?

Smiling, he reached down to help her up, but his face clouded again as he glanced at her hand.

"You're bleeding," he said, nodding at the gash across her palm.

The blood was dripping on the floor and making a spectacular puddle between her feet. The heat traveled up to her ears. She guessed there really was no end, being a fool had taken precedence over everything else.

She tried to catch some of the blood with her other hand, as Will ran to the counter. Reaching around, he came out with the paper towels Uncle Dave always kept on the shelf underneath. She didn't ask how he had known they were there, she didn't trust her voice at this point.

"Here, squeeze it," he said.

"Thanks." She held the paper on the cut and began cleaning the glass again.

Will brought the trashcan closer and they were finished cleaning up the glass a few minutes later.

She took the bag to the back porch and when she came back, found Will by the counter, fiddling with the baseball cards. His face brightened as she came around the counter and sat back on the stool.

"So...you're living here now?" He glanced around the store.

"Yeah, with my uncle."

"That's good, I mean," he reddened and looked at the floor. "I mean it's good, you know, to be with your family." He stopped and looked up, his eyes stricken. "Jeez, I'm sorry, that didn't come out right."

"That's okay."

A measured pause went by, as Winnie whined quietly, wanting another biscuit.

"Is he yours?" Will leaned across the counter.

Kate dug through the bag under the counter and retrieved another treat. Winnie went to work on it immediately. "It's a she. And yeah, I got her for my birthday."

"She's a beauty. A shepherd?"

"Yeah." Kate picked her up, causing the biscuit to fall into her bed and held her up to Will. Winnie closed her eyes and let him scratch her behind the ears, momentarily forgetting her abandoned treat.

"What's her name?"

"Winnie." She rubbed Winnie's back and touched Will's fingers for a moment. A surge of electricity passed between them and her breath caught. She dared a glance up at him and saw the shock in his eyes too.

She withdrew her hand. "I named her after the girl from Tuck—"

"Tuck Everlasting." They said it together and Will smiled. "I loved that book when I was a kid."

The tempting biscuit was too much for Winnie and she kicked her feet furiously to get down. Kate almost dropped her and the dog landed on her side, righted herself and scampered over to her bed to resume slobbering over it.

"Should have named her piglet," Kate said.

Will chuckled.

Another long moment passed between them and then was shattered as Uncle Dave burst into the store, carrying a large box.

Will jumped back from the counter as if he'd been burned.

113

"Man, oh, man. Some people are just not fit to walk upright. You should have heard this idiot, Kate—" He stopped, having seen Will. "I'm sorry, didn't know anyone was here. How're you doing Will?"

"Fine, good," he said and wiped his hands on the front of his jeans.

Uncle Dave squinted a little at Will and smiled. "Well that's good to hear. Your mom send you in for something?"

"No, I was just, um." He looked helplessly at Kate.

"He wanted to know when the next issue of Spy Man was coming out."

Will looked at her and mouthed, *Spy Man?*

She shushed him, grinning.

"Spy Man. I used to read that one," Uncle Dave said, the squint becoming deeper. "I was a big fan, but it just wasn't the same after they got rid of Chieko, huh?" He dropped the box on the floor and something rattled inside. "He came up with the greatest one–liners."

"Yes sir, the greatest." Will raised his eyebrows at Kate, who shrugged her shoulders.

"Well did you set him up with anything Kate?"

"Huh? Oh, no we won't get them in until next week," she said, still looking at Will.

He held her gaze. "Well, I guess I'll be back then."

"Or you could come back in a couple of days. You know," she said, glancing at her uncle, "in case they come early."

"Okay. That sounds good," Will said, backing toward the door. "Guess I'll see you then."

"Yeah, I'll see you..." She watched him walk out to the street, grab his ten–speed and peddle away.

Uncle Dave began unpacking the box, bringing out cases of nails and other supplies. "He's a good kid, that Will."

She nodded and went back to her magazine.

"Yeah, I used to have all those comics when I was a kid," he continued, talking more to himself. "Spy Man, Flash Racer,

Tales of Terror. They were all I would read and it drove my mom nuts."

"Huh."

"Yeah, that Chieko was a crack–up."

"Huh."

"Yeah, funny thing is though," he said, looking up at Kate. "Chieko was in Lightening Man, not Spy Man." He grinned widely, winked and went into the kitchen.

* * * * *

Will was whistling.

Riding down Main Street toward home, his head lifted high, his eyes dangerously preoccupied, he piped out a tune that made the shoppers on the street pause to watch him go by. Packages under their arms, they smiled and pointed out the local boy. A little blonde girl with a swirled lollipop, roughly the size of her head waited impatiently outside the Wood 'n More shop for her mother to decide on exactly which wooden squirrel would look right as a towel rack for the kitchen. She paused in the midst of her candy binge to watch Will, fervently wishing to have a big grown up bike like his instead of the prissy pink one her mother had bought her last Christmas with the stupid ribbons on the handles.

Will came to the end of the street and swerved left. Mr. O'Neil came running out of his house waving his fist, as Will cut across his yard and headed up Galway.

The fact that he didn't know how to whistle or even recognize the tune he was whistling was the farthest thing from his mind. He had seen Kate today and that knowledge filled every available crevice of his consciousness.

In the six years since he met her, not a day had gone by without seeing her face, or hearing her voice. Every girl, who had sparked his interest in those years, had been compared to that scrawny ten–year–old with the melodious voice and the wild green eyes. Will had tried to make sense of it, rationalizing it as an extreme situation that was bound to leave him confused. He tried to reason with his heart and tell himself how ridiculous it was to listen to a boyhood fantasy. Nothing would change the intrinsic truth however; he loved her.

Not a light, flimsy sort of infatuation. A frail, shaky love that collapsed under the weight of its own intensity. Kate had seeped into his soul, not only invading his thoughts, but the very essence of his identity. And up until this afternoon, he had still been trying to deny it. It made no sense and Will was a boy who loved to make sense. His passion was logic. He loved the simplicity of it. The power. His logic told him that it was impossible for him to have such feelings for a girl he didn't know, had only spoke with once and under such circumstances no less. Nonetheless, she enchanted him and the simplicity of that...well, it kept him awake at night.

Rounding the turn up his driveway, Will skidded to a stop, left his bike by the bushes and leapt up to the porch in one stride. His mother was inside finishing the roast they would have for dinner. She bent over the pot, as her ponytail swung to brush her face.

"Your father called, he won't be home for dinner. They want to finish laying the asphalt before that storm comes in." She paused to look at Will. "What's with you? You're all teeth and grin."

"Nothing." He helped himself to a sliver of meat from the pot. "Must be the weather."

"Hey, get your fingers out of there." She swiped at him with the spoon. "It's not done."

He grabbed a can of soda from the refrigerator and sat down at the table. "See those clouds? Looks like we're in for a good one, you can feel the energy."

She glanced out the window to the black clouds accumulating outside. "You always did like bad weather," she said, shaking her head. "Even when you were a baby. You'd lie in your crib cooing and giggling at the thunder until it soothed you to sleep. Must get it from your fathers' side. They're all quirky like that."

Will's eyes danced. "So what are you saying, that all my peculiar traits I inherited from dad's family? That's not possible."

"Yes it is, and all the normal ones come from mine," she said, flicking the spoon at him. Splatters of beef broth flew across the room.

"Hey!" Will ducked, laughing.

"Hey, hey, what's going on in here?" His grandma stood in the doorway, leaning on her walker. "I leave you alone for one minute Julie, and you're starting food fights with my grandson." She limped over to the table and sat down with a sigh, patting Will's hand. "How're you doing, boy?"

"He started it with his obsession about bad weather." Turning the water on, his mother began washing the dishes.

"What's wrong with enjoying the variety the good Lord has to offer?" His grandma said. "I've always felt most alive in the midst of a really nasty storm."

"You see?" His mom said, pointing a sudsy finger at him.
Will laughed.

"So what have you been up to?" His grandmother went on. "You were gone most of the day."

"Just stuff, went into town. It's pretty busy down there for a week day."

"And the festival's only going to bring in more of the buggers." She ran her tongue along her toothless gums. "Wish they'd never come back, the lot of them."

"Frank would be out a job then, Edith," his mom said gently.

"Humph." Grandma didn't like anyone disagreeing with her any more than grandpa had. She began arranging the plates around the table, a smirk on her mouth.

"I did stop by Dave's Supply," Will said, changing the subject quickly. "They've got a new sign out front. You should see it grandma, it's the biggest one in town. The letters must be three feet tall, at least."

Grandma set the plate down slowly. "So you've been to see her then," she said, fixing her wrinkled gaze on Will.

"Who?" Will asked.

"Who?" She repeated, mocking him. "Kaitlin O'Connor. That's who."

Will lowered his head. "Oh, well yeah. She's living there with her uncle now."

"I know that. Lord boy, the whole town knows that. What I'm wonderin' is why did you go over there."

His mother paused at the sink and waited for his answer.

"Well...to see how she was. You know," he finished lamely.

Drying her hands on a towel, his mother came to stand by the table. "Will, I thought your father and I had explained that we don't feel comfortable with you spending time with Kate."

"But you never told me why." After his parents had learned what had happened at the house that night, they grew strangely quiet. His father had stopped just short of forbidding him to see her again, forcing Will to sneak out one night and hitch a ride to see her in the hospital. "What's the big deal with me seeing Kate?" He asked again.

"I told you, your father and I just don't think it's a good idea. She's been through a lot and coming back here must be very hard on her."

"Which is all the more reason to see her. She'll need all the friends she can get."

"But you don't need to get mixed up in all of her problems, Will. She's probably a very troubled girl."

"I still don't get you."

As if she had suddenly become cold, his mother rubbed her arms as she continued. "The kids at your school are bound to make trouble for her and I just don't see any reason for you to be involved."

"You've got to be kidding me. That's so ludicrously shallow, mom. I don't want to get caught on the wrong side, because I might be teased?" He asked scornfully. "I thought you had higher morals."

"That's not what this is about," she said in a low tone.

"Tell me then. What is this about?"

"I'm just trying to protect you from a difficult situation. It's for—"

"If you say it's for my own good, your mother rating really will drop."

"Will!" She fell back as if he had hit her.

He stood and his chair scrapped noisily against the kitchen tile. "I don't want to talk about this anymore." Striding through the kitchen, he went to his room, feeling his mother's hurt eyes follow him all the way down the hall.

He closed his door, careful not to slam it and sat on his bed, looking out the window. Childish disappointment crushed down on him as the wonderful feelings from the afternoon, faded away into painful bitterness. The Kate subject had been a sore one for a while in the Harrickson household. Will had let it go because there was no use arguing over it when she wasn't even in town anymore.

But she was back now, and Will realized that this had to be resolved. If he knew what their problem was, it would be easier to understand. Will was hesitant to believe his parents would blame her for the problems she had. They wouldn't color their opinion of her, based on the towns' perception.

There had to be more.

A knock on the door interrupted his thoughts. "Come in."

"Why are you hiding in here?" It was his grandma's voice.

"I'm not hiding," Will said, not turning.

"And pouting too, no less. Looks like we have the makings of a fine temper tantrum." She chuckled and he heard her walker thump farther into the room. "You know your mother is upset out there. She's throwing God knows what into that pot. Splashing things and making a grand mess. Don't know if I'll be up to eating what she turns out."

He smiled.

"Why don't you get yourself together in here and then go help your mom. She's only thinking of you Will. I can see you bristling at that, but it's true, all the same. You think seventeen is old enough to know all there is to know. That you're a man now with all the answers, but there's not a speck of truth in that. Your grandfather thought it at seventy and he wasn't any more right than you. But I'm falling off my track." She sighed. "Sometimes in life you take what's handed to you Will, and not ask for more. Sometimes you don't want more, trust your ancient grandmother. Your parents and I know what we're talking about with this whole Kaitlin O'Connor situation. It will only bring you pain in the end."

Will finally turned, but his grandmother was already moving out of the room, shuffling her walker across the carpet. He turned back to the window. What was going on here?

* * * * *

The pole to the tent was leaning and Kate caught it just before it dragged the whole thing down on top of them.

"You have that side?" Mrs. Whitmore asked, holding her end.

"Yeah, we're going to have to pound it in farther," Kate said, as a breeze blew under the tent, almost yanking the pole from her hands.

Mrs. Whitmore craned her neck and spoke to the little girl who played in the grass behind her. "Emily honey, go find us a rock. A big one."

Emily smiled and bounced to her feet. "Can I keep it when you're done?"

"Sure," she said and Emily ran off, returning a few seconds later.

"Here Kaitlin, this is a good one because it's so smooth on this side, see?"

Kate took the rock and inspected it closely. "I bet it's the smoothest rock in the park, good job." Hooking the leg of the chair with her foot, she pulled it over and stepped up on it. She pounded the pole farther into the ground and then hopped off.

"Check this out," she said, crouching to Emily's eye level. "Do you see what I see?"

Emily studied the rock, her eyes brightening. "It's a face! Look, ears and a chin."

Kate put it in her hand and pointed to the tent across from them. "I bet if you ask real nice, Mrs. McGrath over there might let you use some of her paints."

Charlotte McGrath was busily painting a red heart on a screaming baby's cheek. She saw Emily smiling at her and waved the little girl over.

Emily skipped to the booth and knelt by her feet, bumping her arm. The brush made a red streak across the baby's face and Emily laughed, saying something about Indians. Mrs. McGrath laughed with her and patted Emily's head, before wiping the baby's face.

Kate walked around the tent to see if there was any sign of Uncle Dave. He disappeared about an hour ago to 'talk shop' with some of the guys. Or so he said. She spotted him, a couple of booths down, sitting in a lawn chair and drinking out of a styrofoam cup. From the way his voice carried and the uproarious laughter from the group around him, she figured they must have been sampling some of the Irish coffee. As she looked around, she noticed that just about everybody was sampling the coffee.

She smiled and leaned against the table. She and Joey had gone to the festival every year, but she didn't ever remember this many people being there.

Cars overflowed the road by Kerry Park and were now being parked on the grass by the banner that read, 'Welcome to Newclare's Festival of Lughnasad'. Tourists, ten feet deep made the rounds at the booths, picking up odds and ends to take back to their homes in the city. Some were gathered around the band that played by the last booth. They played one Irish reel after another, taking short breaks between songs to take a drink from their styrofoam cups. And beyond them, a group of boys scurried about collecting wood for the bonfire that would be lit after sundown.

She and Mrs. Whitmore were manning the jewelry booth. Uncle Dave had sprung it on her last night and she was upset at first, but now she was enjoying herself. Mrs. Whitmore had insisted they dress the part and it had fun this morning getting decked out. Kate wore a long skirt that brushed her bare feet and a short top that hung off her shoulders and left most of her midriff exposed. "You're a beautiful girl, Kaitlin, there's nothing wrong with letting the world see it," Mrs. Whitmore had said when she'd protested. Kate warmed to hear her say that and almost came to tears when Mrs. Whitmore hugged her. Together they picked out jewelry for each other and Kate had ended up with a Runic Cross necklace, matching earrings, a Dragon armband, bracelets on both wrists and a ring on every finger. Kate had never seen so much jewelry in her life and she loved the way she sparkled when she caught herself in the mirror.

"Just get something, Carol and let's get out of here," said the man to her right. He stood behind a woman who ignored him and picked up a pendant, turned it slowly in her hand and then set it down to pick up another one.

The man grunted and dug something out of his teeth. He stared at it for a second and then flicked the piece of crud into the crowd. "What the hell does 'Lug–na–sad' mean anyway?" He asked, nodding at the banner. "Sounds like some German shit to me."

Mrs. Whitmore looked up slowly, having been trying to ignore the man. "It's Irish actually. The founders of our town were Irish immigrants." She gave him a smile that dripped with sweetness. "And it's pronounced, Loo–na–shav. They celebrated it every August first to give thanks for the harvest."

He grunted again. "Give thanks for stealing our country is more like."

"What's this one called?" His wife asked, holding up a necklace.

"Jesus, Carol. Just call it over–priced crap. I can't believe…"

"Chuck, why don't you get yourself a drink and I'll catch up to you later," Carol said with a cool look.

To Kate's surprise, Chuck backed off, muttering under his breath as he drifted into the crowd.

Carol watched until he was gone and then turned back to the table.

"It's a Celtic Pentagram," Mrs. Whitmore told her. "It's the symbol of creation and the way all of life is connected in one way or another."

Carol smiled. "I like that. Do you have anything in silver?"

Mrs. Whitmore led her to the other end of the booth as Emily ran up to Kate, holding out her brightly painted rock.

"Look, look Kaitlin, Mrs. McGrath let me use all her dark colors to make the face and look," she said, turning it over. "She put a fairy on the back and then she put one on me." Emily pointed to her cheek where a tiny fairy had been painted amidst a sprinkling of gold.

"Wow that's neat, she's almost as pretty as you."

Emily beamed. "I'm gonna go show Mamma," she said and ran to Mrs. Whitmore. She almost knocked her down in her excitement and Mrs. Whitmore quickly handed the lady her change so she could give Emily her full attention.

Kate turned to stare vacantly into the crowd. Her foot tapped to the cheerful rhythm of the band and she smiled as she saw Uncle Dave coming toward her.

"There's my Katie girl, where have you been hiding your pretty self?" He asked throwing an arm around her and planting a kiss on the top of her head.

"I've been right here Uncle Dave," Kate said, laughing.

"It's good to see you're enjoying yourself."

"Aye, but I am lassie," he said in a bad accent. "You look like you could use a bit of enjoyment yourself. There's lots to see and do." He pointed to a booth across from them. "Have you tried the potato soup? Mrs. Culloty cooks up a mean pot, hot enough to clean out your innards, but well worth the pain."

She laughed again. "No, but I hear the coffee's pretty good."

"Really?"

"I'm not going to have to carry you home tonight am I?"

He pounded comically on his chest. "No, strong as a bloody ox, I am. Besides, I'm sure I'll be able to crawl." He waved at his buddies, who were motioning for him to come back. Then he stopped with his hand in mid–air and the smile died on his face.

She turned to follow his gaze and saw Mrs. Whitmore standing behind her. She was looking back at Uncle Dave and Kate saw a flash of fear light her eyes.

"Hello David," she said softly.

He brushed back his hair. "Hi Judy, wow, you look great." He looked down to the peasant dress she wore and then back at her face. "It's been a long time."

She flushed. "You look well…"

Emily broke away from her mother and ran to Uncle Dave. "Look, look, I made a face and I got to use all the dark paints. And on this side—"

"Honey, don't bother Mr. O'Connor with that," Mrs. Whitmore said, sprinting forward to pull Emily back and again, Kate caught a flash of fear in her eyes.

Uncle Dave smiled in confusion. "I don't mind," he said, turning his hurt eyes on Mrs. Whitmore. "That's a very nice rock, Emily. You did a good job."

Mrs. Whitmore shifted uncomfortably and looked into the crowd as Emily sat in the grass, pouting.

Kate stood between them for a moment and then bent down to Emily. "Hey, you want to go get some strawberry scones? They have the biggest strawberries I've ever seen over there," she said, pointing.

Emily smiled and nodded, but her mother picked her up. "I'll take her Kate. I'd like to have a look around," she said, not meeting Uncle Dave's eyes. "We'll bring you back some, you don't mind watching the booth, do you?"

"No, that's fine," Kate said and watched her thread her way through the crowd.

Uncle Dave stared after them. "That woman never fails to confound me," he muttered and shook his head.

"What—"

"I'll see you later, sweetie," he said, grazing her forehead with a kiss. He shoved his hands deep in his pockets and hurried off in the opposite direction.

Kate shook her head as she turned to help the twenty or so elderly ladies who had surrounded her booth. They had come together on a bus and wanted one of everything it seemed to take back to their daughters and granddaughters. Kate smiled patiently as she showed the items and explained their significance.

She was arranging their money in the box under the table when she heard a voice from behind.

"Hey kitty–kitty."

Standing, she turned to the boy who stood on the other side of the table. "Doesn't that ever get old?"

Ben laughed. "It *is* you, man I can't believe it."

Kate thumped the lid to the box closed with her foot and shoved it underneath the table. "Believe it."

"Rosie said she saw you at the store, but she's always bullshitting me." He ducked under the canopy to get a better look and Kate suddenly felt squeamish under his gaze. Ricky stepped out from behind him and joined his friend under the canopy.

"Hi Ricky," Kate said, backing away from Ben.

Ricky smiled wide and nodded. His glassy eyes said it all.

Oh yeah, this is fun.

"So where've you been hiding yourself, I haven't seen you

125

around," Ben said.

"Haven't been hiding, just helping out at the store."

Ben held the pole with one hand and let the smile slide further up his face. "Well you're here now and I've got to say, you look good, girl. `Bout time we had some fresh meat around here."

"You're going to break that," Kate said and pulled another box from under the table.

Ben let go of the pole. "Just as cold as ever, man. Here I was hoping you'd loosened up a little, seeing as how I'm free of the Rosie shackles now and you're looking so good."

"Thanks Ben. And you, you're looking...bigger."

Ben had filled out, his baby fat had thickened into hard muscle and he had gained several inches, but his eyes still had the same hardened glint.

"Football. I made the team last year."

Pound on your chest while you're at it...

"Well it suits you," Kate said, taking the necklaces out of the box and arranging them on the table.

"I'll tell you what suits me." Ben followed her to the end of the table and blocked her way. "So what do you say we blow out of here? Come on, there's a truck rally down in Quarryville tonight and if you're nice," Ben said, tugging on the end of her sleeve and pulling it farther off her shoulder. "Maybe I'll take you for a drive."

Kate jumped back, shooting him an icy smile. "Well gee Ben, as much as I'd like to spend the evening, tipping cows and spitting tobacco, I'm pretty sure I have something better to do." She tried to push past him.

He stepped forward, boxing her in between the tables. "I don't think so. You've been gone a long time Katie, and things have changed around here. I've changed," he picked up her amulet and twirled it around his finger. She could smell the liquor on his breath. "You've changed. I figure we've got a lot of catching up to do."

"Think I've had just about all the catching up I can stand,"

Kate said, throwing off his hand and slipping past him.

Ben stormed after her and caught her elbow, spinning her around. "Hey, where're you going? I'm—"

"Now this just can't be good for business," said a familiar voice.

Kate yanked her arm out of Ben's grasp and looked up at Will. He was standing on the other side of the table, hands in his pockets and a grin on his face. She grinned back.

"You might want to find yourself another assistant, Katie. Big Ben here's likely to scare away all your customers." Will made his way around the table and stopped in front of Ben.

"Get the hell out of here, Harrickson." Ben stepped forward and now the boys were almost toe to toe.

"You first," Will said, holding his ground and part of the grin. A dangerous light shone in his eyes and Kate caught a wave of the pleasure he was feeling. He was enjoying himself, seemed to be urging Ben to make the first move. And though his lean body was no match for Ben's football pounds, Kate suddenly had no doubt as to who would come out on top. Will had the confidence Ben lacked. And Ben knew it; it showed on his confused face. But Kate thought more than anything it was the eager expectancy Will emitted that made Ben back off. Ben never moved away, but his shoulders slumped and he was having trouble holding Will's steady gaze.

"Now unless you needed to pick up something for your girlfriend there," Will said, motioning to Ricky. "Why don't you be moving along. I'm sure Kate can handle it from here."

Ricky, who'd been hiding behind Ben, grabbed Ben's shoulder and pulled him away. "Come on man, you're mom's coming," he said, pointing.

Mrs. Easley waved at them from across the crowd. "Benny, Benny where's your brother?"

"She looks pissed, *Benny*," Will said, glancing over his shoulder.

"Shut the hell up, Harrickson." Ben knocked Will in the

shoulder as he brushed past him. "And stay out of my way from now on."

"Benny! I told you to keep an eye on him, where is he?" Mrs. Easley held onto to her straw hat to keep it from blowing away. "You get over here right now and help me find him."

Slapping Ricky on the back, Ben led him away. "Bitch," he said glaring at his mother. "Come on let's get out of here."

Kate tried to sidestep them as they passed, but Ben paused to hold her arm and hiss in her ear. "See you later, kitty–cat."

She jerked away and Ben laughed, heading for the woods at the edge of the park.

"You okay?" Will was at her side, concern pushing aside that strange light she had seen earlier.

Kate let out a shaky laugh. "Yeah, guess I should swoon now, huh?"

Will smiled. "Well, you are in the presence of great manhood."

Mrs. Whitmore was coming toward them, with Emily by her side. The little girl beamed at Kate and Will through a mouthful of strawberries that covered her mouth and ran down her chin to stain the front of her white ruffled dress.

"Don't know what I'm going to do with this monster," Mrs. Whitmore said as she joined them. She dug a napkin out of her purse and went to work on the mess. "Is my Emily under there anywhere?" Emily giggled.

Kate turned to Will and grabbed his hand. "Let's get something to eat, I'm starved."

"I can always eat," Will said.

Kate found an empty table by Mrs. Culloty's booth and saved their seats while Will got the food. He was back, a few minutes later and set the tray down with a flourish.

"How's that for fine dining?" He asked taking the chair across from her.

They ate the soup in silence, sneaking glances at each other and listening to the band. A shadow fell over the festival as the sun dipped below the trees and as if on cue, the park was suddenly ablaze with lightening bugs. But as the sky became a rich blue, the brightest light came from the bonfire that had been lit by the stage. Most of the tourists left at sundown, in a hurry to get back to the city, which meant only the locals gathered around the fire. And the locals knew how to party. It wasn't long before Kate spotted Uncle Dave up on the stage with several other men, a styrofoam cup in one hand and a mike in the other. They were belting out one unrecognizable song after another.

"Is that your—" Will pointed to the stage with his spoon.

She nodded and laughed.

"Well, we'd better go catch up," he said and pulled her to her feet.

The bonfire blazed high over their heads and with the lightening bugs dancing in the air around her, Kate felt as if she had entered a fairyland. Will held her close, swaying to the rhythm and she snuggled into his shirt, enjoying the feel of his hands on her back. The night was sweet with music and her head was light from the sips she'd taken from her uncle's cup. Will stayed by her side, letting them rest between songs and slipping his jacket over her shoulders when he noticed her shivering.

Then the music changed and a cry rose from the crowd. People leapt to their feet to form a circle around the fire and dance to the heavy drumbeat. A girl Kate didn't know caught her by the hand and yanked her away from Will into the circle. She saw him on the other side, looking for her and trying to keep up. Around and around the fire, as she lost sight of Will and felt his jacket fall off her shoulders, to be trampled on by the frenzied feet of the dancers. Their cries matched the volume of the fire and became savage with excitement. Kate tried to wiggle out of the girl's grasp, but the girl just laughed and held on tighter.

When the music ended Kate stood alone in front of the fire. Will faced her on the other side, the flames licking his red face and swallowing him whole from the feet up. His eyes were wide and sparkled in the dancing light. They stood like that while the heat burned Kate's face and fanned her hair.

Someone's watching.

Will felt it as well, because he glanced up to the sky at the same time. Only the night looked down on them, the night with its quiet, knowing presence. But someone *was* watching. Making note of this time and the two of them taking the first few steps down the course set out for them. And waiting.

She looked back at Will and shivered in the cold night air.

CHAPTER EIGHT
IN A KINGDOM BY THE SEA

The storm they had braced for turned out to be more blowing wind than anything else. Rain showered against the window for the entire morning, but by early afternoon the sun had broken up the clouds, the breeze calmed and a little warmth crept back into the air.

Kate took off her sweater and continued stocking the shelves in the thin white shirt she wore underneath. Uncle Dave was out back, working on the truck that had overheated on the way back from Quarryville last week.

She got a better grip on the ladder, before reaching up to set the canned peaches on the top shelf. The ladder teetered under her and she groped for the shelf to keep herself from falling.

"Oh!" She gasped as a pair of hands grabbed her waist.

"Looks like a man's job to me."

She looked around and saw Will standing by the ladder, his hands still at her waist. She jumped off the ladder and faced him.

"Well by all means if you see one, let me know. I could use the help."

He laughed and let his hands drop to his sides. "Is that any way to repay someone for saving your life?"

"Saving my life? Only if you meant to push me off the ladder. Now are you going to help me, or what?"

"I don't know if I can take the abuse."

She dropped a case of peaches in his arms. "I think you'll manage."

They worked for a few hours, finished the stocking and then moved on to clean the windows. Will didn't seem to mind spending such a beautiful day inside, helping her with the chores. He filled the time by telling her about the kids at school and news from around town, who had moved away, who had gotten pregnant, who had spent time in jail. He bent his stories in such a way that made her laugh and feel like maybe she hadn't been the only food for gossip over the last six years. The town was obese with tales enough to satisfy any number of wagging tongues.

"Did you hear about Ernest McGee?" Will moved the candy display to begin working on the front window.

"Who, old Stubby?"

Will laughed. "Yeah."

"What about him?"

"Well, I guess he's been coming home late from working on the bridge and Elsie, well, she thought maybe he was working on something else, or *someone* else and she got angry something awful."

"I bet, they used to come in here all the time and man," Kate said, sloshing more sudsy water on the glass. "That woman could yell. I couldn't even understand what she was saying half the time." She wiped the glass clean and sat on the ledge with a sigh. "Haven't seen them around, though. Not since I've been back."

"Well you're not likely to either, least not Stubby. He's down in the hospital."

"Why?"

Will dried his hands on a rag and sat beside her. "Guess she got fed up with it one night and whacked him upside the head with her roasting pan." He laughed. "Worst thing about it though is that she caught his good hand when she did it and managed to break every one of his fingers."

"That woman is crazy." Kate shook her head.

"Anyway, I don't think he'll be going back to work on the bridge anytime soon," Will said and then chuckled. "Don't think he'll be tying his own shoelaces anytime soon either.

Kate stood and started on the other window. "I don't know why they're tearing down the old bridge anyway. There wasn't anything wrong with it."

"It was old, not to mention, falling apart. My dad said it was only a matter of time before the whole thing just gave out under its own weight and besides, they're going to open it up to two lanes so we can pack in even more of those 'goddamned tourists', or so my grandma would say."

Kate sniffed. "Well, they could have just reinforced it or something. Why tear the whole thing apart?"

"It's called change, baby. Bigger is better, out with the old and in with the new. Where've you been?"

"See, and that's what's wrong these days. Everybody looking for something better, always thinking happiness is at the end of the rainbow and never being satisfied with what they already have."

"So what's wrong with that?" He asked, following her to the other side of the store. "Isn't happiness worth looking for? Life would be pretty dull without it, not to mention...well boring."

She smirked and started cutting open the boxes of magazines. "Happiness is overrated."

"So much cynicism."

"Well, think about it. It only exists under a certain set of circumstances. Whether it's shallow, material things like money and fame, or whatever or even things like love or, or...family." She caught herself staring out the window and went back to cutting open the boxes. "Something that is so dependent on other things, things you won't ever have a hope of controlling well, it's just not worth it. Why take the risk when you're sure to be disappointed? It's better to be satisfied with what you have, rather than wasting your life looking for something you'll never find."

"But what if it's worth the risk?" Will sat on the bottom shelf, hands clasped, elbows on his jean–clad knees. "Wouldn't you want to find out?"

"And if the wanting destroyed what you already had, what then?"

"Well then, what you had wasn't all that great in the first place."

"I don't believe that, I mean if you take the time to create something and if it works even if it isn't the best and even if it could be better, you don't want to take that away. There was a reason for the creation at one time and to tear it apart on the slim chance that something else might be better is not only foolish, but also very selfish." She stopped and looked down at the box cutter in her hand. Running her thumb along the edge, she pressed just hard enough to hurt, but not break the skin. "Foolish to throw away something that still serves a purpose. And selfish to assume that you were meant for something better."

A moment passed and Kate heard Uncle Dave throw a tool against the truck. He had been out there a long time; the truck must be giving him trouble.

She dared a peek up at Will who was watching her with so much kindness. "I'm sorry, I ramble sometimes," she said in a low voice.

"Well your ramblings are much more intelligible than any of my labored gruntings." He put a hand over his heart. "I'm in the presence of genius."

"You shouldn't tease a girl with a sharp object in her hand," Kate retorted, holding up the box cutter.

"I wasn't, really, please don't hurt me," he said, donning a bad southern accent and falling at her feet. "I just wanted to sit and listen a spell. Ma and Pa say it's all hogwash and horse shit, these new fangled ideas of yours but me, I hear the future in your voice."

"You little shit," Kate laughed, "now I will hurt you."

He shot to his feet and took off across the store. Throwing the cutter in the box, she ran after him. Will snatched a roll of toilet paper and threw it at her. Kate scooped it up and threw it back at him, but missed and knocked over a canister of feather dusters instead.

Skidding on the dusters and around the end of the aisle, Will disappeared and Kate slowed, searching for him.

"Aren't we a little old for hide and seek?" She walked down

the front of the store, inspecting each aisle as she went by. "You might as well give it up." She heard a snicker from the end aisle, but didn't see Will. "Olly–olly oxen free."

Will sprung up from behind and spun her into the wall. "There's no such thing as 'too old for hide and seek,'" he said and placed his hands on the wall on either side of her, pinning her in between.

Their faces were inches apart and Kate felt his breath quicken with her own. A simmering fire replaced the giddiness in his face and his eyes dropped to her mouth as she bit the side of her lip. He lowered his gaze to her shirt and she felt the heat from his attention warm her breasts.

The bell jangled above the door as someone came in, making them both jump.

Giggling, she shoved him away. "Get back to work, ace. You need to earn your keep around here."

"Yes, ma'am."

* * * * *

Will came every day and Kate never asked for an explanation, only felt a strange kind of relief that there was no need for one. He planted himself firmly in her life. He made her laugh and his uncanny knack for turning everything she said upside down made her look at life in a whole different light. He made her think, made her question. Made her miss him when he left at the end of each day.

Uncle Dave found him waiting by the door early one morning and he smiled. "She better be paying you well."

Will grinned at Kate. "Yes, sir."

Uncle Dave picked up his battered toolbox from the counter. "Well I'm off to rip that water pump apart." He looked from Will to Kate and back to Will. "Don't let her boss you around to much," he said, slapping Will on the back. He chuckled and disappeared through the kitchen.

Hours would pass with Kate sitting on the stool and Will sitting on the counter, talking. She could whittle away an entire day without ever realizing it. Just the sound of his voice and the way he moved his hands when he talked kept her stomach in a constant turmoil that was far from uncomfortable. He loved to argue with her, liked getting her riled up and then sitting back and listening to the rush of words Kate never seemed to have a problem finding. She fell into his trap every time.

"You don't honestly believe in little green men," Kate said, holding up a science fiction magazine.

"Well you have to admit, it would be awfully arrogant for us to—"

"—to assume we're the only life form in the entire universe. Yeah, yeah, I watched that Nova special too. Where do you keep your 'Welcome Aliens' sign, in your back pocket?"

"It's actually at home. Too big to carry around," he said, grabbing the magazine out of her hand. "We've barely scratched the surface of our own solar system. What makes you think that in all the expansion we have yet to discover, there won't be other forms of life, maybe even similar to our own?"

"Because it all comes down to proof. No matter what kind of faces they discover on Mars, or how many crop circles that appear in Europe, no one had turned up one shred of tangible evidence. *We* are the only intelligent form of life and people who don't believe that just don't want to face the facts."

"How very narcissistic of you."

She snatched the magazine and stacked it with the others on the shelf. "You're developing quite a vocabulary. I must be rubbing off on you."

"You're doing something to me all right," he said, laughing.

Uncle Dave slammed through the backdoor and set his toolbox on the kitchen table. "Well, she tried to argue with me, but in the end, I won."

"As always," Kate said and went to the refrigerator to get him some iced tea.

He took a big swig and wiped his mouth. "It's such a great day outside, why don't you guys get out of here for a while."

Kate took one look at the deep blue sky outside the window and threw the rest of the magazines back in the box.

* * * * *

They headed away from town and toward the creek. The path Will took wound around the bridge, where most of the summer crowd congregated and south, where the rocks and twists in the water created eddies along the shore. The rushing current drowned out the noises from the forest and Kate closed her eyes to let the sounds clear her mind. She sensed Will had stopped behind her.

"You know," she said, slipping out of her sandals to let the water lap at her toes. "I could pitch a tent and live right here."

Will kicked off his sneakers and joined her by the water. "Sounds kind of lonely."

"Really? Look around, how could you possibly be lonely here? With the animals to keep you company and beauty everywhere you turn, I couldn't imagine a better place to wake up to every day."

"Okay, Snow White," Will laughed. "But what about food, or I guess you would learn how to hunt or fish, huh?"

Kate shot him a horrified look. "Never."

"What, you don't like to fish?"

"It's not that, it's just the watching them die part...ick."

Will leapt to the top of a rock and looked down at her. "Oh, come on, that's the best part."

"You beast," she said, scowling. "Figures you'd say something like that."

"So your plan is to pitch a tent by the water and die a slow, painful death and in the end be picked apart by your furry forest friends?"

Kate jumped up beside him. "No, I will be Kaitlin, Queen

of the Creek," she said, prancing from one rock to the next. "And all the forest animals will be my subjects and bring me berries when I'm hungry and guard my castle in the woods where the floors are made of green cotton candy and the walls are alive with the songs of a thousand ancient oaks. And that's where I'll stay forever, dancing and dreaming, save for one day a year when the moon won't rise and the air smells of…" she thought for a moment. "Cinnamon. And then I will venture throughout the lands, touring my kingdom and searching for an unsuspecting fisherman." She glanced behind her and saw Will, struggling to keep up. Grinning, she hopped further away. "And I'll rip him limb from limb and let his blood drip down my arms and flow like wine into the creek and when I'm done, I'll toss his body into the water and let the fish pick the flesh from his bones."

Will made a few running jumps to catch up with Kate and he stood beside her, a dazed look on his face. "Such carnage milady, wherever from the depths of a dark and sinister place do thoughts of such evil manner arise?"

She bounded off the rock. "You know not the depths of the lady's heart."

"'Tis true, but it would do me pleasure to spend a lifetime in pursuit of the journey," Will said quietly and when Kate turned, he held her gaze with a slight smile.

She gave him a slanted smile of her own. "The young sire speaks in bold tongue, for he has yet to fathom the treacherous ground which leads to his prize," she said with her nose in the air. "For only a heart of fire and feet of wings, dare risk the journey."

Kate shot him one last grin before jumping off her rock and heading downstream, not looking to see if Will followed. Leaving only a trail of giggles and wet footprints, Kate sped across the rocks, landing easily on one and jumping off before she knew which one was next. She heard Will grunt behind her as he fought to keep his balance, but she didn't turn. Further and further down the creek she raced until the water deepened into crystalline pools and the rocks became fewer and farther between. She paused at the top of a massive chunk of granite and looked back.

Will was only a few rocks away and he closed the gap quickly, almost knocking her off as he leapt beside her. He pulled her away from the edge and she stood in his arms, gazing into his shining eyes. Streaks of sunlight sneaked through the heavy branches to layer his head in fiery gold. He smiled.

"It was many and many a year ago," he began in a singsong voice that was as warm as the rock on which they stood. "In a kingdom by the sea, that a maiden there lived whom you may know, by the name of Annabel Lee. And this maiden she lived with no other thought, than to love and be loved by me."

Strange tears burned in her eyes while she held his gaze as long as she could and then looked down at the pocket on his shirt. When her eyes cleared, she smiled back up at him and turned out of his arms.

A low hanging tree branch stretched over the deep pool below and after jumping off the rock, she grabbed it with both hands. It groaned under her weight and dipped her close to the water, but only the pads of her feet skimmed the surface, creating twin ripples as she swung across. Her toes caught the edge of the rock on the other side and she turned to wait for Will.

He met the challenge in her eyes and she smiled back, waiting. Glancing up at the branch, Will summoned up a sufficient amount of boyish enthusiasm and made the leap.

It broke almost immediately and the sound of the old wood giving under Will's weight was like a gunshot. He splashed into the chilly water in a tidal wave of girly shrieks and Kate nearly fell in herself, laughing.

"I–I'm sorry," she said, trying to stifle her giggles, but falling into another fit as Will shook out his hair like a dog. "I am, really, is it cold?"

"Is it cold?" Will asked, grinning through the droplets that fell from his hair. The water was swirling around his neck, turning his khaki shirt a dark brown. "I don't know Katie, is it cold?"

Kate squealed as Will threw a handful of water on her bare

legs and she scooted away, but he grabbed her ankles, pulling her in. She landed on top of him and dunked them both under the freezing mountain water.

Coming up with a gasp, Kate pushed her hair away from her eyes and looked for Will. He was gone.

"Will?"

She turned, kicking her feet in the water that was easily fifteen feet deep and started to call again when she felt hands grab her legs. Going under, she floated into Will's arms and he held her for a moment before bringing them back to the surface.

"Getting warmer all the time," he said and ducked, laughing, as she splashed him full in the face.

* * * * *

The sun was setting in a pink and orange haze that seemed to swell up from the end of the creek and the water mirrored the changing sky. A robin twittered overhead, as he settled in for the coming night. Kate leaned against Will's damp chest, watching the day's end.

"Annabel, sweet Annabel," he whispered in her ear. "How she dances in her kingdom by the sea, how she spins and twirls and whirls...so that the angels above would gather round and shudder to see such beauty."

She closed her eyes and let his voice carry her away to a castle in the trees. On a sea of green she floated, swaying to music that rose from the earth and filled the air with its haunting melody. And all around blew leaves of thick moss. They caressed her cheek with a petal–soft touch and flew by her dancing feet, to lift her higher, higher in a spiraling ascent to the sky.

"But how empty the arms of my sweet Annabel as she dances away the years. No warmth to light her days, no laughter to guide her step." He leaned into her hair and his words tickled behind her ear. "The eternity of a hollow embrace, with only the echo of a forgotten promise to fill the silence in her heart. So lovely…and so lonely my Annabel Lee."

His voice faltered on the last few words, so slightly that she wouldn't have caught it, even a few weeks ago. But she knew him now. His body was tense against her back, waiting, hoping…but careful, as if he had come upon a wild animal he was afraid to startle. He shifted his weight, so small a movement that she barely felt it, but now she was free to turn to him and…and…her life was in his eyes. Eyes that were deeper than the pools around them and warmer than a sun–kissed lake on a summer afternoon. She shivered to see the love that swam through those eyes, naked…shimmering and simply and wholly hers. Those eyes that stirred a heat which began at her throat and plunged toward her stomach and as if a fever had touched her, it swam throughout her body, urging its need, pushing her toward him and making her desperate for the soothing relief only his touch could give. His breath mingled with her own and she closed her eyes, feeling the muscles in his arm tremble beneath her hand.

"Kate," he said in a choked whisper, cupping her face in his palm.

His kiss brushed her lips, once, twice and then took her with such sweet passion she softened against him, reveling in the intoxicating flavor of his taste. His fingers traced the line of her neck and then ran through her hair to hold her closer, as his other hand warmed her back. Music filled her ears and the sound of the creek died away…then she was floating, floating toward the sky on wings of moss, twirling and floating to the songs of the forest. And Will was with her. Holding her with his strong embrace, guiding them toward the light at the top of the trees, moving with such fluid grace and confidence. This is where she belonged, with this music, feeling his touch, always and forever under the canopy of his love, protected, cherished.

It was Will who broke it off with a painful little moan that shook his body. Kate opened her eyes, gazing into his for moment, not understanding the tears that were trapped behind them. She reached to caress his cheek, tipping one loose that zigzagged down his face and her thumb wiped it away, as her eyes questioned him.

"I've waited," he said in that same choked whisper and cradled her chin in his hand. "God...I don't know how long..."

She caught his hand and held it, squeezed it, kissed it. "Shhh," she said feeling her own tears burn under her eyelids. "I know."

His arms circled around her and she snuggled into his chest, feeling his heart beat against her back. The crickets had come out of their daytime hiding along the banks of the creek and Kate listened to them take turns serenading each other as the sun sank behind the trees.

And high above them, perched on the tallest branches of the spruce, a robin's twitters were silenced. Down...down it fell, bouncing off the tree and spinning until it landed, only feet behind the couple who sat on the rock. Its empty eyes stared up at the darkening sky.

* * * * *

The light from a passing car crossed the wall and shifted toward the crack in the ceiling. It hesitated by the crumbling drywall for a moment, then dipped into the far corner of the room and disappeared by the window.

Dave watched this, wondering vaguely who would be up at this late hour. Newclare wasn't exactly known for its nightlife, especially in the cooler months. Probably a kid out for a ride. Of course it didn't have to have been a car. A powerful flashlight could have produced the same effect and if the owner of such a flashlight had been standing on the roof of the Wood 'n More across the street, he could have easily—

Oh stop it!

Dave sat up quickly and ran his hands through his hair, the feeling of being watched not receding as he argued with himself.

His heart started racing again and he counted the frantic beats, waiting for it to pass and seeing his father's white face behind his closed eyes.

His father had turned many interesting shades before the chalky white set in, telling him and his mother this time was for real. The old man's hand was still wrapped around his fork when he let out one last gasp and fell face down into the sirloin his mother had served for dinner. He'd stabbed himself in the forehead with the fork, as Dave had seen when Doctor Walsh set him back in the chair. Four perfectly spaced red pinpricks that hadn't bled at all.

His mother had taken the fork from the doctor as they were wheeling him out and Dave could still see her, standing by the highboy and polishing the silver that had been a wedding present, some twenty years before. Her face was turned from him as they stood together, watching the big black car drive away, but there was nothing she could hide in the sudden straightness of her back...the slight tilt of her head...and the sigh she let out as the car turned out of sight.

Slowly and with measured timing, Dave brought his hands down and glanced around. The moon was almost full and it lit the room in a smoky glow. The throw rug at his feet, the easy chair in the corner with an afghan covering its thin fabric, the pile of paperwork beside his lamp he never seemed to get around to...all watched him and waited with an air of expectancy that must be like right before a missile lands and blows everything to bits. Only he was the missile here, whether or not he wanted to be.

His distracted gaze fell back on the lamp. It had been around since before he could remember and though his mother had treated it as if it were diseased, he always kind of liked it, the shiny dark colors of the rock base, the figure standing at he top, coming home from a long day of fishing. But now the little man in the cap was staring at him, waiting, as the room waited.

What'cha gonna do Dave? Huh? Time's a'wasting while you got yer pecker in a scrunch and yer balls tied together.

Maybe there was a time when you could crawl away an' wait out the storm, but that's long past 'cause time's slippin' away, Chicken Boy. Just slippin' away...like a wet fish slippin' through yer fingers... So what's it gonna be Dave?

He glared at the little man and stood to shuffle over to his closet. More papers stacked on the top shelf tumbled on top of him and he pushed them aside, scrambling behind the box of old John Denver records.

He brought out the bottle, wiped the dust from the glass and then wiped his hand on the front of his sweatpants. Eddy had given it to him a couple of years back. Another New Years gone by, standing in the corner of someone's living room, trying not to look bored as the happy group around him counted down to midnight. Eddy had stumbled over to Dave, with his arm thrown around his wife's shoulder and listing noticeably.

"There ya are buddy," he slurred, sending a cloud of toxic breath in Dave's direction.

His wife gave them both a scathing look and slipped out from Eddy's arm, shoving him in the general vicinity of the plaid couch. Eddy landed with a grunt.

"You can have him now, he's useless." She said and then bent over her husband to shout in his ear. "Goin' home Ed and if you know what's good for you, you'll be back before sunup, I mean it now." She slapped him lightly across the face and then charged out of the room.

"Happy fuckin' New Year, ya lucky bastard," Eddy said as Dave sat down beside him.

"Yeah, you too."

Five minutes later he was snoring against Dave's shoulder.

They sat in the truck, hours later, staring at Eddy's house until a light came on in the upper bedroom.

"Time's up," Eddy said and zipped his coat. He felt his pocket and then groaned as he remembered what was in it. "Here you go, keep you warm on these long cold nights." He handed Dave a bottle of gin.

"Oh no, that's okay, I don't actually—"

"Take it, she'll kill me if I bring it in the house and be-sides," he said, looking back at the light in the window. "There'll come a time when you do, trust me."

Dave's hands were trembling, making the cap hard to screw off, but it came after a few tries. He threw his head back and let the liquid burn down his throat. A shudder rocked his body and he took a stumbling step backward to plop back down on the bed. That was better. The shaking in his hands was subsiding and the only thing his heaving stomach felt now was the fire that churned in his belly.

He lay back, thumping his head against the headboard. Now to get some sleep. Nothing ever looked all that bad in the morn-ing, not with the rosy glow of day shining on it. He and Kate were supposed to make a run into Quarryville in the morning, part shopping trip, part need to get away one more time before school started and took her away from him. It was stupid, he knew, but this summer had been so good for him. It had given him the chance to know what it would have been like if…well…she was here now and Dave wanted to spend time with her, maybe take her to lunch on the way back, so they could have a chance to talk.

But now, as he curled to his side and stared blankly at the nightstand, the thought of seeing Kate again had about the calm-ing effect as being hit by a car. It put a fear in his belly even the alcohol couldn't numb.

Closing his eyes, he shivered again, under his sheet and two blankets. When he was old and gray and struggling to remember his own name, much less what they were serving in the dinning hall, Kate's glowing eyes would float up to him and he would pause to listen to his heart hammer against his ribs.

And remember.

His mouth was suddenly dry and he rose to get a glass of water. He stood for a moment and looked at his closed door, be-fore sitting back down on the bed. No need to chance it. God, he would see her in the morning anyway, but by then he was hoping he would have a better grip on the situation.

Situation, my ass. With a shaky sigh, he lay back down and stared at the ceiling again.

The heat was what struck him first as he came down the stairs. Kate and Will had been up late, taking advantage of the last few days of summer and watching a marathon of old monster movies. Dave had gone to bed early, making his exit as gracefully as he could, but shortly after he drifted to sleep, something woke him. He had no idea what it was, he had been sleeping one moment and sitting up in bed with his heart in his throat the next. Thinking he would get a glass of milk from the kitchen and check on the kids, he'd thrown on his flannel robe and headed downstairs. As he reached the landing though, he stopped.

The heat was intense, like walking into an oven. And the air crackled softly, like the sound from a fireplace. In fact, he had a fleeting thought that maybe the place was on fire, but there had been no smell of smoke. As he turned to go to the living room thoughts of fire and pretty much everything else drained from his head. He felt as though he'd stumbled into someone's nightmare and he stood, dumbstruck, trying to make some sense out of what his eyes were telling his mind.

Will and Kate sat on the couch, facing each other and engrossed in conversation, completely oblivious to the chaos that surrounded them. The color in the room had changed. Not the color of the walls or the carpet, but the air itself had turned a deep maroon shade and had changed in consistency. It was rich and charged with an electricity that came directly from Kate and Will, or from the glow which emanated from them. The glow enveloped them like an aura and was turning different colors like a prism held to light.

A streak of color rushed by his head and he started to duck, before it swerved to the ceiling and disappeared. Flashes of light went off all around the room like tiny bursts of fireworks. Some went off and then vanished like smoke. Others exploded and danced merrily around the room, weaving in and out of the furniture before their light slowly faded and then was gone. He watched as what looked like a shiny blue kite's tail soared through the air and paused, hovering above the coffee table. With what looked like a swimmer's leap, it plunged into the wood, turning the table a deep indigo. It swarmed over the top and flew off the edge and towards the open window in the corner before it disappeared.

"I'm sorry Uncle Dave, are we keeping you up?"

He jerked to look at Kate and tried to answer, but was stunned into silence. Her face was calm and as sweet as ever, but her eyes had changed. They were still green, but the shade had turned a brilliant jade. The pupils exploded and swirled like the fireworks swimming through the room.

He swallowed hard.

"Just wanted to make sure you guys were all right." He said, thinking his voice sounded amazingly even.

"We're fine, I was just leaving." Will turned his eyes on Dave and his breath caught again. Will's eyes had the same churning bright color in them, his a shimmering blue. As he rose off the couch, Dave felt the heat go up a notch.

"No rush, I'm going to go to bed." He left as quickly as he could and hoped that they hadn't noticed his fear. For some reason, he felt as though everything would be all right as long as they weren't aware of what he'd seen.

Goddamn it, why did it have to be him?

He sat on the edge of the bed, rubbing his temples, as all hope of sleep left him. It was just so unfair. She had been so different these past few weeks, so sparkling and full of laughter. It was like he had his old Katie back, before all the ugliness came and though he understood the repercussions of what he had seen tonight, there was a voice that screamed denial. She was just so happy.

Tell her.

No. She had been through enough, she deserved this, and she needed this. Enough pain, enough sadness and regret. He wouldn't take that away, no matter what the cost. And he didn't even know for sure. Not really. It would be different if he was sure. He wouldn't rip the floor out from under her again when there was no way he could know for sure.

Tell her.

He had been dreading this moment ever since Maureen had dropped that amulet in his hand. Dreading the moment when he would have to look into the sweet face of his niece and destroy everything she had found good in the world. Including him.

But it didn't have to be that way. Not if he kept his damned mouth shut, because it didn't have to be the way his grandmother had told Maureen. Despite what had happened to his sister, he knew he could keep Katie away from it. Could steer her around it...somehow. Or maybe it was nothing, just some folklore passed down the generations to keep little kids awake at night. And the rest...well screw it. Not everything in life could be explained.

The sun was coming up in the window above his bed. He couldn't remember the last time he'd stayed up all night. Sometime in high school maybe. Kate would be up soon. Would be up and making breakfast for them and if he didn't shake this off right now, she would back him into telling her. She was like that. Her eyes would narrow and she would smile as she worked on him and in the end it would all come out.

He rubbed his face and glanced at the lamp. The cap on the little man's head gleamed from the sunlight, making it look wet.

The little man was looking at him.

"What?" He hissed at it, angry for no good reason.

The little man had nothing to say this time, just continued staring at him.

Dave's hand came down hard and it shoved the hideous lamp off the nightstand and onto the floor. The rug kept it from breaking, as he wanted it to do, so he brought his bare foot down on it. The sharp edges of the rocks cut his foot, but didn't break. He did succeed in knocking the man from his perch and as he looked into its tiny face, laughter erupted from his belly. He rescued the figure and put him in the drawer until it could be glued back on, chuckling the whole time.

The shower went on in the bathroom across the hall and Dave's laughter died as quick as it came. Sighing, he slipped on his robe and went downstairs, thinking he might be able to get in a cup of coffee before she came down.

CHAPTER NINE
A RUMBLING IN THE DISTANCE

Kate flipped her book closed and looked outside. Fresh snow covered the roof of the Wood 'n More shop and the glare from the sun bouncing off the whiteness stung her eyes. Over two feet lay on the ground and they were in for even more, from the looks of the black cloud behind the peak. Her eyes fell again to the book and then to Winnie who slept at the foot of her bed. She nudged the dog with her toe. Winnie opened one eye to give her a very cat–like glare and settled back into her afternoon nap.

"See if you get any more treats," she said.

Winnie twitched a paw and began to snore.

She hadn't left her room in over two weeks and though Uncle Dave had done his best to make her comfortable, she couldn't help but think that the walls were closing in tighter, every day. A fever had spread through her body, leaving her cold with sweat and confined to bed. Bronchitis is what Doctor Walsh had said with his serious doctor eyes and his serious doctor voice. Nothing to do, but rest and wait. Uncle Dave had been wonderful, taking care of her and wiping her face with cool rags. She could hear him even now, down in the kitchen, clanging the pots and pans around, preparing her lunch.

But it was Will who came every day, read to her, talked to her, kept her up to date on the gossip at school. Sometimes she would wake to find him just sitting by her bed, watching her sleep. He stayed at her side constantly during those first few scary days when the pain in her chest was incredible and she couldn't seem to get a breath, just as he had been with her during those first horrific days of school.

She shuddered. The stares, the whispered comments, the rude questions were almost too much, but with Will holding her hand she found the strength to ride it out. He had enough cocky confidence for the both of them and she smiled, thinking about some of the more outrageous comments he'd made in her defense. Nothing threw him and little by little she learned by his example. Learned how to laugh and not be bitter in the face of their cruelty and as her confidence grew, the kids at school backed off.

She hadn't seen him in a few days though and she felt his absence with every loud tick of her clock. His parents had planned a last minute trip into Philadelphia to spend Thanksgiving with friends. His eyes had been dark when he told her, but she didn't question him. His eyes were often dark when he spoke of his parents, parents she had yet to meet.

She sighed and returned to the book.

A short time later a knock on the door made her look up. "What took so long, Uncle Dave, you trying to starve me?" She joked.

The door opened and as if her thoughts had beckoned him, Will stood in the doorway, a tray in his hands. "I's so sorry Miss Kate. I don mean to keep ya waitin', jus ma hands so tired afta shellin' all those peas."

She grinned and yanked the blanket over her thin nightgown. "You see it doesn't happen again."

"Yes'um." He set the tray on her side table and plopped down on the bed to take a good look at her, his eyes twinkling with mischief.

"What?"

"Jeez, you look like crap." He leaned forward to stare at her more closely. "Wow, look at those circles, like rings in a tree stump. I thought ladies on their sickbeds were supposed to look all dainty and pretty. But wow, you really look like crap," he repeated.

"Thanks, I can hack up a mean phlegm too. Want to see?"

He grinned. "No thanks, I'll take your word for it."

"So what are you doing here, except for not trying to cheer me up."

"Just being in my presence cheers you up," he boasted, lying back across her bed and putting his hands behind his head. "I came to deliver good news."

She waited, but he said nothing else. "Okay, I'll bite."

"I like it when you bite."

"Stop it," she laughed and poked him with her foot. "What's the good news?"

"I talked to Mr. Shraver and he said he would let you make up your work over the Christmas break. That way you don't have to repeat the semester. But, there's a catch."

"I'm sure I'll have to bear him a child," she muttered.

"Actually, two." He laughed. "No, as long as you have the work made up in time for next semester, the only other thing he wants is an extra credit essay."

"On what?"

"'Christmas in Newclare.'" Will did a great impression of Principle Shraver, had his prissy mannerisms down to an art. "He wants something for the school paper."

"How very original."

"Anyway, I thought of the perfect place to research it."

"I'm going to have to research this?"

"The Christmas tree lighting," he went on. "It's this weekend. You didn't forget did you?"

"Of course not. I may have been shut in here like a mole for weeks, but I am aware of which month we're in," she finished in a fit of coughs which left her face red and her eyes watery.

He put one hand on her shoulder, his face filling with worry. "You okay?"

She nodded and took a drink of juice from the tray.

"So what do you think?"

"About what?" She asked, setting the glass down.

He sighed. "About this weekend. Do you want to go? I mean, if you're up to it."

One side of her mouth pulled in as she thought about it. "What is this, a date?"

"Date, shmate. Do you want to go?"

153

"I suppose. I mean, if it's for extra credit and all," she teased.

"You'll probably have to do something with your hair, though."

"So it *is* a date," she countered, smoothing a lock of hair behind her ear.

He caught her hand and brought it down. "It looks fine." Still holding her hand, he brought his other hand up to stroke her face. "You know you're beautiful."

She smiled and blushed deeply. He leaned forward until their foreheads touched and held her gaze. His finger traced the side of her face, until it stopped at her lips.

"I think you might still be contagious, I feel feverish all of a sudden."

She grinned. "Do you really?"

"Uh–huh. I'm so weak, I might just have to crawl in bed with you."

"I don't think that would be such a great idea."

"Really? Why not?" His fingers continued toward her neck.

"Because my uncle's coming."

"What—" He stammered, jumping off her bed.

Uncle Dave came in an instant later. "How's the patient?" He asked standing in the doorway.

Kate giggled. "Fine, feeling much better, actually."

Dave looked at Will. "Really? Guess you were just the right kind of medicine, Will."

Will's neck reddened as he avoided Uncle Dave's gaze. "She does look good, I mean better, healthier," he finished hurriedly.

"Well I just wanted to see how you were doing. And to tell Will his mom called, something about a roast for dinner?"

Will groaned. "I was supposed to get that on my way home."

"Well I guess you'd better high–tail it out of here, boy. Don't want to keep her waiting." He turned to Kate. "And you, little lady, need to drink your soup. But I guess I'll have to heat it up now," he said, winking at her.

"Thanks Uncle Dave."

Will started for the door. "I'm glad you're feeling better, Kate. Guess I'll see you Saturday."

"Don't be late," she said, smiling at him.

He flashed her one in return and left.

"I swear, that boy's got a permanent grin on his face, every time I see him. You know anything about that Katie?"

She shook her head, her eyes wide. "Why no, Uncle Dave, not a thing."

* * * * *

Saturday found Kate feeling much like her old self. The cough had cleared and a buoyant energy raced through her veins. She stood in front of the mirror, admiring the color in her cheeks and the sparkle in her eyes. After many false starts, she had chosen a moss–green skirt, which clung to the swell of her hips, hung straight down and brushed her ankles of her short black boots. She fastened a Christmas tree pin to the matching green and black sweater.

"Very festive," she said softly to herself and spun around again.

"Katie," Uncle Dave called from downstairs, "your date has arrived."

Grabbing her coat from the back of the door, she patted Winnie's head and skipped down the stairs. Will stood at the front of the store, a warm smile lighting his face. Flurries of snow drifted by the display window behind him.

She stopped and then turned slowly in a circle.

"I see you fixed you hair," he said.

She swatted him in the chest. "Brat."

Uncle Dave stepped between them. "Now, now, play nice. Will, you take care of my Katie. Have her back by midnight, okay?"

Will nodded. "You can bet on that, don't want a pumpkin on my hands."

"And Kate," Dave continued, turning toward her, "you have fun, but take it easy, okay?"

"I will Uncle Dave, don't worry." She kissed the tip of his nose and gave him a quick hug.

Will held his arm out for her. "Shall we?"

"I'd be delighted," she said, taking his elbow and they headed out the door.

The air was crisp and Kate breathed deep, happy to be out among the living again. Her steps were quick and light, her boots crunching on the powdery snow. She soaked up the frenzied excitement, which always seemed to flow through the town right before Christmas. People bustled about, picking up last minute gifts and preparing for the lighting, which started in less than an hour. Will and Kate stopped at the ice cream parlor on their way to the courthouse. They shared a gigantic sundae, their heads close, their hands touching. She saw little Emily Whitmore sitting with her mother at the next table watching them with wide brown eyes. Kate wiggled her fingers at her and Emily beamed.

Once at the courthouse, Kate lost her breath for a moment at the dazzling decorations. Red and white streamers covered the streetlights, turning them into huge candy canes. White lights twinkled everywhere, in the trees, on the storefronts, strung between the light poles. The police had roped off the block around the courthouse and people milled in the street. Most were visitors from Quarryville. Christmas carols played from the speakers sitting in the trees.

Will bought them hot chocolate from one of the many vendors and they found a place on the stone wall close to the front.

"Joey used to love the Christmas tree lighting," Kate said, taking a sip.

"Really?"

Kate nodded. "Yeah, she always acted like it was stupid to

get excited over something so silly, but we never missed it. She pretended like she did it for me."

Will smiled.

"We sat right over there," Kate said, pointing to a spot down front. "They used to have a set of portable bleachers set up beside the tree. That's where the children's choir stood, at least until the year Laura Pepperson fell off the top and broke her arm. Anyway, Joey and I hid underneath and from there we had the best view of the tree. We could see straight up the middle and wow," she said, remembering, "it was so magical. Those lights just seemed to go on forever."

"Sounds nice." Will put an arm around her and pulled her close. "I hope I can make this just as magical," he said and kissed the top of her head.

Her head dropped to rest on his shoulder. "You already have."

The music ended and the stage lights lit up the courthouse steps. Over a hundred boys and girls of all ages lined the steps, music sheets in their hands. People hushed as Mayor Finley walked up to the podium and began to read the Christmas story from the Bible. When he was finished, the children sang a few off–key Christmas carols, then the lights dimmed and the speakers played a boisterous version of, 'Joy to the World'. The lights on the largest evergreen tree in the lawn lit to a deafening round of applause. Kate clapped and sang along with everyone else, but when she looked up at Will, he wasn't looking at the tree, he was watching her.

When it was over, they walked hand in hand toward the town hall across the street. There was a dance and refreshments planned in the conference room. Will led the way, weeding them through the hordes of people that filled the street.

"Will!" A woman's voice from behind them called. "Will wait!"

Kate turned and watched as a blonde woman in a red coat ran to catch up with them. A man followed a few feet behind, his potbelly jiggling a merry rhythm as he hurried to keep up with her.

Turning, Will's jaw clenched and he stepped in front of Kate. "Oh, sh—" he muttered.

"Will, why didn't you tell us you were coming, we could have all gone together," the woman said, breathlessly.

"I didn't want to mess up your evening," Will said, not looking at them.

Kate moved from behind him, looking at them and then up at Will.

"I'm sorry," he stammered. "Mom, Dad, this is Kate. Kate, my parents, Julie and Frank."

"Nice to meet you." Kate held out her hand and watched as Will's mother hesitated before taking it.

"Hello," his mother said in a flat voice and backed away quickly. His father simply nodded.

"You didn't tell us you were going out tonight," his mother said, directing her eyes only on Will. Her lips pressed together and almost disappeared.

"Didn't I?" Will held her gaze.

"No. You didn't."

His father cleared his throat. "We'd appreciate it if you'd keep us informed of your whereabouts, son. We can't have you gallivanting around town, worrying your mother and me."

Gallivanting? Kate turned to Will.

"Is there a problem?" His voice challenged his father with its sharp edge.

"No, dear," his mother said, putting a hand on her husband's chest. "Your father and I just don't want to worry about you. We shouldn't be, should we?" Her eyes flicked toward Kate.

"Not unless you can tell me a reason why you should be." He raised his eyebrows at her and waited.

"Just don't be too late," she said and they moved away.

Will turned abruptly and pulled her across the street, toward the town hall. His face was flushed and he walked so quickly,

Kate had to run to keep up.

"Will, slow down, what's wrong?"

He finally stopped under the lighted wreath that hung above the double doors. Music floated through the glass. "I'm just so sick and tired of them. Why can't they just tell me—" He stopped and looked at Kate, the words dying on his lips.

"Tell you what?"

He rubbed briskly at his head, looking at the ground and not meeting her eyes. "Tell me when they're going to let me grow up. I mean, God, I'm seventeen now, time to cut the apron strings."

She smiled and squeezed his arm. "They love you, Will. That's all. It's kind of nice that they worry about you, don't you think? I mean, they're your parents."

He gave her a slanted grin. "Yeah, I guess you're right. Just wish they'd do their worrying someplace else."

"Like Fiji?"

"I hear it's nice this time of year."

She laughed and took his hand again. "You sure that's it?"

He nodded. "Yup, that's enough."

"Well then relax," she said, rising on her tiptoes to stand eye to eye with him and smiling. "This is supposed to be fun."

Will smiled back. "Well in that case."

He kissed her full on the lips and Kate shook a little at the strength of it. It was different from their other kisses, intense and demanding in a way that was deeply thrilling. When he broke away, she stared up at him for a moment, trying to find her breath.

"That was..." She trailed off, blushing under his gaze.

Will smiled and was about to speak when a loud *POP* came from above.

Looking up, Kate saw the lights on the wreath were bursting, one by one in a trail that led around the wreath and then down the column where it'd been plugged into an outlet.

Will pulled them away from the shower of sparks and stood with his arm around her, looking up at the smoldering decoration.

"That was explosive," he said, with a nervous laugh.

Kate nodded. Her stomach was twisting into tight knots as she stared up at the wreath.

"Come on," Will said, trying to snap her out of the silence that had settled over both of them. "They're playing our song." He opened the door and she went through first.

"We have a song?"

"Not yet, now come on."

She giggled and let him pull her onto the dance floor.

* * * * *

Christmas came with thoughtful gifts from Uncle Dave and a new dog collar for Winnie. It was pink and studded with rhinestones. Uncle Dave laughed when he saw it and called her 'Biker Dog' for the rest of the afternoon. Kate fixed them a frozen turkey dinner and they sat together in front of the television, watching the parade. Winnie sat in the corner under the tree, chewing on her new collar.

"Isn't there a football game on?" Uncle Dave asked and shoved another bite in his mouth.

Kate sniffed. "You want to watch a football game? On Christmas day? How could you even think it?"

"You're right," he laughed. "I don't know what got into me. Must be something in the turkey." He finished his plate and sat back.

She smiled at him and picked up their plates to take to the sink. "You'd better not change that channel while I'm gone."

When the parade ended a marathon of holiday movies came on. Uncle Dave chuckled, as he saw her check the clock again. "So when's he coming?"

She grinned. "Anytime now, he said—"

A loud rap sounded on the back door. She jumped up and ran to unlock it. Will stood on the porch, a large red box in his arms and a backpack over one shoulder.

"Thought I'd never get out of there," he said, laughing. "When my mom brought out the fruitcake though, I made a run for it."

"Let's go upstairs. I have something for you too." She grabbed his free hand and pulled him up the stairs and into her bedroom. Reaching under her pillow, she pulled out a thin box, wrapped in gold paper.

He took it and shook it. "Hmm. Couldn't be a book, could it?"

"Okay, smarty pants, but which one is it?"

Holding the box to his head, he closed his eyes and concentrated. "I see, I see—"

"I see you, being an idiot. Open it." She sat on the bed next to him.

He tore the paper off and opened the box, his eyes lighting with genuine surprise and pleasure. She had bought him a collector's book of antique model airplanes.

"Thanks, I love it," he said.

"So when do I get to see your collection?"

"Soon, I promise. Now open yours, come on." He put the box on her lap.

She ripped off the shiny paper and in the box, wrapped in tissue paper, was a pair of white ice skates. "Wow," she said, staring at the skates. "Thank you. They're very, uh, pretty."

"You like them?"

"Yeah, they're great, but Will," she paused, trying to find a way to tell him. "I don't know how to ice skate."

"I know, I'm going to teach you. Come on, get your coat."

"What, now?"

"Yes now Chicken Little, let's go."

She pulled on his shirt, bringing him down on top of her and laying back. "Wouldn't you rather stay in, where it's nice and warm?"

He laughed and caught her hands. "Nice try, but you're not getting out of this." Pulling her off the bed, he grabbed his coat and threw her black one to her. "Time's a wastin.' "

There was a place about a quarter mile down stream, where the creek widened into a small lake and it was here that Will led them. Stopping by a hollowed out tree beside the lake, Will set her ice skates in the snow. Reaching into his backpack, he pulled out a black pair of his own.

"Are you ready to learn from the master?" He asked, lacing up his skates.

"Do I have a choice?"

"Nope."

The lake was cleared of snow from previous skaters, though they had it to themselves on this cold, Christmas afternoon. Will led her to the middle of the lake and skated around her in circles, while Kate did her best to stand still and not fall. He laughed and took her hand to help her follow him. After a few false starts and many hard landings, Kate found she could keep up the slow pace Will set. They skated in circles and then in long figure eight's, their fingers brushing through her gloves. The wind rushing by her face and the sound of her skates gliding over the smooth ice exhilarated her and as the afternoon went on, she was able to re-lax and move naturally with the rhythm.

Soon a light snow began to fall and Kate stopped in the middle of the lake to catch her breath and watch.

"There should be a law that it has to snow on Christmas day," she said, watching the drifting flakes. "Don't you think?"

Will came up behind her and put his arms around her waist. "There should be a law that it snows on Christmas day and you have to go ice skating on a beautiful lake with a beautiful girl."

She turned to smile up him and he kissed her, their lips warming against each other. When they parted, she opened her eyes and saw him, watching her.

"Come on," he laughed. "I still have to teach you the triple axle."

"The triple what?"

"It's not that hard." He grabbed her hand and they glided

through the thin veil of snow, their laughter slightly muffled by the stillness that hung in the air.

* * * * *

Kate sprang up in bed, screaming and screaming until her voice gave out. The light flipped on and Uncle Dave was at her side, pushing the hair from her eyes.

"Honey, honey, what's wrong?"

Kate's eyes bounced around the room and then to Uncle Dave who was staring at her with grave concern. Her nightgown was twisted and clung to her damp chest and the blankets were tangled between her legs. Winnie jumped up on her bed and frantically licked her face.

"I'm sorry Uncle Dave. It was just," she said, shakily, trying to find the words. "It was…a nightmare."

"And a doozy if I ever heard one, are you okay?"

"Yeah, it was just so uh, vivid." She smoothed Winnie's fur and set her back down in her box by the bed.

"You want to talk about it? It helps, sometimes."

She shook her head. "I, I actually don't remember most of it. I think I just want to go back to sleep." She pulled the covers up and lay down.

He stood, but didn't leave. "If you're sure."

"Yeah, I'm fine. Sorry I woke you up."

He bent and kissed her forehead. "Try to get some sleep."

"Goodnight," she said and closed her eyes.

He turned off the light and Kate listened as he left, closing the door behind him. Her eyes popped open and she sat up. The clock beside the phone on her side table read, two–thirty–four.

She rubbed her face and swung her feet around to sit on the edge of the bed and bumped Winnie with her foot. Winnie blinked slowly at her.

"Go back to sleep," she whispered and Winnie put her head down. It popped up a second later as the bedsprings squeaked their protest on the other side of Kate's wall. Uncle Dave had gone back to bed.

She pushed back the panic clawing at her brain and reached for the phone. Her hand trembled above it, hesitating. He would be sleeping. She could talk to him in the morning...but still, morning seemed a long way off. Her fingers tapped the receiver playing out a mindless beat as she argued with herself.

The phone rung suddenly, exploding the silence and Kate snatched her hand away. Then she grabbed it, so it wouldn't disturb Uncle Dave.

"Kate?" It was Will's voice and he was whispering.

"Yeah, it's me." She was whispering too.

"You okay?"

"Yeah, are you?" She saw him in her mind and wished more than anything to feel his arms around her.

"I guess so," he said, taking a deep breath. "I just wanted to hear your voice."

She smiled. "Well, I guess I'll see you at school tomorrow."

"Yeah, can I pick you up?"

"I wouldn't have it any other way."

He chuckled softly. "Okay, I'll see you then."

"Bye."

"Bye."

She cradled the phone and stood to walk over to the window. In this early morning hour the world below had a soft, expectant glow. Nothing stirred on the street and no light shone from a window. She sighed and leaned her head against the cold pane.

Three weeks of nightmares had brought her no closer to finding out what was happening. Thoughts of them stayed with her during the day and at night they played with movie–like clarity in her dreams. She shivered, thinking back to that last time she had dreamt with the same intensity. But then it had only been the one dream.

She shook her head and moved away from the window to

lie back in bed. The only explanation she could think of was that something was coming. Something just as bad, if not worse than that cruel night six years ago. And it was that thought which made her tiptoe through her days, waiting and watching. Her world had fallen apart once and she refused to entertain the thought that it might happen again. No, she wouldn't, *couldn't*, let it happen. It she was careful and stayed alert, she might be able to stop it. She had to stop it. She'd worked too hard and too long to let everything slip away now. Not without a fight.

Winnie jumped up on her bed and Kate moved to make room for her. A new resolve firmed her heart and she found that now she could sleep. She was older, she was aware. This time nothing would take away the life she had made.

Nothing.

Chapter Ten
The Fairy Queen

"Hey Will, how're you doing?"

Will took the phone into his bedroom and closed the door. "Good, I'm good Dave and you?"

Dave cleared his throat. "Fine," he said.

A moment went by as static blared on Will's cordless phone. He moved closer to the window and it cleared. "So uh, what's going on?"

"Well, I was wondering if Katie was over there," he said.

"No, I haven't seen her since yesterday."

"Oh."

"Why, what's wrong?"

"Nothing, I mean, I don't know," he stuttered and cleared his throat again. "She was acting strange all morning and when I came back from my friend Mark's house after lunch, she was gone."

Will's hand suddenly felt slippery on the back of the phone. "Really?"

"Yeah, she closed up the store and locked the dog in the kitchen and she left." Dave's voice began to show the worry he had been trying to cover. "She usually leaves a note, you know? Especially if she's going to be gone for this long. And there's something else."

Will swallowed back the sandpaper in his throat. "What?"

There was a long, long pause as he heard Dave take a breath and blow it out. "She uh, forgot her—"

Static drowned out the rest of his words. "Didn't catch that Dave."

"Her coat," he said quietly. "I said she forgot her coat."

The thudding in Will's head became louder as he glanced out the window where a heavy snow was falling. And he heard

167

the man on the radio say they could expect it to continue until tomorrow.

"I don't know what's going on here, do you have any idea where she would go?"

"No," Will said slowly, but as the word came out of his mouth an image flashed behind his eyes. Just a flicker, like a frame of a movie speeding by. And then another. Kate running…Kate crying.

"Because this just isn't like her," Dave was saying. "And it's getting dark now, I'm not sure what to do."

Will strode across his room and poked his head out the door. His father stood in the kitchen, staring at the ceiling as he always did when he became impatient. They were going out to dinner and Will knew he would be hearing about how he had made them late.

"What do you mean, she was weird this morning?" He asked Dave and shut the door again.

"Well, I don't know, quiet I guess and jumpy. I went up to her room to ask her something, I can't remember what and she just about flew out of her skin." He sighed. "It's not like her, not at all."

"Yeah…I know."

"Just wanted to run it by you. If you can think of anything, let me know, okay?"

"Okay."

"Oh and I almost forgot, she got your package this morning," Dave said.

Will smiled. "Yeah? Did she like it?"

"I'm sure she did, she brought it right up to her room. That was nice of you Will."

He heard his mother call for him. "I'll call you if I think of anything."

"Thanks, I'll talk to you later," Dave said and hung up.

Will threw the phone on his bed and went to the closet for his coat. He was glad Kate got the package. He left it on her back porch early this morning as a sort of, after Christmas surprise, but on the way home had worried about it sitting in the snow. He hoped it hadn't seeped through the wrapping and warped the frame inside. His mother had dragged him to a Farmer's Market in Quarryville last week and while he had been waiting for her at the craft booth, one of the cross–stitches had caught his eye. It was a poem, with little winged creatures along the side.

The Fairy Queen

Come, follow, follow me,
You, fairy elves that be:
Which circle on the green,
Come follow Mab your queen.
Hand in hand let's dance around,
For this place is fairy ground.

Something about it reminded him of Kate and he bought it on the spot, surprising his mother, who shot him several strange looks Will didn't bother to answer. After wrapping it with brown paper he waited until this morning to give it to her.

He smiled again, thinking that maybe it had brightened her day, just a little. It was strange when he thought about it. The verse had touched something, had brought visions of children dancing and singing. Had reminded him of summer.

His fingers stopped by the top button of his coat and then dropped by his sides. It had been summer. And there had been white blossoms on the tree outside the open window.

Oh no...

Like a slipping gear finally locking into place, Will heard a *clunk*, as the memory fell into place. He *had* heard that poem before, three or four years ago. And it had been summer. And...and...the sound of a fan whirring quietly came to him and he frowned. Come on, where had he been?

"Will," his mother called through the door. "Your father is

169

waiting."

He finished buttoning his coat and went to the front door. There was a fan...and it kept blowing the pictures off the table. They were pictures of Kate and her sister, Joey and Will picked them up every time, but she wouldn't let him move the fan, because she was hot.

That was it.

"Will? Honey, we need to go, now."

He stepped away from the door, slowly and ran his hand through his hair as the stupidity of what he had done crashed down on him.

"Will?" She rapped on his door.

They would play in the backyard. They loved it back there with the flowers and all the trees to play hide and seek with. I would be working in the kitchen, but I could still hear them. Being silly and playing their games. And there was a rhyme they'd sing, what was it? They'd sing it over and over, screaming and laughing. I can almost remember...

"Will, I mean it now, let's go."

He couldn't breathe. Someone was sitting on his chest and he couldn't get air enough to even answer his mother.

"Will!"

Will opened the door and brushed past her.

"There's no excuse for keeping your mother and me waiting, Will," his father said as he entered the kitchen.

"I can't go, there's something I need to take care of." He found his boots by the door and yanked them on. His shaking fingers gave him trouble as he worked on the laces.

"There's nothing you need to take care of besides getting yourself inside the car, right now."

Will recognized the tone in his father's voice, but shook his head anyway. "You don't understand, I have to go."

"Your mother and I have been tolerant of your disobedience, until now."

Will turned and glared up at his father, who had moved toward Will and within striking distance. He'd never hit Will in his life, never laid a hand on him in anger, but something in his father's face told Will there's always a first time.

"What do you mean?"

"This Kaitlin O'Connor situation. That is where you're going, isn't it? I believe we made it clear how we felt."

"Kate is not a situation, I don't know why you keep calling her that. And no, I don't believe you made anything clear." Will balled his fists, but kept them at his sides.

"Will."

He looked around his father's bulky figure and saw his grandmother standing in the doorway.

"Son, listen to your father. He knows what's best in this case. You need to learn to trust...and not question," she said.

"Why Grandma?" Will asked, turning his anger on the old lady. "Because it seems to me it's you who thinks you know best. So why don't you tell me why you're pulling the strings in this family all of a sudden?"

"You mind your tongue, boy," his father growled, blocking his view. "And mark my words. You're done. Finished with her *and* her family, you hear? No more sneaking over there when you think we don't know. No more phone calls, no nothing. You'll be home, straight away after school and when you're at school, you'll stay away from her, far away. If you see her on the street, you go the other way and you stay the hell out of her uncle's store and if she calls here, I'll tell her myself how it's going to be." His father's jaw clenched as he spoke the next. "And you'll mind me. Or so help me god, I'll put you in the car and drive you down to that military school they've got in Philly."

Blind rage blurred Will's vision, as he stared up at his father. His hands began to hurt and he flexed them behind his back, not taking his eyes off his father, who was staring back and panting like a caged animal. His mother sagged against the stove and made a noise that sounded like a sob, but said nothing. Will moved to look around his father and saw his grandmother turn to go back to her room. Her walker clicked on the linoleum floor. He looked back up at his father.

"Go to hell," he said and ripped open the door. It slammed behind him as he ran into the forest to find Kate.

* * * * *

The snow had started again, making it hard to see much more than ten feet in front of him. It stung his cheeks and burned his eyes with icy gusts of wind that blew up his coat, making his bones ache. The landscape changed as he plowed along and ditches hidden in the snow tripped him over and over again until he was covered from head to foot. He stopped to catch his breath against a tree and surveyed the land, trying to get his bearings. Nothing was familiar. He was lost.

Closing his eyes, he thought about Kate. Thought about the way she ran like a spooked horse whenever she was in trouble. He put himself in her mind as she opened the package this morning and read the cross–stitch. Felt her panic as her eyes raked over the words, over and over, in stunned disbelief. Saw the tears coursing down her face as her thoughts turned to him, lost and betrayed.

Where are you?

Deeper, deeper…now he saw her running through the woods. Her hair was white with snow and she was crying. One of her shoes had fallen off and an angry scratch burned red down her cheek. She moved with purpose through the woods, a destination in mind.

With his eyes still closed, he turned in a half–circle, like a blind man sensing light from a window. He could feel her. She was close.

He opened his eyes and began to run.

"Kate!"

There was a rise just ahead and Will ran to the top of it. He barreled down the other side and burst out of the trees, almost shooting off the side of the cliff. He fell, knocking a pile of snow off the edge and when he looked after it, he saw the creek about fifty feet below. Icy, black water carried broken branches and gray chunks of ice in its swift current. The branches dipped and bobbed and slammed into the shore, only to be dragged back in and rushed downstream. He looked to his left and saw only more snow and trees. Then he looked to his right.

Kate was standing fifteen feet away.

Her tears had subsided and she appeared much calmer. The wind blew her long, dark hair away from her face and Will was struck for a moment by power of her beauty. Her green eyes stared raptly at the creek and her gray–tinged lips were slightly parted, tiny clouds puffing through them with each breath. Her slender fingers worked into fists, relaxed, balled up again. She stepped closer to the edge and Will saw she wore only one shoe.

"Kate!" Will shouted, but she gave him no response. He took a few steps towards her and shouted again. "Kate!"

Now she did turn and Will stopped in his tracks. Her eyes had turned a brilliant, phosphoric green that seemed to glow with fire. They swirled and shifted and Will could see streaks of black sliding over the color. Like little worms, the black raced over her eyes and mixed with the green, turning it a sluggish, dull color. Will shivered, but didn't back away.

"What are you doing out here Kate? It's freezing." He spoke in an even tone, trying to ignore the madness in her eyes.

She turned toward the edge again. "Go away Will." Her voice was barely audible above the gusting wind. It was stiff and brittle, as it might break if spoken too loudly. The sound of it scared him even more. He didn't know that voice.

"You're freezing," he repeated, though he didn't see her shivering, despite the missing shoe and no coat. He shrugged out of his own coat and held it up. "Come on, I'll take you home."

She shrank away from him, holding up her hand and slipping on the loose snow. He pulled away quickly.

"You stay away from me, you just," she hesitated, "stay

173

away," she said, not taking her eyes away from the creek.

"Okay."

They stood like that in the snow while the sound of the angry creek rose up from the canyon. Stood like that for a long, long time. Until Will's feet went numb and his fingers felt arthritic when he flexed them, but he didn't move.

"It never stops," she murmured, more to herself it seemed, than to him. "Never stops, never goes away, just goes on and on…"

"Kate—"

She jerked around, her strange eyes swimming with tears and threw something on the ground by his feet. It was the cross–stitch.

"Tell me it's not what I think it is Will."

He stared at the cross–stitch, guilt hanging in the air with every passing second. No words came.

"Why? I don't—" Her trembling fingers ran through her hair, pulled it away from her face and then held it at her neck. "Why?"

Let me get this right, please.

"I didn't do it to hurt you," he began. "And I haven't gone in a long, long time, since way before you came back."

"You think that makes it better?"

"No, no, I'm just trying to explain it in some way that won't make you hate me more," he said and for a second, he thought he saw something in her eyes that encouraged him, so he rushed on. "When you left I couldn't believe how much I missed you. I mean, I hardly knew you. I thought about you all the time and I played that night over and over again in my head until it just about drove me nuts." She was still listening, good. "I was just a kid and I didn't understand what was happening, all I knew was that I wanted to be with you, wanted to feel you…and, and touch you again. And then one day my mom went with the church down to Quarryville for some volunteer work and I went with her. She left me in the office while they visited with the residents and I saw a lady, sitting in the garden." He hesitated, planning out his next words.

"So what," she fired. "It was just like a do–gooder mission for you? Slumming with the crazy's?"

"No, it wasn't like that at all." God he felt stupid. And he felt her pulling away from him with every stupid word that fell out of his mouth. "When I talked to her I felt closer to you. She's changed, Kate she's—"

"Don't say it!" She slammed her hands over her ears and scrunched her eyes shut. "God don't say she's changed, don't say her name, don't say–say anything, I can't, I can't," she sobbed harshly and Will started for her again. She whirled around and took a step backwards. "Go away Will. I don't want you here. Please, just go away."

"I'm sorry Kate, I'm so sorry, I never—"

"God Will, how could you? How could you, you were the only one, I trusted you," she choked out.

"I know, I know and I'm sorry, please. I know how upset you are, but this isn't helping." A pounding started in his head as he watched her gaze over the edge.

Her fingers fumbled inside her shirt and she took out the necklace she always kept next to her skin. Will had only seen the charm that hung from the end once or twice, but never asked her about it. He could never find a way that didn't seem prodding. She wrapped her hand around it and took a deep breath. "Get away from me Will."

"I'm not going anywhere without you." He spoke sternly, trying to hide his terror at how close to the edge she was now.

The snow picked up and her figure faded a little in the swirling whiteness. He felt as though she was slipping away from him even as she stood, not ten feet away.

"You don't have a choice." She was staring at the bottom again and Will chanced another few steps closer. He could almost reach out and touch her now. A whiff of honeysuckle blew by his nose and he glanced around at the snow–covered landscape in confusion.

"Let me help you, we can get through this," he said, trying to concentrate. A fluttering, pink shape caught his eye at the bottom. He peered over the side and looked down, but could make out no discernable object.

Kate moved forward, her toes now hanging over the edge. "I think it's time I helped myself."

Another gust of wind blew by, the scent of honeysuckle stronger this time and Will saw the fluttering pink again. He crouched down a little and squinted his eyes. As it formed an identifiable shape, he felt an icy hand close at his throat.

Falling back, he fought to keep his balance and then lunged forward to verify what his eyes were telling him. Panic crawled through his brain and for an instant his feet twitched to run, run as fast and as far from here as he could get. His saw his journey through the woods and toward home where he could hide under his covers like he did when he was five and had woken from a nightmare. He'd stumbled into Kate's nightmare and it was unlike any he had before.

A girl lay at the bottom of the gulch.

Her body was spread over the snow–covered rocks and dead branches that were scattered along the shore of the creek. One leg rested on a hollow log and her hands were almost folded at her stomach. The pink pajamas she wore were stained with mud and grass. Her head sat at an odd angle, leaned against her shoulder. Her glassy eyes were open and seemed to be smiling up at the falling snow.

Oh God, oh God. What hell is this?

He put his hands to his face and rubbed at his eyes. That was no ghost. No sad, forlorn figure looking for an eternal resting place. This was a memory. Kate's memory. A memory carefully preserved to be kept alive and growing. Every detail, every nuance had been captured and held in a dark vault in the depths of Kate's mind. It had been stored and shielded from time and reason. She had taken it out to look at it again and to possibly try and make peace with it.

Make peace with it.

He looked up and saw Kate with her eyes closed and her arms outstretched. Her face was lifted to the gray sky, snowflakes brushing her long eyelashes. She lifted herself up on her toes and began to sway forward.

"NO!" Will leapt forward and caught the back of her shirt in one hand. She swung at him, trying to break free, but he tightened his grip and pulled her away.

"Stop it, let go!"

He trapped her arms at her sides and clasped his hands together at her stomach. She kicked and thrashed in his arms, her one sneakered foot connecting with his shin over and over again until it went numb. Dragging her away from the edge, he stumbled on a rock and fell, bringing her down on top of him in the snow. The back of her head banged against his nose and hot pain tore through his head. He pushed her off and rolled over until he straddled her between his legs. She screamed and bucked, trying to throw him off.

"Stop it! God damn it, I said stop it!" He grabbed her wrists and shook her hard. Blood sprayed from his nose, showering her face and shirt. His angry, threatening tone broke through her hysterics and she stopped screaming.

"What the hell are you thinking?" She tried to pull her hands away, but he held them firm and bent down to look directly into her eyes. They were clear now, all traces of the black gone. "What the hell was that?"

"You don't understand. Please, just let me go." Her pitiful eyes stabbed at his heart, but his anger overrode everything else.

"No, I won't." He did let go of her hands though and saw red marks where he had been holding her. Keeping his knees on either side of her, he went on, "and don't tell me I don't understand. I was there, remember? I saw the whole thing. I saw Joey—"

"Don't please, Will—" She turned away and started sobbing

again.

"Stop it, listen to me." He moved her face so she was forced to look at him.

"No, no," she moaned.

"I watched her die."

Her sobs subsided and confusion filled her face. "But, how could—"

"From behind that boulder." He stabbed the air in that direction with his finger. "I stood and watched her roll down the hill. I saw her hit the bottom. I saw you start to go after her, my God, I saw you start to go after her." He let go of her face and looked down. "And I stood there like an idiot, frozen with panic. I just—I couldn't believe what was happening." He sniffed and shook his head, sending blood flying where it landed in the snow beside them and melted into the ground. "And then after, in the house. Kate I was there, I do know how is was... what she did."

Kate closed her eyes, tears squeezing from between her swollen lids and sliding down her face to wet her hair. "You don't understand, Will. Not really. I had her hand. I had it and I thought it was going to be okay, I–I really did. She was almost to the t–top. But I didn't hold tight enough and she slipped and she fell. And I watched her...I watched her fall all the way down. I watched her eyes...and she was s–so scared. I just, I didn't hold on tight enough..." Her voice faded away and she rolled her head to the side.

"I'm so sorry," he said, sitting her up and holding her against his chest. "The one thing in the world I would never want to do is make it worse. I didn't mean to, I know how it's been for you, how hard it's been, but you have to get past it, you have to try because it'll only hurt more if you don't."

Her body stiffened in his arms and she moved away, standing up and brushing the snow from her jeans. "Like you did?"

He dropped his head. "Kate—"

"No, no more excuses. I'll get past it because I don't have any other choice...but I'll do it alone."

"It doesn't have to be that way."

"Yes it does, it does and it's your fault...it's the only way for me now. So from now on Will," she stopped, looking at her feet as she tried to get out the next words. Words Will knew would drive them apart forever. She looked back up at him and he saw bitter resolve shine in her eyes. "From now on, you stay away from me, Will. I don't want to see you, I don't want to talk to you, I don't–don't want to know you anymore. And if you really mean not to hurt me any more than you already have, then you'll listen to me and you'll stay away."

She turned with a little sob and ran into the forest. Will watched her until she disappeared into the whiteness and then he put his head down.

So that was it. Yeah...that was it. He should have known...it was only a matter of time.

He dug the rock he'd stumbled over out of the ground and hefted it. It was cold as was everything on this late, January evening and he chuckled at the irony. Something so warm and beautiful that started in the sweet days of summer had came to a wrenching, brutal halt in the hard, lonely days of winter. It was funny, really.

The tears that broke through his closed eyes burned his face and his sobs grew like fire in his throat. Not fair...god it was not fair, but she was right. It was his fault, his stupidity, and his burden. And now, she was gone.

"Goddamn it all to hell!" He roared and threw the rock over the edge. He never heard it land.

Chapter Eleven
And So It's Told

The second semester of school started with the usual drudgery of tests and homework. Kate dove into the work with relief. Her marks were high and her teachers gave up their sympathetic looks to treat her with the respect she was earning. Uncle Dave was impressed with her eagerness, though she could tell he questioned her motives. He noticed the new hardness in her face, the purpose in her walk

"I'm fine, just tired is all. I haven't been sleeping well," she would tell Uncle Dave when he asked.

And that wasn't far from the truth. Her night terrors had reached the point where she spent more time wrestling with her sheets and kicking poor Winnie off the bed than she did sleeping. The dreams were always the same. Oh, maybe they would start out differently, under the guise of something sweet and innocent, but they would always end the same way, with the monster who chased her, destroying everything in his path. But it was always her fault somehow. Something she could have done or should have done if she had the strength, but in her dreams, she never had the strength. She was just a spectator to her own demise. And *he* would win, again and again and she would wake up, screaming.

Uncle Dave listened to her nocturnal horrors, but didn't ask anymore. He would be there with his soothing words and gentle rubs and sometimes he would sit on the edge of her bed until she slept again. But the strain was wearing on him. He had aged the past few weeks. The lines around his mouth had deepened and the gray in his hair spread with alarming speed to cover most of his head. His eyes never changed, though now they were dark with worry most of the time. Kate's sadness grew to see her uncle, once so bright and alive, shuffle around the house like an old man. But there was nothing that could be done. A shroud rested over the house and as they went through the motions of life, it only became darker and heavier with each passing day.

And Will's absence did nothing to ease the tension. Again, Uncle Dave said nothing, leaving her to work it out on her own, but he let her know, in his own way, that he would be there when and if she wanted to talk about it. A part of her did want to bring it into the light and beat the problem into some sort of shape she could handle. But doing so would bring Will into the light as well and that was just too hard.

Sometimes, for a painfully brief moment, when she first woke in the morning and the fuzziness of sleep still surrounded her, she would forget. She would wake thinking about Will and she would smile. And then it would be back, like a hand squeezing her heart and she would lay back in bed to fight back the tears so she could face the day. Because for as much as she avoided Will at school, her thoughts were never so kind.

It turned out she didn't have to try that hard at school. Will was gone for the week after their meeting and just as she started to get really worried about him, he was back. She saw him in the halls, never talking to anyone and always with his head down. He ate lunch alone, as did she and walked home alone. She thought he must have been taking a different route because she never ran into him. He'd listened to her, all right and until one strangely warm day a few weeks into February, she had seen nothing of him except for the back of his head as he hurried away.

She had been sitting in the truck while Uncle Dave went inside to pay for the gas and slowly pulling up the ripped upholstery on the seat. It came up in neat little strips that she tossed on the floor. A car horn blared behind her and she snapped out of her daze, brushing the pile under the seat before her uncle could see it.

She turned to see who was honking and when she saw the boy on the bike, she ducked down. It was Will and he was glaring at the man who'd honked at him. The driver waved him off and swung around to park behind the truck. Now she could watch without being seen. Will stopped by the air hose and climbed off his bike. He grabbed the pull–cord and gave it several hard yanks before the compressor started with a tired putter.

Kate rolled down the window and peeked around the gas pump for a better look. He had changed too these last few weeks and she had the uneasy feeling of time rushing by her with a crushing speed.

Oh Will what's happening...

A frown line wrinkled his forehead and shadows darkened the hollows under his eyes. His clothes just seemed to hang on him and there was a slump to his back that twisted the pain in her chest. And his hands, his hands that were once so strong and sure had a tremor to them as they worked to screw the hose to the tire.

Uncle Dave came out of the store and caught her gaze before she could look away. He got in and started the truck, but didn't pull away.

"You know," he said, without looking at her. "Why don't you go talk to him. Nothing's ever resolved without that at least."

She shook her head. "No, we've done enough talking."

"But not the right kind." Uncle Dave turned as Will rode by without seeing them.

"Yeah, I know," she said, watching him in the mirror.

Sighing, Uncle Dave put the truck in gear and pulled out.

"There's a lot you don't know you know, a lot about Will," he said a few minutes later.

"What do you mean?"

"Well, after everything happened and you left, he came to see me."

"Really? Why, I mean he didn't know you, did he?"

Uncle Dave cleared his throat. "No, not at first, but he came almost every day and we had some good talks."

"About what?"

"Well you, mostly."

"Oh."

"He wanted to know about you, your life, your interests. What you were like when you were little. I guess he wanted to know *you*." He chuckled. "That boy could sit and listen to stories for as long as I let him. I'd be chasing him home half the time because we'd lose track of time, you know? And I told him just about everything I remembered. All the mischief you and your sister caused. You were quite a little punk back then," he said and ruffled her hair.

Kate smiled.

"Anyway, I just wanted to tell you and I'm glad I did now. You decide for yourself, like I know you will. I'm not excusing what he did, but just keep it in mind that whatever he did, he did because he loves you."

She wiped her eye with the back of her hand and looked back out the window. "You think?"

He laughed. "I may be an old geezer, but I know it when I see it, though I can't say I've ever seen his kind. That boy loves you, Kate. You'd be a fool to throw it away…and my Katie is no fool."

She leaned to kiss him on the cheek and rest her head on his chest. "Thank you."

"I just want you to be happy. It's the only thing that matters to me. You deserve it."

Something in his voice made her look up at him, but he hid whatever it was behind a smile. She grinned back.

"So does this mean I can finally have my Saturday nights back?"

"Oh, you are so bad," she said, laughing.

* * * * *

The next day found Kate walking down the path that led to Will's house. She held a small box in her hand; a present she hoped would repair some of the damage she had helped to cause. His house wasn't far from town and she hurried, anxious to see him now that she had decided. For once she'd been up all night and it had nothing to do with the dreams. She couldn't stop thinking about him and twice during the night, she had put her shoes on and was halfway out the door to see him before she stopped. No sense in making a fool out of herself in front of his parents when she could wait one more day. His parents just didn't seem like the type to appreciate someone dropping by at three in the morning. Especially his dad.

When she arrived, the house was quiet. No cars were parked out front and the drapes were closed. Thinking maybe only his parents were out, she stepped up to the porch and knocked on the door.

"You won't find anyone home," a voice from behind her said. Kate turned and faced an elderly lady, dressed in a long, flowery dress that tied in the middle. She wore gardening gloves and her white hair was pulled back in a loose bun. "They've all run off to Quarryville to put the Jeep in the shop."

Kate stepped off the porch and started back down the driveway. "Oh, well I'll just come back later."

"Hey, hey, what're you running off for? Why not sit a spell. I've just been out in the garden, taking advantage of this warm stretch we've been having and I could use the company."

"Oh no, that's okay," she said, backing away. Something in the old woman's face was not as casual as it tried look and Kate felt the need to go home, now.

"You're Kaitlin O'Connor, aren't you?" The woman said, stepping closer.

"Yeah," she said quickly. "Um, can you tell Will I came by?"

"Sure you don't want to stay? I could make us some tea and we could sit by the garden. It's too nice a day to be inside."

Kate looked doubtfully at the gathering clouds. "No, I really need to get home. Maybe another time."

The woman spoke quietly and Kate almost missed her next words. "You think an old woman has nothing to say maybe, nothing a young girl like you would be interested in. But you might be surprised, the things I've seen, but more important the things I could tell you. Things about that charm you've got hung 'round you neck there."

Kate stopped and turned slowly. Will's grandmother stood with her hands on her hips, her head nodding triumphantly.

She reached for the amulet, which always hung beneath her shirt. Only the rope showed at her neck.

"You'd be surprised, child," the old woman repeated.

"I don't know what you're talking about and I have to get home," Kate said, as forcefully as she could and began to walk away.

"Things about the man in your dreams as well," she went on.

Kate stopped. Cold fear froze the blood in her veins as she turned, one more time.

The woman held her hand out to her and motioned. "Come, come, let's sit and talk a spell. The weather's so right for it."

Kate moved forward, as if in a dream and let the old woman lead her around the house and to a bench that sat at the edge of a vegetable garden.

"Now you wait right here and I'll get us some tea. You like lemon and sugar?"

Kate stared at her.

"Right, me too," his grandmother went on. "I reckon I could weather just about anything with a good cup of lemon tea." She left for the house, passing a walker that stood outside the back door.

Kate sat and looked at the small box in her hands. A breeze shook the trees overhead and she could smell the rain, heavy in the air. Thoughts of Will flashed through her head. Will teaching her how to ice skate. Will holding her hand at the Christmas tree lighting. Will kissing her so tenderly at the creek.

She looked into the woods. She could just leave. Just walk home from here and forget about the crazy old woman who was in the house, fixing her tea. Indecision made her hesitate and his grandmother came back before she could make up her mind.

"There now," she said, handing Kate a thick mug. "Isn't that better?"

"Thank you."

She sat down in the wooden chair, opposite Kate. "Can't remember when I felt this good last. Must have been a year, or more. I woke up this morning and I said to myself, 'yes, this must be the day.' Lord sure is good to be giving me the strength for this even if it won't last. It's good, to be up and around again," she muttered, mostly to herself.

"Must be what day?"

"Why the day I meet you, of course. I've been waiting for this, longer than you can imagine, I'm sure."

Kate set the mug down beside her. "Mrs. Harrickson, why would you think you'd be waiting for me?"

She gave Kate a harsh look. "So you think the old woman's gone a little daffy, eh? That what you think?"

"Well, what would you think?" Kate said evenly.

His grandmother laughed. It was a pleasant, broken in sound. "I like you, girl. You've got what my mother would call, grit. I was hoping I wouldn't though. Would have made it easier."

"Made what easier?"

"What I've to tell you. I was hoping also I wouldn't have to, but it seems you and Will are intent on seeing that I do." She sat back and closed her eyes.

"What does Will have to do with anything?" Kate sat forward on the bench.

"All in good time. Let me tell it my own way. The way I need to tell it so as you'll understand."

"All right, I'm listening," Kate said.

His grandmother sat with her eyes closed until Kate thought she might have fallen asleep. Then her eyes snapped open and Kate saw the faded blue in her irises had brightened and become almost translucent. Deeper colors swam in a circle around her pupils and Kate found she couldn't look away.

Kate squeezed her eyes shut and when she looked back the old woman's eyes were back to normal. For the most part. The brightness hadn't dimmed and there seemed to be energy in them that hadn't been there before.

"That man in your dreams was called Lordon Harrick," she said with a voice that mirrored the energy in her eyes. "He was born in the city of Galway, which lies on the western coast of Ireland. The year...was seventeen hundred and forty–nine." She paused and looked closely at Kate. "You'll hold your questions and your arguments 'till it's done."

Kate nodded.

Satisfied, she went on. "He came to America in the belly of a cargo ship bound for Richmond, Virginia when he was nineteen. Hid in a storage compartment and slept with the rats. Ate whatever slipped through the cracks from the decks above. He stayed in Virginia for a few years, doing odd jobs and making lots of enemies. He was a scattered, fruitless soul, who took what was offered to him and stole what wasn't. More'n one reward hung on his head by the time he left, mostly from men whose wives he'd taken and then cast aside. When he ran, he came here," she paused and looked around. "To Newclare. A few years passed as he took a wife and she bore him three children, two boys and a little girl.

"By this time he was deeply involved with the Druid cult that had migrated from Ireland and was living on the outskirts of town. The founders of our town here may've had their roots set in Ireland mind you, but the Protestants had Pennsylvania pretty much settled by then. And they didn't take kindly to the strange ways of the Old World, so a better way to put it might be that they'd been banned from the town. They lived in shacks in the woods, but not Lordon, he enjoyed his small place in the community, so he'd sneak out under the cover of night to meet them.

"Lordon'd been interested in the Druid culture since he was boy. His father had been part of the cult in Ireland, had in fact, and spent years studying their gentle ways and beliefs. Lordon grew to despise what he thought of as a weakness in his father. Their love of nature and peaceful habitation with the earth, it sickened Lordon, but other aspects of the cult interested him. Their spells, incantations, their knowledge of the underworld and...of the future."

She leaned close to Kate and spoke in a confidential tone. "Rabbits," she said. "They used them to tell the future. Now they didn't hurt them or anything, they'd just watch them and then they'd have their visions." She laughed a little. "Can't say I've seen anything as supernatural as that in the pesky things. Leastwise not while I'm chasing them out of my garden."

Kate nodded, but something was ringing in the back of her head. Rabbits...or was it just one rabbit? She almost had it and then it was gone, as the woman began talking again.

"But I'm falling off my track," she said and sat back. "As a boy, Lordon would follow his father to the woods and hide while he watched and learned. It was the only thing that he respected. What he considered to be honest and true. But, as they say, a little knowledge is a dangerous thing." She said the last and shook her head.

"As I said, Lordon's father was in training. It takes years, sometimes twenty years or more before he could've been considered a Druid priest. And his father struggled with the peaceful nature of the people. And failed, many, many times. On one occasion, while having dinner with a friend, they got into an argument and in a drunken rage, his father attacked him. The man's wife ran to help her husband and his father turned his anger and confusion to her. He raped her repeatedly and in the end, accidentally killed her. They hung him for it, not for the rape and murder of the wife of course, but the injuries to her husband. Lordon watched his father dangle from the rope without a tear in his eye and then went home. On the way, he found an iron pipe by the side of the road and when he got home, beat his mother within an inch of her life with it. He'd been eleven at the time and his mother lived in fear of him until she died of pneumonia four years later."

Will's grandmother took a deep breath and Kate could see her energy waning, but her eyes remained bright and glowing. "The Druids were like a second family for Lordon. He fell in love with the power their beliefs offered, but again, resisted the calm, harmonious lifestyle. He always saw the possibility for more and because of that eventually got himself kicked out. That didn't stop him, though, he continued practicing on his own. Scribbling in his little journal and staying out whole weeks at a time. By concentrating solely on the spells and the teachings of the under-world, he progressed faster, much, much faster than he should have.

"Gone was his unfocused nature, now he had purpose and with this purpose came change. More and more his family felt him pulling away, or being pulled away. He looked at them with disgust now, as if after seeing the wondrous visions of the dark spirits, his family repulsed him. They lived in fear of him, waiting for the spark that would ignite the fire they saw smoldering in his eyes.

"Then, on one dark and starless night, he stormed into his son's room and grabbed his eldest, Garret out of bed. His brother Ennis, who'd been six at the time, and his sister Anya, a year younger, woke to the commotion and watched as their father dragged Garret out of the room. Their mother met them in the hall and her screams were cut short as she got a look at what the two younger ones had seen in their father's eyes. There was blackness in them and the blackness possessed his eyes like worms, swarming on a rotten apple. You see," she said, leaning forward. "He had the evil in him already then. It was in him, just waiting to get out. Anyway, when their mother found her voice again, she screamed desperately for him to hand over her child. She pulled and scratched at him, trying to take back her son, but Lordon wouldn't be stopped. Finally, she fell, sobbing at his feet at the top of the stairs, blocking his path.

"He did stop then and as he looked down on her he said, 'The due must be paid.' With that he pulled back his foot and heaved her down the stairs. She tumbled all the way down and landed at the bottom with a loud crack, as her neck separated from her body. Lordon continued down the stairs, past his dead wife and out the door, the child in his arms screaming in terror. Ennis and Anya stood alone in the house for several minutes, while their young minds tried to comprehend what they'd just seen. Then they ran after their father.

"Garret's screams led them to a part in the forest where five large rocks surrounded two metal posts, secured in a ditch. A fire raged around the posts, nearly consuming them. Ennis found a spot behind a tree and sank to the ground, his young sister, leaning against him. Their father was busy hog–tying Garret with the end of a chain. And Garret was screaming. Oh yes, he was screaming. His face was red from effort and his voice had become scratchy, but he never stopped screaming. The tying done, Lordon crossed to the other side of the fire and picked up something hidden in the brush. It was only now that Ennis saw the chain led directly into the fire. Garret realized this and his screams were fed with fresh terror. Closer and closer he was pulled toward the fire and Garret did everything he could to stop it, even...even sank his teeth into the ground at one point, but nothing would stop Lordon. Garret was held fast against the poles, in the heart of the fire and the flesh began to melt from his bones. The wind carried his screams all the way back to town, but by the time help arrived it was all over. Ennis watched, his cries matching the pitch of his brother's. But little Anya, she buried her face in Ennis' back, refusing to see the horror. And then, little by little, Garret was finally silent.

"Lordon appeared out of the darkness and stood by the fire for a moment, as the wind rose and the fire lifted to brush the lowest branches of the trees surrounding them. The night was suddenly filled with voices, evil, seductive voices that stirred confusion in Ennis's soul. Lordon began to laugh, with the black madness in his eyes, and then he was lost in a tirade of nonsense words and phrases, broken only by bursts of screams and laughter. Lordon stood, his arms outstretched, his head lifted to the heavens, waiting. And as he waited it came. A dark cloud formed in the sky directly above and the wind howled like screaming children through the trees. In its breeze blew smells, stinking and rotten, like things old and forgotten. The cloud, if it could be called a cloud, shifted and eventually began to turn, slowly and then faster and faster until it swirled with a mindless power that caused Ennis to resume his screams. And the wind, instead of blowing the fire out, as it should have, as the laws of nature would have demanded it do, the wind blew the fire higher and higher. It caught the branches of the overhanging trees, but stopped before racing through the forest, as if containing itself. Lordon noticed none of this as he stood below the cloud, still laughing.

"And then, just as suddenly as it'd come, the cloud receded. It wasn't gone, though, it rose to a distance Ennis could no longer see, but he could still hear it. Lordon looked around in confusion. It wasn't finished, but he didn't understand why it'd stopped. And it was then that he saw them. The eyes staring at him from the darkness of the trees. They surrounded him and his fire and as he began to understand, the townspeople emerged from the forest. News had spread through the town and something of a posse had been formed to catch Lordon. Shouts rose and Lordon made a pathetic attempt to run, like the true coward he was, but they captured and tied him quite easily. Someone was able to retrieve poor Garret from the fire and the chain was then attached to Lordon. He started his chants again; this time in the rambling, frenzied voice of one that knows the end is near. On and on he went as he was pulled into his own fire and just before his hair went ablaze, the cloud once more came to rest above them. Lordon saw this and laughed as he shouted out his final words. 'T'will come a time when the fire burns not here, but in the hearts of Newclare. A dark hour indeed when the fruit of my loins are brought together as one, in the power of the twelfth generation. And from their joining will I arise, reborn to seek vengeance on those who would destroy.'

"And then the cloud came to claim its own and Lordon was taken. The essence of his body was stripped away until all that was left was naked and pure and then gone, just like that." She snapped her fingers and Kate jumped, nearly falling off the bench.

The old woman sat back, clearly out of breath and looking into the woods with her bright eyes. Kate watched, as the fire died in front of her and the heavy curtain of night lifted to reveal the Harrickson's backyard and the garden in which they sat. The clouds had come in with intent now and Kate shivered as the wind blew against her skin.

Just as she thought the old woman was done she spoke again, her voice low and tired. "When it was done, the fire had swallowed almost an acre of land. The townspeople did their best to control it and by morning, the fire was out. The land had been scarred, though. And over time it became clear that it had died. No life could be sustained at the site and eventually it became the burial ground it is today."

His grandmother closed her eyes and breathed deeply, relieved to have finally told it. When she opened her eyes again she stared at Kate quietly and waited.

Kate looked past her into the thickness of the trees and listened to the wind. It seemed she could hear a child screaming in the rising and falling gusts. She shivered again.

"You haven't told me everything," Kate said in a low voice.

The woman leaned closer and peered at her with interest. "Haven't I?"

"No." Kate held her gaze even while her feet twitched to get up and run. Run as far and as long as she could to get away from this woman and her evil tales.

His grandmother sat back again, still watching her. "What more would you have me tell you?"

"This man, Lordon, what was his plan? What happened to him, what did they stop him from doing?"

"Seems from the look of you, you've got a mind as to what it might have been."

"You're not telling me what I want to hear," Kate repeated.

The woman chuckled. "Don't think anything else I've to tell you is likely what you'd want to hear. But," she paused and took a sip of her tea. "If you want it colored, so be it." She gazed again into the trees as she tried to find a way to tell it. "The forces that rule the world are basic, pure natures that, when tried to be understood, can overwhelm a man in their simplicity. Lordon understood this and he saw beyond the inner workings to the perfection that lay beneath. When stripped of all their disguises, the forces are flawless with truth. And our world lies between like a metal ball placed between two magnets. We live in the balance they create." She leaned toward Kate again. "Now, what would happen if you took one of the magnets away?"

Kate nodded, understanding.

"If evil could be touched. If hate could be drunk like bad wine and power held in a fist. That was Lordon's truth. The truth he'd come to realize and to desire more than life itself. He needed to purge and cleanse himself from the last of his weakness." The grandmother's cup emptied and she set in on the ground. "That's where Garret came in. He was the last semblance of balance Lordon hung onto. In that act, he forever left the truth that we live in, for the mysteries and darkness that lived in the power for which he so craved. Because what he craved was really quite simple. How better to attain the power and strength of demons, than to become one of them?"

Thunder rolled in the distance and Kate glanced at the sky, the wind blowing her hair wildly about her face. Her fingers clenched around the small package on her lap. She looked down at it, forgetting for a moment what it held.

"Unfortunately for Lordon, he wasn't able to complete the ritual." The woman went on. "And everything he'd worked for so hard and so long was taken from him because of the interference of the townspeople."

Kate waited for her to continue, but she didn't. "So he died. That's it?"

His grandmother dropped her head to her chest. "As hard as I tried, I still didn't get it across to you any, did I?

"You've told me a horrible story, one I'll probably never forget. But I still don't understand why you felt the need to tell it, or why you told it to me."

She looked up at Kate, her eyes burning with urgency. "The soul, girl, I'm talking about the soul. It goes on and still does to this day. What Lordon started that black night in these very woods is not over. It was unable to be contained. And it lives on."

She shifted in her wooden chair and came closer to Kate. "After that night, Ennis was...changed. His young mind was incapable of holding all he'd seen and until he reached the age of eighteen, he stayed in a place where there were others like him. Slowly, over time, he came out of it and when he did, he ran. Spent his life running, as did his children and theirs, always trying to escape something that couldn't be escaped from. It lived with them, in them and from Ennis was born generation upon generation of wanderers. Never staying in one place, never setting down roots, though over time, they wouldn't even remember why.

"And little Anya. She was shipped down to the city to live with her mother's people. But before she left, she and Ennis had a visit from an old man who identified himself as a friend of her father's. That is, before all the strangeness came. He'd known their father when he'd still been with the cult. Seems this man witnessed part of that night and when the crowd left, helped himself to a handful of the ashes. He fashioned that charm you've got hung at your neck with them and gave it to Anya. It's a Runic Helm; hexed to protect the little girl and her family from the black evil he'd seen that night. It hung around little Anya's neck until her little girl was old enough to wear it. It kept the evil from spinning out of control, but never stopped it. No, it never stopped it."

Kate picked the amulet out of her shirt and looked at it, turning it over and feeling the familiar tingling sensation. "Then why am I wearing it?" Her voice was barely a whisper.

"Child, don't you see? The evil never stopped. Ennis ran from it for the rest of his life, moving from one city to the next, but never escaping. And Anya, she came back here to Newclare, when she was old enough, to live close to her roots. She told no one who she was and lived a simple life with her husband and children. Her children stayed on after she passed and so it was carried, one to the next, not in the genes, but in what some calls the 'windows to the soul'. Skipping over generations from time to time, but always surfacing, somewhere down the line. Never diluting or becoming weaker with each transfer, but getting stronger and more powerful as the twelfth generation neared. On and on and on, until it reached that man your mother called Father and then on to her and finally—"

"No!" Kate shouted, putting her hands over her ears. "I don't want to hear any more. Please."

His grandmother reached out and pulled her hands away with surprising strength. "But you must. You have no choice. Not listening isn't going to make it go away, but it may make it worse. It is your heritage and who you are." Now she stroked Kate's hands, holding them softly. "Your legacy."

Fat tears rolled down Kate's face as she stared back into the wrinkled face of this stranger.

"Lordon lives on. He lives in you, in the evil he created. And your dreams, your dreams are a warning of things to come. You still have balance and that's good. It's that balance that's using the dreams to try and stop what will happen. But as I look at you, girl, I see something. And that something tells me it's only a matter of time before your balance begins to tip as well. Only you can breathe life into him. You and the power the two of you can create. Because you see, *you* are the twelfth generation.

Twelve is a very powerful number in the Druid religion and that is why Lordon chose it. So you must understand, that you are the twelfth generation and it's your generation that will bring the curse to pass. But you can stop it before it happens."

"I don't understand," Kate said, her voice thick with tears.

"He waits and has waited for hundreds of years. But I think you know as well as I, that his wait is almost over. That's why I've told you this. And warned you. Because if you're not careful, you'll set in motion things that can't be stopped."

"What are you talking about?"

"I'm talking about Will," she said her voice suddenly stern. "Surely you've figured it out by now."

Kate drew back. "Will?"

"How do you think I knew to tell you?"

"But he—"

"He is who you know him to be. A descendant of Ennis."

Kate snatched her hands away. "No."

"I can't say I understand the manner of nature that pulled the two of you here, only that what's been done can't be undone. But it can be stopped. There's still time." Her voice softened a bit. "You know what you have to do."

Kate said nothing, as tears blinded her eyes.

"Well, good. I'm glad we've had this little talk." She glanced up at the dark clouds. The sky lightened as a crack a thunder burst overhead. "Looks like you should be moving along, though. Don't want to get caught in this storm."

Kate couldn't move. The weight that pressed on her shoulders glued her to the bench and she struggled to breathe. With an effort she stood and the package slid to the ground, unnoticed. A strong gust of wind hit her back, propelling her forward, past the old woman, past the garden and into the woods. The rain finally came and it hit her face in stinging slaps. Her hair flew out behind her and her feet pounded the ground. With every step, Kate felt the horrible pressure lift. The faster she ran the more it lightened and soon Kate felt as if she were flying over the terrain. Her voice lifted in retching screams that rose from the pit of her belly. Over and over again, as if she could rid herself the pain through her throat. Hot tears mixed with the cold rain that continued to pour down through the trees. Just when she felt like she could run no more, she came to a clearing and fell to her knees. Her face lifted to the sky and she bellowed her hatred to the clouds above until her voice gave out and she could only scream hoarse curses. Her strength was soon washed away and she collapsed on her back in the tall weeds. She laid, spread eagle, letting the rain drench her face and the mud soak her clothes.

And she cried.

Chapter Twelve
A Fragile Balance

Will lifted his hand and rapped lightly on the door.

After a few moments it opened and Dave stood in the doorway. He wore his bathrobe and slippers.

"Hey Dave, how you doing?" Will asked.

Dave's pale face brightened. "It's good to see you again, Will," he said. "It's been too long, come in, come in."

Will hedged in the doorway. "You sure? I mean, I wasn't sure if I should come."

"You're always welcome here, you know that," Dave said, ushering him inside.

Will shut the door behind him. "Thanks."

"So what brings you out in this weather?"

"Well, actually, I came to see Kate." Will rubbed his head. "Do you think, I mean, is it okay? How's she been?"

Dave turned to light the stove, but Will saw his face tighten as soon as he'd said Kate's name. "I was kind of hoping you'd come to see her," Dave said.

"She's all right, isn't she?"

"Yeah, she's fine. She's up in her room right now."

"Thanks."

"Hey Will?"

He stopped. "Yeah?"

"I don't know," Dave said. "There's something going on with her. Something she can't handle on her own, but she won't talk to me. She's cut me off entirely." He looked at the floor and then back up at Will. "See if you can't find out what's going on. I know you guys have had some problems lately, but it's more than that and it's really worrying me."

Worried himself now, Will nodded. "Sure, thanks for telling me."

Dave nodded at him and went back to the kitchen.

Will continued up the stairs and stopped in front of Kate's door. It was closed and he paused a moment before knocking on it.

"Come in."

Her voice was different. It was hesitant and weak in a way Kate had never sounded. It was the voice of someone much older than he knew.

He pushed the door open and saw her sitting with her back to him on the bed. He could see only the side of her chin behind her dark hair that had turned black in the low light. An unopened textbook lay in her lap and she was staring out the window. The first signs of sunset were visible over the building across the alley.

He said nothing for a moment and as he waited, a wave of dread came over him. It was stupid to be thinking that way. It was only Kate. But still, he said nothing.

"What do you need, Uncle Dave?"

"It's me," Will said softly.

He heard her sharp inhale of breath and wondered why she would be afraid of him. She was angry, he knew that, but the fear confused him.

"Kate?" He took a few steps into the room, but stopped several feet away from her.

She turned, slowly, as if the motion pained her. The book slid off of her lap and she put her feet on the floor. Her eyes stared straight ahead.

"What are you doing here, Will."

Her response startled him and he blinked back the tears that suddenly stung his eyes. "I um, came to see how you were." He glanced around the room, wishing she would look at him. "I tried to call."

"I've been busy."

Will looked down at his scuffed sneakers. He should go. He never should have come, she said stay away, why was he here?

But he couldn't leave her, not like this. Anger, he could handle. Hate even, but not this. He forced himself to move forward, but she made no move to make room on the bed, so he stood, shuffling his feet and feeling like an idiot.

"What's going on Kate?"

She shook her head, still not looking up. "I told you, I've been busy."

Running his hands through his hair, he walked over to her dresser and leaned against it. "No, I mean with us. I feel like, I don't know, you're confusing me."

Now she met his eyes and he fell back. There was anger there, all right, but so much more…so much pain he didn't understand.

"Well god forbid I should confuse you," she said in a hateful voice.

"You want to tell me about this then?" He took the package from his coat pocket and held it to Kate. "You hate me, I know that. You don't want to see me, I know that too, but this? Do you know how I felt when I saw this? I thought, well I guess I thought that…"

She glared down at the picture and for a second he saw her face soften. It was a picture of Kate. One he had taken on their skating trip in the woods. She stood, her arms at her sides, in the middle of the lake with snow swirling around her like a gentle tornado. Her hair fell down her back in soft waves, lightly sprinkled with snow, as he face lifted toward the sky. Her nose was red with cold and her eyes twinkled with excitement. A soft smile played on her lips. It sat in its oval frame by his bed where it would be the first thing he saw when he woke in the morning.

"I guess I thought you were trying to tell me something," Will continued. "I thought maybe you'd forgiven me, a little."

"Why would I do that?"

Will blew through his mouth and shoved the picture back in his pocket. "I don't know Kate. Why'd you give it to me then?"

"Where did you get that anyway?" She asked, packing up

her books.

"Where do you think? My grandmother. Why did you leave it with her? You could have given it to me yourself."

"Probably because I didn't think it was a good idea for us to see each other. And it sure as hell isn't a good idea right now, so why don't you just leave, Will." She was slamming the books inside her bag and they kept falling out.

"No, I'm not going anywhere until you explain yourself," he said and folded his arms.

"I don't have to explain myself to you."

"Yes you do, you owe me that at least."

She shoved the last of the books in her bag and turned away from him. "I owe you nothing."

He caught her shoulder and spun her around to look at him. "Yes you do. That's not fair to drop something like this on me and then offer no explanation."

She glared down at his hand on her shoulder until he put it back at his side. She moved away from him and dropped the bag.

"Fine, fine if you want to hear it, then fine." She met his eyes, dead on. "Maybe I thought something could have been salvaged. That's why I gave the picture to you."

"But now? What's happened?"

"I was feeling weak and I made a mistake is all," she said and turned away again. "I thought I was missing you, wanting you back, but then I remembered. *You* are the reason I feel like this in the first place. It's your fault we're not together. Your sneakiness, your lies, your mistake that ended everything and I don't know why I thought anything would ever change. I just came to my senses finally and I realized I don't need you anymore. I don't want you anymore and I guess I don't know if I ever really did."

Will hung his head while he listened to this, giving her the time she needed. Now he lifted his head and met her eyes. "Crap."

The look on her face might have been comical if not for Will's mood. Her expression changed several times, confused, angry, shocked. She settled on angry.

"Crap? What the hell are you talking about? I'm trying to…"

"What you're trying to do is fill my head with more of your crap." He shook his head and made a slow circle around the room. "I never thought I'd say this, not to you. You're lying."

"What? I am—"

"You are, it's written all over your face and even now while you're fiddling with your hands there. God Kate," he said and glared back at her. "This world has too many liars already, you were the one who was always truthful with me. You've always been that at least, it's something I've admired."

She held his glare. "Your mistake…again."

"Tell me what's going on Kate, I don't—"

"Oh come off it Will. It's only your ego talking anyway. Your massive male ego that refuses to believe you did anything wrong. Will screwed up? No way, there has to be another answer, there has to be something else. But guess what? You *did* screw up and no matter how you think you can fix this, you can't. You've finally run into something you can't fix, nobody can fix it, so just leave it broken, okay? And move on, I'm sure there are plenty of other girls you can use that charm on, so stop wasting your time on me. And so what if I'm lying anyway?" She spit out at him as she picked up her bag. "Ask me if I care."

He grabbed her arm as she pushed past. "We're not finished here."

Her eyes narrowed. "You have no idea how finished we are."

And then she was gone in the slam of her bedroom door. Will stared at the poster she taped to the back of the door, as he listened to her stomp down the stairs. It was an ocean scene with whales and dolphins and fish all swimming around each other. The longer he looked at it, the more he felt as if there were too many things going on. It was too confusing with its melding images and sharp colors.

203

He sighed and lowered himself on her bed. Her smell lingered on the sheets and he picked up her pillow, breathing in her scent. The sound of the backdoor slamming made him jump and when he looked out the window, he saw Kate hurrying away. Her book bag bounced against her back with every angry step.

* * * * *

Kate looked at the clock above the door and then back at Mrs. Fenter, who stood on the other side of the counter, holding two different brands of stewed tomatoes.

"I just don't know," the woman said slowly.

Sighing, Kate turned to the magazine on her lap.

"The last time I tried this one, I think it was a little too tangy." Mrs. Fenter furrowed her bushy eyebrows and turned the can over to read the ingredients. "Or was it too sweet?"

"Uh–huh," Kate said, wishing she would move her big head, because it blocked the early morning light from the door.

Mrs. Fenter's large head was only made worse by the curls she rolled on top of it. She had worn the beauty–shop helmet for as long as Kate could remember; though it did nothing for her beakish face. The curls exaggerated her long neck and threw her little body off balance.

Mrs. Fenter tilted her head to the side in her pursuit of the alien ingredient and Kate had the sudden urge to strap her down and buzz it all off. Just buzz her bald, down to her flaky pink skin and she wouldn't stop until every last curl covered the floor at her feet. She heard Mrs. Fenter screaming in her mind, as her precious hair was stripped from her head and Kate started to giggle. Her wailing sounded more like a bird screeching.

"But this one had stems or something nasty in it," bird woman said, turning her attention to the other label. "There were hard little chunks that Mr. Fenter said gave it a better consistency, but I don't know. It just didn't taste right to me."

Kate suppressed the urge to leap over the counter and beat

204

the woman with her stewed tomatoes.

"How much was this one again?"

"It's two–fifty–nine."

"Two–fifty–nine…" Mrs. Fenter squinted distastefully at the second can. She shook her head, but the curls never moved. "And this one?"

"Two–sixty–nine."

More shaking while the curls stayed in suspended animation. "Two–sixty–nine, hmm," she said. "But why would this one be more?"

"Probably because that one has more rat eyes in it. You know, for better consistency."

Mrs. Fenters' eyes widened in shocked anger and she slammed both cans on the counter. "You have quite a mouth on you, young lady. You should be trying to make friends in this town." She grabbed her purse from the counter and whirled around. "Especially after all the trouble you've had," she muttered, as she threw the door open, slamming it against the window and huffing out to the street.

Kate heard Uncle Dave laughing behind her and turned around. "You know Kate, the idea is to sell her the tomatoes," he said.

"Somebody should sell her up a river," Kate muttered and grabbed her coat from the closet.

"Hey, I was wondering if you'd like to take a ride into town after school. I have some errands I've been putting off and then I thought maybe we could catch dinner."

"Sorry, I've got a big test tomorrow." She slung her bag over one shoulder and headed for the door.

"You sure? We don't—"

"Gotta get to school, I'll see you later Uncle Dave," Kate said and the rest of his words were lost behind the closed door.

She breezed across the street and hopped up to the sidewalk. The sun was shinning and its glare stung her eyes, so she almost ran into Mr. Bowing as he emerged from the Wood'n

More shop.

"Whoa, slow down there Katie," he said. "Too nice a day not to stop and take notice."

"Sorry." Now the man walked in front of her again, blocking her path and Kate tightened her hands into fists.

Mr. Bowing glanced up at the sky and tucked his hands in his apron. "Yup, the bears are smiling today, sure to be a mighty fine one."

Kate stared at the carved wooden bears that he set by the doors and shuddered. They *did* seem to be smiling. "Gotta get to school, Mr. Bowing," Kate said, moving around him again.

"Have a good day." Mr. Bowing bent to arrange the tallest of the bears more toward the street.

Kate slipped on her sunglasses and stepped up her pace so she was almost running. Past the Wood'n More, past the bank. Farther and farther away from the store until finally, she could breathe.

Uncle Dave's intent wasn't lost on her, though she knew he thought he was being discrete. He was worried and he wanted to talk and blah, blah, blah. This touched a part of her, but for the most part she was annoyed. At heart, his motivations were selfish, as were the kind words from her teachers and the sappy sympathy from the few friends she'd managed to make. Be happy Kate, smile Kate, and let us know you're okay so we can feel better about ourselves. And by god if you're not okay, at least put on a good front so we all can play the game together. It made her want to puke.

Three more months. Three months before school was over and she could crawl in a hole and die for the summer if she wanted. There would be nobody in her face, telling her how to feel or asking her to *talk*, for Christ's sake. As if they knew what the norm was and if she wasn't reaching it, something must be wrong with her. What they didn't know was that she *was* the norm. That was the secret to the great joke called life. This was how it's supposed to be. It's supposed to be hard and it's supposed to make you want to scream and the only end in sight for the hole miserable lot was the white silk lining of your own coffin.

"Kate? Kaitlin, are you with us?"

She was pulled away from scene outside the window by the voice of her fifth period English teacher.

No, not really...

"We're on page one–twenty–four, The Last Works of Poe. I'd appreciate it if you could stay with us please," Miss Shea said. She spun the ring around on her finger as she always did when she was forced to speak harshly.

Kate rolled her eyes and stared back out the window. A single, sagging tree stood in the middle of the brick courtyard and its branches nearly swept the ground. In the spring, purple blossoms sprouted from the branches, but it was still winter and the spidery twigs looked dead. The snow had melted in the past few days of warm weather and a puddle of last years' leaves were gathered at its trunk.

Ms. Shea started the class on their assignment and then approached Kate.

"I just don't understand what happening here, you were doing so well in the first part of the year," she whispered by Kate's shoulder.

Kate sighed, but remained silent.

"Now I know you've had some...stuff to deal with." She twirled the ring faster and faster around her finger. "I know it's been hard for you, but we can't let you work suffer. Days of no homework and then there's that essay on Poe I have yet to even see a draft of. There's college to think about you know, and a career. We have to keep the big picture in mind." The ring was moving at warp speed now. "I just want you to know that if you, well needed to talk, about anything, you can come to me. My door is always open."

Kate slammed her pen down on the desk.

"You know, Miss Shea, have you ever thought that maybe

207

it's you and not me?" She asked in a loud, strained voice.

Her teacher's pencil–thin eyebrows rose to nearly meet her hairline and the ring stopped in mid–spin. "What? I don't—what are you—"

Kate smirked. "Did it ever occur to you that it's next to impossible to complete any of the work you assign because I'm so incredibly frustrated by your pathetic attempts to interpret one of the most brilliant poets ever read?"

Miss Shea stood quickly, as if Kate had slapped her. Kate stood as well, gathering her books, but not missing a beat. "In fact, you've actually ruined any hope of my writing something we've covered in class so I've decided to analyze a poem from off the reading list. You'll get the draft by the end of the week."

Miss Shea's face was now a rich shade of red and her breath came out in short, uneven bursts. The class was staring at Kate. Every pencil hung over a paper and every mouth was open in stunned disbelief. The bell for next period rang, but no one made a move to leave.

Kate smiled sweetly at Miss Shea and for some reason her smile seemed to drain the red from her teacher's face. "'Oh, the moaning and groaning of the bells,'" she said, rolling her eyes to the ceiling. The door thumped closed behind her.

Once out in the hallway, her steps quickened as she threaded through the students moving like a herd to their next class. She could see the light from the door at the end of the hallway and in her hurry to reach it, she plowed over several innocent bystanders.

The fresh air hit her face like a splash of cold water when she reached the steps outside and she paused a moment to catch her breath.

Now there would be a note. Little Katie's disrupting class and being quite the bitch, what to do? And after the note came the conference. Uncle Dave in his one nice suit sitting beside her in Principal Shraver's office and picking at the crease in his pants. And then it's back to the guidance counselor for poor, disturbed little Katie.

She wanted to scream.

Instead, she tied her coat around her hips and stared for home. Uncle Dave was gone. He went to his friend, Mark's house on the last Friday of every month to go over the accounts for the store, so she would have the place to herself.

"Hey, *Kat*lin!"

She heard the voice and shuddered even before she turned and saw Ben and Ricky coming down the street toward her.

"Never thought you'd be cutting class." Ben said when he caught up.

"Well Ben, never thought you would either." Kate started walking again and the boys followed her.

"Are you kidding?" He said, missing her sarcasm. "You'd have to chain me to the desk on a day like this. That place is just a waste of time."

"Yeah, 'cause you have so many better things to do, right?"

He grinned. "Exactly. See what I mean Kate? We think alike. Why can't you see it?"

"See what?"

"That it's us, we need to hook up. I like you, you know and we've known each other since, like kindergarten. You've always been, I don't know…better than those bimbos at school."

She pulled her lip in and gave him half a smile. "Yeah…thanks Ben."

"You know what your problem is," he said, taking a running step to catch up to her.

"Enlighten me."

"You've been hanging out with soccer boy so much you don't even know what's its like to be with a real man."

She stopped with her hand on the gate and was quiet for moment. Ben stared at her with curiosity and then backed away a little as she stepped up to him. "You know, you're right."

"Really?"

She looked him straight in the eye and continued. "Yeah. I

mean, here I've been wasting my time on a boy, when I could have had a man all along, but you know," she said and drummed her fingers over her lips.

"What?"

"I'm just not sure that you are…you know, a man."

He stared at her. "I, I'm a man," he stuttered.

Ricky tittered from behind.

"Really?" She lowered her eyelashes and plucked at a button on his shirt. "Well I'm unconvinced," she said, opening the gate and backing into the backyard, keeping her eyes on him. "Maybe you'd like to convince me."

Ben and Ricky followed, both reeling from their good fortune. Kate led them to the picnic table and hopped up, leaning back on her hands. Ben came around slowly, his face filling with color. He dared to put one hand on her knee and she smiled as she wrapped her leg around his to pull him closer.

"I've been waiting for this for a long, long time," she whispered.

He grinned, a big toothy one that turned into a drooling leer. "I knew it. I could tell you wanted it even under that nice–girl routine." He slid one clammy hand around her waist and pulled her closer. "Didn't I fuckin' tell you Ricky?"

Ricky stood a few feet behind him, trying to look over Ben's shoulder. "No, you always said—"

"Shut the fuck up, Ricky," he said and dug his fingers harder into her waist. "Where's that uncle of yours?"

She ran her hands up and down his chest. "Gone," she said, tossing her hair over her shoulders. "He won't be back for hours."

He grinned again and leaned to plant his thick lips on her mouth and then slithered his tongue toward hers. She turned her head and he moved farther down her neck. His hands roamed freely over the front of her sweater and she laughed, deep in her throat as she arched her back toward him. He trembled between her legs and she felt a surge of heat rush down her stomach.

"Oh yeah," he muttered in her ear. "That's good." Grabbing

her under one thigh, he pressed himself closer to her and she felt the bulge under the zipper of his jeans.

Her fingers traced the back of his head and curled into his hair. She opened her eyes slightly and then closed them quickly so Ricky wouldn't see anything that might make him cry out a warning. Her other hand reached into the back of her jeans and fingered the switchblade that was clipped inside. It was a simple Swiss Army knife that had only one blade tucked neatly inside a black cover. She had begun carrying it shortly after the dreams had started. The weight of the metal against her skin had been oddly comforting. Flipping out the blade, she held it for a second before putting it back.

Nobody said she couldn't have a little fun first.

* * * * *

Will stomped through the snowy puddles and his boots created small tidal waves that sloshed up to the sidewalk. His backpack was heavy with work he missed from doing exactly what he was doing right now, but he didn't care. School was a joke anyway and the only thing that kept him going was the fact that it would end soon. He hefted the pack higher on his shoulder. It was warm today and Will glanced at the cheery sky, muttering a curse under his breath.

They were having people over for dinner. Just some co–workers of his dad's, but Will felt slightly ill at the thought. He would have to sit at the table and smile and talk and pretend to be the good son. He and his dad weren't on speaking terms, not since that night when Will had told him to go to hell. And his mother, well she was just beside herself with all the tension in the house and had tried again and again to talk to Will. There would be other girls, she would say. Forgive your father. Will had stopped short many times from telling her to go to hell as well.

His pant leg was soaked with muddy water and Will stepped up to the sidewalk. He heard a shout from behind and turned to see two men standing in the road, yelling at each other.

"What the hell's wrong with you? You blocked me in you asshole." One man said as he kicked at the tire of the other man's car with his boot. His cheeks were bright with anger and the look on his face made Will stop in his tracks.

He'd seen that look before, that blank, unfocused rage. The face of a woman drifted before his eyes, but she was gone before he could put it together.

"Well if you knew how to drive that piece of shit, you'd be able to get out," said the second man, stepping closer. The brim of his hat almost touched the forehead of the man in the boots.

"If I knew—" he stuttered.

Will glanced around to see if anyone else was watching, but the street was empty. Their voices faded away as he continued on and soon he realized he was a block away from Dave's store. The arguing men and the familiar look were pushed to the back of his mind as he felt the old flutter in his stomach.

It was a stupid habit. More like pathetic, if he were to be honest with himself. He would pause in the alley that ran alongside the store and look into her window. He had seen her only a few times and each time his breath caught as he watched her moving around the room with that elegant grace he remembered and so missed. Once, he took a few steps toward the backdoor, wanting to see her closer, thinking maybe she might talk to him. But, he stopped, just in time and continued down the alley. She wouldn't talk to him; it was over.

Turning into the alley, he slowed and looked into her window, but saw nothing. Disappointed, he shuffled his feet and waited. She had to be in there and Will had no problem waiting. Then again, she was probably still in school. He had no idea what time it was, or how long he had been wandering around town.

Muffled voices floated from the backyard and he peered over the fence to see who it was. A pound of lead landed in his stomach as he identified the two boys and the girl, sitting on the picnic table. He took a step back and then came closer to put his hands on the fence; sure his eyes were playing tricks on him.

But no, it was Kate and she was sitting with her legs wrapped around Ben Easley. He barely saw Ricky standing a few feet away from them as the anger welled up inside him, turning his entire body into a pillar of rage.

He should just go, but his feet wouldn't move. With sickening disgust, he watched as Ben's hand slid under her sweater and she moved toward him, moaning. Now he did turn to leave. Just as he did however, his eye caught something shiny that poked out of the back of her jeans. He paused as she pulled it out. Her fingers fumbled with the catch and then the long silver blade sprang out. She turned it in her hand until she held it in a fist.

Will dropped his pack as understanding crashed down around him.

"Hey!" His feet flew over the pavement, around the fence and through the gate. The couple on the picnic table jerked their heads up. Ben's face filled with confusion and then anger when he saw who had shouted.

"Get the hell out of here, asshole," he yelled at Will.

Will ignored him and looked at Kate as she turned her strange eyes on him and smiled. Will felt his stomach shrink. The blackness was back, as it had been that day by the creek, but now it covered her eyes completely. No color showed through its greasy shine.

She hooked her foot around Ben's leg and pulled, yanking him to the ground. Ben fell and Kate landed on top of him, her arm pulled back and the knife held tightly in her hand. Will shot across the yard and threw himself at her, shoving her off of Ben and into the bottom of the fence. Kate kicked and scratched, but Will brought his fist down hard on her arm, knocking the knife out of her hand. He grabbed it and backed away, breathing hard.

Ben lumbered to his feet, holding his arm, which had a patch of dark blood spreading on his white shirt.

"Fuckin' psycho bitch!" He shouted at her and grabbed Ricky's arm. "Let's get out of here, man."

213

They disappeared through the gate and Will heard them running down the street. He waited until the sound of their pounding feet died away and then turned to Kate. She slumped against the fence, staring blankly at a patch of dead grass and blinking slowly.

"What the hell's going on here Kate?" He tried to sound reasonable but the knife in his hand burned cold through his fingers. "Kate, answer me."

She sat up slowly, but didn't look at him. "I don't," she stopped and shook her head.

He crouched down beside her. "Kate, look at me. What is this?" He asked, shoving the knife in her face. She ignored him and he reached out to grab her chin and point it toward him. The black was fading from her eyes and she looked like she was waking up from a dream. Her eyelids drooped and her face was pale. "You've got to tell me what's happening. How can I help you if you don't tell me what's going on?"

She moved out of his grasp. "I don't know. I felt so…I don't know," she said in a daze.

He stared at her, not knowing what to say. She ran her fingers through her hair and wiped at her face.

"I don't know what you want me to tell you, Will."

"How about the truth? That would be a change," he said. "I've already heard all your lies."

She pressed her lips together and shook her head. "You don't want to hear the truth. Why don't you go back to your perfect little life and just leave me alone?"

Hate seeped into her words and Will struggled not to slap her.

"I care about you Kate, although right now I can't remember why," he said, putting his hands on her shoulders. "Please, tell me what's going on."

"It's nothing you need to worry about. I can deal with it on my own," she said, stubbornly.

He scoffed. "Yeah, I can tell."

"I don't need this. I'm really tired, go home Will." She stood and started for the backdoor.

"Kate, please—"

"—Kate."

The little hitch in his voice made Kate look around. She saw the anger in his face was gone, all that was left was sadness.

"Nothing's been right for so long," he said softly, walking closer to her. "And I try to pretend it's okay, I try to go back to the way it was before you came home, but it's no use. You fill up my days, you make me laugh. Your touches, your smile...without them, all my days are dark. You're my light Kate, you have been for so long now." His eyes glistened over. "I miss you."

Oh Will, I miss you so that I can't breathe....

"Tell me what to do and I'll do it, tell me what to say and I'll say it, just don't shut me out, please," he said.

Tears sprang to her eyes. "There's nothing Will, there's nothing either of us can do."

He took her hands and leaned down to her face. "There's got to be something," he hissed. "I can't just walk away, not from you, Kate, can you?"

"No," she whispered.

"Then don't, please."

She shook her head. "It's not that simple."

"Yes it is, it can be. We can make it that simple." He held her face, his fingers stroking her hair. "We can do it together."

"Oh, Will—" She let her head fall on his chest and breathed deeply the scent that was only his. He held her silently, running his hands up and down her back. Her eyes closed and she swayed slowly in his arms. The world faded away, the light, the sounds, until only the feel of his hands and the beating of his heart remained. Darkness surrounded her and she clung to it, this secret haven she had found. Down and down, into the darkness that swallowed the pain and covered the guilt. Falling, floating, drifting in a sweet sea of nothingness.

Then, rising up out of the dark was the face of the old woman, her wrinkled eyes bright with warning and fear.

She squeezed him tightly to her, kissed the side of his neck and with a sob that tore from her throat, shoved him away.

"We can't do this," she said her voice breaking.

His face hardened with disappointment. "I won't let you go, Kate."

Turning, she ran up the steps two at a time. "You don't have a choice."

She left him in the yard and ran inside the house.

CHAPTER THIRTEEN
THE MESSAGE

A week later, Kate sat behind the counter, waiting for Uncle Dave to come back from Quarryville. A magazine rested on her lap and she ripped through its pages with increasing impatience, trying to find ideas. Uncle Dave's birthday was in a few days and she couldn't believe she had forgotten until today.

Not an another watch, she'd done that for Christmas, she flipped to the next page...not a tie and certainly not one with red and white checks, ugh...not a wallet...not a pair of turtle cuff-links. Who would wear those revolting things? And when she looked closer, she saw the turtles were grinning at her with a mouthful of tiny teeth.

"Ick," she said and slammed the magazine shut.

She wanted to find him something good. Something that might make up for the way she had been acting lately. He never said a word about it, but she saw the pain she was causing in his eyes. She picked up the magazine again. There had to be something that—

The bell above the door jingled.

"How can I help—" she began out of habit and then saw who it was.

"Hi Kate," Will said with a small smile.

His cheeks had patches of red from the cold, which had come back in force over the last few days. Her body tingled from the energy that seemed to fill the room whenever Will was near.

"Hi..."

He held up his hands. "I come in peace. I just wanted to pick up some things and see how you were."

She let out a breath she hadn't known she had been holding. "Okay."

The bell jiggled again and Uncle Dave came in struggling

with two brown boxes. "Hey Will." He looked at Kate, a question in his eyes and then back at Will. "Can you give me a hand?"

Will took the box on top and followed Uncle Dave to the back of the store. She heard them speaking in hushed tones for a minute before Will came back out and stopped in front of the bin of craft supplies. He picked out some glue and paints and brought them to the counter. After she rang up his purchases, he stayed by the counter, making small talk about school and homework. He was careful not to touch her hand, which lay close to his and never held her gaze for longer than a few seconds. She stared at the counter as well, fiddling with the candy display. Her eyes were stinging and she blinked several time to clear them.

"Oh, hold on a sec," she said as she saw Mrs. Whitmore come in with Emily. The little girl was dressed in a long black coat that belled at the bottom and had her blonde hair pulled back in a French braid.

"Hi Emily," Kate said, waving to her.

Emily smiled back, her whole face lighting with happiness. "Hello Kaitlin. How are you?"

"I'm fine thank you. You doing some shopping?"

She giggled. "Momma says we need some flour for our cake. She says I can help her frost it when it's done. It's going to be pinolapple."

Kate laughed. "Pineapple?"

"Yeah, she said I can't help her put it in the oven, 'cause I might burn my hands off, but I can lick the bowl when we're done."

"That sure sounds like fun. I'm sure your cake's going to taste very good."

Mrs. Whitmore put a hand on Emily's shoulder. "Come on, Mommy's in a hurry today."

They walked to the rear of the store and Kate turned back to Will. He began giving her a progress report on the new model he was working on. He got the idea for it from the book she had given him for Christmas. Just as he pulled out a piece of scrap paper to show her a rough drawing, a loud voice from the back of the store startled them.

"I told you Emily, I don't have time for this today. We'll have to do the cake tomorrow." Mrs. Whitmore was plowing through the stacks of canned goods, knocking some to the floor, where they rolled under the shelf.

The little girl's eyes fill with tears. "But you promised. We were going to make it from scratch, you said."

Her mother sighed. "We'll make it tomorrow. I told you I have that meeting tonight."

Emily stuck her lower lip out and folded her arms across her chest. "But, I don't want to go to Mrs. Ferguson's, her breath smells. And we can't do it tomorrow, you're going to dinner with Mr. Bowing tomorrow."

"Where did you hear that?"

Emily hung her head. "I heard you guys talking in the store."

Mrs. Whitmore snatched Emily's face by the chin. "You've been eavesdropping on me?"

"No, I jus–just heard. I'm sorry Momma."

"You know better than to listen to other people's conversations," her mother said. "Quit your pouting, now. We'll do it another night."

Emily looked at the floor and muttered softly to herself. "I don't know why you have to go to that stupid PTA meeting, anyhow."

Mrs. Whitmore brought her hand down hard on the side of Emily's face. "Don't you talk back to me. You hear?" She shook Emily's shoulders, making her head flop back and forth. Her voice raised a few more octaves. "Do you?"

Will looked into Kate's equally shocked eyes and she shook her head. Uncle Dave heard the shouting and hurried out of the kitchen. "Judy?" He asked stopping a few feet away. "Is everything all right?"

She turned to him and Kate saw her eyes were full of fury,

but under the anger was something else. Mrs. Whitmore looked just as confused as Uncle Dave. "Why don't you mind your own damned business."

"I just think maybe you should calm down." He reached for Emily's bright red check and rubbed it.

She yanked the girl away from him and Emily let out another yelp. "I don't think I need parenting lessons, especially from *you*." Grabbing Emily by the upper arm, she led them to the front of the store.

As they passed, Emily looked at Kate through a pile of blonde hair that had broken loose from her braid. Her eyes were wide and glassy and then she was gone.

Mrs. Whitmore slammed out the door with Emily running to keep up with her. Kate and Will watched through the glass door, as her mother bent down to eye level with Emily and yelled until her face turned red. Emily was crying uncontrollably and Kate could see her saying sorry, over and over again. Then Mrs. Whitmore grabbed her arm and pulled her farther up the sidewalk, out of sight.

Will whistled. "Man, what was that all about?"

"I don't know," Kate said, shaking her head. "But there's something going on with her." She looked at Uncle Dave, who was still staring out the window, pain and loss written clearly on his face. Then he lowered his head and went up the stairs.

"Yeah, I guess so. I've never seen her freak out like that," Will said.

"No, it was more than that." She felt something twitch at the back of her brain and thought for a second she might...as soon as she tried to grab it though, it shifted out of reach and was gone. "I don't know."

* * * * *

Kate went to bed that night thinking about Mrs. Whitmore and the way her eyes had glittered when Uncle Dave had been

220

talking to her. There was definitely something off in the woman, but Kate couldn't put her finger on it. She couldn't understand why it was bothering her so much either.

Frustrated, she swung her legs over to the floor and sat up. Another sleepless night made her body feel heavy and her eyes burn. She yawned and glanced out the window. The glow of pre–dawn was creeping over the town, lighting the buildings in its rust–colored warmth.

A quiet laughter from behind made her jump off the bed, as her heart was yanked through her throat. Her eyes darted around the room, but she saw nothing out of the ordinary. Winnie looked at her from her box on the floor and then waddled over to lick her bare foot. Kate patted her head and told her to go back to sleep.

The prickly feeling of the back of her neck was going away, but she couldn't shake the thought that someone was watching her. She was sure that it was lack of sleep and the pressing quiet of the house, making her hear things. The shadows in the far corner of her room had no maniacal stranger lurking in them, waiting to pounce. She shuddered.

A bird crowed loudly outside her window, greeting the morning sun. The bird flew away and the silence set in again.

"I gotta get out of here." Pulling on a pair of jeans, her old sneakers and a sweatshirt, she threw her hair up in a ponytail and patted Winnie's head. "I'll be right back, girl."

Thinking a jog was just what she needed; she padded down the stairs and to the kitchen. The house was darker downstairs because all the shades were drawn. Walking carefully, so she didn't bump into anything that would wake Uncle Dave, she made her way to the backdoor and let herself out.

The cool air instantly revived her and she took a deep breath. A second later she let it out in one choking gasp and fell against the closed door. Her eyes bounced from the porch, to the yard, to the fence, back to the porch. Each time they became wider and wider until she could feel her lids stretch painfully at the corners. A loud ringing began in her ears and drowned out everything else, disorienting her and making her dizzy. She shook her head, trying to clear it. A soft breeze blew through the backyard, chilling the sweat that had broken out on her face and neck. She squeezed her eyes shut and clenched her hands into fists. She knew they would go away. She had seen other things that weren't real and she knew this was the same. This was the same. When she opened her eyes, the backyard would be okay again. She would go on her jog and laugh later about what an imagination she had.

She opened her eyes.

The rabbits weren't gone, in fact there seemed to more of them than before. They lay on the porch, several by her feet and more by the stairs. One hung off the edge of the porch, its head dangling. Farther into the yard, the picnic table was covered in blood and brown fur. One of the little bodies had been pinned under a leg. Uncle Dave's truck was parked beside the table and Kate's stomach turned as she counted, one, two, three rabbits splayed across the hood. Their bodies looked strangely thin, as if they'd been crushed by a rolling pin. They lay in what looked like a puddle of pink goo. More heads peeked out at her from the top of the tires, playing a sick game of hide and seek.

Her horrified gaze shifted to the fence surrounding the yard. Weaved through the chain links were more rabbits. Their heads shoved through the small holes, their fur blowing gently in the wind. Some hung on the top, the metal speared through their necks and jutting out the other side. Blood trickled from their bodies and glistened in the rising sun.

He was here...he was here, oh God, he was—

Kate fumbled inside her sweatshirt and pulled out the amulet. The warmth immediately seeped into her fingers and spread up her arm. She closed her eyes again and held it tighter, tighter, until the metal cut into her skin and her palm was suddenly wet. Concentrating on the warmth that spread through her body, she felt her heart begin to slow. Her breath came more regularly and the ringing in her ears subsided.

Feeling more in control, she opened her eyes and surveyed the scene before her. A focused calm flowed through her and she realized that the calm enabled her to stop her shaking limbs. The yard seemed to grow brighter as she stood there and she thought she could trace the movement of the sun across the brown grass.

Then she realized something else.

Turning, her sneakers slipped in a puddle of the Jell–O–like sludge and she grabbed the doorknob to catch her balance. She threw the door open and crossed to the cupboard under the sink, leaving bright red footprints behind her.

Yanking the cupboard doors open, she fell to her knees and began rummaging through the plastic containers and dish soap until she found the box of heavy duty garbage bags. She ripped off two black bags and then searched for the work gloves Uncle Dave usually kept down there. They weren't there this morning, though so she gave up and went back outside.

The stench of blood hit her harder now that she was moving around and it burned her nose and throat with its sickening sweetness. She started with the rabbits on the porch, prying their bodies off the boards and dumping them in the bag. Their pitiful eyes looked up at her, little black orbs that had burst and run down their fur. She stared at one for a moment, feeling the panic spread over her again, but then shook herself and threw it in the bag.

The sun was lifting higher in the sky, lighting the ghastly yard in a cheerful glow. A warm drop fell on the back of her neck and she looked up just as another landed on her forehead. A rabbit swung from the roof of the porch, hung from one of the nails Uncle Dave used to hang the Christmas lights. Blood dribbled down its stomach and was dripping off its paw. She stood and jumped up to grab it, feeling it tear in her hand.

She shoved the rabbits one after the other into the bag. There were just so many. So many of the wretched things and the sun was rising higher and higher above her, soon to wake Uncle Dave, soon to wake the whole town. She finished the porch, at least with the rabbits, but it was still covered in blood and goo. The goo was under her fingernails as well and then became smeared in her hair when she brushed it from her face.

Dragging the now heavy bag across the yard, she began sweeping the bodies off the picnic table and into her bag. Some were cold and stiff and stuck stubbornly to the wood, forcing Kate to peel them off with both hands. Others were still warm and pliable and looked as if they were sleeping, but for their runny eyes. It was the warm ones that made Kate wish she had Uncle Dave's gloves. As she lifted the table and reached to get the rabbit that was trapped beneath it, she heard the front gate squeak open.

She whipped her head toward the side of the house and felt a snap rip down the back of her neck. The pain went unnoticed though, as she shot to her feet and took two blind steps toward the gate. She had no idea what she would do when she got there, only knew that she had to stop whoever was coming, any way she could.

Before she could take a third step, Will appeared. He stood, staring at her with naked shock and horror. She could only stare back at him, feeling her face itch with blood. The bag slipped from her fingers and she opened her mouth, but no words came out. She closed it and continued staring at him.

His eyes took in the blood that covered her gray sweatshirt, the bag of dead rabbits beside her and the yard, still littered with dozens of bodies. His face continued to pale, as he rubbed his head like he always did when he was trying to say something. He said nothing however, just scanned the yard again until his gaze landed back on her. The shock was fading and something more intense and frightening filled his eyes.

Without a word he pulled the sleeves of his black sweater up past his elbows, walked to the porch, grabbed the other bag and went to the fence. He pulled a rabbit from the chain and began filling his bag.

She watched him for a moment, and with a sigh that shuddered through her entire body, she went back to work.

The picnic table was cleared, so she started on the truck. They worked continuously until all the bodies had been dumped in a bag and then Will went to the shed. He came out a moment later with some rags and the cleaning solution Uncle Dave used to get the grease and oil off the driveway. Will poured some of it on the porch and then got on his hands and knees and started scrubbing. Kate crouched beside him, scooping handfuls of the slop in her cloth and emptying it into the bag. When the porch was clean, they moved to the table, pouring the cleaner over the top so it ran down to the benches. Kate's hair stuck to her face as she scrubbed with the rag and she spit it from her mouth over and over again, tasting the blood that soaked the strands.

Next they washed the truck. Kate worked on the hood as Will cleaned the mess from under the fenders and tires. The fence was the easiest, the blood just melted off the metal when they poured the cleaner over it. As Will was finishing up, Kate ran inside to wipe her footprints from the kitchen floor.

When it was done, Kate checked again for any remaining signs and saw that everything was shiny and clean. Maybe Uncle Dave would just think it had rained.

Will went into the shed with the bottle of cleaner and came out with a can of gasoline and two shovels.

"Let's go," he said, picking up one of the bags.

She hefted her bag over one shoulder and followed him through the broken length of fence and into the woods. They walked for over half an hour and Will never said a word. He kept his eyes forward and stayed a few steps in front. They headed south, away from town and toward the creek, but he swerved around it, taking them farther and father downstream. Kate slowed as she realized where he was headed.

"Will?" He didn't turn. "Will!"

The break in the trees was closer now and Kate stopped, watching Will. His back was straight and his pace never faltered as he moved toward the clearing. He wouldn't wait for her and she wondered if he even knew she wasn't with him anymore. She cursed under her breath.

Why Will? Why here?

Taking a quick look behind her, she picked up her bag and followed. She ran as fast as she could to catch up with him and they entered the Badlands together.

It hadn't changed since she had seen it last with Joey. If anything, the bare trees had grown thinner and taller. They hunched, one over the other, permanently crippled with time. The ground was hard and cracks ran through it like lines in an old woman's face. Kate felt the silence descend the moment they entered. Then she realized it wasn't completely quiet. The sound of the breeze winding through the twisted branches created an eerie orchestra of wind instruments, all playing a melody she couldn't understand, but made her shiver anyway.

Will kicked his way through the brush to the far end, stomping on dead branches that exploded in clouds of dust. And then he stopped, so suddenly that Kate nearly ran him over. She pushed past him.

They stood before a circle of five large rocks.

The bag slipped from her hand and fell to the ground, spilling out several dead rabbits. Her fingers wrapped around her neck as she took a deep breath and tried to calm herself before she joined the rabbits on the ground. The metal posts were gone, as was the chain, but the rocks...the rocks were still there.

Will tossed her a shovel and dropped his bag. He cleared away the dried pine needles and branches and began digging in the middle of the circle.

Kate worked beside him, wiping the sweat that blurred her vision and trying to keep up with the frenzied pace Will set. She felt her back jar several times as she pounded away at the hard earth.

When the hole was a couple feet deep and six feet wide, Will threw down his shovel and picked up one of the bags. He emptied the rabbits and gooey rags into the pit, threw the bag in and then did the same with her bag. Kate stood aside watching, as he opened the gas can and poured a liberal amount on the whole mess. Closing the can, he set it a safe distance away and pulled out a box of matches from the pocket of his jeans. The rabbits lit easily and Kate was forced to back away from the sudden heat.

She watched the flames lick the brown fur, curling and dancing around the pile of butchered rabbits.

Child, don't you see? The evil never stopped...

Will's eyes met hers over the blaze of the fire. His image was hazy with heat and smoke and for a moment, his face changed. It was the face of someone she had never met, but immediately recognized. The hollow eyes that questioned her, accused her. The eyes that stirred a guilt deep within her soul. Guilt she resented and denied without thought.

She turned from him and stared silently into the fire.

* * * * *

"Katie, you okay in there?"

"Yeah, I'm fine."

"Well when you come up for air, come on down. I made some rabbits for breakfast."

The soap fell out of her hand and spun crazily around the bathtub basin. "What?"

"I said I made some omelets for breakfast."

She let out a shaky laugh. "That's okay, I'm not that hungry, thanks though."

"Suit yourself."

Reaching to adjust the knob, she turned it just a bit hotter and let it flow over her face. The water burned her neck and chest, streamed over her stomach and collected in a small lake at her ankles. The pipes were bad and the water was usually halfway up her calf by the time she was finished. She'd washed her hair three times now and was satisfied that it was clean. Her scalp felt raw from the scrubbing and the hot water, but she didn't mind.

The smoke lifted from her skin in the rising vapors and she could smell the strong smell of gasoline come off with it. Under those smells was the sweet scent of blood and it was that smell that made her dump more shampoo on her head and begin a forth washing.

Ten minutes later she was standing naked in front of the mirror over the sink. She wiped the foggy mirror until she could see her face. Her cheeks were bright and itchy, her neck blemished with patches of red. She smoothed her wet hair away from her face.

A night of lost sleep and the exhausting activities of the morning should have left her feeling drained, but she didn't. In fact, she felt as if she could run for miles. Energy tingled through her body and her mind was sharp and alert. Leaning over the sink, she stared closer at her face. Despite the events of the morning, she found less fear in her eyes than there had been even yesterday. Not that she wasn't scared. It was just...she felt something coming, knew with each passing day it came closer and closer and the waiting was making her restless now. She was ready to stop running.

She wrapped herself in a towel and went to her room to get dressed. Thank God it was Saturday and she wouldn't have to see Will again for two more days. His questions might rush her into saying something she wasn't sure she wanted to say. No, she needed time to think.

"Kate, you dressed?" Uncle Dave called through the door.

"Just a second," she said and tugged the sweatshirt over her head, before opening the door. "What's up?"

Uncle Dave stood in the doorway, Winnie at his heels. "Well first of all, your dog here says she can't go out with anyone but you and I think she really needs to go."

Kate smiled and pulled her hair out of the collar of the sweatshirt. "It's a girl thing. We're very particular about our bathroom habits."

"Say no more," he said and patted Winnie's head. "And

also, I was wondering if you wanted to help with the inventory today."

She thought about it for a moment. "You know, I was actually planning on going to the library today."

He nodded. "Okay, it's been so slow lately, it probably won't take very long anyway."

"You sure?"

"Of course. You know I did manage by myself somehow before you came," he said, wagging his finger at her.

"How, I'll never know."

"Get out of here, but don't forget about Miss Picky." He gestured toward Winnie.

Kate scratched her behind the ear. "Like I could."

After taking Winnie for a quick trip around the block, she was soon headed for the library. The day had turned dark, the bright sun of the morning had been chased away by the clouds she had seen gathering above the peaks. Kate pulled her coat tighter around her body. It was good to be moving. Now that she was finally taking some action, however small, some of the hopelessness she'd felt for weeks seemed to fade away.

Jumping off the curb and over a pile of old snow, she crossed in the middle of the street and headed for the library.

It was usually busy on Saturdays and today was no exception. She recognized several kids from school, hanging out on the benches between the front doors and then seated, inside at the tables. She headed straight for the back of the building for the books on religion. It only took her a few minutes to find what she was looking for and after grabbing a few at random, she settled on the couch by the window. Ten minutes later she was lost to the world.

* * * * *

"Miss?"

A hand tapped her on the shoulder. "I'm sorry miss, but the

library's closing."

Kate looked up, startled. "Oh," she said, glancing at the window behind her. It was black and only her face stared back through the glass. "Okay, thanks."

Kate closed her book and then bent to separate the ones she would check out. It had been a disappointing day. She found plenty of information on the beliefs and customs of the Druids, but nothing specific. Nothing she could use. She sighed. What a waste.

After checking out a few books she hadn't had the chance to look through, she stepped out into the night. It had begun to snow, the first snow in weeks and she stopped a moment to look up at the swirling flakes. She loved the way they created little storms within themselves and danced in the wind. They looked like playing children. She pulled up her hood and started down the sidewalk toward home.

She would just have to keep reading and looking until she found something that helped her. Maybe she would get Uncle Dave to drive her to the library in Quarryville. That one had to be twice the size of Newclare's. She could tell him she was doing a report at school and—

"Katie..."

She looked down the sidewalk behind her. There was no one there, so she turned slowly and continued. It sounded just like someone had called her name, clear as a bell, she heard a voice say—

"Katie..."

She whipped around again, slipping a little in the fresh snow. The street was empty with only a few cars parked along the side. The snow made it hard to see more than a few feet and the bright streetlight she was standing under didn't help. She squinted her eyes and tried to look through the veil, but saw nothing.

A little slower now, she started again. Must have been a hard day if she was hearing voices. But considering the way her day had started, she wasn't surprised. She guessed she was lucky that was all she was hearing.

"Katie girl..."

Her hood was muffling the voice so she ripped it off to shout into the white. "Hello? Who's there?"

Nothing, for a long moment and then...a quiet laughter her ears barely caught. It was slow and deep with a touch of easy familiarity. Then she realized...the laugh was familiar. From this morning.

"This isn't funny," she heard the waver in her voice and struggled to keep it even. "Who's there?"

The laughter was gone, though she could still hear it in her mind. Her steps quickened and for the first time, she realized how far the library was from Uncle Dave's store. She ripped the switchblade from the back of her jeans and flipped it open. The weight of it in her hand calmed her but didn't slow her steps.

"Katie girl, my Katie girl..."

She spun around and kept walking backwards. "Is that you Will?" She asked, knowing he would never scare her like this.

Something knocked her feet out from under her and she landed hard on her rear with a shriek. Her heart pounded for a moment then she saw that she wandered off the sidewalk and tripped over a rock in Mr. O'Neil's yard. Grabbing her bag of books, she jumped to her feet and went on. It was quiet now.

Rounding the corner, she started toward the store. She passed dark windows on her right and empty buildings on her left. Uncle Dave was the last one in town who actually lived in his store. Most of the storeowners had a house outside of town, so after closing time she and Uncle Dave were the only ones left for blocks. Uncle Dave said he like it that way, no one to hear if he wanted to work in the shed at all hours of the night. And no one to hear now, if she decided to say, start screaming at the top of her lungs.

The wind picked up, blowing the snow from the sidewalk up in her face. She squinted against it and then stepped off the sidewalk, into the street.

"Katie girl, my sweet, sweet Katie girl..."

She broke into a run and crossed the street in five long strides. Jumping up to the curb, her foot slid and she caught herself with one hand. Not looking behind her, she ran up the sidewalk, closer and closer to the store.

"—my sweet, sweet Katie girl..."

The light from Uncle Dave's large front window shone brightly on the snow–covered sidewalk. Four more steps—

"—come to me, my sweet Katie girl..."

Hot breath on her neck, a clear voice in her ear. Two more—

"—stay with me, my Katie girl..."

She yanked open the door and heard the welcome tinkle of the bell. A hand brushed the back of her jacket and the scent of rotting apples was suddenly strong in the air. She ran directly into Uncle Dave's chest, dumping her books on the floor.

"Whoa, slow down there," he said, holding her by the shoulders. "What's wrong?"

She looked behind her out the glass door, but saw nothing except for the reflection of the two of them. "I heard, I mean I thought I heard—"

Uncle Dave looked at the panic on her face and then past her, toward the door. "Is somebody out there?"

"I don't know, I was coming home from the library–" She had to stop and catch her breath. "—my name, he knew my name."

His eyes widened and then he led her to the back of the store. "You stay here and sit down, I'll be right back."

"No, don't go out there—"

"I will be right back, now you do as I say and sit," he said.

She sat.

He returned to the front of the store and walked behind the counter. Kate leaned out far enough to see him take the ring of keys from his belt and unlock on of the bottom drawers. He pulled out a gun, one she didn't know he had and then slammed the drawer shut with his leg.

Coming around the counter, he held up his hand to her and then went to the door. He paused for a moment, listening and then went out, locking it behind him.

She watched him go with a plunging feeling in her stomach. Minutes passed. Five. Ten. He wasn't coming back. He was never coming back. He'd walked out the door and into oblivion. And it was her fault. All her—

With a cold gust of air, the door blew open and Uncle Dave was back. She leapt to her feet and ran to hug him.

"Sorry I was gone so long. I wanted to go around the whole block and then I checked behind the store." His face was red from the cold.

"Did you see anything?"

He shook his head. "No, but I did see Mrs. Fenter's cat. She said it got out the other day." He smiled a little. "Seems Muffy's shacking up with Mr. O'Neil's tabby these days. Are you okay?"

She nodded, running a hand through her tangled hair.

"What was going on out there?"

"I don't know," she said. "I thought I heard something, I don't know now, it was probably nothing."

He furrowed his eyebrows in disbelief. "Are you sure?"

"Yeah, it was dark and late and I must have got a little freaked out, I'm sorry."

"No, no, it's okay, I just want to be sure you're okay," he said, reaching to hug her to him.

She snuggled against the warmth of his chest, sighing. "I'm fine, Uncle Dave, just a little tired."

"Why don't you get up to bed, I can close up here."

"Thanks." She gathered her books and started for the kitchen. "See you in the morning."

"Goodnight," he called after her.

"Goodnight."

"Kate?"

She stopped by the stairs. "Yeah?"

"If there's ever anything you want to talk about, let me know. I may be old, but I have learned a thing or two in my life." His eyes sparkled with something she couldn't name. "You'd be surprised."

Her breath caught on the familiar words and she stared at him intently for a moment. Then she shook her head, trying to clear her thoughts.

"Thanks," she said slowly. "I'll keep that in mind."

"And Kate?"

She stopped again.

"You know I love you."

She smiled and felt it ease her tired face. "Me too."

CHAPTER FOURTEEN
"HAPPY BIRTHdAY, UNClE DAVE..."

Dave sighed and wadded the paper into a tight ball before tossing it toward the trashcan. He missed.

Pale sunlight came through the front door of the store. It was barely enough to light up the litter of receipts and inventory lists that lay on the counter in front of him, but he didn't turn on the overheads. Having the lights on in the daytime always depressed him somehow and today had been depressing enough. Numbers had never been his strong suit, which he always thought was ironic for a man who ran his own business. The numbers that covered four sheets of paper in his ledger didn't match any which way he ran them. Sighing again, he pulled out a fresh sheet and began punching buttons on his calculator.

The heater kicked on and a streamer rustled in the warm air that blew from the vents above. He glanced up and smiled at the decorations Kate had put up for his birthday. Blue streamers ran from one end of the store to the other and then wrapped around the front door. Balloons of all different sizes and colors hung from the streamers and on the walls. The kitchen was decked out as well, with a giant basket of flowers arranged on the table with a helium balloon tied to it that read, 'Happy Birthday'. He figured she must have started decorating around five this morning since it had all been done by the time he came down for breakfast. She had given him a quick kiss and told him she had a surprise planned for later, then ran off for school.

"Damn," he muttered and threw down his pencil. It rolled across the counter and onto the floor.

The end of the month usually brought him to Mark Hudson's house and that's where he had been that morning. Mark was an accountant who worked for a firm in Quarryville, but managed to get most of his work done at home, on his personal computer.

They'd grown up together and had been in the same classes in school. Dave actually looked forward to these monthly visits because Mark was a great guy who had a surprisingly light sense of humor for an accountant.

This morning had been a different story however. Mark had opened the door with three days worth of beard growth on his face and eyes that told of nights of restless sleep.

"Hey man, how's it going?" Dave asked.

"Not so great actually, what's up?" Mark looked past him at the street and then back at Dave, his face barely hiding his annoyance.

Dave held up a box of papers and receipts. "Is this a bad time?"

"Oh, shit," he said, slapping his forehead. "I completely forgot, can you come back later?"

"Yeah, no problem, whenever's good for you."

Mark moved back to close the door. "I'll have to call you."

Dave heard Mark's wife shout from inside the house and then the faint sound of breaking glass. "Hey, is Cindy alright?"

Mark narrowed his blood–shot eyes and Dave saw they were dark, too dark, despite the shadows of the house. "Yeah fine, look I said I'd call you."

And with that, he slammed the door.

Dave stared at the house for a moment, listening to the shouting from inside and then shuffled down the sidewalk and climbed into his truck. Shaking his head, he started the engine, giving it just the right amount of gas to keep it from stalling.

He drove down Galway toward the store, passing Mr. O'Neil's house on the right. As he began to make the turn his eye caught something in the man's yard and he slowed to a stop, peering out the passenger side window.

It was Mr. O'Neil and he was dressed only in a black and red stripped bathrobe and slippers. He held a box in one hand and a metal garden trowel in the other. Dave recognized the box from yesterday when the man stopped by the store for two cases of nails. He asked Dave for his entire stock, not offering any explanation. And Dave, not wanting to engage the man in conversation, had obliged.

Now, he watched as Mr. O'Neil poured a scoop of nails onto his lawn. He sprinkled them over the dead grass as if they were seed, then reached into the box for another scoop.

Dave leaned over and rolled down the passenger window. "Hey Irwin, what are you doing there?"

He looked up, startled. "Oh, hello Dave," he said and walked over to the truck.

"What do you have there?" Now that he was closer, Dave could see the brightness in his eyes. The man was pumped about something.

"Oh these," he said, looking at the box in his hands. "They're nails."

Dave sighed. "I can see that Irwin but...what are you doing?"

He looked up at the sky. "Thought I'd take advantage of the weather, before that storm comes in."

Dave stared at him and his eyes widened as Mr. O'Neil turned to throw another scoop. "Still not getting you," Dave said, half–smiling.

Mr. O'Neil put his head through the window and spoke in a confidential tone. "Well Dave, I'll tell you. I'm fed up with it and so I've decided to take matters into my own hands."

"What are we talking about?"

"Those piss ant little demons. The ones who cut across my yard because they're too damned stupid and lazy to go around." He looked from side to side as if someone else might be listening. "They're killing my grass you know. It's turns brown and then just shrivels up. And my roses. Every year at least two are killed, sometimes more. There's no respect, none at all. I tell them, 'go around, stay out of my yard', but do they listen? No, they laugh at me, because they know they can get away before I can catch them. But not anymore," he laughed suddenly, a sharp, harsh burst. "But not anymore, no…I'll have the last laugh and my roses will be safe."

Dave stared at the man again. "Irwin are you okay?"

Mr. O'Neil went on, ignoring him. "They whiz through here on those slick bikes of theirs," he said and made a whooshing noise with his lips. "And next time…pop! That'll be the end of the little fuckers."

He laughed again, jiggling his box of nails and leaning farther into the truck, so the glare of the sun was no longer in his eyes. And that's when Dave saw it. The strange swirling blackness that swam like worms through the man's eyes.

Dave lost his thoughts for a moment and when he spoke, his voice shook. "Ir–Irwin what's—"

"Those cock–sucking mother fuckers won't even know what hit them—"

"Irwin!"

"—they'll know better than to fuck with me. Those god-damned little piss ant fuckers, I'll teach'em to—"

Dave had rolled up the window and driven away quickly, leaving the man to his ramblings on the side of the street. Now, as he stared at the jumbled numbers in front of him, all he could think of was the blackness in Mr. O'Neil's eyes. It had to be a trick of the light. That's all.

He bent to tackle the numbers again, when his head snapped up and he looked around.

Apples?

The room was empty and as far as he knew, there hadn't been apples in the store since they went out of season last fall. He put his pencil down and looked toward the ceiling. A vent was directly above his head and he lifted his face to it. The smell was definitely coming from there. Apples in the attic?

He was thinking about taking a look up there when the bell above the door jingled.

"How're you doing today…" He trailed off as he turned toward the figure standing in the doorway.

238

DARK LEGACY

The faint light from outside outlined the figure in a dark sil-houette, though it did more than that. It shone *through* the man, giving the impression that the man lacked substance and Dave almost laughed. Getting spooked by a shadow, that was good.

Before the laugh could reach his throat though, the shadow began moving toward him. It wore a long coat that reached the top of his buckled boots. And as he approached the counter, Dave saw his brown pants were tucked inside the boots. The shadow now stood in front of Dave but still, it didn't speak.

"Can I help you?" The familiar line helped to calm him, helped to reassure his screaming mind that this wasn't a shadow he was talking to. Just a trick of the light, is all.

Dave continued staring at the strange looking pants. They were made of a soft material that looked like thin leather, but weren't. He tried to ignore the way the pants showed through to the cans of peas on the shelf behind the man and the boots that, that...well, didn't seem to connect with the floor. Tried to ignore the overwhelming smell of apples in the air, the smell that had turned into a heavy, almost sour scent. He folded his trembling hands behind his back.

"Oh, I should think in a great many ways."

The voice had a thick accent Dave couldn't place. His words danced in the air around Dave, blending into each other with a musical quality. There was a familiar ring in the voice that took him a moment to recognize. Then he caught it. It sounded like Kate's voice, but at the same time was drastically different.

"Are you looking for something in particular?" He could feel the man willing Dave to look at him, but he kept his eyes on the counter. Moving closer, the man splayed his fingers out on the counter. His hands were pasty white, with no visible veins through the thin, shadowy skin. There were rings on every long, gnarled finger. Red, blue, brown stones in settings Dave had never seen before. Carved in the gold around the stones were snakes and spiders, twisting and winding around his fingers. One of the rings on his left hand had what looked like a tree trunk

239

along the length of one knuckle to the next and a bright green stone at the top. He moved that finger back and forth, playing the light into Dave's eyes.

"Why yes actually, I am," the man said, as the heater kicked off.

Dave sat down abruptly and started punching numbers into the adding machine. His fingers missed the buttons and only non-sense came up on the screen, but he continued anyway. "Well, let me know if I can find anything for you."

The man leaned over the counter, folding his hands in front of him and spoke in a quiet voice. "I should think you would know what I've come for, Mr. O'Connor."

I should have warned you, Kate…I should have told you…

The stench of apples gagged Dave now and his stomach be-gan to swell. His eyes flicked toward the front door and saw the sun had come out from behind the clouds. The light beckoned him, but he didn't move. He saw his useless flight across the store and out the door and knew from the fluid, easy way this man moved, shadow or no, he would have him before Dave even got out from behind the counter.

I'm sorry Katie…so sorry…

The hands moved across the counter, brushing off invisible flecks of dust. Dave stared at them with rapt attention, until his eyes were drawn upward, toward the man's face. A silver chain hung around the man's muscular neck with a charm on it he rec-ognized. Feathery white hair lay across his shoulders.

I love you…

Up…up…up to his sharp chin, a tiny brown mole with a hair growing out of it, the thin gray lips…

"Yes, I think you have exactly what I need," the lips said.

Up…up to the hollowed cheekbones, the long straight nose, until he met the dark pits which were its eyes.

Dave never looked away.

* * * * *

Kate set the bag on the sidewalk and rearranged its contents, feeling foolishly traitorous. She'd picked up the things she needed for Uncle Dave's birthday dinner at the only other store in town that sold food products. The Hometown Grocer had opened up the year after she left and though Uncle Dave had never said anything outright, she could feel the tension every time Mr. Richards, the store manager, came into Uncle Dave's store. They would comment about the weather, how business was doing, and act as if the fierce competition between them were nothing. She knew the thing that irked Uncle Dave wasn't even the suspiciously familiar green and white awning out front, but the name of the store. As if there were anything 'Hometown' about them. They were a chain of larger stores hidden behind many different names. But she thought he would forgive her this one time for conspiring with the enemy since it was for a good cause.

Satisfied that the can of corn wouldn't punch a hole through the plastic bag, she picked it up and continued toward home.

After hours of pouring over the cookbook she picked up at the library, she finally decided on a meatloaf, mashed potatoes and corn. It seemed like her best bet, no simmering, no whisking (whatever that was) and nothing that asked for an eighth of a teaspoon of anything. She could just dump everything into a bowl and mash it up. After staring at a bag of potatoes for several minutes in the store, she had thrown them back and grabbed a box of instant. The meatloaf would be a challenge enough and besides, she didn't want to throw Uncle Dave's taste buds into shock.

She crossed Galway Street and not being in the mood to get yelled at today, was careful not to cut into Mr. O'Neil's yard. The grocery bag in her hand was heavy and she thought she probably should have dropped off her schoolbooks before buying the food. But then she would of have to explain where she was going and she wanted to surprise Uncle Dave. She just hoped it came out all right and she didn't burn the store down. Now that would be a good surprise.

241

A car passed on her right and she recognized it as Mark and Cindy Hudson's, Uncle Dave's friends. Looking closer, she saw they were both in the car, talking animatedly. The red pinto was weaving back and forth down the street and then came to a stop with its tail end still in the road. Cindy jumped out and yelled into the car.

"You son of a bitch, if you don't want to see my mother, why don't you just go home." She kicked the side of the car with one high–heeled black shoe and Kate winced, feeling it on her toes.

Mark got out and slammed the door shut before rushing to her side. "Why would I want to see her, when she's right in front of me every day. In my home, in my bed," he yelled back and punched the window with his fist. Kate saw the glass crack down the middle.

"Fuck you, look what you did to the car," Cindy screamed, shoving him in the chest, her blonde flying back and showing dark roots.

"You think that's bad, how about this?" Mark kicked the fender, crushing it in.

Cindy gave him a savage look and for a moment the light caught her eyes. Kate took a step back, not believing what she was seeing.

Blackness swam in her irises.

"I think it's about as weak as you are," she said and reached inside the car to pull out the ice scraper. She hit the windshield with it, causing a star that spread all the way across.

They took turns tearing apart their car in a game Kate would have thought was funny, if it hadn't been so deadly serious. There were a few people on the street watching, but no one did anything to help. Kate tried to think of a way to stop them, but the flash she caught in Cindy's eyes stopped her cold. All she wanted to do now was get as far away from them as she could.

She hurried down the street. Their voices faded behind her and the some of the people who were watching went back inside.

Finally reaching the store, she took a deep breath and reached to open the door, but the sign in the window made her hesitate. It read, 'Closed, sorry we missed you.' Uncle Dave didn't tell her he was going anywhere today and he knew she had something planned. It was probably just a quick errand; he would be back in a minute. Something felt wrong about the whole thing though and it was then that she realized she had been standing outside and thinking about it way too long.

She stared at the doorknob. *Just go in, Kate.* But she couldn't. There was something wrong and the longer she thought about it the more wrong it became.

She stared at the doorknob.

It's going to be hot.

It is not going to be hot. And where did that come from anyway? She shook her head and stared again at the doorknob. It was probably locked. Uncle Dave never went anywhere without locking at least the front door. She should go around and to the back, but her feet didn't move.

She stared at the doorknob.

A breeze blew her hair away from her face and over one shoulder. It was getting cold and she could smell the snow in the air. It would snow tonight and her home–cooked dinner would taste even better with the wind and the snow blowing against the building. It would be cozy.

The bag weighed heavy in her hand and she moved her fingers so the circulation wouldn't be cut off. Uncle Dave went to see someone or drop off something and he would be back as soon as he was finished. There was probably a note on the counter and here she was standing in the cold like an idiot, wondering about it when she could just go in and read the note.

Trying the door anyway, she was surprised to find it open.

"Uncle Dave?"

The lights were off and the only sound was the rustling of the streamers in the breeze of the heater. As the sun dipped behind a cloud, the store darkened, covering everything in a shadowy haze. She closed the door behind her and walked further inside.

One of the streamers had fallen off the ceiling and she brushed it aside to go to the counter and get the tape. She stepped on something that broke under her foot and looked down to see the sunglass display lying upside–down on the floor. Frowning, she picked it up and put it back, fixing the sunglasses back on their pegs and tossing the broken pair in the trash.

The note must be here somewhere. She looked behind the candy display and then by the register. Maybe it was in the kitchen. She started in that direction and then stopped.

There was a pair of legs hanging off the kitchen table.

She looked away and back at the fallen streamer. Better get that back up before someone trips over it. She grabbed the tape and then stepped up on a shelf to reattach the streamer to the wall. That's much better, it looks festive in here again. With that done she glanced around the store and tried to remember what she was going to do next. Oh yeah, dinner.

She picked up the bag and headed for the kitchen. Walking past the legs on the table, she set the bag on the counter. The refrigerator was a little full and Kate spent a moment rearranging things so she could fit in her groceries. After the milk and butter were put away, she turned to empty the rest of the bag. She left the ground beef on the counter and dug through the cabinet over the sink for some candleholders. She found some pretty silver candles at the store and was looking forward to setting a nice table for Uncle Dave. The holders were hidden behind a stack of bowls they never used and she reached on her tiptoes to get them. The candles fit perfectly inside and she went to the table to set them out.

But there wasn't any room on the table, so she returned to the refrigerator and put them on top.

The clock above the sink told her it was close to dinnertime. Uncle Dave would be hungry when he came back from wherever it was that he went and when he came home, he would be so surprised that she had everything ready and they would eat together and he would tell her about his day and where he had gone. And she would tell him that she forgave him for worrying her like this. If only she could set the table.

There was a large mixing bowl in the cupboard by the refrigerator and she placed it on the counter. She hoped Uncle Dave wouldn't be home too soon. The recipe had said it could take up to an hour to cook the meatloaf. That would okay. They could just hang out together. She would make some tea and they would sit and talk. Because Uncle Dave was out doing some errands. He wasn't laid across the table with flowers in his eyes...oh, oh God...in his eyes...

Her fingers pierced through the plastic wrap and sunk into the cold meat. Uncle Dave with flowers in his eyes. Uncle Dave with dirt sprinkled across his blue flannel shirt. Uncle Dave with the 'Happy Birthday' balloon strung around his neck and tied so tight, the string cut into his skin. She watched the balloon dip and bob and spin wildly in the wind from the heater.

Uncle Dave was not going to eat her dinner, because Uncle Dave was dead. She dropped the meat on the floor and turned slowly to shut off the oven. Uncle Dave was dead because there were flowers in his eyes. And the flowers were pink, not Uncle Dave's color at all because Uncle Dave's eyes are brown. They're brown with little flecks of gold that glitter when he's happy. She stared at the pink flowers in confusion.

The heater kicked off and the balloon settled. The clock ticked softly and then louder and louder until it boomed in her ears. And then she could hear something else. It sounded like someone screaming. It was loud and harsh and it hurt her throat as if she were the one who was screaming.

She stumbled across the floor and fell into the chair by the table. Leaning her head down to his arm, she cried. Her body shook and strangled noises rose from her throat, but no tears broke from her burning eyes. She lay on his arm and let the strange, dry sobs flow from her, feeling fresh the loss she thought she had come accustomed to.

"Nooo," she whispered and lifted her head. His face was pale, but not all that changed. His lips were closed and natural looking, and his other arm was laid causally across his stomach. There was more dirt scattered on top of his hand and inside the crevices of the pinky ring he always wore.

She'd asked him one time where he had gotten the ring and he just smiled. "'Some of the sweetest things in life are better left, untold'" he said. She had told him she thought he was weird.

With gentle hands, she brushed the flowers from his eyes and gasped. There were only hollowed places were his golden–flecked eyes had been. Two hollowed–out pits with what looked like tiny raisins in the center. She gripped her stomach and looked away.

The heater kicked back on and started the balloon dancing again. She watched it, smiling and laughing down at her and felt something rise out of her numbness. In a vicious burst of anger, she ripped the string from Uncle Dave's neck and stomped on the ridiculous balloon, popping it under her foot.

She stood and got the dishtowel from under the sink. Placing it over Uncle Dave's hideous eyes, she bent and kissed him on the cheek.

"I'm sorry…I'm so sorry," she whispered beside his ear. She listened to herself breathe for a while, listened to the reassuring whistle of her mouth taking in air. And then she wiped her nose and sat up.

"I have to go now Uncle Dave." She closed her eyes and took another deep breath. The familiar scent of his evergreen cologne filled her lungs. "I love you."

She pressed her lips together and picked up the truck keys from the hook by the door. She opened it and then stopped, another idea creeping into her head. She looked back at Uncle Dave and hesitated, not wanting to touch him again, but then felt the horror of that thought. She would never touch him again. He would never tousle her hair…or give her a goodnight kiss.

Something began to sting her eyes and she forced it back with an effort. There was time enough for that later.

Carefully, so as not to move him, she wound the big ring that held the store keys off his belt loop. She flipped through the keys to find the small gold one, as she hurried back to the front of the store. There were three gold ones, so Kate tried them all in the drawer below the register. The third one opened it and she picked up the gun with both hands. It was cold and heavy and felt as if it had a purpose of its own when she hefted it. She stood and stuffed it down the back of her jeans, next to the knife.

She opened the back door and stepped out into the crisp air. Pausing a moment on the porch, she took a deep breath. Yes, this might turn out to be a good day yet. It just might. She tossed the keys in the air and caught them with one hand as she jumped off the porch.

PART THREE

Chapter Fifteen
A Moment of Clarity

The door handle on the truck was jammed so Kate yanked it twice before the door opened suddenly, sending her flying backwards and landing on her bottom. She brushed herself off and climbed in.

There were only two keys on this key chain, one for the lock box in the back and one for the truck. She slipped the second one into the ignition and turned it. Nothing happened. She looked down at the three pedals by her feet. It was the one on the left she was supposed to push. She hoped. After pressing it to the floor, she tried the key again. The truck sputtered and stalled. Okay, okay...gas. She turned the key and tapped the pedal on the right. With a thunderous shake, the truck roared to life.

Now she looked at the shifter on the steering wheel. Taking a guess, she moved it down a notch and let out the clutch. The truck lurched forward and hit the shed door, buckling it in the middle. Okay...that must be first. She slid the lever all the way up and let it out again. Her head hit the steering wheel as the truck jerked backwards. After stalling it two more times and taking out part of the gate, she was out of the yard. She cranked the wheel to the left and tried to find first again. The truck bounced off the sidewalk and crawled down the street.

There was no one else on the road, which was good because she couldn't seem to drive in a straight line. She saw the Hudsons about a block away, their car still half in the street. The pinto was hopelessly crushed with most of the windows smashed and one tire flat. As she approached, Cindy jumped on top of the car and began beating the roof with her ice scraper. Clumps of blonde hair covered most of her face and the front of her blouse had been ripped open, revealing several cuts on her neck and chest. So lost was Cindy in the blank rage that had overcome her, she wasn't

251

aware of any of this. She continued to bludgeon the roof of the pinto, as her bare feet slid down the cracked windshield.

Mark had found a hammer and was working on the back fender. Kate couldn't see his eyes, but had a good idea of what she'd find if she could. It was told in the fury of his hammer. The mindless purpose, the desperate need to smash and destroy everything, anything that wasn't his wife it seemed. His body shook as if on the verge of a great explosion and his voice was ravaged by hate. He shouted unintelligibly over and over again with each ear–splitting clang.

Another car came from the other direction. It stopped behind the Hudsons and the driver waved his hands at Mark and Cindy. Kate slowed the truck to maneuver around them and then cursed when it stalled. She looked out the side window and saw Mark and Cindy paying no attention. Then she looked at the other driver.

His face was red all the way up to his receding hairline and his cheeks were puffing in and out like a fish. He waved at her and screamed curses she was glad she couldn't hear. She turned the key again.

"Come on, come on." Nothing happened and a burning smell wafted up from the engine.

The man in the other car pounded the steering wheel, then slammed his car in reverse and backed up a hundred yards. With his body hunched over the wheel and his face the color of an overripe tomato, he gunned it and sped toward the Hudsons' car.

Mark saw him coming at the last second and managed to leap away. Cindy however, was knocked off the roof of her car, arm in mid–swing and thrown to the pavement. There was dead silence for a moment, then the man got out of his car and stormed over to Mark. Mark saw him coming though and in a running leap, tackled him, bringing them both down to the street.

Kate turned the key again, mouthing a silent prayer and trying not to give it as much gas. The starter caught and she guided the truck past the insanity on the street and farther down the block. Glancing in the rear view mirror, she saw Cindy sit up slowly, rubbing her head. When she took her hand away, she stared at the blood that dripped from it and then looked up at the sky. Kate watched as long as she dared and then turned back to the road just in time to slam on her brakes to avoid hitting the boy crossing in front of her on his bike.

The truck stalled again.

"Shit," she muttered, trying to start it. Then she stopped, as her neck and arms broke out in a prickly rash. She looked up at the boy.

Will was staring back at her, his hands on the handlebars and his feet on either side. He smiled for an instant and then narrowed his eyes.

"What the hell are you doing, Kate?"

She glared at him through the windshield. "Get out of my way."

"No, not until you tell me what you're going."

"Get out of my way or I swear to God, I'll run you over." Her fist came down on the steering wheel and she jumped as the horn blared.

Will jumped too.

She turned the key and thumped on the gas pedal. What stupid luck to run into Will right now. "Don't think I won't," she yelled.

He walked his bike over to the curb and threw it on the sidewalk. She ignored him, cursing at the truck and pounding on the pedal. The passenger's side door opened and Will climbed in beside her.

"You're giving it too much gas," he said, slamming the door shut.

She glared at him again, then rolled her eyes away and tried the key with less gas. It started.

"There, now let the clutch out, slow...good, now press on the gas, but just a little."

The truck took off much smother this time and soon they

were on the outskirts of town, headed down the mountain on Kerry County Road. After a few minutes, a loud roaring noise shook the truck and she began to think something was going to explode.

"You need to shift to second," Will said quietly.

"Where's second?" Kate pushed in the clutch and yanked on the shifter.

Will leaned over, brushing his arm against hers. "Here, you just pull it toward you and down—hey, watch the road."

She swerved off the shoulder and back to the road. The truck stopped shuddering and picked up speed. Cold air rushed through the cab, blowing hair in her eyes. She let go of the wheel for a split second to push it away.

"You want to tell me where we're going?" Will was staring out the window at the trees rushing by.

"No."

He looked back at her. "Now third."

"Huh? Oh." Pushing the clutch in again, she fiddled with the shifter.

"The same thing, you just—"

"I know, I know," she said, waving him away.

The odometer inched up to thirty and Kate felt her heart pound as the road flew by, but she didn't let off the gas.

"So what is it?" Will asked.

"What's what?" She asked and stepped lightly on the brakes. The guardrail came dangerously close to the truck as she made the turn.

"What's so important that you needed to steal your Uncle's truck?" He kept his voice casual. He knew her well enough not to back her into a corner.

"I did not steal his truck."

"A minor technicality," he said. "Where is he anyway, does he even know that you're gone?"

She pushed harder on the gas. "Will…if you want to come with me, keep your mouth shut."

Something in her voice cut off Will's reply and he turned to look out the window again.

She switched on the radio. It was as old as the rest of the truck and the reception was lousy. After flipping the dial from one end to the other, she found a song she liked. She turned it up and let the driving beat fill her head as she sped mindlessly down the mountain.

* * * * *

Skidding to a stop in the gravel parking lot, Kate turned off the headlights. Will sat beside her, a stunned look on his face, one he'd carried ever since they had driven past the entrance and he realized where she was headed.

"Hey," Will said, as she opened her door. "Before we go in there, you have to promise me something." The lights from the entrance shone on half his face, leaving the other half in shadows.

She sighed and sat back in the seat, one foot dangling outside. "What?"

"You've been hurt so many times, Kate and I can see in your eyes that you've been hurt again, today," he began.

She looked away and stared at the building. So close now.

"Promise me you won't do anything that'll make it worse. I mean, I don't know what you hope to accomplish here, but I can't imagine anything you've got in mind is going to help the situation." His eyes followed hers, toward the building. "Are you sure you've really thought about what you're doing?"

"I don't need to think about it," she said and hopped out of the truck. She slammed the door behind her.

Will took a few running steps to catch up with her and his hand brushed her back. "Hey, can you hold on a—"

Spinning around, Kate scooted out of reach before he could feel the gun in the back of her jeans. "Look," she hissed. "I'm sick of your whining. If you want to wait in the truck then go ahead, but if you're coming then shut up, because I'm going, no

255

matter what you say."

"Fine, I'm with you, okay? But look." Will pointed to a sign by the glass door. "Visiting hours ended two hours ago. They're not going to let you in anyway and if you go rushing in there like this they'll know something's up."

Kate read the sign and turned to take out her frustration on the small bush by the entrance. It fell over with one kick. "Damn it anyway," she said and looked back at the truck. The parking lot was cast in darkness, made fuller by the clouds above that had yet to open with snow. Kate could smell it in the air though, the brisk, thin scent that promised a heavy storm.

She turned back to Will. "I don't care, I'm going," she said and started for the door.

"I know you are, but hold on." He grabbed her arm and pulled her back. "Let me go first, all right? And whatever you do, keep your mouth shut."

Kate nodded and followed Will through the double doors.

They walked into a lobby area with plush burgundy carpeting. The walls were covered in soft cream–colored wallpaper and the vaulted ceiling had a large crystal chandelier that hung from the center. Three leather couches circled around a marble table with a statue of Gabriel sitting in the middle. Kate took in this splendor with a sour taste in her mouth. How much had Uncle Dave been paying for this place?

Will led them to the receptionist on the opposite side of the room. She sat behind a glass wall and pressed her lips together in a slight grimace as Kate and Will approached.

"Can I help you with something?" She cocked her head to the side and the bun that sat atop layers of blonde hair shifted precariously.

"Well, I hope so," Will said. He gave her a cheesy smile before continuing. "We've had some bad luck with our truck and I was wondering if we might use your phone."

The receptionist gave Kate a wary look and Will quickly stepped between them. She turned back to Will. "Well, you can't use this one, it's for office use only."

"Is there another one in the building? I hate to bother you, I know how busy you must be, but that storm'll be here in a while I think and I'd hate to get caught in it."

She was taken in by Will's sickening sweet tone and smiled back at him. "By the restroom," she said and pointed with one bright pink nail. "Just around the corner."

"Thank you so much, I can't tell you how much we appreciate this Miss...is it Shanty?" Will squinted at her nametag.

"*Shaunty*." The receptionist corrected with a grin.

"Miss *Shaunty*. You're a lifesaver." Will gestured toward Kate. "Why don't you take care of that and then freshen up while you're at it." He jerked his eyes toward the set of double doors and tapped her shin with his foot. "I can wait here."

Kate walked in the direction he pointed and then past the restroom door. A gentle push opened the double door and she slipped through.

She was at the end of a long empty hall which was glaringly white compared to the warm colors of the lobby. Patient doors lined either side and Kate made her way quickly, reading the names on the doors as she went by. Since it was after dinnertime, she figured most of the patients were already in bed. She zigged–zagged back and forth and was nearly at the end of the hall but still she didn't see the name she was looking for. This was taking too long. Will wouldn't be able to occupy that woman all night.

There was a door on the right and taking a chance, she opened it.

The room was dark and spacious, much too spacious to be a patient room. Windows lined the far side and metal folding chairs were set up in a circle in the middle of the room. A piano stood by the wall on her left next to a small couch. She backed out of the room and had almost closed the door before noticing the woman in the wheelchair.

Kate went in and closed the door softly behind her. The woman faced the window; her straight black hair hung down her back and brushed the wheels of her chair. Soft light lit her high cheekbone and her skin glowed with a healthy richness. A silk blue bathrobe covered her shoulders, draping to the floor under the afghan that lay on her lap. She wore matching slippers on her feet.

Walking further into the room, Kate never took her eyes off the woman. She stopped just a few feet behind her and tried to catch her breath.

She knew the tilt of this woman's head, the straight line of her back. Knew her voice, though she spoke no words, only continued staring out the window.

Kate stepped closer and pulled the gun out of her jeans.

Her voice. She could hear her voice, cold and hard and scratchy with hate and suddenly Kate backed away. Her mind screamed at her to run...run, how could she even be in the same room with this woman? Breathe the same air? Fear, slick and sweet raced through her body as she stared at the woman in the wheelchair. The gun shook in her hands and she gripped it tighter so it wouldn't slide through her damp fingers.

I will not be afraid of you. Not anymore. You are the weak one, not me. You let it take you, you let it control you, you loved it more than you ever loved us. You made your choice.

Kate leveled the gun at the back of the woman's head and released the safety.

You opened the door the night Daddy died and everything, everything since has been your fault. You didn't fight it, you didn't stop it. You could have stopped it before it was too late. But now it is too late and you're here and everyone else is gone...they're all gone...and it's your fault, it's always been your fault. You made your choice...and you never chose me.

Kate slipped her finger over the trigger and steadied the gun with both hands. Her body tensed against the coming blast...but it never came. Her fingers refused to obey and the gun began to shake again. Come on, come on. She willed her fingers to move but nothing happened. The room turned smeary and dark and

Kate blinked several times to clear her vision.

"Katie? Is that you?"

Kate froze, with the gun still hanging in front of her.

"Come here honey, it's such a beautiful night," her soft voice said and Kate obeyed. She took one shuffling step after another until she stood before the woman.

The gun dropped to her side and then clattered to the floor.

Glassy eyes stared out at the starless sky and a smile played at her lips. Not a wrinkle lined her soft skin. Not a brush of gray streaked her black hair. Not a worry darkened her sparkling eyes. Those eyes that told of warm summer days and happy endings.

Kate followed her mother's gaze out the window and stared into the night. The clouds that had been gathering all day had finally given them some snow and it came in soft, twirling drifts. Kate closed her eyes, as tears slid down her cheeks.

"Will it snow all night, Mamma?"

"I don't know honey, maybe. That would be an awful lot of snow."

"That's okay, then me and Joey can go sledding all day tomorrow."

"Well then, I think you'd better rest up, if you're going to do that much sledding."

"Just a few more minutes please, it's so pretty to watch at night. It's like they're dancing."

"Okay, just a little while longer..."

Kate reached for the little girl that sat by her mother's knee, but she vanished like smoke and all that was in her hand was a piece of her mother's bathrobe. Kate knelt by her feet and moaned as a gentle hand rubbed over her head...around her face. The hand pulled Kate's head to her lap and she laid on the soft silk, her tears wetting the material.

"Shhh honey, nothing's ever all that bad."

She sobbed harder and let herself be rocked back and forth as she listened to the quiet humming...a lilting tune she knew well. Years and years washed over her in a rushing torrent of

259

memories…picnics, walks in the woods, she and Joey dancing with her mother to some silly song in the kitchen. Everything she'd lost everything that had been taken from her. Her mother, her childhood…Joey.

Her tears came in quiet waves until she heard a rustling noise from behind. She leapt to her feet and whirled around.

Someone had come in. She cursed herself silently and grabbed the gun from the floor to shove it back in her jeans.

After glancing around the room though, she realized they were still alone, but now the smell of apples was suddenly in the air. The smell was familiar…

A brief gust of wind blew the hair from her face and she turned toward her mother again to come face to face with the man who stood on the other side of her wheelchair.

He wore a long coat that brushed the top of his boots and his white hair seemed to glow in the darkened room. He *was* glowing in fact, or maybe it was just a trick of the low light that made it seem as if he was more shadow than anything else. The outline of the window was visible through his torso. When she looked again at his boots, she saw they didn't touch the floor, though he didn't float…it was as if parts of him just weren't there. And for some reason, she thought of the apples, the heavy, sweet scent that was beginning to gag her and inexplicably she understood that it smelled of those apples and deep, moist earth, where he had come from, where he was still *continued* to come from. Her sluggish gaze lifted up…up to the amulet with the strange writing strung around his thick neck. Up…up to his face that was shrouded in darkness, but she saw the small smile he gave her. His teeth were almost as white as his hair.

He came around to the front of the wheelchair and stood, staring at her mother. His shadow darkened her face, but her smile never faltered. She stared through him and out the window at the snow that was now slamming against the glass. The man put his hands on each armrest of her chair and bent eye to eye with her.

Her mother didn't move.

The rotting stench of apples was thick in the air now and Kate felt a little woozy. She backed off one more step and glanced at the door. It seemed a mile away.

The man began to shake the chair, bouncing her mother around in it. He tipped it back, lifting it off its front wheels. Her mother's head flopped back and her hair touched the floor, then he brought the chair back down with a bang. She heard him laugh, or at least it sounded like a laugh. It was a low, scraping noise that hurt Kate's ears.

She glanced at the door again.

He caught her movement and looked up. Kate's eyes traveled slowly back, back, until they met his. The door was forgotten. The smell of the apples was forgotten. Her mother was forgotten.

Her hand fell away from the gun and she stood, unmoving, drinking in the pureness of his eyes. The sheer and beautiful power of the perfection that shone in his eyes. Not a trace of conflict or doubt or caution clouded the sparkling orbs of energy that drank her in as she did them.

"Do you hear it?"

She wasn't sure he'd spoken because his lips never moved, but that didn't matter because she realized she did hear it. A single commanding voice that gathered up all the jangled and discordant noises in her head and smoothed them into one resounding tone that rang true in her heart. It told her to let go, *let go*...so she did. She felt the burdens of years slide off her shoulders and as she let go of her remaining doubts, a drifting peace came over her. No longer did she feel torn between guilt and anger. There was no more struggling, no more floundering in the confusion of her own conscious. She was freed and now...now she could breathe. Her hate was let loose from the shackles of morality and the weakness of her fear. After six years, her hate was finally complete.

No healing.

The man held one gnarled hand over her mother's head.

No regrets...no forgiveness.

He lifted his eyebrow at her and waited.

No love.

Kate nodded.

He turned to her mother and cupped her chin in his hand. One thumb rubbed tenderly over her cheek and he smiled. Kate watched as her mother's eyes cleared and she saw the man for the first time.

"Wha—"

"Shhh," he murmured. He rubbed her mother's hair with his other hand and tilted her head back.

Her mother tried to twist away and she pushed at his chest, but he tightened his grip on her chin, sinking his fingers into her cheek.

"Get away, get away from me, please," her mother said and tried to yank her head out of his grasp.

He chuckled. "But you have something I need..."

Kate watched her mother's terrified eyes dart around the room, searching desperately for help. Kate stood back, out of her sight.

You thought it was Joey, Mamma but it was me, it was always me...

The man came closer to her and her mother screamed, a small pitiful sound that made Kate's heart soar. Oh, the sweet satisfaction that she was aware. That her mother would understand the horror before it would happen. And Kate got to watch every moment of it. A little thrill passed over her.

He pulled her mother's face to his and forced her to look into his eyes. As their eyes met, she stopped struggling.

The sparkling colors in his eyes brightened and began to spin. They spun and spun in an incredible tornado of light and flash and then they leapt from his eyes and toward her mother. In a shimmering stream, they stretched across the distance until they met her mother's eyes. There, they stirred her mother's colors and spun with them faster and faster until her colors merged with his. Her mother's mouth opened in a silent scream and her lips widened until Kate could see every one of her teeth. Her fingers gripped the armrests of her chair and dug into the metal, folding her nails back. The power in the room was fantastic. Kate's hair stood on end with electricity and the blood raged through her body. The colors spun in their whirling tornado and then all at once, leapt back into the man's eyes and were gone.

Her mother fell into a lifeless heap on the floor.

"Kate!"

She heard Will's frantic voice behind her but paid no attention. The man was looking at her. He was smiling at her and holding out his hand.

"How I have waited for you, my Katie girl." His voice was warm with love and she knew that yes, he loved her without reservation or condition. His voice welcomed her and told her that finally, finally she had found home. All her pain and loss were washed away in the soothing comfort of his voice.

She took a step toward him and bumped something with her foot. She looked down at her mother. Her mother was dead. And that was good. Her mother wouldn't hold her anymore. No...no. Kate shook her head. She wouldn't *hurt* her anymore. Confusion trickled back into her mind and she looked desperately into the eyes of the man for the tranquility she felt just a moment ago. But she found herself instead, staring down at the body of her mother.

"Oh my God," she breathed.

The man stepped in front of Kate and took her face in his cold hand. Her mother's body on the floor was all that separated them. "Just look at me, my child," he said. "And you will be well."

She searched his eyes and found nothing, nothing but death, dark and lying and jealous. His breath was hot on her face and the stench of rotting apples was back, full force and hitting her in the stomach. The sparkling colors in his eyes had dissolved into muddy pools that turned black. She backed away and his hand slipped from her face.

She took another step back and stared, gaping at the floor. Her mother's hair was draped across her face and her body was twisted with one foot still caught in the footrest of her wheelchair.

"'Tis who you are, don't fight it," the man said and began to circle around her mother, closer to Kate.

"Nooo..." She shook her head again, moving further away. Will tugged on her arm.

"We gotta get out of here Kate," he said in a rattled voice Kate didn't recognize. "Come on—"

The overhead lights switched on, blinding her for a moment. She turned toward the door and saw Ms. Shaunty standing with her hands covering her mouth. Her pink nails dug into her cheeks.

"What's going on here?" She asked in a high, squeaky voice, looking at the body on the floor. "What's going on? Mrs. O'Connor..." Her voice was lost in a decibel Kate's ears couldn't pick up.

Kate spun back around and looked back at her mother, then over at the piano, by the couch, the chairs, the window. The man was gone and so was the scent of apples.

"What have you people done?" Ms. Shaunty was staring at her and then at Will, her eyes widening with fear. She stepped out of the room. "What have you done, oh my God, oh my God, Bill," she shouted down the hallway, not taking her eyes off of them. "Bill, come in here I need you!"

Kate heard heavy footsteps pounding down the hallway, getting louder and louder. Will grabbed her shoulder and pulled her toward the door at the opposite end of the room. "Come on, come on, time to go."

She followed him out of the room and down the hall. They ran the length of the hall and made a left at the end. Will skidded to a stop and pulled her back around the corner as she saw the doors at the end of the hall slam open and two security guards jog toward them, their keys jingling on their belt loops. She looked behind her and heard Bill nearing the end of the other hall.

Trapped.

"Come on," Will said and pulled them into a room across the hall. He closed the door softly behind them and leaned against it, listening.

"Do you see'em Bill?"

"No, but they ran this way, start checking rooms and I'll start at this end."

She heard a door open and the rustle of a curtain as they pushed it open to look under the bed. Kate backed away from the door and looked around the room.

Photographs lined every available space on the walls and cluttered the surface of the dresser and nightstand. The drapes were open and the sill was lined with six pots of flowers. Their orange and yellow blossoms glowed strangely against the snowy night beyond.

On the other side of the neatly made bed, sat a man with a newspaper. He sat so still in fact, that Kate thought for a moment he was dead. But the man raised his head after a moment and gazed evenly at them. He followed Will's eyes to the window.

"If you wouldn't mind moving my marigolds?" He asked quietly.

Will nodded and began placing the pots carefully on his bed. Kate ran to help. When they were done, Will ran his hand around the frame of the window, searching for the latch.

"You can't open it," the old man said. "They're too afraid we'll all just fly away."

A door slammed in the next room and Kate heard footsteps approach.

"Get back," Will said, barely giving her enough time to jump away before he brought the heavy metal chair down on the window. It shattered, sending shards of glass at her face.

"Go!" Will was up on the sill, holding an arm out for her.

Kate jumped up and out the window, landing on her hands and knees on the sharp rocks below. Springing to her feet, she followed Will around the side of the building toward the parking lot.

"Keys, keys," Will was shouting at her.

She dug in her pocket, pulled out Uncle Dave's keys and threw them at Will. He opened the driver's door and let her slide across before hopping in and starting the engine. It started on the first try and Will spun out the tires, leaving the parking lot in a cloud of dust. The truck shot down the gravel road, bouncing over the dips and skidding on the turns. He made a left at the end of the road and picked up speed on the blacktop.

"Hey, the highway's back there," Kate said, pointing behind them.

"Yeah, I know." He glanced in the rearview mirror. "Do you see them?"

She twisted in her seat and peered down the road, watching the entrance to the home. No car with lights and sirens came careening out of the driveway and racing toward them, but she watched until Will made a turn and it was out of her sight.

She settled back in her seat and risked a glance at Will. His face was red and his body was bent toward the wheel, trying to see the road through the blinding snow.

"Will—"

"Don't," he said harshly. His eyes never left the road.

She nodded and slumped against the window.

Chapter Sixteen
Lost in the Deep

Will drove for miles and miles, making one unthinking turn after the next, pushing the truck as fast as he dared on the slick roads. Hours went by with only the sound of the windshield wipers skipping across the glass to break the silence. Kate fell into a restless sleep, awakening only when the truck stopped.

"Where are we?" She rubbed the sleep from her eyes and looked around, confused for a moment. Then the events of the day fell like bombs, one by one back in her head and she moaned, wishing she could go back to sleep.

"I don't know." Will revved the engine and she heard the back tires spinning out. His face was even redder than before. "The pavement gave out back there and I thought this might lead out to another road. I should have just turned around." He gunned the engine again. "Damn."

She sat up and rolled down her window to look outside. The trees, heavy with snow, hunched over the road creating a dark tunnel and all she could see was white. No lights, no other cars. She rolled the window back up.

"Does your uncle have a shovel?"

"Yeah," she said. "It's in the back."

He climbed out of the truck and slammed the door. Several minutes went by and then Kate heard a terrible banging on the back of the truck. She looked out the back window, but the snow was too thick to see anything. With a pounding heart, she opened the door and stepped into the cold.

"Will?" She called. "Will, what are you doing?" He didn't look up at her, but continued beating the rim of the wheel with the shovel. "Will!"

"Goddamn it Kate, what's going on here?" He swung again.

She ran to him, trying to catch the shovel in her hands and

as he brought it up for another swing, she felt the air rush by her head. She screamed and jumped back.

He stopped and looked at her, his face frozen with shock. Then the anger washed over him again and he turned to whirl the shovel into the forest. She didn't hear it land.

"What's going on Kate, I feel like I'm losing my mind."

"You're not," she said quietly.

"I'm not? You sure about that? Because what I saw back there didn't leave me with a whole lot of other options."

She looked away. "I know."

"So if I'm not losing it, then what the hell's going on? And this time you'd better tell me, because I've about had it with all your lies and your secrets." His eyes turned hard on her and she backed away.

"I don't—"

"Don't, don't you say that," he shouted and in two powerful steps, crossed to her and grabbed her by the shoulders, pushing her up against the truck. "Don't you say you don't know, or that it doesn't concern me, 'cause where I'm standing in the middle of nowhere and stuck in the snow, it sure as hell feels like it concerns me."

His fingers dug into her upper arms and she bit her lip to keep from crying out. "You're hurting me."

He glared at her a moment longer and then shoved her away. She fell against the truck and slipped, falling on her hands. Will stormed down the road, kicking up snow as he went and eventually disappearing in the cloud. She heard him yell something unintelligible and then come running back.

"That man, that man back at the home," he yelled and stopped a few feet from her. "For the last two months I've had nightmares every night and that man back there has been in every single one of them. So what the hell? You going to keep saying that it has nothing to do with me?"

She brought the amulet out of her sweater and held it between her fingers. "No."

"Then talk, goddamned it Kate, would you just—"

"What do you want me to say, huh?" She shouted. "You want me to tell you something you can make sense of? Something you can work your mind around and come up with some sort of brilliant explanation? Well I can't, okay? I don't know what's going on, I don't understand any of it."

"But you know more than me. And you have, for a long time. You've been lying to me and I want to know why." Will said in a deadly low tone.

"Don't you understand? None of this," she said, waving her arms out. "None of it was my idea. I just wanted to be left alone. I wanted to live my life in peace and I wanted to be with—" She glanced up at Will bit off her last words. "It doesn't matter what I wanted. It never has."

The amulet sliced into her palm as her fingers closed tighter around it. Then she ripped her hand away and punched the truck. "God it's not fair! I did everything she said, everything and it still didn't make one damn bit of difference," she shouted and kicked the tire. The blow wasn't felt on her already frozen toes. "I can't change anything, I can't stop anything. I did exactly what she said, but it still didn't matter. I lost it all anyway."

Will stood beside her and took her shoulder, this time much more gently and turned her around. "Not everything."

She looked up at him and felt drowned by his eyes. The eyes that were ravaged by pain, but shining with love, abiding and true. She held fast to that anchor and felt it edge away the hopelessness that clung to her with cold, spidery fingers. He kissed her, driving his maddened heart into hers and taking them both into the spinning dark abyss that Kate fell into with relief. She let the darkness of denial wash over her and hide them from bright glare of truth. Pushing further and further until all that existed was the forever in the moment they had created. His lips…his hands…his love she had denied herself for so long.

Then, with a sobbing cry, she shoved him away and stumbled to the back of the truck. "You don't understand," she shouted. "We can't let this happen, *I* can't let this happen. I can't lose you."

"I won't let that happen," Will said, trying to gather her in his arms. She shook him off.

"You won't be able to stop it, there's nothing you can do." She covered her face with her hands.

"There is something you can do, you can tell me what you know," he said and pulled her hands down. "You can tell me what you know and then we can get through this. Together. No more secrets."

She looked at his trusting, confident face and could have died for what she had to tell him. The wind blew snow in her face and she looked down and saw her feet were covered. She couldn't feel them anymore.

"No more secrets," she said and walked slowly to the cab of the truck.

* * * * *

A line of water zigzagged down the foggy windshield, mixing with larger pools of moisture, where it gained speed and raced to the bottom of the window. Kate watched this phenomenon with vacant eyes.

Will was staring at the windshield, but Kate didn't think he saw anything through the glass. "I'm sorry about your uncle," he said in a thin voice.

"Yeah."

"So how long?"

"How long what?"

"How long have you known?" He turned to her and she looked away from the fresh pain in his eyes.

"Since the day I dropped off the—"

"The picture yeah, I should have known, man," he said rubbing his head. "That was like over two months ago."

"It feels like a lot longer than that."

"Yeah…" He crossed his arms on the steering wheel and rested his head on them. "My God Kate, what are we going to do?"

"I don't know."

He was quiet for a while and Kate wiped her window to look at the snow that still fell outside. It was an early morning hour, but no light shone through the thick clouds above. She watched the snow, her mind finally quiet and didn't notice when her breath fogged up the glass again.

"I don't buy it." His voice was quiet, but there was an edge to it.

"What do you mean?"

"Well if what my grandmother said was true, then what's happening now? I mean you did what she said, right? But hey," he scoffed. "It looks like this guy made it back just fine without us. So what's up with that?"

She shook her head. "I only know what she told me."

"Maybe she's wrong."

"So what if she is? Do you want to chance it?"

"I don't think we have any choice. I mean look at what's already happened, do you want to wait any longer? We need to take some action, all this sitting around and trying to avoid whatever's happening is doing nothing but making it worse. We need to get rid of him." He looked out the window and then let out a short burst of laughter. "We need a priest."

She stared at him. "You're kidding."

"Why not? Assuming the earth is flat, that the bogeyman is carrying away children by the cart–full and demons are romping through the forth dimension messing with our heads. Why not?"

"You're not helping."

"Well why don't you tell me what I can do then. 'Cause as far as I see it, this guy's got no reason to leave. There's nothing to stop him and God knows what—" He stopped, his mouth open.

"What?"

"We've got to get back there," he said and began pulling on

271

his parka.

"Why, what's wrong?"

He stopped and tried to speak slowly. "Don't you get it? First he shows up at the store and then at the home. What do you think he's doing, visiting old relatives? I heard what he said about your mother having something he needed and I guess your uncle must have too." He zipped up his parka and put one hand on the door handle. "What if my grandmother does?"

She stared at him as the realization dawned in her head.

"My parents went into Philly for the weekend, but my grandmother, she's home and she's alone. We've got to find that shovel, come on," he said and ran out into the night with Kate close behind.

Away after a long, cold search they found the shovel in a ditch about a hundred yards, and went back to dig out the truck.

They drove for an hour before hitting blacktop again. It was still pretty slick, but at least now it was flat. Will stopped at a gas station and went in to get them something to eat while Kate made the call.

"What did she say?" Will asked when they met back at the truck. He tossed a wrapped sandwich on her lap.

"Nobody answered your phone, so I called information to get the number for the police department. I was going to tell them I thought I saw someone breaking into your house."

"Yeah?"

She sighed. "The lines are down, Will. Because of the storm."

"The whole town?"

"It doesn't take much, you know that." She unwrapped her sandwich and stared at it, realizing she wasn't hungry anymore.

"This is nuts, damn it." He sat for a moment and then thrust the key in the ignition and roared out of the parking lot.

They drove in silence for a while. The day had brightened but only by a little. Turbid sunlight filtered through the black clouds, not even giving enough light to turn off the headlights.

The snow continued.

"They block the road at the base of the mountain, you know," she said quietly.

Will kept his eyes on the road. "I know."

By midmorning, they turned off the highway and into Quarryville. The town was shut down. They passed only three cars and a snowplow on their way through. Not a soul had ventured out in what the man on the radio was calling the worst storm in nineteen years. All the convenience stores were closed and only an occasional light could be seen in the houses they drove by. On the far end of town they passed several message board signs that flashed, 'Warning Kerry County Road closed ahead'.

Will never slowed.

It was another five miles before they hit the roadblock. A police car sat with his lights and flashers on in the right lane and orange and white barricades blocked the rest of the road.

"Here we go," Will said and slowed the truck.

One of the officers saw them coming and climbed out of the car. He was tall, so tall that the hood of the cruiser came to his waist. Another officer came from the passenger's side, much shorter and with narrow shoulders. They both wore regulation hats and thick black coats.

The tall one tapped on Will's window. "You're going to have to turn it around and go back, son," he said when Will rolled down the window. "Road's closed, case you hadn't noticed." He was chewing something and spat it on the ground when he finished talking.

Will smiled and shrugged his shoulders. "We live in Newclare, we're just trying to get home, we've got the chains there."

The officer leaned in the window and smiled back. "Road's," he said slowly. "Closed."

Kate watched the other officer walk to her window and peer in. She didn't roll it down, but stared straight ahead, trying to shake the feeling that the man on her right was licking his lips at her.

Will flicked Kate a quick glance and then turned back to the officer. "We have to get home."

"You don't want to do that," said the shorter man by Kate. His voice was muffled through the glass. "Just came down the mountain myself and you don't want to be in Newclare just right now." He grinned, showing off a gold–capped tooth. "Trust me."

Will turned away from the grinning policeman. "You don't understand. My grandmother is sick and there's no one—"

"No, you don't understand, son," the officer on Will's side said. "The road is closed, so you're going to have to turn it around and—"

"Oh, screw this," Will muttered and threw the truck gear.

The man on her right pounded the window with his fist and Kate shrieked, jumping back. Their eyes met and she screamed again. His eyes had thick blackness swimming in the irises and faint red veins around his lids. He had drawn a gun from his side and the grin had widened.

Will covered her with one arm, peeled out the tires in the snow and pulled away. The barricades flew up over the hood and hit the windshield, but didn't crack it. A second later an incredible bang ripped through the air and the back window shattered. Kate ducked and held her ears.

"Was that a gun shot?" Will leaned down and could barely see over the wheel. "Holy shit, was that a gun? Are they shooting at us?"

Kate inched up the back of the seat and peeked out the shattered window. She saw the taller officer lunge at the smaller one, making his second shot fly wild in the air. The smaller one threw him off and...and...oh God. This wasn't happening. She didn't see him shoot the taller man and she didn't see the taller man crumple to the ground and disappear in the snow like the earth had swallowed him up. Oh, oh no...she couldn't have seen that.

"What the hell are they doing, they're shooting at us?" Will jerked the wheel suddenly, making her slide into the door. "Are

274

they following us?"

Will made another turn and she couldn't see the parked cruiser anymore. "I don't think so."

The truck began to slide and Will steered into the turn to bring it around. They straightened and continued on the snow–packed road. The plows hadn't been here, because of the closure, so the snow was easily a foot deep, two in some places. The wind blew it around and Will was having a hard time staying off of the shoulder.

"At this rate they could catch up with us on foot." He down shifted and thumped on the gas. "As long as we don't stop, we should be fine. Well I don't know if I could say fine though. Oh my god, did you see his eyes, Kate? Did you?"

Kate was digging under the seat for something to plug up the hole in the back window. "Yeah." She found one of Uncle Dave's old work shirts and stuffed it in the hole. "He's not the only one either."

Will shook his head. "What? But how?"

"I don't know. Will," she said, reaching into the glove box to get a tie to pull her hair back with. "I don't know if going up to Newclare is really the best idea right now, I mean whatever's going on only seems to be getting worse."

He was silent for a moment. "It's catching, like a virus."

"What?"

"Look, I don't see what choice we have, my grandmother's up there." He glanced in the rearview mirror. "And it's not like we can go back now anyway."

"I'm sorry, you're right, but I don't know what we think we're going to do when we get there."

"We'll have worry about that when we get there, if we get there."

The truck was dropping speed and spinning out in the snow as they climbed the mountain. The trip from Quarryville usually took a little less than an hour. They had already been on the road twice that. Kate saw the landmarks that told her they had more than halfway to go. Will had turned the heater off, thinking they might get more power out of the truck and she was shivering with cold. Freezing air seeped through the spaces around the plugged hole and hit the back of her neck. She wished she had thought to get the blanket out of the lock box back at the gas station, because Will refused to stop the truck.

"What does that sign say?"

It was early afternoon, though the only way she knew was because of her watch. The sky hadn't lightened and if anything had actually gotten darker. She leaned forward, but couldn't see the sign through the snow. Rolling down her window, she poked her head out and squinted. "Four miles."

"We're going to make it," he said with a glimmer of a smile.

She nodded. "Should we go to your house first, or—"

"Hang on," Will interrupted and tried to slow the truck. They were rounding a bend on a slight decline and the back tires had locked up. Will pumped the brakes and turned the wheel slowly, but the guardrail was coming up fast and Kate braced for the impact. Her seatbelt kept her from hitting the windshield, but her head bounced off the back window. The world exploded in a stunning array of stars.

The engine sputtered and stalled.

"Will?" She opened and closed her eyes several times until the stars went away. Will's head was resting on the steering wheel so she pulled on his shoulder to sit him up. Blood flowed down his face from a deep cut above his eyebrow. He moaned softly and fluttered his eyes.

"Oh God, Will." She sifted through the junk Uncle Dave kept in the glove box and pulled out a pile of napkins. Being as gentle as she could, she pressed on his head and tried to stop the bleeding. Her hands were soon drenched in his blood and she pushed up the sleeves of her sweater.

"Thanks," he said, watching her. "But I always thought angels of mercy had blonde hair," he said, his eyes twinkling. "And

I thought they'd be a lot cleaner too, look at you, you're a mess."

She shoved a clump of hair that had broken out of her ponytail behind her ear. "Bet you thought angels never popped anyone in the head either, huh?"

"I'm sure there's a rule somewhere."

"Wouldn't count on that." She took his hand to put it over the napkins. "Hold it for a second, I'm going to see what we have in the back."

He leaned his head on the seat and closed his eyes. "Don't be too long, you know how I hate to wait in the car."

She stared at him a moment, then smiled and jumped out of the truck. It had slid down the shoulder and was jammed against the guardrail. The snow was waist high on this side, where the wind was blowing it off the road. She waded to the back of the truck and used the tire to step into the bed.

Getting stuck in the snow was something that happened to the locals almost every year and Uncle Dave took pride in stock piling the truck with supplies. She unlocked the box and pulled out a gray wool blanket and the first aid kit. Iodine, bandages, tape, everything she needed, good. Her fingers were fast becoming numb with cold so she worked quickly to lift up the cans of gas and grab the snowshoes from the bottom. Uncle Dave had bought the second set of shoes shortly after she'd come to live with him. It had been important to him to get them right away, as if he wanted to make sure she knew their living arrangement was permanent. Her eyes welled up with tears as she stared at the shoes. Funny, that the first tears she shed for Uncle Dave would be over a pair of snowshoes.

She gathered up her things and went back to the cab.

"Wow, you're a handy girl to have around," Will said, seeing what she had.

"Don't you forget it." She patched up his cut as best she could and then put everything back in the kit.

Will inspected her work in the mirror. "Not bad, you might have a future here, Miss Nightingale, I wouldn't—"

The truck rumbled beneath them and Kate heard a soft explosion. She looked at Will whose face paled even more as he peered out the back window.

"What—what was that, Will?" She looked out the window behind her, but saw nothing but more snow. "Was that an avalanche?"

"I don't know, I've never heard one before," he said and began to button up his coat. "Let me out, I want to see."

She opened her door and he slid out after her. He climbed up the ditch and stood on the road, looking east, toward town.

"You wait here, I'll be right back."

"Yeah, you're funny," she said, and threw the blanket over her shoulders. "I think I've heard that in a movie once or twice."

After closing the door, she joined him on the road. Her feet sank in over a foot of snow.

Will narrowed his eyes and whistled softly. "Look at that," he said, pointing.

Rising up from the little valley where Newclare lay, was a huge plum of smoke. She couldn't see any of the buildings through the snow, but knew the area well enough to know that the smoke hovered directly above the town.

"What is that?" Her voice was hushed in the cold air.

He shook his head. "Couldn't tell you, it might just be a whirlwind, kicking up the snow." He walked further down the road. "I can't tell from here."

"Maybe we should circle around to get to your house," she said, watching the cloud rise in the air and begin to dissipate.

"That would take us miles out of the way, we'll freeze to death before then." Turning to her, she saw his eyes were small with worry. "We might anyway, here put this on." He took off his parka and took the blanket from her.

"What are you doing?"

He wrapped the blanket around himself. "We're going to have to walk into town and I won't make it if I have to carry you, so put it on."

She stared at the green parka for a moment and then reluctantly slipped it on. It covered her hands and hung nearly to her knees.

"Good, now I'm going to get the snow shoes and then we'll get out of here."

He returned a few minutes later and after strapping on the shoes they were on their way. Despite the thick coat, Kate felt her cheeks and nose go numb almost immediately. Will's blanket was soon white with snow and he fought to keep it closed against the rushing wind. She urged her feet to hurry even as her mind asked her what she was hurrying to. They rounded a bend and could no longer see the town, but the question weighed heavy between them. There was a whirlwind down there maybe, but maybe not the natural kind.

They crossed the bridge and Kate stopped for a moment, overwhelmed by the beauty of the scene before her. The creek was covered in snow and the trees were white drooping shapes that hung low over the channel. The trees met in the middle and cast the creek in a tunnel of almost complete darkness. A flash of lightening lit the sky above the bridge and she heard thunder only a second later. She ran to catch up with Will.

"Is that a sign?" Will was pointing to a shape on the side of the road. It was covered in snow, so he ran to wipe it clear.

Newclare, one mile.

Kate gave him a nervous smile.

"Hey," he said, giving her a quick hug. "It's going to be okay, you hear me? Whatever happens, we'll be together and that's the way it'll be from now on, right?" His words came out slurred because of his numbed lips.

"Yeah."

"Then let's go find my grandma. I bet she knows a little more than what she told you." He took her hand and they walked into town.

The smell of smoke hit her first. Before the screaming and shouting, and before the alarms. The smoke was strong and it stung her eyes. They turned down Main Street and stopped.

Several cars blocked the road, covered up to the bumpers in snow and the traffic light which hung above the intersection was draped across one of the cars, its red light still flashing. Will and Kate stepped over the wire and continued up the street. Buildings on either side had alarms blaring and windows broken out. She could see at least two farther down that were on fire. Only the burned out shell of Olan's Automotive had been left, untouched.

And faintly, barely audible above the alarms, was the sound of shouts and screams. Far, far in the distance, but Kate knew what they were all the same.

"Keep moving." Will shoved her in the back, forcing her to run in the deep snow.

Another block into town found them across from Mr. O'Neil's house. He was in the yard, wearing his bathrobe and covered in snow and paint. He held his paintbrush up to the sky and was doing a little dance. His mouth was stretched in a wide smile and she could almost hear the tune he was humming. Two limping steps to the left, one to the right, a half circle away from them. He waved his paintbrush in the air above him and Kate took a step back. That was no paintbrush. It was a garden trowel and the red that covered it and Mr. O'Neil was not paint. He turned again and his black eyes landed on Kate.

"My roses are safe," he yelled in a joyous voice and raised both of his blood–stained arms in victory.

Will smiled sickly and nodded at him, yanking Kate down the sidewalk. She watched as they hurried away and saw Mr. O'Neil go back to his dance. She watched him until he disappeared in the thick, white snow and was gone.

Chamberlain's was coming up on the right. Its roof was gone. Some of it was scattered in the street and some of it hung off of the buildings on either side. Ashes swirled in the air and the smoke was strong from the fire that still burned inside.

As Will and Kate passed, they saw movement inside the blown out windows. Dark, fuzzy shapes that darted around the store with startling speed. She heard a woman shriek with rage and a thunderous crash that ended with another shriek.

"We'll cut through the alley on the other side of your uncle's store and then head for my house." His voice was too loud and she saw somewhere deep inside, he was screaming. Screaming and begging to be let out of this nightmare. His lips were blue with cold and his chin shook so that she could barely understand him. A tiny spot of blood had seeped through the bandage on his head.

"I'm going to run in and get you a coat," she said. They passed the Hudsons' overturned pinto and she stopped in front of the store to untie the snowshoes.

"Okay." He started to open the door, but she shook her head.

"No, I want to go in alone, please." The empty eyes of her uncle flashed in her head and she steadied herself on the door handle. After a moment, she opened her eyes and looked up at Will. With relief, she saw the understanding she needed.

He nodded. "Okay, I'll wait out here for you, if you're sure."

"I'm sure. I'll be right back," she said and gave him a quick kiss on the cheek that made his mouth relax. He held the door open for her and she stepped inside.

It was much warmer in the store and her hands and face burned in the heat for a moment. The air was stale and heavy with the scent of perfumed flowers. She turned her mind from thoughts of flowers and continued into the store, toward the counter where Uncle Dave usually threw his coat when he came home. There were no lights on and the gloom outside had turned the store into a tomb. At least it was a festive tomb. The streamers hung across the ceiling like a celebration for the dead and the balloons, having fallen off the walls, spread before her in a sea of color. *Hey guys, the party's in here, who brought the maggots?*

She stopped and ground her fists into her eyes. Enough. Just get the coat and get back to Will.

She didn't want to get any closer to the kitchen than she had to so she reached over the counter and rooted around on the shelf for his coat. Nothing. Lifting off of her feet, she slid on her stomach onto the counter and felt again. She drew her hand back quickly and jumped away from the counter.

That was hair. Oh God, that was hair. There was hair under the counter. Silky, thick hair with just a hint of wave. Her chest tightened and her short breaths whistled in her ears. Why was there hair under the counter and why was she still standing here, thinking about it?

She took three steps to the door when she stopped. Will had been through enough today. And whatever was under the counter wasn't moving. She looked back, undecided. He needed the coat. He was freezing to death out there and besides, she wasn't going anywhere until she found out what was under there.

With a confidence that surprised her, she walked around the counter.

Huddled under the cash register, her blonde curls' partially covering her face was a little girl. She leaned against something furry with her knees pulled to her chin and her head resting on one shoulder. Her bruised mouth worked anxiously, trying to speak and then biting down on the lip. Tear stains streaked her cheeks and her eyes were closed in an exhausted, but restless sleep.

Kate took her by the shoulders and shook her gently. The little girl opened her eyes and jerked away.

"Shhh, it's okay, don't be afraid." She brushed the hair from the girl's face and gasped. "Emily? Oh honey, what are you doing here?"

Emily recognized her and immediately burst into hysterical sobs. "Oh Kaitlin, I'm so glad I found you, I didn't know where to go, I'm sorry, I'm sorry," she wailed and collapsed in Kate's arms. "I was so scared and I ran and ran, but nobody was here and I didn't know what to do."

She held the little girl, stroking her hair and rocking her

gently. Movement under the counter made her look to see the furry thing Emily had been resting on.

It was Winnie. Oh no, she'd forgotten all about poor Winnie, all alone for so long. She reached to bring her out and the dog let out a low growl.

"Hey, it's okay," Kate said. "Come here girl."

Winnie staggered to her feet and limped out from under the counter. Kate gasped as the low light fell on the dog.

In the last twenty–four hours she'd lost most of her body weight and developed a list that was usually reserved for animals ten times her age. And her little face. Kate brushed the matted fur from Winnie's eyes and fought back a scream that rose in her throat. Her shiny black eyes had turned the color of dirty ashes and the tender skin around them was swollen and raw. She looked up at Kate with quiet acceptance and then mercifully closed her eyes.

"Just calm down and tell me what happened," Kate said turning away, not understanding Winnie, and not wanting to understand Winnie. "It's okay now sweetie, just tell me what happened."

Emily sat up, still holding Kate as she took a hitching breath. "My–my momma. There's something wrong with mamma." She swiped her nose with the sleeve of her black princess coat. "I don't know what happened, but she got so mad at me and she was yelling and saying horrible things and then and then," she lost her breath and dissolved in a fit of sobs. "She–she started hit–hitting me and I got so scared, so I just ran and I didn't know where to go and so I came here, but there was nobody here so I hid and oh, I'm so glad you're here Kaitlin, I was so scared."

"You're okay now, honey," Kate said, holding her tightly. Emily buried her face in her neck.

"It's better now that you're here." She drew back and looked up at the ceiling. "Are you guys having a party or something? Because I—" Her eyes widened into saucers and her face paled a shade.

"What? What's wrong?" Kate followed her fixed stare and turned around.

Ben Easley stood behind them at the end of the counter.

His face was pink with excitement and his naturally curly hair, which he usually kept tame with gel, was tossed crazily about his head. He wore an orange parka, zipped to his chest and brown combat boots. The front of the parka was splattered with blood, as were the cuffs above his thoroughly washed hands. And his eyes...his eyes were the color of night.

"Hey kitty–cat."

CHAPTER SEVENTEEN
SEEKING SHELTER

Kate pushed Emily under the counter and stood, facing Ben.

"What are you doing here?" She asked with more defiance than she felt.

He smiled and his tongue slithered over his teeth. "Well, I thought maybe we could party together, but from the looks of what I found in the kitchen, I'm thinkin' you started without me."

A furious burst of anger ricocheted through her head. She glanced down at Emily who was sucking on her knuckle and rocking back and forth. Her eyes had filled with fresh tears as she stared up at Kate. This was too much. Kate looked back at Ben. Just too much.

"We can get rid of the kid and have some real fun," he said, taking a step toward her. "We got interrupted last time."

"Why would you think I'd want to do anything with you?" She took a step away from him.

He grinned and looked down at Winnie, who had never made it back under the counter. Ben glanced up at Kate and kept his black eyes on her, as he brought his steel–toed boot down on Winnie's neck. It snapped like a pencil.

Oh…can't breathe, I can't breathe…Winnie…

"Well if that's the way you want it, I think I'll like it better if you fight." He kicked Winnie's lifeless body under the counter where it hit Emily in the legs. The little girl screamed. "You should really clean up around here Katie," he said, taking another step toward her. "It can't be good for business."

She reached behind her and ripped the gun out of her jeans. She pointed it directly at his chest.

Ben looked at the gun and the smile fell from his face.

"You…stay…away," she said in a gravely voice. Her blurred vision kept falling to the dead dog at her feet and she fought to stay focused on Ben. She raised the gun to his head and then back to his chest.

"Well, this is just getting better and better," Ben said and leaned against the counter. His smile had returned.

Kate blinked her eyes again and nudged Emily with her foot. "Emily honey, go get Will, he's right outside and then you stay out there, okay?"

Emily nodded and crawled out from under the counter. Ben blocked the only way out, so she stepped up on a shelf to climb over the counter when her foot slipped and she started to fall. Kate caught her by the back of her coat and helped her up, just as Ben shouted and ran toward them. He grabbed at Emily, but Kate shoved him away. Emily had been thrown off balance though and teetered on top of the counter for a split second before she fell, on her back, on the cement floor.

"Emily!" Kate reached for her as Ben ripped the gun out of her hand and pushed her into the corner where the counter met the wall.

"Now," he breathed in her ear. "This is more like it, we're going have some fun."

She struggled against him, but he shoved her harder into the counter. She felt the edge dig into her back. "Get off me," she shouted, bucking and kicking at him. "I'm going to kill you, you sick son of a bitch."

Ben thought about it for a second and looked down at the blood on his parka. "You know, that's the same thing my mother said." He wagged a thick finger in her face, the insane smile on his lips and nothing but death and murder in his eyes. "Have you two been talking?"

"Shit," she muttered and glanced at the door. "Wi—"

He slammed a heavy hand over her mouth. "No, no sweet kitty. That would spoil all the fun now wouldn't it?"

The bell above the door jingled and Ben looked up, bringing the gun around to point it at the front of the store and loosening his grip slightly. He pulled off one shot that flew wild into the ceiling because Kate bit his other hand and shoved with all her strength. He let out a tiny yelp and backed away, giving her the chance to clasp her hands together and strike him square in the jaw. He took a few more stumbling steps backwards and fell.

She scooted over the counter, pushing the cash register onto Ben just as he started to get up. It landed on his shoulder and head and Kate heard him moan once before he fell back and was silent.

She leaned over the counter and saw his eyes were closed. His hand relaxed and the gun fell to the floor. Then she looked at Will standing by the door. His face was pale and one hand still held the door handle.

"You just let me know next time you need some rescuing," he said in a shaky voice. "'Cause you know, I'm your man." He threw the blanket on the floor and walked toward her. "Do I have, 'shoot at me' written on my forehead today? Because I swear—"

"Come on, we have to help Emily." Kate fell to her knees and gathered the girl's head in her lap. When she pulled her hand away and she looked in horror at the blood that covered it.

"Oh man," Will said. He rushed over and stood above them. "What happened?"

"She fell. Go get some towels from the kitchen, get one of them wet," she said, waving toward the kitchen. He left and returned a few seconds later with the towels, his face a shade whiter. He had seen the kitchen table.

She wiped the blood away and was relived to see the tiny cut that had caused so much blood. Pressing on it, the blood slowed and eventually stopped. Emily's eyes fluttered open and Will helped her sit up.

"You okay? Can you stand?" He pulled her to her feet, but didn't let go of her.

She swayed and leaned against him. "Don't feel good," she said into his chest.

Ben moaned behind the counter and Kate met Will's worried eyes.

"Okay honey, we have to go." He scooped her up and

headed for the door.

"Hold on," Kate said and went around to get Uncle Dave's coat. She looked down at Ben for a second and then picked up the gun. He groaned and moved a little under the register.

"Come on," Will said, starting for the door.

She looked again at Ben. Then she looked at Winnie. Only her paw could be seen from under the counter. She looked back at Ben and brought her foot down into his side where it connected with a satisfying thud. She brought it back again when she felt Will's hand on her shoulder.

"Time to go," he said.

She nodded and followed him to the door.

"Give me that thing," Will said holding out his hand. She dropped the gun in it and handed him the coat, taking Emily so he could put it on. The air outside was shockingly cold and the snow stung her face. Will began to lace up his snowshoes when Kate tapped him on the shoulder.

"Unless of course, you would rather walk," she said and pointed to the snowmobile parked by the side of the building.

"Small favors," Will muttered, taking the key from Kate and starting it up. After settling behind Will on the seat, she put Emily on her lap and they headed down the alley.

The ride was long with the wind blowing against them. Kate kept her head down and leaned into it, grateful for the big hood on Will's parka. They left the chaos of the town behind, though the deceivingly serene peace of the forest was unsettling. It was as if the trees held their breath for the events to play themselves out. As if it had all been told again and again and whatever course she took would lead her to the same place. A force stronger than she permitted her to wonder occasionally but always guided her back.

"Almost there," Will called back to her. She squeezed his arm in return.

There was work to do before the day was done. And when it was over she would be gone. She knew that now. Even as she sat on the back of her dead uncle's snowmobile with a child on her lap and a man she didn't know at the wheel, she slipped further away. Shedding the last semblance of a lost childhood and the sweet comfort of innocence. What would be left? If she could see through this day. If only she could see through this day.

Will slowed and came to a stop. "Kate, look at this."

She peered around his shoulder and her breath stopped.

His house was still there. Thankfully, his house was still there and at first, Kate didn't understand the fear in Will's voice. It wasn't on fire or broken into in any way. And then she saw she was wrong about that. Every window in the house was broken and the shards of glass were scattered over the yard. But...but the glass was on the outside of the house, as if the windows had been broken from the inside. Shaking her head, Kate turned toward the garage. Only the jeep sat in the driveway, since his parents had taken the car.

But the driveway...she could see the driveway...and she could see the glass in the yard, because in spite of the miles and miles of two and three feet high snow they had passed through today, Will's house and the area around it...was cleared of snow.

Kate got off the snowmobile and handed Emily to Will. She stepped off the bank of snow that surrounded the house and onto the dead brown grass that was the yard. The roof, the porch, the tree that hung over the house, all were dark with wetness, but without a speck of snow. She crouched down and felt the grass.

"It's warm." She turned to Will.

He stood behind her, holding Emily and staring at his house, hurt and fear shading his eyes. He raked his fingers through his hair and glanced back at the snowmobile, then back at his house.

"All right, all right," he said, starting for the porch. "So we go in."

The house was dark and Kate knew before Will flipped the switch that the power was out. As her eyes became adjusted to the light, she saw the overturned table in the middle of the kitchen.

Dishes had been pulled from the cupboards and were thrown on the floor and the refrigerator laid on its side, blocking the entry to the living room. Will strode through the kitchen, kicked aside one of the chairs and climbed over the refrigerator.

"Hello?" He called and waited a moment. No answer.

Laying Emily on the couch, he surveyed the damage to the living room. Lamps, tables, books were strewn all over. The television had a large hole in the screen and was resting on its side in the corner. But there was more, much more wrong with the room that skidded around her mind until she realized what it was. It was the ceiling. It sloped in the middle and if Will reached up he could have easily touched it with his hand.

"Will..." They both heard the voice and Will pushed past her to his grandmother's room down the hall.

Kate stood in the doorway as Will kneeled on the floor beside his grandmother. She was lying on the floor with her nightgown hitched up to her bony thighs. Will pulled it down and yanked the afghan from her bed to cover her body. His grandmother's eyes were closed and her chest moved only slightly with each breath.

Kate stuffed a pillow under her head and tried to hide her shock. Covering his grandmother's forehead and eyes, down to her cheekbones and across to each ear was a network of thick, blue veins. They pulsed and throbbed like tentacles grabbing her face. Kate was afraid to move her too much because the thin layer of skin that covered the veins looked like it could easily break.

"Will," she said again in a voice that was faint and hoarse. "You're here, my boy...I've been waiting for you." She opened her eyes and Kate jumped back. The whites of her eyes were blood red, but the irises glowed with brilliant colors. Just as in the garden, they spun and danced with life and energy.

His grandmother took Will's hand and squeezed with feeble strength. "It's good that you're here boy, where's your Kaitlin?"

Kate took her other hand. "I'm here Mrs. Harrickson."

"What happened Grams?" Will asked gently.

Dark Legacy

His grandmother brought Kate and Will's hands together on her stomach and patted them softly. "He was here, child." She shifted her dazzling eyes to Kate. "In this house, with his black madness and his dirty smell. He came to me and whispered his evil; he played his games and told his lies. He tried to take it. He did everything he could to take it, but I wouldn't let him," she said with a little smile. "I felt my mind slipping and buckling, but I held on and I stayed strong until he tired. And oh, did that anger him. He went into a rage and stormed the house before he left in a wind as black as night." Her voice gave out to a whisper and her eyes closed.

"Grams?" Will squeezed her hand and looked up at Kate. "Grams—"

"Shhh, boy, I'm not gone yet." She smiled and went on. "I've this to tell the both of you. He can be stopped. I was wrong before Kaitlin, what I told you. Wrong and scared, but I'm not anymore. The evil that walks the earth can be stopped and I reckon you and Will are to be his downfall. He doesn't know it yet and that's to your advantage because there is a power, a power that is greater than his and it lives in the two of you. This power burns in pure white fire and in its vapors is everything good and true. It's the fire that holds the balance, you remember Kaitlin, about the balance?"

She nodded.

"Good. Don't forget, don't ever forget. Because he wants that fire. The power in the fire to add to his own. This is his savage attempt to correct the mistake so many years ago. You cannot let him have it, you must face him and you must win. He cannot be allowed to live again and now you must stop him."

Her voice was fueled with sudden strength and Kate saw the colors in her eyes fly like sparks from a pan of cooking bacon.

"But how?" Kate asked, looking up at Will but his face reflected her own confusion. "How do we stop him?"

His grandmother closed her eyes and took a wheezing breath. "There is something, something I was a fool not to tell you before. A book. The journal that belonged to that madman. It has been passed through the generations, along with the story. Now I don't know what's in the book, it's written in a language our family lost a long time back, but it's the only link you have." She turned toward the closet in the corner of the room. "And it was here, right under his nose," she smiled, one of sneaking pride.

Will rose to his feet and rummaged in the closet until he found a small, leather–bound book on the top shelf. He returned to his grandmother's side and dropped the book in Kate's lap.

Kate opened it and flipped through the pages. They were yellowed and frayed at the edges and tore easily as she turned them. Faded words and symbols covered the sheets, carefully crammed together and running from one side to the other with no margins. She shut the book with a sigh. It would take her a year of study to decipher the thing.

"Now I know what you're thinking, but that's no matter. What matters is that you have it. And you do with it what you can. You *use* it how you can," his grandmother said. "I wish I had more, but it's all I can offer. You take your chance and you do your best, but if it turns sour, you run like the dickens and you don't look back. The both of you. You hear?"

They nodded and she patted their hands again.

"It's good to've seen you grown, Will. Your grandpa would be proud. I'll give him a hug from you…when I see him…" Her words faded away. Her breathing slowed until Kate heard a clicking in her chest and then…nothing.

She looked at Will and saw his face harden to stone. A glaze spread over his eyes and his lips disappeared. She reached for his arm and he shied away.

"We gotta go," he said and left the room.

She turned back to his grandmother. Her eyes were closed and the veins on her face were fading. A tiny smile touched her mouth. "Thank you," she whispered and pulled the afghan over her head.

Dark Legacy

Will pulled the snowmobile onto Main Street and slowed to a crawl. The town was eerily quiet in the light snow that had started again. A single car alarm blared in the distance and the wind had calmed to barely a breeze. Chamberlain's was empty, though no tracks could be seen to show anyone had left. Will stopped in front of her uncle's store.

"You see anything?" He cupped his hands to peer inside.

Kate did the same and shook her head. "No, but I think the back door's open."

They leaned back and Will drove past the windows, toward the alley. "Let's get warm and then we can take a look—"

His last words were lost as the snowmobile was knocked over and they fell, headfirst into cold. She pushed herself up, coughing and sputtering and groping for Emily who had disappeared into the powdery whiteness. Kate felt the girl's coat and had clasped hands with her before a hand from behind clamped down on her upper arm and yanked her out. She struggled to her feet then fell again as she tripped over a rock, hidden in the snow. The hand grabbed the back of her hair, lifted her up and pulled back, baring her neck to the dark sky above. The cold steel of a knife was placed below her jawbone.

"Kate!"

Will leapt forward as she felt the serrated edge of the knife slide into the top layer of her skin. Warmness flowed instantly down her neck.

"Not so fast, lover boy."

Ben.

"Let her go, now," Will said, eyeing the alley behind her. She heard Ricky's familiar snort and turned slightly to see more of Ben's gang forming a half circle around them. Using her free hand, she pulled the switchblade out of the back of her jeans. Slowly, slowly, she lifted the blade out of its case and turned it

293

in her hand. And waited.

"I'll give her back when I'm done, I promise," Ben said in a mock attempt to sound reasonable. "But you know, it may be a while."

Emily crawled out of the snow and looked up in a daze at Kate. She took in the scene for a moment and then fixed on the knife at Kate's throat. Her mouth opened and the still air was shattered by piercing screams as Emily let go in a fit of terror.

Will flicked the little girl a glance and then looked back at Kate. Something was breaking inside him. Something was ripping apart the confidence and sensibility on which he based his life. It glowed sickly on his face...and in his eyes and suddenly Kate felt more afraid for Will than she did for herself.

"I said, let her go." The words were savage and Kate felt Ben hesitate before remembering *he* had the knife. His grip tightened around Kate's body and the knife slid farther down her neck. He began to walk backwards, pulling Kate along with him.

"And I said, you can have her when I'm done...if there's anything left." He stumbled on the rock and let go of her arm to catch his balance. Kate shoved her knife into his side and pushed away. She heard his scream, but never saw his fist coming until it exploded into the side of her head. She went down on her knees and then to her hands. The white snow in front of her turned an ugly gray color before she fell into it.

She landed on the side of her face and fought the fuzzy feeling that went with the throbbing in her head. Ben. Ben was still here...somewhere. Opening one eye, she stared into his red face, high above her as he hefted the massive rock over her head and prepared to drop it. Her eye closed.

BANG!

The shot ripped through the air and hung over her like a bad smell. The wind stopped, the snowflakes hovered above the ground, undecided. Emily's screams were cut off in mid–breath. She counted her heartbeats and listened to the wheezing of her lungs. Then...many, many heartbeats later...a tremendous thud shook the earth beneath her. It rumbled for a moment then all was still.

Emily's voice rose again in a shriek that seared Kate's aching head. She pushed up on her hands and looked up in confusion at Ben, who still stood, the rock forgotten in his hands as he blinked through the steady stream of blood that flowed from his head. His hands lowered and Kate scooted away as he let the rock fall to the ground. He touched his head where the bullet had grazed it, and a puzzled look came over his face when he brought his hand down and stared at the blood.

As her mind cleared, the world seemed to speed up, rushing along and dragging her in it's current.

Will lowered the gun and took a step back, his face a tight mask of horror. He opened and shut his eyes several times as he looked at Ben and then at the body in the snow, then at Kate. The black was fading, but was still visible above the colors in Will's eyes.

It was slowly sinking into the rest of Ben's gang as they stared down at Ricky's body. Then they turned to Will and Kate with faces that changed from hatred to murderous and bloody. Lips that curled and sneered, black eyes that narrowed with vengeance.

"Kate!" Will shouted.

She jumped to her feet and started to run, but stopped as she spotted something half buried in the snow.

"Will, the book!" It lay in a drift a few feet from the snowmobile, its pages open and blowing in the wind.

"Leave it, come on!" Will jammed the key in the ignition as Kate dragged the screaming Emily back onto her lap. He turned it, but nothing happened. Again and again, as Ben turned his head and finally saw them, desperately trying to get away. He motioned to his friends and they started to run. Will cranked it one more time and it started.

"Go, go, go," Kate yelled in his ear.

The snowmobile skidded away, leaving Ben and his gang

in a cloud of snow. Will raced down the street and to the other side of town. The speed was terrifying as they soared past the parked cars and buildings. Kate leaned close to Will, peering over his shoulder and hanging on as best she could.

"Whoa, hold on," Will said as he came up on the turn for Kerry County Road. Three overturned cars blocked the road with a ripped fence lying across them. He made a sharp left.

"Where are you going?" She asked as they left town and headed down the deserted road.

He didn't answer and just as she began to think he had no idea, a building appeared out of the haze. Drifts of snow piled high against the red brick, reaching the lower windows. Will shut off the snowmobile.

"Let's see if there's a way in," Will said swinging his leg over and starting for the door.

"You're going to break into the church?"

Will set Emily to her feet and told her to walk. As he turned back to Kate, the dressing on his forehead flopped open and he tore it off. "I thought I might try the door first." He threw the bandage aside and walked up to the church, not waiting for her response.

Kate wrapped the coat around her blood–covered neck and trudged through the snow to Will. He banged on the door once and was lifting his fist again, when it opened.

The man who held it for them had the kindest face she had ever seen and even though she stood in two feet of snow, she felt instantly warmed.

"Get on in here and out of that cold," the man said, ushering them inside. "You 'bout going to catch your death."

Will led Emily past him and into the foyer. He stomped off his shoes and patted Emily down, trying to shake some of the snow from her clothes.

"Come on, in you go," he said to Kate who still stood by the door. He flashed her a set of large white teeth and put a gentle hand on her back. "That's a bitter wind out there."

He closed the door and picked up a candle from the shelf behind it. "I's starting to think maybe God Himself was beating on our roof. Never heard a wind so loud."

Kate walked through the foyer and into the dim sanctuary. Candles had been placed on ledges by several of the windows and an oil lamp sat on the pulpit. Christ's Church of Newclare served all of the town's residents, Baptist, Lutheran, even a few grumpy Catholic's. She and Joey had visited the church a few times growing up, usually when their mother felt the need to cleanse her soul after a wild Saturday night. Kate had never listened to the long, boring sermons, but always perked up when it was time to sing. She loved the way the voices rose in unison reverberating off of the gigantic stained–glass window of Jesus holding a lamb above the pulpit. The window had always held her attention. No matter where she sat in the congregation, the glassy eyes of Jesus seemed to be on her, but instead of making her nervous, it comforted her in a vague way. His eyes were the same, every time she saw them.

She moved further into the sanctuary and saw several of the townspeople gathered in the pews.

Miss Shea sat next to Rosie Parker who slumped over the pew with her head to the side. The left side of her body looked charred and her shirt was ripped at the neck. Her teacher talked softly in Rosie's ear, but the girl gave her no response.

Adam O'Mally sat under the window. Kate had only seen him once or twice since she had come back to town. He dropped out of school a few years back and was working at Chamberlain's. She always thought he had the nicest smile, one that reached his eyes and spilled into his words when he spoke.

He wasn't smiling now though. She could only see a portion of his dirty face, as he leaned against the wall with his chin resting on his knees, but it was enough. Soot covered his entire body and the hair on the left side of his head had been burned off.

In the pew across from Adam, Mrs. McGrath sat with

Raymond Kerrisk, Ricky's dad. The two didn't appear to be speaking. Mrs. McGrath's head was down and when she looked closer, Kate saw she had a rosary in her hand. Her mouth worked silently.

Mr. Richards, still in his grocers smock, sat in the far corner, by the kitchen, smoking a cigarette. Or at least he was trying to smoke a cigarette. The ash was long, as if he'd only been staring at it.

Kate took in the sad little group and shook her head. They all had the same vacant eyes, the same stunned faces.

Mrs. McGrath saw them come in and hurried to give Kate a quick hug. "My dear, you look exhausted. But it's good that you're here."

Kate gave her a thin smile.

"Well, who is this?" She asked, directing her attention to Emily, who stood slightly behind Will, sucking on her knuckle. "You're Judy Whitemore's little girl aren't you, I'd know those blonde curls anywhere." Mrs. McGrath crouched down to her eye level and fingered one of Emily's limp, wet locks. "My, you're just a little ice cube," she said, taking Emily's free hand. "I bet I know just what will warm up those bones. We have some hot chocolate in the back, do you want some?"

Emily glanced up at Will who patted her on the head and nodded. She turned back to Mrs. McGrath. "Do you have any marshmallows?"

"I bet we do, you want to help me look?" She asked, holding out her hand. Emily took it and let Mrs. McGrath lead her to the kitchen behind the baptismal.

Will came up behind her, putting his hand on her shoulder, as the man held out his hand. "Name's Jacob Benning. I'm the one who keeps things running around here, guess you'd could call me the resident handyman."

Will took his hand and shook it once. "Will," he said. "And this is Kate."

"Nice to meet you."

Jacob led them down the aisle and leaned on the back of a pew while Kate and Will sat down.

"I came up here last night to wait out the storm. My place's breezy as a cardboard box these days. Figured this as good a place as any to freeze my tail off, might as well be in good company." He set the candle down beside him and Kate saw his hand shake. "Mrs. McGrath was the first to come. She blew in here like a whirlwind all in a mess about her husband. Seems breakfast came out burned and he came after her with the hacksaw." Jacob shook his head. "Right around that time was when Chamberlain's went up." He nodded to the boarded up window beside them. "Broke one of the windows and almost knocked Ol' Bessy off her kilter. I had go down there and shut her off 'fore she exploded."

They all looked up as Mr. Kerrisk stood and began to pace at the front of the church. "He got here just before you all. Face white as a sheet. He woke up this morning and heard his son, Ricky, going crazy in his bedroom. Throwing stuff around and screaming like crazy. He tried to calm him down, but got hit in the gut for his efforts. After Ricky run off, he went into town and had some kind of bad business at the police station. He wouldn't say what. Then he came here."

He lowered his voice and spoke in the tone of a man who had seen and heard these things, but didn't quite believe them. "There's a bad wind blowing here in Newclare. Don't know if I understand the half of it." He shook his head again. "Heck of a time for Reverend Bishop to be down in Quarryville, bingo–ing with the old folks."

Will had been surveying the sanctuary and when he spoke his voice was on automatic. "What kind of supplies do you have? Flashlights, batteries, blankets."

"Just about anything you might want would be down in the basement, I'd assume," he said nodding toward a door to the right. "Bring up a couple more lamps while you're at it. We could use the light."

Will left, walking in a stiff, awkward gait that hurt Kate to see.

Jacob watched Will until he disappeared through the door and then turned back to Kate. His chocolate–brown eyes widened as he really saw her for the first time. "You're just soaked straight through. Come on, I got a blanket in the back." He peeled off her coat and his eyes widened even more. She was confused for a moment and then remembered the cut on her neck. Pulling away, she tried to cover it with her hands. He looked down at her with a sad smile, a hundred questions bursting in his eyes. "I'll be right back."

After grabbing a blanket from a closet in the foyer, he led her to a pew in the front row. "I kept this out handy, thought I might have a use for it," he said, pulling a box from behind the pulpit. From it, he pulled out tape, some gauze and a pair of scissors. With a tenderness that surprised her, he cleaned the blood from her neck and taped it up. When it was done, he wrapped her in the blanket and sat down.

She stared up at the window above the pulpit. The gray skies outside had turned the panes dark, somber colors but again, the eyes…the eyes were the same.

"Amazing, isn't it?"

"What?"

"His face. I ain't never seen a picture that had so much love in His face. Don't know how they did it, but somehow, just looking at it, it makes me feel like everything going work out all right."

Staring up at the window, a tear slipped down her face. "Not everything."

He took her hand in his. "Don't want to hear none of that talk. No matter what's been happening, or what's to come, He's up there, lookin' out for us. And when it's time, but only in His *own* time, He's going to put an end to it. You just gotta have faith, you got to believe."

She looked down and saw how pale she was against his

rich, dark skin. Another tear splashed the top of his hand. "Maybe for you, but you don't know what I've done," she whispered.

"You right, I don't, but He does and He still lookin' down on you with all that love." His voice shook with emotion. "He's in you, you just gotta let Him out. Cause when you do, you can feel it. Just like a fire, eating up all the bad, 'cause the fire, it burns pure and then sets you free."

Kate's thoughts turned to someone else who had spoken of the fire that day. Had it only been this morning? It was already becoming vague in her mind. She was tired. So tired and the weight of it seeped all the way through to her bones. Her eyes closed briefly and then shot open as Emily returned with her hot chocolate.

"Look Kaitlin, we made one for you," Emily pointed to the cup Mrs. McGrath held. "And there's lots of marshmallows in it."

Kate smiled. "Thank you, I think that's just what I need right now."

Emily sat beside her and the two of them drank the hot chocolate while Jacob went to speak with Mr. Kerrisk and tried to get him to sit down.

"Where's Will?" Asked Emily, a hint of worry darkening her eyes.

"He just went to get some more—"

Her words were cut off as a strange whistling noise rose from outside. Later she realized she couldn't have possibly heard the rock that broke the stained–glass picture of Jesus. Yet she did, because she looked up in time to watch it shatter.

Chapter Eighteen
The Bells

Several others joined Emily's scream as a split second later another rock, the size of a baseball was thrown through the window on their left.

"Get down!" Jacob shouted and Kate threw herself over Emily, dragging them both to the floor. Their mugs of hot chocolate shattered, as she shoved Emily under the pew and then crowded in beside her, holding her tightly. Emily had stopped screaming, but shook uncontrollably, her face blazing with the terror she'd carried with her all day. Kate covered her face and jerked as more rocks landed above them. Glass flew everywhere and suddenly she smelled smoke.

"Kate!" That was Will's voice.

She pried Emily's arms from around her neck to look toward the back of the church.

Will and Adam were stomping on something that burned in the middle aisle and Jacob was running toward them with a blanket over his face to shield himself against the flying glass. As he reached the boys, he threw the blanket on the fire, extinguishing the last of the flame.

Kate turned back to Emily. "You stay here, no matter what, don't move until I come and get you, do you understand?"

Emily nodded mutely and shut her eyes.

In a hunched run, Kate joined them behind a pew. Adam crawled to the end of the aisle and strained to see outside. She heard angry voices and shouts, but couldn't distinguish any of the words. Then Ben's shout rose above all the others.

"Throw out the bitch and the killer and we'll leave you alone."

Will and Kate met eyes and then ducked as another volley of rocks came through the window.

"Friends of yours?" Adam asked, covering his head with his hands.

A liquor bottle came flying through the window with a piece of newspaper shoved inside. The flame didn't catch though and the liquid poured out harmlessly, wetting the carpet.

"We gotta board up that window," Jacob said, crawling toward the toolbox under the window he boarded up earlier. "Ain't got no wood left though."

He glanced around the sanctuary and then at Will. Will nodded and the two of them stood simultaneously, brought up a foot and kicked out the back of the pew. It snapped with a loud pop and fell.

Emily screamed at the front of the church.

Kate ran to help Jacob pick up the splintered wood as Will worked on the next pew. A rock whizzed by her head on her way back to the broken window and she choked back a scream.

Jacob drove in nail after nail, dodging rocks and tearing up his hands on the chunks of wood. Once the windows were as covered as they could be, the three crawled to the others side of the church and worked on the rest. Nothing could be done about the high, stained–glass window above the pulpit.

A minute of silence went by. Then five.

"Are they gone?" Kate asked, peeking through a slit in the boards.

In answer to her question, a pounding sounded on the front door. Someone tried the handle and then cursed to find it locked.

"I'll be back asshole, you're goin' pay for killing Ricky." He threw one more kick at the door and then it was silent again.

Kate stood up and looked around. Glass was everywhere. On the pews, and all over the carpet. In her hair. She shook some of it out and only then did she see Mr. Kerrisk standing behind Will.

His face was pale and his body trembled with rage. And his eyes…oh no, his eyes…

"Will look out!"

He turned just in time for Mr. Kerrisk to hit him in the face. Will staggered back a few paces, but was able to block the next blow.

"You killed my boy! You son of a bitch, you're going to die for that, I'll make you beg for mercy, I'll—" Mr. Kerrisk's face went placid and then he slumped to the floor. Jacob stood behind him, a fire extinguisher in his hands.

Will rubbed his cheek. "Thanks."

"We'd better find something to rope him up with. Expect we'll only have more trouble with him when he come around."

"I saw some cord downstairs," Will said.

He returned a minute later with the cord and helped Jacob flip Mr. Kerrisk over on his stomach. When they finished, Will laid one of the blankets over him and sat down. Kate moved to sit next to him, when she heard a soft whimpering from the front of the church.

"Emily, oh no," she moaned. On swift feet, she made her way to the little girl, still huddled under the pew. Her eyes were closed and her fists were white at the knuckles. Kate touched her arm and she leapt back.

"Hey, it's okay now, you can come out."

Emily opened her eyes. "Is it over?"

How she wished it was. "Come here honey." Kate pulled her up to her lap on the seat and spread the blanket over them.

Emily wrapped her arms around Kate's waist and closed her eyes. "I want it to be over," she whispered in a tiny voice.

The weight of her warm body was comforting to Kate as she leaned her head against her shoulder and closed her eyes. "I know honey, so do I. So do I..."

* * * * *

"Nigger!"

Kate's eyes snapped open and she looked around.

"Ugly nigger dog, you stinkin' son of a whore..." On and

on it went as Kate picked up Emily who had awakened from her fitful sleep, crying the tears of an overly tired child. She met Miss Shea in the kitchen.

"I'll make her up a bed in the corner, she'll be fine," she said as Kate sat Emily at the table.

Kate returned to the sanctuary and found Jacob standing over the tied Mr. Kerrisk. Jacob's eyes were bright with pain, but she couldn't tell if he felt it for himself, or for the cursing man on the floor.

"His son's gone, he don't know what he's saying," Jacob said above the onslaught of shouts.

Kate picked up one of the blankets and ripped it with her teeth. "Well it doesn't mean we have to listen to him," she said.

"Hey, hey, what are you doing?" Mr. Kerrisk shouted as she came around behind him. "What are you, the nigger's whore? Get away from me, hey!"

He kicked at her but she managed to stay clear as she brought the strip of blanket over his mouth and tied it secure at the back of his neck. He growled and then was silent.

"Where's Will?" She asked, glancing around the sanctuary.

Mrs. McGrath was now huddled beside Rosie in the back pew and Mr. Richards was smoking a cigarette and staring blankly at the ceiling.

"I don't know, he's here a while ago. He's a good boy, Kate…just, thinks too much, you know?"

She smiled. "Yeah, I know."

"You go find 'em if you want, I'll keep Mr. Kerrisk company."

Mr. Kerrisk snarled and kicked at Jacob. He missed.

The foyer was empty, so she tried the door opposite the kitchen. It led to a short hallway that ended at the back door. She opened the door to the reverend's office and closed it quickly. The next door opened to a flight of stairs. She stood in the doorway for a moment, staring into the blackness.

Will is up there. She can feel him. But she can feel something else too. Something that flutters like—
(power of the two)
—a leaf spinning in the wind, but it slips away and suddenly she's hearing bells—
(what a tale of terror now, their turbulence tells...)
—ringing higher and higher—
(to the mercy of the fire...)
—until she throws her hands over her ears with a little shriek.
They are silent.
She opens her eyes. She wipes her palms on her jeans. She looks back up the stairs.
Will is up there. He is calling her. He needs her.
Her feet are on the stairs.

There was anger in the room and she felt it before she reached the top step. This was the bell tower, a perfectly square room with a sharply slanted ceiling that came to a point in the darkness high above. A bell, turned green over the years, hung in the center of the room, above a square hole that opened to the first floor. The monstrous bell was her height and was as wide as it was tall. She crept toward it and stood with her toes at the edge, looking down. A rope hung from the middle and disappeared into the blackness below.

She made her way around the bell, tracing her fingers around its frozen rim. There was a window on the opposite side and as she came out from behind the bell a cold breeze hit her face. A figure stood by the night–filled window, his back to her.

The floor creaked as she inched toward him, but he didn't move. He stood, stone still, staring out the window. Little clouds formed by his mouth with every shallow breath and firelight from the blazes in town danced on his twitching face. His hands grasped the sill, curling into fists and scraping the paint up under his nails.

Her hand hesitated above his back and then pulled away. "Will."

She didn't think he heard her and was about to speak again when his whisper floated by her ears.

"So much death, so much hate…emptiness…"

She moved to stand beside him and rested her hands on the sill, brushing away a dried up bird's nest. Its inhabitants were long gone on this stormy April night.

"How can we go on?" He continued in the voice of someone who had been screaming all day and now had no breath left. "Where is there to go from here? Here is nowhere, we're in the throes of nowhere and I can't even see anymore to get out. How did this happen…how did it come to this?"

Swallowing hard she put a hand on his back. It felt warm even before she touched it. "Will—"

"No," he said, jerking.

She backed away, from his eyes…from his eyes that were too dark, even in the shadows of the room.

"I can't see you I can't see anything, I'm so far down all I see is the pain and the hate and the rage I've become and *that* is the only thing that makes sense to me now."

"No, don't say that, this will end, it will be over and we'll—"

"NO!" He crossed in two powerful steps to grab her by the wrists. The blanket fell from her shoulders. "I've killed, don't you understand? I've killed someone, there is no *over* for me," he roared. "My hands are covered in his blood and that smell will never wash off. Whether or not we get through this. I'll live with the stink of what I've done for the rest of my life."

"But you can't blame yourself for that, you did what you…"

"I didn't! I didn't do it because I had to. I did it because I wanted to. And so help me God, but I wish I hadn't missed! I wanted Ben to die, I wanted to kill him because he touched you, because you let him!"

"You don't mean that," Kate cried, pulling out of his grip.

"No?" He asked, following her around the bell. "Well you're wrong, Katie. Just like you've been wrong about so many things."

The light from the emerging moon fell on his face and Kate let out a choked cry. The black was in his eyes, spinning in a gleeful little dance that left nothing at all of the Will she knew. And he was smiling at her.

"Now do you see, now do you understand? I *liked* it Kate. I *enjoyed* it Kate. And if I had the chance I'd do it again, only this time I wouldn't miss. This time I'd jump up and down on his bleeding body and I'd scream and laugh. The power, my God!"

He shoved the bell toward her, with a surprising surge of strength. She leapt away and felt its breeze on her face.

"The power is incredible. I've never felt anything like it. It races through my veins like burning lava, more intoxicating than anything I've ever experienced," he rambled on as Kate circled the bell again and made her slow way toward the stairs.

"I can do anything, be anything and take what I want without fear. Can you imagine that Kate? Can you?"

He saw her slinking toward an escape and jumped over the hole as the bell made an upward swing. Landing beside her, he yanked her away from the open stairwell.

His face was inches away from hers and his breath was hot on her lips. "Can you imagine the power in that feeling? The absolute invincibility, the utter greed. Everything I see is mine, for the taking," he finished and then pressed his mouth against hers. His kiss was demanding, his lips, hungry and eager to fill an emptiness that ached inside him. She pushed him away, but he grew only more insistent, raking his hands over her back.

She shoved again, taking him off balance and nearly throwing him down the stairs. "Stop it Will," she shouted, scrambling away. "What's wrong with you?"

He caught himself on the rail and turned, the smile still

twisting his face. "There's nothing wrong with me, Kate. Not anymore. For the first time in a long time...I feel great." He started walking toward her.

"Get away from me."

"No, I don't think so, Kate. Because the way I see it, we're in this together."

She shook her head. "What are you talking about?"

"Oh, come on." He jumped behind the bell, blocking her. "This, us, the whole fucked up mess. It's meant to be, you know? Preordained." He hopped up in the window and walked its length. The light from the fires gave him a red glow. "Why do you keep fighting it when it won't do any good?"

She shook her head again. "That's what he's waiting for. You have to keep fighting it Will, we both do, because he's waiting for us to give up. Can't you feel it?"

He jumped down from the window and landed in front of her. "Yeah, I can feel it, I can't feel anything else and that's just it, Kate. I don't *want* to fight it anymore."

His black eyes glittered down at her, as he took one step forward for each of hers back. She glanced behind her and saw the stairwell was only a few feet away.

"That's...that's just a stupid thing to say," she said inching closer.

"Oh, Kate. You disappoint me. I was sure you could come up with something better than that."

She glared up at him. "You're right, I can." Not wanting to chance another look, she took a shuffling step, feeling with her foot. The stairwell had to be close. "It's a stupidly pathetic thing to say that the Will I know would never have let come out of his mouth. You want to give up? Fine. But you're doing it alone, because I won't have any part of it. And I'm not going to stand here, listening to you, when all you want to do is try and scare me."

She turned to go downstairs when she felt his hand on her back. He pushed her off balance and then caught her sweater before she could fall down the stairs. Yanking her back, he threw her across the floor and she rolled off the edge of the hole under the bell. She screamed, catching a broken piece of board before tumbling over.

"I'm scaring you?" Will roared and grabbed her ankle. He pulled her away from the opening and Kate felt several splinters ram into her stomach as her sweater bunched under her arms. "Am I scaring poor little Katie?"

"*Get*! *Off*!" Her foot connected with his shoulder. He lost his grip on her ankle and Kate shot to her feet.

He chased her to the other side of the bell and pined her against the wall with his leg between hers. "You're mine, Kate. You always have been, no matter what you say. And I want what's mine."

His lips crushed hers and she couldn't breathe under the weight of his body. On and on he plunged into her mouth as his hands squeezed her arms until she felt her hands tingle. She squirmed and writhed in his iron hold, but Will wouldn't be stopped. He was gone now. Taken from her and thrown into the clutches of the evil that had waited for them their entire lives.

And suddenly she realized she was tired too. Tired of fighting something that would win in the end anyway. And tired of denying what was rightfully hers.

Will's body began to shake in violent waves that seemed to originate from somewhere, deep inside him. He slumped against her and when he rolled his face over hers, he wet her cheek.

"I can't see you Kate," he sobbed into her neck. "I–I can't feel you..."

She reached for him...trying to fill the ache that was pulling him away from her. When he tugged her sweater over her head, she didn't resist. And when she felt his bite on her collarbone, she didn't flinch away. He caught her wrists above her head and held them there, as he traced down her arm with his tongue. He brought her off the floor, crushing her in his maddened embrace. His lips dove into the darkness of her breasts and the roughness of his unshaved face chafed her skin. Then he was on his knees, fumbling with her jeans and tearing at the zipper in a frenzy of scathing kisses that burned across her stomach. The jeans tossed aside, he pressed into her, his hands kneading the soft flesh of her buttocks. His hot breath and rapacious mouth lit a fire that leapt through her body, leaving her weak and trembling. A cry rose up in her throat and she bit down hard on her lip, tasting the blood she drew. Now she fell and they were rolling and rolling until her back was on the blanket and she sunk further down, plummeting into the fire that consumed them both. And his hands, his furious hands were everywhere and where they missed yearned for his touch. He devoured her, molding her body to his, lifting her in waves of writhing desire. She opened herself to him, to his painful, throbbing lust and now she did cry out, as the tides of ecstasy grew too large to contain. On and on it went, rising and falling with each merciless thrust until the fire exploded, blazing everything in its path. She arched her back and felt the heat burst through her chest.

And when the flames subsided and dim light of the room came back into focus…there was Will…as there always had been Will, looking down at her, his body still quivering and shining with sweat. "I–I'm, are you…?"

She nodded and pulled him close.

They lay, intertwined in each other's arms, staring out at the dark night as a wolf howled in the distance.

And somewhere…the bells were silent.

* * * * *

"Get some rest, sweetie, things always look brighter on a full night's sleep," Miss Shea said as she pulled the blanket over Emily's chin.

Emily didn't want to get some rest, she wasn't tired, not anymore and she doubted anything would look brighter in the morning, whether or not she got a full night's sleep. Her eyes narrowed and Miss Shea mistakenly took that for compliance.

"Good girl, I'll be right here if you need anything." She settled back at the table, her head bent over the Reader's Digest she found under the sink.

She liked Miss Shea well enough she supposed. She was someone her mother would call, 'a do–gooder, prissy–type' whose eyes smiled so much; you could never tell what was behind them. But she did make good hot chocolate and used twice as many marshmallows as her mother did.

Emily's eyes teared up thinking about her mother and she hugged herself, ducking her head under the blanket. She wondered where her mother was and where she would sleep tonight. There wasn't a time she could remember when Mamma didn't kiss her goodnight and blow her another one before she shut the door. Emily would stare at her ballerina nightlight as she fell asleep, listening to the low noises of the television in the next room.

Thinking about Mamma brought that scary feeling in her stomach, so she thought about Kaitlin instead. She liked Kaitlin, mainly because she talked to her like she was a big kid and not in that baby voice most of the adults used. But also because her eyes did that funny light–glow thing sometimes, like Emily's did. And that made her feel good. Whenever Emily came into Kaitlin's store, she would listen to her stories about school or about anything and one time, Kaitlin gave her a book. It was all about this puppy and how he got lost in the woods and had all kinds of terrific adventures. Mamma read that one to her almost every night and Emily never tired of the happy ending when he finds his home and everyone had missed him so much. She wished somebody would read her a story right now, but she thought Miss Shea was too busy with her Reader's Digest.

There was a terrible crash in the sanctuary that made Emily hug herself tighter. Miss Shea threw down her Reader's Digest and went to the door to peek out.

"She's not breathing," she heard Mr. Benning yell. Miss Shea shot a worried glance at Emily, who shut her eyes quickly and held her breath.

"Get her up on the pew and get me some…" Miss Shea said as she went into the sanctuary, closing the door behind her.

Emily opened her eyes. Someone had stopped breathing out there. Someone wasn't breathing and that meant they would be dead soon. And even though it sounded like everybody was trying to help whoever had stopped breathing, Emily knew it wouldn't work. There were bad things happening today and the bad things wanted people to be dead. Emily knew about 'dead' and it gave her that scary feeling too, almost as much as thinking about mamma, so she decided to stop thinking about it.

She was she glad to be alone. Some of her friends were scared of the dark or of being alone, but Emily didn't mind. The silence was comforting; she could do anything or be anything she wanted when she was by herself. She knew her mother worried about that; knew she was an 'only child' and that she might have a hard time in school, but Emily never worried. She had the most beautiful garden parties with Bonny Bear and Janie, who would giggle if you pushed her belly and snore when you laid her down. Her mother would stand in the doorway sometimes and watch her with a funny look on her face. She would stare at Emily, or maybe something in Emily's eyes and then she would get upset and go to her room.

Emily heard her crying a lot in there and knew it was because her Daddy had been taken to that 'better place'. Everyone had told her about that 'better place' but she never understood why it was so better if it made her mamma cry. It sounded like a bad, bad place and she would be happy when her Daddy could finally come back. Maybe then her mother wouldn't cry so much.

Someone started to cry in the sanctuary. Emily thought it was probably Miss Shea. She had that look like she was about ready to burst. All of a sudden, she was scared again. Miss Shea was her Sunday school teacher and if she was crying out there, something bad must have happened to her too. But Kaitlin never cried and that made Emily feel better because that meant Kaitlin knew everything was going to be okay.

Emily threw off her blanket and sat up. She hadn't seen Kaitlin for a long time. And she hadn't heard her voice out there either. She slipped on her sneakers and went to the door. Miss Shea and Mr. Benning were standing with their backs to her over someone who was lying on a pew. Mr. Kerrisk met her eyes and growled a little, but the others didn't notice. Emily stayed as far from him as she could while she searched the room for Kaitlin.

She wasn't there. She wasn't anywhere and the scary feeling was getting bigger in Emily's stomach. If she couldn't find Kaitlin, she would be alone and that kind of alone *did* scare her. But it was okay because she would find Kaitlin 'cause she knew Kaitlin would never just leave her here. Unless…unless something bad had happened to Kaitlin too. Oh, no…she had to find her, now.

Her feet padded lightly on the thick carpet to the door on the other side of the pulpit. She opened it and stepped inside, closing the door softly behind her.

She wasn't supposed to be in here. This is where Reverend Nolan stayed until the singing was over. She always imagined it to be a garden with bright flowers and giant butterflies where the Reverend sat as God talked to him, telling him what to say in his sermon. She had known it probably wasn't like that, but never guessed it to be this little hallway. God wouldn't want to talk to nobody in here; it was too dark.

The door to her right was open and she saw the desk and bookcase, but not Kaitlin. The door on her left was closed, so she tried it.

"Emily…"

She turned around. That wasn't Will's voice, at least she didn't think it was.

"Hello?" She drifted toward the door at the end of the

hallway. "Is somebody there?"

"Emily...come here," the voice asked from the other side.

"What do you want?"

"It's mighty cold out here child, open the door." A noise shuffled against the door as the man leaned in to speak into the crack.

Emily glared at the door. "Why don't you go to the front and Mr. Benning can let you in."

"There's no time, you're mother's waiting," he said.

Mamma! She slid the lock over and opened the door. A blast of cold air hit her and she started to close it, but the man held it open.

"I've come to fetch you, to bring you to your mother," said the man in the big black coat. His face was in shadows, but she thought she wouldn't have recognized him anyway. He talked weird, like the guy on her mother's cooking show and certainly not like anybody here in Newclare. And the tourists never came up in the winter unless they were lost.

"Come, come she's waiting, she'll be wanting to see you, she's been worried."

"Is she okay, where is she? Did she get hurt?" Her mother must be hurt if she didn't come herself, that's why she would send this strange man who smelled like the apples in her grandmother's orchard.

The smell was getting stronger as she waited for the man to answer and now she thought maybe he didn't smell as good as the apples at her grandmother's.

"She is hurt a bit, but not bad, not bad at all, but she'll be getting more worried as we stand and talk."

The apple smell was starting to sour and Emily backed away. "I have to get my coat..."

"There's no time, come I'll carry you," he said, opening the big black coat and bending toward her. As he did his eyes did that funny light–glow thing and Emily relaxed. Maybe he would know where Kaitlin was too. She let him pick her up and wrap his coat around her and then she realized...he did smell just like grandma's orchard.

CHAPTER NINETEEN
ON ROCKY GROUND

"Kate! Will!"

The voice shocked Kate out of a heavy sleep and she untangled herself from Will's arms to sit up.

"Kate! You two up there?" It was Jacob's voice at the bottom of the stairs. It was getting closer as he walked up the steps.

"Yes, what's wrong?" Will was awake now and frantically pulling on his clothes as he threw Kate's to her.

"It's Emily, she's gone!"

Icy panic landed in Kate's stomach and somewhere in a dark corner of her mind...she wasn't surprised. She forced her hands to fasten her jeans. Was there no end to the nightmare of this day?

"We're coming," Will said slipping on his shirt.

Jacob's voice faded as he went back down the stairs. "Don't know how long she been gone, so you'll want to hustle it."

Kate was tying her shoes, her fingers working awkwardly with the laces. Tears blinded her sight and she growled in frustration as the knot tightened.

Will caught her hands, squeezed them gently, then worked on the knot and finished tying her shoes.

When it was done, he took her face in his hands. "We're going to find her, do you hear me? This is enough, enough for one day. We're going to find her and we're going to bring her back, so get that look off your face and help me."

"Okay." She wiped at her nose and blinked away her tears, as Will pulled her to her feet.

Downstairs was a madhouse of people rushing in every direction, calling for Emily and yelling to each other. Miss Shea was sagging against the far wall, crying.

Kate stormed across the sanctuary and grabbed her by the shoulders. "You were watching her goddamn it, where did she go?"

Miss Shea shook her head. "I–I don't know, I was only gone a minute."

"You were gone long enough for her to disappear. How could you leave her alone? How could you just leave, when you—"

"I went to help Rosie!" She snapped and threw Kate off. "Emily was sleeping and I went to help the others. I didn't th– think that..." She trailed off in a fit of tears.

Kate left her and went to find Will. It figured that it was Rosie who was responsible for Emily's disappearance. That girl always had to be the center of attention. She had been like that ever since they were kids and even now, she wouldn't change. Kate glanced in the kitchen, but didn't find Will or Rosie. She wanted to find Rosie and tell her what she thought of her stupid antics.

She walked to the back of the church, but found no one in the foyer. Spinning on her heel, she walked back into the sanctuary and stopped when she spotted something in the corner.

It was a brown blanket. There was a lumpy shape under it and as Kate stepped closer, she saw a lock of fluffy red hair, peeping out from its folds. She stared at the lumpy shape and then backed away. She wouldn't be telling Rosie anything now. Neither would anyone else.

"Hey, over here!"

It was Mr. Richards. Kate rushed to the back door, where she found Mr. Richards, Will and Jacob standing in the open doorway.

Jacob's flashlight lit up the churchyard.

Kate's heart sank. Those were tracks all right...big tracks, with a long stride, much too long for Emily's little legs.

"Oh God, he's got her," Will said in a voice far different from the one he'd used upstairs.

"What? Who's got her? Hey, hey!" Jacob shouted, as Will pushed past him. "Where you going with no light?" He asked, holding Will back by his shirt. Will yanked free and raised his fist to Jacob who held his ground until Will backed away.

"We all want to find her son, but we got to be careful. Ain't no use losing somebody else out there," Jacob said. He patted Will on the shoulder and turned toward the sanctuary. "Let's get the rest of them flashlights."

* * * * *

The tracks led away from the church to the clearing behind it. Single file, they stomped through the snow, the light from the flashlights bouncing off the fog and blinding Kate. She almost ran into Will when he stopped.

The tracks were gone.

"What the—" Jacob sounded very far away even though he stood, only a few feet in front of her. He searched the clearing, scanning the light back and forth, but there was nothing. "All right," he said, his distant voice trembling. "We got to split up. Mr. Richards, if you want to take your group up toward the highway, we'll head south, to the creek."

Kate met Will's eyes and he nodded slightly at her.

"If you don't find anything in a half hour or so, come on back. She couldn't have gotten any farther than that anyway."

Mrs. McGrath and Miss Shea, leaning on each other for support followed Mr. Richards, as Will, Kate, Adam and Jacob watched.

"Let's head out," Jacob said, breaking the silence that had fallen over them.

Jacob broke the path in front, taking them toward the forest at the end of the clearing. Kate knew there was forest at the end of the clearing, but the fog made it impossible to see more than ten feet, as it swirled around her flashlight like cold smoke.

Adam brought up the rear. She could hear his anxious

breath coming faster and though she could barely make out Will and Jacob talking in front of her, Adam sounded like he was blowing right in her ear. Then he began to talk to himself. Mad ramblings about the cold, about the fog, about the noises he thought heard. He started in a hushed voice, but then became louder and louder until he was almost shouting.

"We have to go back," Adam yelled.

Jacob and Will turned.

"Don't you feel it, any of you?" His eyes danced around in the dark, as he looked at whatever he saw through the fog. "It's in the forest, listening to us, waiting for us, we have to go back!"

Jacob took a few steps toward him. "You need to calm down, boy, there ain't nothing out there 'cept maybe a little girl. Keep it together man."

But whatever was straining Adam's mind had broken now. This is how it would end, Kate realized as she looked into the fog and *did* feel something, waiting for them in the forest.

"You guys are nuts, all of you," Adam said, pointing his finger at them. "It's out there, I know it is, I can smell it, it wants us—"

"Adam, you stop this, now!"

"What is wrong with you people! I'm not going to get my-self killed over some kid," he said, backing away. "No, no way!" He disappeared, his flashlight bouncing as he ran until it too, was gone.

The fog settled in heavier around them and Kate, Will and Jacob huddled together.

Then there were three…

"All right, all right, close your mouths and let's get a move on," Jacob said and started again.

The trees of the forest did nothing to break up the fog, which was growing thicker as they walked on. It hung under the branches and shrouded the ground at times in murky waves. They called for Emily, their voices dampened in the thickness, but amplified in Kate's ears. They called and called until they went hoarse, for the little girl they knew they wouldn't find. Kate tried to pinpoint when she knew they weren't meant to find Emily and found she couldn't. It was just a feeling; a feeling she knew that was shared by the others as met their eyes by the tree stump where they stopped to rest.

"Guess that's it," Jacob sighed, saying it first. "We need a search team out here, with dogs and such. Just gotta pray the good Lord take care of her 'till then."

Will stared at him, anger lighting his eyes. "What the hell are you talking about?"

"You gotta face facts, we—"

"You just want to leave her out here to freeze to death, while you wait on the *good Lord*?" Will picked up his flashlight and started to walk away. "I'm not putting my money on those odds."

Jacob ran after him, circling around the tree trunk. "I was just saying—"

And then he was gone...just...gone, in a puff of snow. He was running after Will and then, gone. Or fell. Her mind caught up with her eyes and she realized that Jacob had fallen.

"Jacob!" She shouted running toward the spot where she had seen him vanish.

"Kate, stop!" Something in Will's voice made her to come to an abrupt halt.

She held up the lantern, but could only make out a vague image of Will, standing by the tree trunk.

"I can't see how big it is," he said in a quiet voice, walking slowly toward her.

Kate looked down at her feet. Oh... Oh God. A mine shaft. Or a sinkhole. She had never seen a sinkhole in her life, but the name alone created enough of an idea. The lantern shook in her hand. She could be standing above sixty feet of hole, with just a thin layer of snow to cover the opening. She was suddenly dizzy.

"Just take a step back, Kate." Will was right behind her, calm and steady.

She took a deep breath and inched away. Will brought his hand to her back and she swayed toward him. Far, far below, they heard someone moan.

Will set her away and behind him and then felt his way forward with one foot. In a strange, lurching dance step, he made his way to where Jacob had fallen and held out his flashlight.

"Sweet mother—"

Kate followed in Will's footsteps and crouched beside him. She saw immediately what had shocked him. Jacob hadn't fallen into a hole. He slid down the side of a cliff and landed by the creek she heard very faintly at the bottom.

The creek.

Layers of thick fog lay in front of them. Thick enough to walk on it seemed, but when she held the lantern out, she could just make out where the snow stopped and the fog started.

"We need some help," Will said, lying on his stomach and shinning his light into the white. "Go get the others, they're headed for the highway, find them and bring them back, but don't go into town, don't go anywhere near town. And if you can't find them, see if you can drag that lunatic, Adam back here. And bring some rope, if you can find it."

"Where are you going?" Kate asked, already knowing.

He looked at her and shoved the flashlight in his mouth. "Go, go!" He shouted through clenched teeth.

Kate ran. Back into the trees and over the trunk, the light from her lantern jerking crazily before her. Her legs carried her swiftly through the deep snow, faster and faster until the cut in her side began to ache and sweat poured down her face, blurring her vision and still she ran. Between the trees and over the rocks, she ran, sobbing and screaming.

And then something was following her, crashing through the bushes and gaining fast. Closer and closer it came, panting and cursing and grinning through its slobbery white teeth. More and more speed she put in her feet and still it followed, reaching for her with its blood–red fingernails.

324

Dark Legacy

Get back here you little bitcheeeeees!

Up over the rise and into the clearing where the thorns cut her legs and tangled her steps. Her bare feet stung from the rocks and the pain in her side was becoming unbearable. She ran. As the cool, honeysuckle sweetened air rushed by her face and Joey's eyes followed her through the trees. She ran.

And then she fell. She went down, flat on her face, the lantern shattering on the tree beside her. Flipping on her back, she kicked furiously with her feet. Grunting and screaming at the powdery snow until the last of her strength was spent and she collapsed, staring up at the strange gray fog.

* * * * *

It was cold. And the cold was making Kate tired in a stealthy, apathetic way. She sat up to brush the snow and glass from her coat. The fog had lifted some, darkening the forest around her. She stood and leaned against the tree. Winds wound through the forest, its song promising the stronger gales she knew were still to come. She watched, as it swept over the last of her tracks in the snow.

She should have brought some breadcrumbs, then smiled ruefully and remembered how the breadcrumbs had worked out for Gretel. Keeping one hand on the tree, she circled it, searching for something, anything that could lead her out of the forest. There was nothing, just tree after nondescript tree in every direction. And now she wasn't even sure of which way had brought her to this one. She looked to the branches above. They obliterated any stars she might have used to guide her way, had she been able to tell the Big Dipper from Orion's Belt. The blackness of the night weighed on her with its pressing, knowing quiet. So dark...so alone. She fumbled for the amulet in her sweater.

Holding tightly to the jagged metal, she closed her eyes and concentrated. The familiar warmth stole through her cold limbs and steadied her thumping heart. She dove deeper into the darkness, brought Emily's face to the front and focused in on every detail. The splattering of freckles across her cheeks, the dimples under her eyes that appeared when she smiled, the faint lemony scent of her hair.

The amulet fell from her hand and bounced against her chest.

It was *him*.

Rushing out of the darkness, she felt him as clearly as if he stood before her. The irresistible, all–consuming power that drew her, beckoned her and she felt herself weaken with all he had to offer. The resolution, the release from this spiraling free–fall of anger and guilt.

She opened her eyes. He was near…and he was waiting. She dropped the amulet back into her sweater and strode through the trees, her steps quick and sure.

* * * * *

"Jacob!"

Little by little, Will scooted down the side of the snow–packed cliff. He held the light between his teeth, pointing it in front of him, but it was no help. The fog was thickening as he made his descent and even his legs were beginning to get lost in the mist. How was he ever going to find the man down there?

His foot slipped and he began to barrel down the cliff on his back with his arms flailing. He built up more speed as the snow road up his coat and his hat took flight into the darkness. With a less–than–manly shriek, he flipped to his stomach and dug his hands into the snow, clawing at the frozen earth. The ride slowed and soon his foot landed on a rock. He shivered and waited for his heart to stop pounding.

"Jacob! Jacob, can you hear me?"

Holding his breath, he waited. Nothing, not even the rustle of the wind.

He's probably gone already. No way could anyone take that kind of fall and not end up like ground beef at the bottom. His empty stomach turned. He should have gone to get the others and left Kate here to mark the spot. This was stupid. He wasn't thinking and that scared him, because as things were getting more and more crazy, there was no room for error. He'd promised Kate he would get them out of this and what did he do? The first chance he got, he sent her off into forest to get lost...or worse. And something in her eyes had told him she shouldn't be alone. There was...something, right under the surface and if he hadn't been so damned out of control, he might have caught it sooner.

"Shit," he muttered and slammed his fist into the ground, catching himself before he started to slide again.

They never should have split up. And now he would pay for that mistake. Things were falling apart fast, rushing by him with brutal speed and building momentum. Where would it end? He was beginning to think he didn't care, as long as he and Kate were far, far away when it did.

His feet touched bottom and he stood, shaking the snow out of his coat. Depending on how he had tumbled down the cliff, Jacob should be close by, but hell if he could see a thing down here.

"Jacob," he called, picking a direction and trudging through the snow. "Jacob, where are you?"

Ice cracked under his foot and he leapt away, tripping over something behind him and landing hard in the snow.

"Jacob?"

He shined the light in the man's face, but didn't see it move. Jacob lay half–covered in snow with his legs twisted beneath him. Will brushed him off and tried to find a pulse in his neck. Either he was dead, or Will's nursing skills needed work.

"Goddamn it." All the way down here for nothing. He sat back and rubbed his head. So alone, he felt so alone and as he tried to push it away, it slunk back, cold and knowing. All alone in an invisible forest that breathed and waited high above.

He needed Kate. Needed to hear the easy beats of her voice, needed to feel her slender fingers between his. But she was gone and the more he thought about her, the more she became a pale, flimsy image in his mind, too soft and beautiful for the cruel horror of this day.

Jacob stirred and groaned in pain. Slipping his jacket off, Will laid it over Jacob and tucked it around his shoulders. Will looked down at him with confusion, hating himself for wishing Jacob were already gone. He had watched enough people die today. He shook his head in disgust. What was wrong with him that he turned so selfish and calculating?

"Hey man, you okay?"

Jacob smiled. "Gonna be sore in the morning, that's for sure." A thin line of blood broke free from one eye as he rolled them up to Will. It traced the crease by his cheek and puddled up in his ear.

Will shined the flashlight away from his face and farther down, trying to hide his shock as it lit up the lower half of Jacob's body. Jagged, white bone had broken through his pants in three different pieces and dripped with flesh and blood.

Will brought the light back to Jacob's face. "Kate's getting help, you just hang in there," he said, knowing that the fear rang loud and clear in his voice, even if Jacob couldn't see it in his eyes.

"Don't expect I'll be needing much of that, it's in the Lord's hands now." He coughed gently and a blood spilled from his mouth. Will wiped it with the cuff of his shirt.

"It won't be long now," Will lied, glancing at the unseen ridge above them.

"It's okay son. Ain't nothing I didn't know was coming for the past forty years or so," he said, following Will's look. "Just has a way of sneaking up on you."

"Stop talking like that, they'll be here soon and then we'll get you out of here." Will panned the light into the darkness around them and then back to Jacob as he spoke again.

"I know your fear," he said quietly and Will drew back from the pity in Jacob's eyes.

"What are you talking about?"

"Don't think I don't. Lived most my life with the fear that can choke you at times. Oh, you won't call it that, you'll call it anger or confusion, but it don't change what it is." He coughed again, spitting up more blood. "Your heart's hard and rocky and it makes you weary, son. It drains you, it owns you and it don't give nothing back, ever. You need to open it up and turn it over to someone who can fill it with something good. Let Him lead you where you need to go and have the faith that He'll see you through."

Will shook his head. "You've got to be kidding. I mean, 'have a little faith and it'll all turn out right?' I'm sorry, man, but come on, how'd it turn out for you?"

Jacob smiled. "He don't make no deals, ain't no compromising. Besides, you think it matters any to Him? Our little battles here on earth, shoo," he said, his lips widening into a grin. "Win or lose, live or die, what difference do you really think it makes to Him? He lookin' at your heart, son. That's where He see you, that's where He hear you. That's where it matters. And when He come for you, all He gonna care about is how you lived. You remember that when this mess here all settles. You remember what I told you, 'cause in the end that's all it is. What you make of what He gave you."

Will wrapped his arms around himself and looked down. "I wish I had that. That conviction. Then maybe all this crap would make some sense."

Jacob closed his eyes, as his breath quickened. "It's not always about making sense. There's worlds of knowin' that you and I'll never see. It's about trust and faith and doing the right thing, even when it hurts. And you can have that, it's yours, for the takin'. All you gotta do is open your eyes and *see* it, 'cause it's right there in front of you." He coughed again and it sounded like something tore loose in his lungs. Will wiped up more blood from Jacob's mouth. "You'll know what I mean, you'll know it when it happens and then you'll spend the rest of your days feeling stupid that it took you so damned long..."

Will smiled. "Well, I'm good at feeling stupid, so I guess I'm ahead there," he said, but Jacob didn't hear him. His eyes rolled away and his breathing became more and more shallow. A low gurgling noise came from his chest, as he took in the air through a layer of liquid.

Will sat beside him, staring into the fog, his mind peacefully quiet. After a while, the fog began to lift and he could see the outline of the ridge above. An icy wind blew through the canyon and Will shivered in his thin shirt. Kate had been gone a long, long time. And she wasn't coming back, but Will realized he knew where he could find her. With great care, he closed Jacob's eyes and put his coat back on. He stood there for a moment, tears filling his eyes as the wind blew snow over Jacob's body. Then he walked back to the cliff wall and worked on finding a way back up.

* * * * *

Kate broke through the trees and didn't miss a step as she entered the cemetery. When she reached the building, she crouched in the shadows and listened. It was hard to see if there were any lights inside through the boarded windows, so she stood and cupped her hands at the glass.

Nothing.

She moved to the next window. This one was cracked and one of the boards had slipped, leaving a gap. She put her nose to the gap and felt warm air rushing by her face. Why was it so warm in there? If only she had something to stand on, then she would be able to see more than just the ceiling. This side of the sanctuary was dark, but there was light coming from where the pulpit stood. A huge shadow moved across the ceiling and Kate jumped back. She held her breath and waited, but heard nothing.

She sat down against the building, not wanting to chance putting her face back up in the window. She needed a black ski mask, so her skin wouldn't glow so much. She glanced down the length of the building and then up at the roof. Yeah, that and a cat suit, then she could be Bat Girl and climb to the windows upstairs. Or maybe Bionic Woman would be better. She could just jump. She was wondering if it would work without that cool, techno sound effect when the front doors of the church blew open.

She heard them slam back and then bounce closed again. Her heart stopped and she waited, but no one came out. Had they been locked when everyone left? Inching down the wall, she peered around the corner. The doors were closed, but not latched. The wind was stronger on this side and it banged them together loudly.

The doors had been locked. She pushed her hair behind her ears and stepped up to the doors. Her hand hesitated on the doorknob.

It was warm.

And when she opened the doors, the heat tingled over her body. She took off her coat, folded it in half and placed it on the bench. She did this, all the while aware of the eyes that absorbed her every movement. The deliberate eyes that were held…enraptured by the soft tremble of her hands…the smooth motion of her tongue as she wet her lips…the whispered hush of her quickened breath…

She turned and walked down the aisle, her eyes cast to the midnight–blue carpet. Mr. Kerrisk lay on the floor by the window, his face no longer angry, but filled with fear. He jerked his eyes to the front of the church and grunted frantically as she walked by. Ignoring him, she went on, passing the lumpy figure that was Rosie under the blanket and stopping halfway down the aisle. Only then did she look up.

There he sat, Lordon Harrickson, knees apart, on the bench

behind the pulpit. No part of him was anything, but solid flesh and bone now and the scent of apples was gone. The pulpit had been pushed over and now lay across the stairs. Five candles were placed in a half–circle by his feet. Wind blew through the broken stained–glass window behind him. Wind that had been warmed by the time it touched Kate's face.

"And so you've come to me," he said in a voice, deep and satisfied. He dropped his head, just a bit and watched her with his brilliant eyes.

"Had I any choice?" Nice and steady.

A flash went off in his eyes and she caught herself before backing away. There was something so familiar about the way he was watching her. Oh God. Will looked just like that when he teased her. He had the same flashing eyes that twinkled and danced with mischief.

"Ah, but we all have choices, that's what makes life so grand. Don't you say? It's the mystery in the choices we make that give its flavor."

A moment passed between them as he watched her with his dancing eyes.

Kate broke the spell and looked away. She stared at the broken window above him until she felt she could look back.

"Where is Emily?" Her voice was not as steady this time.

Her question made him smile. "Just like an angel come from Heaven, that child," he said. "And so like you, the spirit, the beauty. But lacking, in so many ways."

His hand jerked as he pulled on a rope she hadn't noticed he held. At the same time a bundle of some sort rose from the pew beside her and soared into the air. Kate screamed, jumping back as it swung toward her. She felt the cool softness of hair brush against her face. And the hair carried a lemony scent.

"Emily!"

It was Emily. Emily with her mouth gagged and her hands tied together at her waist. Emily with a rope wrapped under her arms and her shiny white shoes poking out of the folds of her dress. And as she made her ascent toward the ceiling, the little girl's eyes opened. They looked down on Kate and they screamed. Her eyes were screaming and Kate screamed with them, reaching for her. But Emily rose higher and higher, stopping only a few feet from the rafter the rope had been thrown over.

"Her rearing's what tamed her, dampened the fire that blazes so rich in you." He looked up at Emily's swinging body and clicked his tongue.

"Let her go!" She lunged at Lordon.

He let go of the rope and several feet slid through his fingers.

"NO!" She ran back to Emily as her body plummeted toward the floor, but she would never make it in time. Emily was going to die and it would be Kate's fault. She couldn't get to her fast enough, not fast—

Emily came to a stop just above Kate's head and was pulled back up like a yo–yo. She rose up, up, up, so quickly that Kate thought he would bash her head on the rafter. But he stopped her in time and Emily again swung back and forth, thirty feet above.

"And so you've seen the way of it, eh?" Lordon gave the rope a tug to keep Emily swinging. "T'would be a shame for any harm to come to one of my own. I'd return her to you…"

Kate tore her eyes away from Emily and glared at Lordon. "Then do it."

"Aye, but I'd be happy to," he said, clicking his tongue again. "There's just the one small matter."

"What?"

"You've come into possession of something you've no business having and now, you'll be returning it."

"I don't know what you're talking about."

"The journal, child. The journal. Let's not play games, now." He was beginning to loose his smile. "That old hen had no business giving it to you and you've no business having it now, so I'll say it again. You'll be wanting to return it."

"But I—" The image of the book Will's grandmother had given them, lying in the snow flashed through her mind. "I don't have it, I don't know—"

"Enough!" He pounded on the back of the bench and Emily bobbed, high above. "Your lies sicken me."

Shifting his black eyes away from Kate, he raised his head to the ceiling. The hand that didn't hold the rope curled into a fist as he took in a deep breath and blew it out, slowly. The already warm room now became unbearable. The air crackled with heat and the wind from the stained–glass window blew like a blowtorch against Kate's face. Emily let out a low moan, the first sound she heard her make.

Then, as soon as it came, the heat dissipated. Like a door had been opened, the air cooled instantly and Kate could breathe again. Lordon opened his fist, one finger at a time and looked down.

"A bitter, bitter thing it is, bad relations between family." His smile reemerged. "I'll have none of that, so," he said letting out the rope, hand over hand. "As a gesture of good will..."

Little, by little Emily was lowered until Kate could grab her and untie the rope from her chest. She sat with the girl in the middle of the aisle, working on the knot around her mouth. When the gag was off, Kate hugged her close and kissed her red cheeks. Emily looked up at her, but said nothing. She was in a place without words now and Kate wondered if she would ever be able to find her way back.

"Beautiful, beautiful child," Lordon said. He had been watching them and his voice had an air of reverence to it. "Softness and beauty in such a small package. 'Tis a deceptive package, though. Her father's blood is what rages through her veins. It's what'll hold her and in time, she'll come to see freedom of it."

Kate ripped at the knot at Emily's wrists. It was wound around several times in a combination Kate couldn't untangle.

"My dear," he said, when she didn't speak. "You haven't guessed it, have you? Look at her, look at her and see her for who she *is*."

Kate's hands stopped, as she looked into Emily's sweet face. Her full, petal–soft lips were all her mother's, but...

No...oh no.

The tiny cleft in her chin, the tilted, almond–shaped eyes, even the little fairy nose...all a smaller, more delicate version of someone she knew and loved. Or had known. Uncle Dave.

Lordon laughed, a full belly laugh that filled the room with its arrogance. "Do you see?" He asked, rising with a swiftness she hadn't anticipated from such a large man. "The eyes...oh, the eyes. I see potential, I see possibilities in those marvelous eyes." He drifted down the first few stairs, coming toward them, getting closer...closer and the heat intensified again with each step.

Kate leapt to her feet, pulling Emily with her. "Yes, yes, I do see, but you don't want *her*, do you."

He stared at her oddly and for moment and Kate thought she saw hesitation flicker in his eyes. Then it was gone and he smiled again.

"Alas, I've underestimated you, you...my own blood."

He returned to the bench. Kate took several steps back, toward the open front door behind her. She stopped as Lordon sat and began talking again.

"'Tis not this limp rag doll, holds my interest," he went on. "But the wren *Cliodhna* that stands true as life before me. The melody of your voice has haunted my dreams for half an age." He rested his temple on his forefinger and sighed. "So many, many wretched years I've watched go by as I've waited for the one who will bring to pass all that I've seen. And here you are, my child, my blood. Every bit the gem for which I've waited so long..."

Kate held Emily behind her and took a few more creeping steps down the aisle. "What are you talking about, all you have seen?"

"T'would fill a lifetime of dreams, what I've come to know." With his first two fingers, motioned toward the doors behind her. They slammed shut.

Kate jumped but held his gaze. "Well sorry to disappoint you, but it looks like you've waited an awful long time for nothing. You'll get no help from me."

"But you already have, you see," he said, chuckling. "You and the boy both. More than I could have hoped for and when the time comes, you'll serve your purpose, but first, there are other matters I must attend to." His face tightened and his eyes showed some of the darkness that hid behind his smiles.

"Which are?"

"All in good time, it will be shown to you, but only when it is time."

"It wouldn't have anything to do with the crazies running loose in town, would it?" Kate said, trying to get Emily to stand on her own. Emily needed to stand. Emily needed to be able to run. "So that's the big plan? Drive everyone nuts, just for your stupid revenge?"

Lordon smiled. "Oh my dear, I've simply lifted the veil from their eyes, given them a taste of the world and life as it 'tis. Without the guise of all this pretence and piety."

"Crap," Kate said, setting Emily on her feet. The girl stood, but shakily. "You've shrouded it to suit your own twisted ideas. You think the evil that controls you, can control anyone. But that's where you're wrong."

Movement in the hall behind him caught her attention, but she pulled her eyes away, quickly. "You can do what you can to make everyone crazy enough to kill each other off. God knows, they didn't have far to go." Careful, oh careful not to look away from the being who was watching her so intently.

Will! Thank you, thank you. You've never left my side...

"But it would only happen, because you made it happen," she ended.

DARK LEGACY

He thought that over, staring up at the ceiling and again, Kate thought she saw a flicker in his eyes. "I can see we have far to go here, Kaitlin. But no matter. A willing student is a learned student and that's why I've saved the best for you. There is much to be learned from the final hours here in Newclare and when it is finished we—"

"When it's finished, what? This is just a power trip for you, isn't it? Just an elaborate production to show off." She heard herself rambling, but didn't care. Anything, anything to keep his sharp eyes on her and away from Will. "You're power hungry, is all. And what does power want, but more power? So why don't you tell me? Where does it end?"

Will stood in the doorway now, the gun drawn in his hand.

She stepped forward, dragging Emily along. Lordon's eyes were riveted on her. "And who would be left to see it anyway, after you're done blowing up the world. Who will be left to watch you gloat? Doesn't sound like you've worked this out very well, for all those years of planning and waiting."

Will was only a few feet behind him now, his face red with excitement.

Shoot him.

"And what is this 'we' shit anyway? What makes you think I want to be in the same room with you, let alone—"

Lordon began to laugh, throwing his head back and clapping his hands. "You delight me," he said and with a wave of the same two fingers, the gun flew out of Will's hand and hit the wall. A shot went off and Mr. Kerrisk wailed behind her.

"You really do, I don't know what pleasures me more, your boundless amount of verve, or your bumbling henchman over there," he said as Will was driven away from the stairs. And driven was what it was—as if something had pushed him. "But in answer to your question," he continued, coming around the candles to stand at the head of the stairs. "You *will* come to see the way of it, because it is in you to do so. You will come to feel the truth in the power and know the triumph of fulfilling your destiny, for it is this, for which you are here."

Kate shook her head. "No, that may be why you're here, but no matter what you *think* you saw, I am more than just a means to an end. And I won't let anyone or anything control me like it does you, not that you would understand," she said, crossing her arms. "You're nothing more than a glorified ghost."

He brought the side of his mouth up in a slanted smile and again she could see Will's handsome face hovering, just slightly below his. "Aye, but I'll give you that," he said, chuckling. "Made flesh and bone by none other than the two of you. Which is why our young lad, William is still here. Been useful to me, he has." Turning toward Will, his smile disappeared. "'Till now."

"But the fact is you are just a ghost, a ghost with a bag of magic tricks. And you use your ticks like a magician would, to distract us from what you really are, which is helpless and pathetic—"

"Enough!" He roared, throwing up his hands.

She jumped back, stumbling on top of Emily.

Lordon closed his eyes and after a moment his face relaxed. "'Tis only your fear talking. You fear what you do not understand." His eyes turned bright with desire. "My Katie girl, don't be afraid of it, don't run from the part of you that cries out for it. You feel it, I see into the watery depths of your soul. You yearn for the peace that it offers. Welcome it, embrace it, as an end to your fruitless struggle."

Kate stared into his sparkling eyes and felt him digging at her mind. Emily's hand fell from her waist as she stepped forward, watching the amazing colors of his eyes. "You're right," she murmured.

"Kate no," Will moaned.

Lordon held up his hand and Will winced in pain.

"I'm sorry dear, go on," he said.

The flaming colors in his eyes were so beautiful. "You are. Everything I have endured, all the loss, all my failures. It's just so much...too much." She shook her head, but didn't look away.

"It would be so much easier to live without the guilt. Without the knowledge that only more is to come. You're right. I do feel it and the strength it takes to resist is unbearable at times."

Lordon smiled and held out his hand. "Don't resist. Let it take you. Let it wash away the guilt and pain and join me. At my side, our power will be limitless and you will know ecstasy beyond your comprehension."

"But," she went on, smiling back at him. "I think I would rather spend ten lifetimes in the fruitless struggle, than spend one more minute here with you."

And as she spat that out, she fired up the power he touched within her and turned it around, to him. She could feel the colors leap to her eyes and they sizzled and sparked with brilliant energy. Drawing deep from a well of old, old strength, she pulled at him, reaching into his eyes, thirsty for more, more of what had in riches. Lordon took a step back and...yes...that was fear, his fear she felt and the fear heightened the taste. She reached farther...and now she no longer had to pull. It filled her, completed her, and pleasured her like nothing else.

Ohhh, this is what it is...waves of pure energy you can touch and taste...so beautiful, so satisfying...

But suddenly she pulled away, severing the stream and blinking her eyes, the feeling of being full enough to explode strong in her mind. She had taken him to the edge, but he was strong, so incredibly strong and she could take him no farther.

Kate smiled again, a wide, bright one that stretched her face like plastic. She hoped it covered the fear she was sure he had felt. "You might want to take care of that," she said, nodding behind him.

Lordon spun around and Kate saw that the tail of his coat was consumed in flames. He roared, loud enough to shake the remaining glass in the window above the pulpit free from its frame and send it crashing to the floor. The candles by his feet fell over as he thrashed around, trying to put out the fire.

Will jumped up on the front pew and leapt over three more

to reach Kate.

"Come on!" He shouted and grabbed her hand.

Kate held fast to Emily as the three raced for the doors. Almost there, just a few more steps and then they were in the foyer.

"Noooo!" Lordon's voice was close and Kate looked back.

He was storming down the aisle toward them, with his burned coat flapping behind him. Fixing his fiery gaze on Kate, his lips curled into a sneer and she caught a glimpse of the man who had thrown his own son into a fire to die. This man would let nothing stop him and he was coming, oh god he was almost on them...

His hand reached to grab Emily when something rolled into the aisle and blocked Lordon's path. It was Mr. Kerrisk, still tied and gagged and as he lay at Lordon's feet, his eyes gestured wildly at the door.

Get out, get out while you still can, go, go, go!

Will pushed on the closed doors, but they held fast. Taking a step back, he brought up his foot and kicked them open.

"Kate! Come on!"

Kate turned to pull Emily to her feet and saw Lordon back away from Mr. Kerrisk. He pulled his boot back and drove it into the man's head. The boot connected with the bottom of his chin and his neck snapped as his head flopped back and thumped against his spine. It then rolled to the floor, attached now, by only the thin skin at his neck.

She covered her mouth with one hand and yanked on Emily's arm with the other. Will grabbed the back of her coat and they made it to the doorway before Lordon looked up at them.

"I said no," he said in a booming voice that came not from his mouth, but from the rafters above him. He raised his hand, palm out and Emily's arm was ripped from her grasp.

"Emily!"

Kate threw herself toward the little girl, but was stopped

by a wall of heat. The heat burned her hands like hot coals and created a thunderous wind that blew the hair from her face. Emily's figure turned watery through the wall and she saw the girl backing away, back, back toward Lordon.

He jerked his hand, just slightly and Kate was driven through the door. She landed in the snow outside, on top of Will who was buried in the four–foot drift. The wind blew out of the church and over them, sweeping the snow away from the porch. Kate shaded her eyes against it and struggled to hold up her head.

When it passed she looked up in time to see Emily watching them. Her body was calm, though her shoulders slumped and her tied hands seemed to be too much weight for her to hold. But her eyes... They stared vacantly at Kate with all the overwhelming horror that had finally become too much for her to bear.

"Emily, no!"

Kate bolted to her feet but wasn't able to take a step before Lordon lowered his hand and the doors closed, trapping Emily inside.

"Emily!"

Kate pounded on the doors, but they were hot, so hot and the heat was buckling the wood. "Emily!" She grabbed the doorknob and screamed as the burning metal seared her palm.

"Get back," Will said and kicked the warped doors. Again and again he kicked and then with a running start, he slammed his body against them. But the heat had expanded the wood and now they were wedged too tightly.

Will pulled on her sweater, dragging her away. "We have to find another way—"

The wind was back. It swept through the doors and rushed at them like an invisible fireball. Kate threw up her hands to cover her face, as it blew over them and then she was tumbling down...down...down the steps with Will's arms around her. The back of her head exploded in a thousand tiny lights and then was gone as the fireball washed over them. Its force moved over her body with the strength of a boiling tidal wave...she couldn't move...she...couldn't breathe. On and on, it crashed down, crushing her chest, her stomach, trapping her limbs under its power. And the noise...it roared through her head like a tornado, sucking all thought, all reason from her mind and just before she felt the last of herself slip away...

Will...where are you? I can't see you...don't leave me, please don't leave me here...Will...

But then she was gone, swept away in the current that no longer crushed her, but dragged her into its boiling depths.

Chapter Twenty
The Breaking Dawn

"Kate! Kate wake up, come on."

Will. Will was here.

"Can you hear me? Kate?"

His voice began to clear her fuzzy mind and she tried to sit up.

"Hey, hold on a minute," he said, gently pushing her back down. "How's your head?"

Kate blinked her eyes several times and Will's three faces slowly converged into one. "Fine. I'm fine," she said, but the voice she heard sounded far, far away. Her head pounded out a slow, steady beat and the back of it felt warm. It was the only thing on her body that felt warm, as she lay, shivering in the snow.

Will tilted her head to the side. "The bleeding stopped, that's good."

She felt the gooey blood that clotted her hair, but it was her hand that made her wince. Will helped her to sit up and she looked at her hands in the thin light of the moon. Her palms were blistered and the tips of her first three fingers oozed puss. "Emily," she said. "We have to get Emily."

Will nodded. "I know, I know and we will, but not yet."

"What do you mean, not yet? We can't leave her in there Will. We can't—"

"We're not going to Kate, but we can't do anything about it right now."

"Maybe you can't, but I'm not leaving her in there with that maniac," Kate said and struggled to her feet. The world darkened and spun crazily.

"Kate," Will said, grabbing her before she fell. "Listen to me, listen." He turned her toward the church. "Look at that, do

343

you see? There's nothing we can do to help her right now, but we're not going to leave her, I promise. We just need to think. I need some time to figure out what we're going to do. And she'll be okay, if you think about it. He won't hurt her, he really can't, because he needs her."

Kate listened to Will's words, but stared at the church. It stood, a few hundred feet away and glowed like hell itself. The brick base, the porch, the roof, glowed with the heat that Kate could feel again, even so far away. And the snow around it was gone, just like at Will's house, but the building was different. It burned bright red and pulsed like a throbbing heart.

"I know," Will, said turning her back around. He lifted her chin toward his face. "I know, and we're going to find a way to get her back. But I need your help Kate. Can you help me?"

She nodded.

"Good, good." He let go of her chin and rubbed his head. "Now let's think. When I came in earlier he was talking about a book, do you remember?"

"Yeah, the one…from your grandmother."

"Right. We need that book Kate, do you know where it is?"

He was fading again into dark, ugly colors and Kate lowered her head. The pounding was so heavy…she couldn't—

"Kate!" Will shook her. "Think Kate, come on."

"The store, it's back at the store."

"Okay." He walked a few paces away and then came back. "Okay, so we go get the book."

Kate looked at the church. Emily was alone in there…with him. Choking despair rose in her throat. She promised Emily she would take care of her, that she would get her through this, but now…

"We'll be back," Will said from behind. "I promise you that, we won't let him hurt her any more, but right now we need to go."

She turned toward him and saw the promise hardened in

his eyes. "Okay."

Taking the snowmobile was out of the question, it was parked too close to the church and already the metal had begun to melt, so Kate and Will began to walk toward town. Uncle Dave's coat now covered her shoulders. Will walked beside her, shivering in his sweater, his hand holding hers in a grip that stung her burned palm and numbed her fingers, but she said nothing. Will was with her and nothing else mattered. He would see them through this, she saw it in his eyes...the steely determination. Regardless of everything that had happened, his eyes told her he would see them through this and she held onto that thought as they entered Main Street.

The town was quiet now. The alarms were silent and even the wind ceased to blow through the streets. They passed one burned out building after another, each with their windows blown out and insides ransacked. Furniture littered the street. A couch had been pulled onto the sidewalk and set on fire...a table thrown through a window, like the remnants of someone's wild party, but the guests had all left. Kate and Will passed through the town without seeing a single person, but she felt them, watching her from the dark buildings. She moved closer to Will and quickened her steps.

A block from her uncle's store, Will was forced to lead them around the cars in the street and up to the sidewalk. Mark and Cindy's Pinto was gutted by fire and smoke still rose from its engine. Mark was nowhere to be seen, but she saw Cindy. Her foot hung out the backseat. The nylons had been burned from her legs, along with most of her flesh and Kate caught a wisp of charred barbecue as she hurried by.

"Okay," Will said as they came up on the store. "Where was it?"

Kate ran into the alley and dropped to her knees. She dug through the snow, the pain in her palms sharpening as they touched the cold.

Turning, she started to dig behind her. "It was right here," she said, digging faster. The snow flew all around, covering her hair. "I don't understand, I saw it." She glanced at the buildings on either side, marking the spot. "It was here, I know it was."

Will worked by her side, shoving aside piles of snow with his arm and feeling through the rocks underneath. They cleared the area between the buildings, but didn't find the book.

"Come on," Will said, getting to his feet. "It's not here."

Kate stood and turned in a slow circle. "But it was, I saw it."

"I know you did, but there's only one place it could be now," Will said quietly.

She looked at him for a moment and then nodded. "But why would Ben take it? That doesn't make any—"

"Shhh!" Will took her arm and led them closer to the building. "Did you hear that?"

"No I—" But she did hear it…the high tinkle of a woman's laugh. She turned toward the sound and saw movement in the alley. Two dark shapes skittered over the fence and ran into the yard behind the store.

"We have to get off the street," Will said. "There're more of them, I've been hearing them ever since we got back into town."

Kate pointed across the street. "There, come on."

They ran into the Wood'n More shop and shut the door behind them. The display windows were broken, but the store was untouched by fire. Kate kicked aside the debris at her feet and followed Will to the counter.

"Flashlight, flashlight," Will muttered, rummaging in the shelves. He threw open the drawers under the register. "Don't tell me they don't—ha! Here we go."

Tossing two candles on the counter, Will reached in the back of the drawer and retrieved a box of matches. After lighting both candles, Will wrapped the ends in papers towels and handed one to Kate.

She held up the candle to take a closer look at the store.

The display racks had been shoved through the window and lay on top of each other, half in and half outside the store. Several deer heads sat in a pile in the corner of the room and blankets from the shelf above covered most of their glassy eyes. Kate moved away from the counter and held the candle up to the marks on the wall.

Deep groves were scattered across the wood panel and when she walked further down, she saw they covered the entire length of the wall. Frowning she turned back to Will and tripped over something in the aisle. It was a woodcarving, one of the bears that usually sat outside the doors. She lowered the candle and gasped. Only the body lay on the floor, its head was gone, hacked off it looked like, by the same instrument used on the walls. She lifted the candle and saw more of the same. All the way down the aisle lay a variety of decapitated woodcarvings, deer, squirrel and birds, piled up next to each other in a perplexing array of carnage. Kate shook her head. Where are the heads? And who would do this? She picked up the body of a butchered raccoon and held the candle up to its severed neck.

"Kate!"

She tossed the raccoon into the pile and hurried back to Will.

"Let's head upstairs," Will said when she returned. "I don't like these open windows"

"Okay." Kate held her candle up to Will's face and saw fresh fear in his eyes. "What's—"

He shoved the candle away. "Nothing, it's safer upstairs is all."

His body blocked her view behind the counter and Kate pushed him aside.

"Kate don't—"

Ignoring him, she walked to the end of the counter and held the candle over her head.

It was Mr. Bowing, Mrs. Whitmore's assistant. He wore the same outfit he had worn since she was a girl, blue shirt, jeans and a white apron.

The apron was a dazzlingly white and spotless, for all the blood that covered his face. His gray hair was soaked in the mess and there must have been a slant in the floor, because the blood had flowed downstream, toward the front of the store. Kate held her hand over her nose. Why hadn't she smelled him before now? The light shook over his body as Kate stepped closer. Mr. Bowing's feet lay slightly apart with his toes pointed away from each other and his hands still held the hatchet in a kind of suspended–animation death grip. The hatchet was buried in what remained of his face. The blade had caught him between the eyes, but not before ripping off half his nose, which hung by a flap of skin on one open eye. The eye was filled with blood.

"Happy now?" Will asked from behind her.

She lowered the candle so fast the flame flickered out.

He picked up a bag from the counter and guided her toward the rear door. "Come on, let's get out of here."

They walked behind the counter and Kate had opened the drawer to grab more candles, when Will hit her from behind, dragging her to the floor.

"What—"

He slammed his hand over her mouth and held a finger over his lips in a silent warning.

A few seconds later she heard it. The running feet that were muffled in the snow, but coming closer as she and Will waited. They reached the store and now Kate heard laughter, loud and frenzied. Nothing rational could be heard in their high–pitched squeals that sounded like the javelinas Kate had seen on National Geographic. There were five of them, at least, and they ran back and forth several times in front of the store with no apparent purpose before a rock crashed through the remaining glass in the display window. There was more screaming laughter and then the thumping of their running feet as they headed down the block.

Will held her for another minute and then poked his head

over the counter. "They're gone."

She stood and brushed off her jeans. "You sure? 'Cause if you're not, please, feel free to throw me to the floor again, I'm getting kind of used to it now."

Picking up his candle, Will struck a match and lit it again. "Don't be such a baby," he said grinning at her.

She grinned back. "Admit it, you enjoy knocking me on my ass."

He picked up the bag and opened the door to the upstairs. "I refused to answer the question in the event that I may—" His words were cut off by the barrage of objects that tumbled off the stairs and into Will's feet. His candle blew out when he jumped and the room went pitch black.

"What the…"

Kate heard him fumbling for a match, but she was able to light hers first. She held the candle in the doorway and they both leaned over the round objects that had been piled against the door.

"The missing heads," Kate said and began to laugh.

"The what?"

She kicked enough of the wooden animal heads away from the stairs so they would have a clear path to the second floor. "Never mind."

Will nodded. "Yeah…never mind," he said and locked the dead bolt behind them.

* * * * *

"I don't like it."

Kate dipped the knife in the jar and spread more peanut butter across her bread. She couldn't seem to stop eating, now that she had started.

On the other side of the candle sat Will. The flickering light danced over his face, giving her brief glimpses of the welt Mr. Kerrisk had given him by his jaw. It was beginning to swell and turn a nasty shade of purple.

"It doesn't really matter if you like it or not, Kate."

She heard the tone in his voice and saw his tightly folded hands in his lap. Will had stared into the flame, during the entire conversation, not meeting her eyes once as they spoke. And he hadn't touched the food they found downstairs.

"Yes it does," she said, trying to shove away her childish anger. "If you want me to go through with it, it does."

Will sighed. The lines had deepened around his eyes and he looked tired, so incredibly tired. All she wanted to do was bundle him up in a blanket and put him to bed. How long had this been going on? She couldn't remember anymore.

"I can't do it without you, so unless you have a better idea…"

"I do," Kate said. "We go into Quarryville and we get help. This is too much for just the two of us, we need help."

Will dropped his swollen chin to his chest. "What are you going to do Kate…fly?"

"No I—"

"Phone's are gone and the roads won't be back up until next week," he said, finally meeting her eyes. "By then it'll be too late."

She wished he hadn't looked at her. Up to this point, she had done a good job of denying the truth that was so obvious in his eyes. Gone was the twitching fear, now only deep resignation showed in his face. He would do this with or without her.

Kate wrapped up the bread and put everything back in the bag. Her appetite was gone.

"Okay," she said. "After we get the book, assuming we *can* get the book, what then?"

"We go find Lordon."

"Yeah. That sounds easy enough." She stood and walked to the far end of the room. The smell of smoke blew in the open windows and Kate stared down at the street. It was empty now; the only movement was the smoldering fires down the block.

"Do you even know how you sound?" She asked with her back to Will. "Delusional for starters. What are we going to do when we find him, if he's even still here."

"He's here, he's not finished yet and besides," Will said. "I can feel him."

Kate nodded. "Yeah, I know what you mean. It's like we're connected…somehow."

"Right, so we get the book, find Lordon and then we get Emily back."

"He's not going to let us just walk out with her," Kate said, turning. Will was staring into the candle again.

"I know."

"Great, you know. So what're we going to do about it, huh?"

Will rose, slowly, like an old man with arthritis in his back. He stood at the opposite side of the window and looked down at the street, as Kate did. "You said it yourself," he said. "We're connected to him, joined in some twisted way…we're his family." He laughed and Kate winced at the sound. "We may have brought him back, but like my grandmother said, we can get rid of him too. And that's what we're going to do, we're not running from him anymore. We're going to put an end to it, an end to him and nobody else is going to get hurt."

He moved away from her, just slightly, but Kate felt the distance. "You're not giving him the book, Kate. I can't let that happen, *we* can't let that happen. I just need you to distract him long enough for me to get to Emily and then you two are going to run. And fast and you don't look back."

Kate looked at him and heard his voice ringing in her head. From the bell tower.

There is no over for me…

"What about you, Will?" Her voice cracked, as the last of her breath escaped her lungs.

He didn't answer.

She crossed to him, two quick steps and put her hands on

his shoulders, pushing him, forcing him to look at her. "What about you?" He kept his eyes on the street as she shook him, his arms crossed over his chest. With boiling rage, she slapped him across his already swollen face. "Talk to me damn it, talk!"

She pulled back for another blow and he caught her hand in his.

"*We* may have brought him back, but it was *my* fault," he said, not at all upset by her outburst.

"What?"

He nodded, still hiding his eyes. "It's true, you tried to stop him. You did everything you could and I just caved."

Kate was shaking her head. "No, that's not true, you're not thinking straight."

"But I am, finally." He sighed. "It was my fault from the beginning. I knew something was wrong after Christmas, but I didn't press it. My pride didn't want to press it. I left it all in your lap, I was selfish and stupid and blind. I just didn't want to admit what was happening." He finally turned and Kate saw his eyes were bright with unshed tears. "And then yesterday, I knew things were bad, but I still let you drive right, straight to him. And then I left you. I'm supposed to be watching out for you, what the hell is wrong with me? And then there's Ben, god I almost got you killed."

"But none of that—"

"And Emily." His words came out harshly, like they'd erupted from his throat. "He's got her. Right now and it's because of me. That connection, that joining we share with him? It's ten times stronger with us and tonight...tonight I completed it. I closed the circle, exactly what my grandmother was trying to prevent. That was my doing, don't you see? My selfishness, my weakness, but I can fix it."

Kate pounded on his chest, trying to stop his frightening words. "No, no Will! It's not true, you can't believe that, you can't possibly believe that, I won't let you!"

He pulled her toward his chest and she struggled against

him, but he was stronger and his arms held her tight. She sagged against him, listening to the steady rhythm of his heart and when he spoke, she heard his muffled voice through layers of clothing.

"It's not up to you to change the truth, Kate," he said. "Neither of us can do that, but we've been given this chance to help Emily and we have to take it." He gathered her closer, his hand running through her hair and a hundred kisses rained on her head...her face. "She's one of us, like us, you know that, don't you? And she needs us right now; she's counting on us to get her out of this. And then, later...she'll need your strength, your courage to see her through."

He pressed her against his chest and when he spoke again, his words were sad...so lost. "So when I tell you to run, you run hard and you run fast and you don't look back, do you hear me? Not ever. And you leave me to do what I can to correct my mistakes."

He held her for an unknown amount of time, as Kate let her mind go peacefully blank. Then, with wrenching deliberateness, she pulled away and stood at the other end of the window. He was gone from her now, out of her reach and she could think of nothing to bring him back.

She stood beside him, looking down at the dark street and found herself wondering why someone would have windows with no glass. They would have such a beautiful view, but it would be cold with no protection from the wind. So cold.

"When?" Her voice was gone and all that came out was a hoarse whisper.

"Sunrise," was Will's brisk reply. "We'll need the light and also...he'll be weaker then. I don't know why I know that, but, I don't know, it feels right."

She nodded and the motion hurt her neck. "Sunrise."

A blast of cold air rippled her clothes, but Kate didn't move. Maybe they had known what they were doing when they left the glass out. They could feel the world as it really was and not pretend to live a life of warmth, when in reality, a bitter wind blew outside.

She felt Will watching her, studying her with so much love and admiration. He moved to wrap his arms around her shoulders, but she shrunk away.

"Don't, please..." She shriveled into the corner, away from the comfort that was no longer hers to claim.

He nodded, returning to his spot to stare again at the street below.

* * * * *

Kate couldn't feel her face. The cold had started her nose running and when she swiped at it, she didn't feel her hand against her skin. She sat by the window with her arms wrapped around her knees and her chin resting on the frame. Her muscles ached from sitting, crouched on the unforgiving wooden floor for so long and a definite pounding shot up her back, but none of that bothered her much. There was no place else to sit, no place that wouldn't hurt just as much.

Will. He was somewhere...behind her. She heard him rustling around occasionally, pacing, sitting, and getting up to pace again. But his noise, his presence was only slightly affecting to her. He was slipping away. Slipping into that place where she lost so many others and though her mind heard his noises, her heart heard nothing.

And Kate...she was in a dark, frozen place, where the light never came and the silence was broken only by distant screams. Nothing...she felt nothing, not the pain, not the loneliness...only the cold. The creeping, stealthy cold that seeped, deep inside and turned everything it touched to ice.

Will was moving again. His steps came closer...closer, to stop behind her and then he was beside her, his breath on her neck, his hands on her shoulders.

"Come here," said Will's voice and Kate felt something break. It fell out from under her and now she was falling... falling into his arms, into the shelter and love they offered, they had always offered. She clung to him, tighter and tighter, proving to her unbelieving heart that he was here, he wouldn't leave, and he wouldn't let her go on without him. Not without Will...please, not without Will...

He pulled the coat to cover both of them and she settled against his chest. She heard his breathing in her ear and closed her eyes. Yes...this is how it would be, she and Will, holding each other, warming each other with a love that defied reason, that only strengthened in the years to come. She and Will, dancing forever to music too beautiful to be heard, and too powerful to ever be stopped. It would guide them, stay with them until the end of their days...the end of time.

A sudden gust of wind blew through the window and the candle Will had set beside them, flickered out. The wind continued into the room, rustling loose bits of paper and whistling through the cracks in the old walls.

Kate reached for the matches in her pocket, but Will laid his hand on hers.

"No," he said in a low voice. "It's okay."

She followed his gaze out the window and toward the mountain that stood above the town.

The darkened peaks stared down at them, three massive chunks of rock, with the tallest shaped like a fist. A red glow lit them from behind and spilled over the countryside to touch the tips of the evergreens that surrounded the town.

The candle wouldn't be needed. Sunrise had begun.

Will pulled her back onto his lap and used the coat again to warm their chilly bodies. She felt his heart thump faster against her back as they sat together, watching the sun emerge from behind the mountain. She searched for his hand, lost in the folds of the coat and held it, squeezed it and pressed it against her own heart, so he could feel them beat in the same rhythm.

He leaned his mouth close to her ear and his words shook with emotion. "And neither the angels in heaven above, nor the demons down under the sea, can ever dissever my soul from the soul of the beautiful Annabel Lee."

A glimmer of white poked through the ridge between the peaks and shot across the distance to bathe the roof of her uncle's store in gleaming sunlight. She looked down at her hand, enclosed in Will's and saw the gray, night–color of their skin begin to turn a richer pink. She closed her eyes against the harsh light and let Will's voice calm her drumming heart.

"For the moon never beams, without bringing me dreams of the beautiful Annabel Lee...and the stars never rise, but I feel the bright eyes of the beautiful Annabel Lee," he whispered, bringing her face to his.

His kiss was light on her mouth, skipping across her lips like waves on a shore. He cupped her face, blocking out the breaking dawn and enclosing them in a circle of darkness that knew no light, but the light they made together. Skin slid over skin from tears they both shed and somewhere...far, far in the darkness...she heard music.

The kiss ended, but their faces remained touching, seeking comfort in the warmth they created. Will intertwined his fingers with hers and she curled closer to him, desperate to lock his scent into her memory.

"I'll never leave you...."

Will's words lifted promise in her heart and she felt the ice give way to warm sunshine. She raised his hand to her lips and with Will's body, strong and sure against her back and the scent of him breathing through her mind, she opened her eyes to greet the rising sun.

Chapter Twenty–One
The Way of Things

She stood, with her head tilted down and her hands balled into fists at her sides. Two feet of snow covered her shoes, though Will knew that wasn't why she didn't move. She was waiting, gathering her flying thoughts and smoothing them into a deliberate order.

You can do this Katie, come on...

One by one, her fingers uncurled and slowly, an inch at a time, her head lifted. Will sat back on his haunches, feeling his heart press against his ribcage. The rising sun brushed the tip of her nose and cheekbones in brilliant color and washed over her dark hair like molten lava. The power, the beauty, everything he knew and loved and admired in her, shone like a blinding light on her face. Her delicate shoulders squared and now she opened her eyes. She was ready.

Will leaned around the decorative iron formations that hung above the sign of the Wood'n More and crawled further down. He crouched again, behind the two–foot high brick wall that lined the top of the building and brushed away the snow that blocked his view. That was better. He could see from the turn–off to Kerry County Road and all the way to where Main Street dead–ended at the courthouse. He looked down at Kate, who had begun to plow through the snow.

"Ben?"

Her voice rose up to him with eerie clarity. The aftermath of the storm had left a pocket of bitter cold hanging over the town. No wind blew and the silence that had descended was a stark contrast to the frenzy of last night. Will found himself missing the gales of snow that had disguised the ruin and destruction he saw below.

Fire had destroyed most of his town and anything still

standing was only crumbling ruins. Beside him, the roof of Chamberlains was gone and it looked like a bomb had gone off in the bank to the right. Bits of wall lay in the alley below, but its three–story structure still stood. He surveyed the damage, his gaze resting on one building after another and then he stopped on the school. It was still there. Its east wing was blackened by smoke, but the building was intact. Will shook his head and a tiny smile creased his mouth. Figures the only building left in town would be the school.

"Where are you Ben?"

Will turned back to the street and saw Kate pass below. She waded through the snow with determined speed and again, Will felt overwhelmed by her endless amount of strength. More strength than he could imagine, more than he had. And she didn't even know.

"I know you're here somewhere, Ben. Stop hiding and come on out." She shoved a garbage can aside and continued down the street. "I just want to talk to you, you wouldn't mind that, would you?"

She was teasing him, drawing him out and inviting him to play with her. Will shook his head at this newfound talent. She was quite the little actress.

"It's awful cold out here, Benny. Wish you'd come out so we could go get warm somewhere," she said, as she rounded the block and started back. "I'm really sorry about before, but you know how it is. I want to make it up to you."

She glanced up at him, frustrated. Just a quick look, so as not give away his hiding place. She continued past her uncle's store.

"Come on Ben, I said I was sorry, where are you?" She stopped at the alley, looking, but finding nothing. "This isn't very nice you know," she said, moving past the alley. "Here I am, of-fering an apology and you won't even come out so I can give it to you. That's just no way to treat—"

She stopped. Her body stiffened and he watched her take a

deep breath before turning. She walked back to her uncle's store and looked up at him, hesitating with one hand on the door. Their eyes met and Will shook his head vigorously.

No, don't Katie. Don't go in there, don't do it—

But she was, with a little shrug of her shoulders and a raise of one eyebrow, she was gone...swallowed up by the darkness inside.

"Shit." He leaned over the wall and tried to peer into the broken window, but saw nothing. "Shit, shit," he muttered, jumping to his feet. He took two running steps toward the door that led back down to the second floor before he stopped.

Lordon stood in the doorway.

The fiery sunrise lit across his hair and shoulders, but didn't touch his face...his ghastly pale face, that was smiling at Will.

Walking out on the roof, he gave a tug on the rope he held and something came thumping up the stairs, onto the roof. That's when Will saw her.

Little Emily lay at the end of the rope. Snow covered her blonde hair, was caked in her coat and her stockings were full of holes, as if she had been dragged miles and miles across the countryside. The rope was wound around her wrists and had cut off the circulation Will saw, because her tiny balled hands had turned a dusty blue. But her face was pale. So pale...and so still.

Will retraced his two steps, not feeling himself move, not knowing he did. Only one thought remained in his brain now. "Kaaaaaate!" He shouted, turning toward the wall. "Ka—"

The word was ripped from his mouth as a weight landed across his back. It felt like a sack of potatoes, but potatoes wouldn't be this hot...this excruciatingly hot and jagged against his back. It crushed his lungs, squeezing out all his air and just before he fell, he caught of glimpse of Lordon standing behind him.

He was laughing.

* * * * *

"Kitty cat…"

She stopped as the voice drifted by and felt her stomach tighten with panic.

No…I'm in control here, just breathe…breathe…

Turning, she backtracked toward the store and stopped at the door. She looked up at Will, watching her from the roof across the street and saw his wide eyes, saw him shaking his head frantically at her.

"Here kitty–kitty…"

One shot. We've got one shot at this.

She yanked on the door and stepped inside.

The smell was incredible. It shot through her nose, creating a terrible pain between her eyes and choking her like the water from the creek used to, before Joey taught her how to swim. She took another step and her foot flew out from under her and she landed on her back. A gunshot ripped through the air and Kate lay on the floor hearing it echo in her ears and spread through her body. Waves of agony radiated from her spine, to her head, down to her feet.

Slowly, so slowly with each move accompanied by a mind–numbing streak of pain, she sat up and looked down at herself.

No, not shot…no blood…no hole. She stared at her glistening palm and turned, hearing the creaks in her neck. A popped balloon lay in a puddle of liquid where her head had landed. The liquid covered the floor, dripped from the walls and ceiling…and finally, her overloaded senses kicked into gear.

Gas. Oh god, it's gasol—

"There you are."

Ben stood by the register, still wearing his bloody parka and combat boots. Three red containers sat on the counter beside him. Kate recognized them from the shed. Backups for the long mountain winters. More of the containers were thrown haphazardly by the door, some with gas still spilling out of their nozzles.

"Thought maybe you weren't coming," he said with a smile.

It made his black eyes shine like two pools of oil.

Kate leaned forward on her hands and pushed herself up. The pain intensified, blurring her vision and she staggered back several steps. Catching herself on the overturned display rack, Kate forced her mind to stay focused on Ben. "Why wouldn't I come?"

"Oh, I don't know *Kate*." Her name spit from his mouth with obvious hatred. "Maybe because ever since we were kids you've been jerking me around. You were always there, in my face, walking around here like you were better than me. Did you think I didn't know Kate? Did you really think I didn't know what you and your skank whore sister called me behind my back?"

Any time would be great Will, any old time now...

She smoothed her wet hair in what she hoped was sheepish guilt. "Come on, Ben. We were all kids back then and that was a long, long time ago." Willing her feet to move, she walked toward him, each step bringing her closer to the wild sheen in his eyes. "Everybody grows up and we did too," she said quietly. "Why don't you give me a chance to prove it to you, show you that I've changed. You can't tell me you haven't done things you're ashamed of. We all have."

Ben picked up a gas can and banged it on the counter, twice, three times and then threw it into the others, like a bowling ball, knocking them all to the floor. "And here I thought you'd only come back for this," he said, shoving his hand into his parka. He drew out the book and held it up to Kate, bobbing it over her head. "But you came to make friends. That's good, friends are good, they come in handy sometimes, huh?"

"Yeah," Kate agreed, transfixed by the book he swung around in his hand. "Friends are good and we can be friends Ben, you and me. I want that, I really do."

"You do? Well I can't tell you how warm and fuzzy I feel right now," he said and threw the book in the air. He caught it with his other hand. "You don't even want this thing do you. Do you!"

"No I—"

"What? I can't hear you Kate. Did you say you didn't want this?"

"I just thought we—"

"Good," he shouted above her. "Then you won't mind if I get rid of it, so we can get down to being friends."

He reached into his pocket again and pulled out a book of matches. 'Top of the Day from Newclare, PA' was written in florescent green lettering across the lid. "That okay with you Kate? Would that make you happy *Kate*?"

Kate fixed her gaze on the tiny box he twirled in his hand. In, over, under, flip...faster and faster he wove the box between his fingers and she couldn't look away.

Will! Will where are you?

"You don't want to do that Ben," she said, inching toward the door. Her foot slipped on the wet floor and she grabbed the counter, but her hands slid in the slimy lake of gasoline that had collected on the warped counter. God...it was everywhere, on everything...

"No? Why not?"

In, over, under, flip.

"I mean, that is why you came here, to make friends? It has to be."

He switched directions and the box wove an opposite pattern. Under, over, in, flip.

"It has to be. Unless...unless you were a *lying, teasing whore*."

"No...that's not true Ben, I'm not lying, I'm not," she whispered.

The path of the box came to an abrupt stop and Ben slammed it on the counter. A little wave of gasoline rippled across to Kate's hand. She snatched it away with a screech.

"You're not lying?" He slid the box open and he pulled out a wooden match. "Then where are you going Kate?" His fingers were shaking and the box slid across the counter as he tried to light it. He tucked the book under his arm and grabbed the matches.

Run you fool! Run, run!

But Kate couldn't move. Panic froze her limbs and all she could do was stare at the end of the match as Ben struck it across the side. He hit it too hard and the wood bent in half. He threw it down with a grunt.

"Huh? Where're you going in such a hurry?" Another match came out of the box and this time he was more careful. It lit with the sound of a hissing snake. He held it up and the flame danced in front of his face...was mirrored in the shiny blackness of his eyes. "Where...the fuck are you *going!*"

"Ben please..." Her voice came from a distant region of her mind. "Please..."

"I don't think you came here to make friends, *Kate*," he said, spitting out her name again and now he was moving, walking toward her.

Run, run, run!

The flame was close enough that Kate could feel its heat on her face. It flickered and jumped on the end of the stick, growing bigger...brighter as Kate watched.

"No." Ben's voice was loud and it echoed between Kate's ears. "I don't think you came to make friends at all..."

Finally and with dream–like slowness, Kate turned and ran. She slipped in the gas, but kept going, plowing into the display rack and landing on her side. She sprang to her feet and made a dash for the door.

Ben roared. She heard him take two thundering steps and caught a glimpse of him from the corner of her eye. Red faced, mouth open, arm raised with match in hand. She skidded to a stop and her rear landed with a thump in a puddle.

Wrong way! Wrong way!

Her feet kicked wildly as she made the turn, her hands sloshing in the gas and her wet hair slapping against her face. She scrambled to her feet and bolted toward a surprised Ben.

The match was already out of his hand and flying like a missile toward its target. It whizzed by her head, as she skidded around the corner and dove for the dry floor behind the aisle.

Whoosh!

The force rocked the store and blew over the shelving where she hid. It landed, propped against the wall and Kate lay with her hands over her head in the tiny space between.

She looked up, choking on the smoke and trying to see through the brilliant haze of light. A rushing noise came from the other side of her hiding place, faster and faster it came, in a hungry, frenzied hurry. Kate wiggled on her belly to the end of the aisle and poked out her head.

A wall of fire consumed the front half of the store and it was coming, racing down the trail of gasoline that stopped by the end cap of her aisle.

Up on her feet again and screaming through the store, Kate ran for the kitchen, tripped on an overturned chair and landed on her face. She rolled over and looked up at Ben.

He stood in the doorway, the left side of his face, a melting mess of flesh and blood and the hair around his ear smoking in little curls that drifted toward the burning ceiling. He still held the book in a fist.

"You lying bitch!" He screamed and the book exploded into the side of Kate's head. Blinding lights burst like fireworks before her eyes, but she found she didn't need any vision at all, as she kicked out with her foot, catching him in the shin. He let out another roar and crashed down on top of her.

"Get off me!" She screamed, kicking and bucking, but he remained, one knee on either side of her body. White panic flashed through her mind and she brought her knees up as hard as she could. He jerked and she missed.

"*Get! Off!*" She screamed again and lunged up at him, aiming her fingernails for his face. Pieces of burned skin came off under her nails and she reached up again to dig her fingers into his eyes.

He shoved her back to the floor and slammed his hand against her throat, pinching off her windpipe, like he had pinched off a hose. Thick fingers squeezed around her neck and she heard his distant ravings through a rising sea of blackness.

"Gonna blow your house down!" Were the crazy words that reached Kate's ears. "Gonna huff and I'm gonna puff and I'm gonna blow your fuckin' house down! You goddamned lyin' bitch!"

His ugly face swerved out of focus and she felt herself begin to sink. Farther and farther away she sunk, away from the smoke, the heat, the maniac spouting nursery rhymes at her. With the last of her strength, she raised one knee and brought it straight up.

This time she didn't miss.

Ben released her neck with a tiny gasp and fell off and onto the floor. Kate rolled away, choking and barking like a seal. The kitchen came back into view with a bang, as the blood rushed into her head and she sat up.

The fire had passed with lightening speed over the gas and was now working on the wooden paneled walls and ceiling. The concrete floor where Kate sat in her squishy jeans felt hot.

Out. Out now, thank you...

She pulled herself up with the overturned chair and stumbled toward the backdoor. Ben rolled back and forth on the floor, a litany of curses flying from his mouth and Kate made a wide circle around him. Bumping something with her foot, Kate stopped. She picked up the book and shoved it triumphantly in her pocket, resisting the urge to kick the squirming Ben.

The door was lost in smoke that thickened by the second, so she felt around, her hands skipping over the small window at the top and then down, down. She found the doorknob and yanked.

Nothing.

She collapsed in a fit of coughs, doubled over and held her stomach, until they passed. The lock. She had to unlock it first.

Spinning the lock so it laid horizontally, she yanked again.

Still nothing.

"Damn it, come on!" Kate jiggled the knob, shaking it harder and harder and then brought her fist down on it. Over and over again, until the doorknob fell off and clattered to the floor. It bounced off her foot, but Kate felt no pain. Slipping her fingers through the hole, she pulled with all her might, gaining leverage with her foot against the wall, but the door didn't budge.

It's jammed Kate.

That was Will's voice, but Kate didn't question. She dropped to her knees and felt with her hands. A broken piece of board was jammed through the small space at the bottom of the door and Kate grabbed it. Wiggling it back and forth it started to come out when she heard Ben scuffle to his feet and she turned.

Ben's hulking figure emerged from the smoke.

"Here kitty," he croaked, stumbling toward her. "Here kitty–kitty…"

He couldn't see through the smoke where Kate crouched on the floor, so she crawled past him, coming within inches of his boots and then got to her feet and ran.

The window above the sink wasn't locked. She slid it all the way open and was climbing onto the counter when Ben barreled toward her. Using his fist like a hammer, he aimed at Kate, but she dodged away. The vase of dried flowers in the windowsill shattered, as she jumped down and ran around the table where Uncle Dave lay. Ben followed.

"Don't run kitty," he said in his frog voice. He cornered her on the other side.

She lunged to the right, but Ben saw her fake and almost caught her on the left. Out in the store, part of the ceiling caved in and sparkling ashes blew through the doorway. A handful fell on Uncle Dave, who lay, drenched in gasoline. He lit immediately and Kate ducked, but Ben didn't seem to notice.

"Kitty–kitty–kitty," Ben said again. "Don't run little kitty, 'cause I'm only gonna catch you."

Kate looked down at her flaming uncle, up at the fire that was fast approaching the kitchen and then finally...back at Ben.

"No," she said, giving him a hard smile that penetrated the blackness in his eyes. "You never could catch me Ben."

Bringing her foot up, she shoved the table and it teetered on two legs, before the weight of Uncle Dave's body shifted and it crashed to the floor, bringing Ben down with it. He screamed from under her uncle's body and then his face was gone in the flames. They raced over his head, gobbling up the last of his hair and then leaped down his coat, melting the fabric to his skin. Ben scrambled to his feet and stood, amazingly enough, for now there wasn't much *to* Ben, just fire and burning clothes. Like a roasted marshmallow gone wrong, he stumbled around the room, beating at himself and wailing through the flames.

Kate tore her eyes from this spectacular sight and raced again for the door. Ben saw her movement and stomped, on two burning legs after her, yelling and waving his flaming arms, a machine set on automatic. Kate screamed, jumping up the stairs with Ben only inches away and her hair...god her hair was on fire, it crackled in her ears and the heat sizzled against her neck. She smacked the back of her head as she ran up the stairs and slammed the door behind her.

Is it out! Is it out!

She couldn't tell, but kept bashing herself in the head and holding the door. The thumping came up the stairs and banged against the door, just once and then thumped back down the stairs, this time faster and more confused. It ended with a loud thump at the bottom.

Kate leaned against the door, catching her breath and smelling the awful stench of her burned hair. It lay over her head like bits of charred twigs and still smoked profusely. Stronger and stronger the smell became until Kate let out a little shriek and jumped away, slamming into the wall.

The door was hot. The fire had taken over the kitchen and was now blazing its destructive path up the stairwell. The smoke wasn't from her hair; it was seeping through the cracks around the door.

Think, goddamn it Kate, think!

But her mind was cringing in a small, dark hidey–hole, screaming back. *Fire! Fire! It's going to get us, it's going to eat us all up Joey, what are we going to do! It's going to eat us just like Daddy, oh just like Daddy—*

The attic.

Will's voice again, but she heard it loud and clear through the jumbled mess of her thoughts. She ran down the hall, jumped with both feet and caught the rope that hung from the ceiling, pulling the trapdoor down.

After climbing into the attic, she turned and pulled the stairs up, cutting off the steady stream of smoke that rose through the hole.

The attic wasn't much more than a crawlspace and as Kate looked around, she realized that Uncle Dave had been quite the packrat. A table stood on end beside her, its broken leg bent in a waving position and dozens of wicker baskets were balanced on top. She recognized the baskets as those that the apples came delivered in every year and it looked as though Uncle Dave had been collecting them since he opened the store. More wicker sat on the other side of the trapdoor and all around her were stacks of magazines, newspapers and boxes. Boxes piled atop boxes, piled atop boxes, all filled with personal records, receipts and accounts for the store.

She took in this dizzying array of flammable objects and began to dig her way through the mess toward the dormer window on the far side of the room...toward the only window in the house that would lead out and around to the roof.

The window was stuck and didn't want to move after years of staying closed. Kate found a metal rod from some shelving in one of the boxes and used it to pry the window open. Tossing the rod aside, she crawled, feet first out to the roof, stepping carefully on the four–inch ledge that surrounded the dormer.

The cold hit her immediately, chilling her fingers and making it difficult to get a firm grasp on the framing. The wind had picked up again, rushing and crackling in her ears and blowing her off balance. She took a step back, feeling with her foot down the slopping roof for secure footing. Ice and snow gave way beneath her and she gripped the framing tighter. Just a little farther…she let out her arms and lay against the roof, her toes reaching for the level roofing around the second floor. Just…a little…farther…

"Kate! Watch out!"

Now that *was* Will's voice and when Kate turned, she lost her hold on the frame and began to slide down on her belly. Screaming, she clawed at the siding, digging her fingernails into the wood until her feet landed on level roof. Letting out a frustrated sigh, she turned…and screamed again.

What was left of Uncle Dave's bedroom, burned in white–hot flames below her. The roof had caved in, dampening some of the fire under the debris, but the room was already destroyed. The floor had fallen into the store below and she saw through the leaping flames, Uncle Dave's mattress lying on its side against the counter in the store. Other pieces of furniture lay scattered among the wreckage, burned beyond recognition. The fire was strongest on the street side and as Kate watched, a chunk of wall broke from the far corner and the fire was now free to spill into the sidewalk.

The wind shifted, blowing the intense heat toward Kate, but it was the smoke…the smoke that rammed down her throat, choking and gagging her. The roof, the fire, everything around Kate vanished in the blinding smoke and she turned away, covering her nose and mouth and holding her breath. The crackling of the fire rose up higher and higher behind her and her head began to pound, but still, she held off the poisonous fumes.

And then, like the wave of a hand, the wind shifted. Cold air rushed past Kate and she took a gasping breath.

"'Tis good that you could join us, Katie."

The voice cut through the deafening roar of the fire and the rushing wind to reach Kate with its smug satisfaction.

She turned; dropping her hands and again, faced the burning pit of fire below. Her gaze lifted, up, up to the street and as the wind gusted once more, she had a clear view of the building across from where she stood.

Lordon stood in a puddle of melted snow on the roof of the Wood'n More shop. He took a few steps to bring him closer to the wall around the roof, his boots creating small tidal waves that flowed over something he pulled along. She couldn't distinguish the lumpy shape that lay so still behind him, but had a fair idea of what it was.

And Will...where's Will?

Her frantic gaze skipped over the roof and then she saw him, huddled in a little pile against the wall, his face pale and drawn with pain. A trickle of blood ran from his ear and his face was a mess of cuts and scraps. But his eyes. They were on Kate and through the horror that surrounded him, she saw relief in those eyes...relief that she was okay and Kate felt her heart burst with love.

A crash from below made her scream and jump back. The far wall of the bedroom was gone, in a crumbling pile of fire and ash. Hungry for more, the fire crept closer to where Kate stood.

"Quite a shame that you've brought us to this, Katie," Lordon shouted above the wind and fire.

Kate stepped away from the deteriorating roof and edged toward the side of the building, by the alley. Her face burned with heat, yet her back shivered in a biting wind and she continued to move away from the pit until the heat lessened. There were several feet of untouched roof on this end and Kate was able to stand without gripping the sloping part of the roof.

"You have something of mine," Lordon was saying, but Kate ignored him, while she studied the side of the building. Smoke rose from behind it, telling her that the porch had caught fire and she grimaced. Only way to go was up now—

"Kaitlin!"

Lordon's voice shot across the street and it had lost all semblance of the earlier smugness. Kate heard his frustration and fought back a smile.

"The book," he shouted. "Return it now!"

Kate reached into her back pocket and drew out the book. It felt small and unimportant in her hands and she flipped through it, her eyes scanning the nonsense within its pages. All this trouble for what looked like a bunch of rambling junk. She glanced back at Lordon.

He was watching with eyes that couldn't hide their eagerness. It was Christmas morning in demon world.

Kate closed the book with a snap and was pleased to see him jump. "Let them go," she shouted back. "If you want your stupid book, then let them both go."

Lordon quickly recovered from having at last seen his book. "Toss it over the side," he said, gesturing toward the snow–covered alley. "Do it now or you will suffer my child, I promise you that. You will suffer beyond your scope of imagination and so will they." Raising an eyebrow he nodded toward Will and Emily. "You need only toss it over the side and we'll all go in peace."

Will was getting to his feet. Slowly and dragging his right side as if he had a stroke, he finally stood, leaning heavily on the wall. He looked up at Kate.

He's a liar Kate. We both know it and that won't change after you give him the book. A liar and a thief, but underneath it all...he's a coward. You know what you have to do.

Kate kept her eyes on Will, saw his small nod, saw the tiniest smile turn his lips. She looked back at Lordon.

"You want the book?" She asked, holding it up and was that...yes...fear, shone on Lordon's face, bright and shaking and oh so delightfully *human*. She held the book higher, giving him a clear view. "You want it? Then you can have it."

And with a smile she felt all the way down to her toes...she tossed the book.

It fluttered in the cold air, spinning as it rose toward the sky and then came to a split–second stop and made its descent into the fire. It landed on its spine in the burning rubble by the sidewalk. The book fell open and Kate saw the fire swarm over the pages, turning them into little bits of ash that soon were lost with the rest.

She looked away from the burning book and back at Lordon. He watched her as well.

And the fear was gone from his face.

"You'll regret that little Katie," he said with a voice that had no need to shout. "Yes...you'll regret that foolish act very much indeed."

Kate froze, the smile dying from her face. She had known, yes she had, but to see it, to have it finally happen, was too much to bear. And as she watched the anger on Lordon's face give way to boiling rage, Kate hovered in a safe place, high above, cringing from the monster who had begun to lift his hand.

The heat changed in consistency and she knew immediately that it came, not from the pit of fire below, but from the demon across the street. She could touch it now, if she cared to, weave her fingers between it like dense fog...fog that steamed with a smothering, deadly heat. It seeped into her lungs, choking her worse than the smoke and it lit another fire, one that would burn her from the inside out. She felt it bubbling in her stomach, her lungs, her throat and the pain...the scorching pain was racing through her body...tearing through her body...ripping out her insides and chewing them up with fiery little teeth. She hovered, looking down on herself, watching herself stumble back, knowing there was no escape, no escape from an evil that could reach across time and reason and destroy from the soul out.

And that's when she saw him, from that high up place. Her love, her life...running, through the pain that crippled his body, through the tears that blinded his eyes. Tears for her...running for her...saving her, one last time. Only one word came from his mouth.

"Kaaaaaaate!"

Lordon never saw Will coming, so intent was he on destroying Kate. His eyes blazed with hate and his hand was nearly level with his shoulder when Will hit him, running full force, throwing them to the ground.

Instantly, the heat left Kate's body and she fell into the roof, grabbing hold of a loose board to keep from slipping off. She regained her balance quickly and ran to the edge of the pit.

"Will! No!"

But her screams didn't reach Will as he wrestled with Lordon. The men rolled over the cement roof splashing in the melted snow, a flurry of black trench coat and flying fists. But Will was no match for Lordon and within seconds, Lordon threw him off.

Will skidded to a stop, shook his head and turned, slowly, trying to find Lordon. He spotted him, still crouched on all fours and Will sprang again, but this time Lordon was ready for him.

His hand shot out, knuckles curled, body shaking. Will was able to run one more step before he was stopped, his head flying back as if he had been hit by an invisible wall and he started to fall to the ground, as Lordon thrust his other hand toward him. Will was picked up and thrown backward. His heels scraped against the cement, bouncing on the small rocks and litter until they hit the wall surrounding the roof and went flying up to his waist. Up, up, he was thrown, across the tiny alley and against the third floor wall of the McInerey Bank of Newclare. His body smashed into the brick and Kate saw his face relax and his eyes close...mercifully close, before Lordon dropped his hands and Will slid down the length of the three story building to land with a small thump in the alley below.

Kate watched this with no breath in her lungs. No feeling in her body. No thought in her head. That was Will, lying in a tangled heap beside the garbage can. That was Will's shoe that poked through the snow and pointed up at the sky. Will's hand that dangled so uselessly. Her Will...her Will...

"No..."

what I can to correct my mistakes...
"—no, no..."
The wind blew snow over his dangling hand, snow that would cover him soon, encasing him in a blanket of cold.
"—please...no...Will..."
my sweet, sweet Annabel Lee, sweet Annabel...
"Will..."
for the moon never beams...never beams...
"Will!"
Her scream shattered the air, rising above the wind, above the fire to lift to the mountains with breaking sorrow. On and on she screamed until her throat was raw and her jaw ached and still she screamed, feeling over and over again the ripping in her chest, the pounding in her head. Still she screamed.
And then she stopped. And the air rushed back in to fill the places her scream had been. But nothing...nothing filled her heart, her beaten and broken heart. Darkness, thick and still surrounded her and Kate snuggled inside, shutting doors, one by one, jumping each time one slammed, until it was all done. All closed. Now she could sit and wait. Wait for the end that would take her and then it would be over...finally over.

* * * * *

Far, far in the distance...a voice. A small, weak voice that called, pleaded for her to come back...please...come back...
"Kaitlin..."
Kate opened her eyes and saw that she was lying, huddled on the roof, her head dangerously close to the gaping hole that was the roof before her. She lifted her head, careful to avoid the alley and looked across the street. Looked at the roof across the street. Looked at Lordon. And looked again at Lordon.
He had changed and for a moment Kate thought she was only imagining his figure still there. But he was there...only changed. Or, more accurately...something had changed him.

374

Kate got to her feet, ignoring the pounding in her head and keeping her eyes on Lordon. A piece of roofing collapsed beneath her feet and she jumped back, only slightly understanding that the roof was almost gone now. Fire had at last conquered the building, only the central support frames still stood and those would be gone soon too.

But Kate saw only the other roof, the one that held Lordon. The one that she could see...*through* him. The one that was entirely visible through his body and as Kate took in this incredible sight, she realized...Lordon did as well.

Lordon still crouched on his knees on the roof, his hands out in front of him now as he inspected their newfound lack of substance. He turned them over, as if to see something different on his palms and them turned them again, shaking his head in disbelief. And when he turned toward Kate, she saw something else. Something that went beyond the shaking fear from before, this was deeper, ingrained in his soul and stamped across his forehead.

Kate groped for the amulet, buried beneath her sweater. Pulling it out, she held it between her hands, running her fingers over the jagged metal. It was cold to her touch. It was dead weight in her palm.

You have something I need...

It had been broken. The link, the connection, Kate no longer felt his presence in her mind and for the first time since the nursing home, she saw him for what he was. Pale, weak and needing. He had been feeding off of them, she and Will and now, his supply had been cut off. In a fit of childish rage, he bit the hand that fed him and now he was defenseless...and desperate.

The desperation was unmistakable in his shaking hands and his roving eyes...eyes that didn't glitter half as brightly as before. He was searching...searching like a wild, hungry dog for something that would replace what he had lost, anything that would give him back the power for which he so craved. And when he found it, he stopped shaking.

Kate stepped forward, her heart picking up where it left off and slamming against her chest. "Emily! Emily no—"

The roof gave again and this time Kate went with it. She fell into the hole, reaching at the last second for the wooden siding. She grabbed hold and pulled herself up, coughing on the sudden gust of wind that blew smoke up from the store. Crawling on her hands and knees, her sneakers slipping on the wet siding, she climbed up on the overhanging roof of the window. Another deafening crash brought the rest of the roof into the fiery pit and Kate could only stand on the window and watch.

The wind shifted again, clearing her view. Lordon held Emily between his big hands, pointing her still face up at his. His lips were draw back with effort and she saw his thumbs cutting into her plump cheeks. And then she saw the colors. The colors that shot from his eyes toward hers and all at once, Emily awakened. She stared into the face of a demon from hell and she opened her mouth to scream, but no sound came out. Her feet kicked furiously and her fists beat him at his head and shoulders, but none of this penetrated Lordon's focus. The colors spun faster and faster in his eyes and then...Emily's colors began to spin.

"No!"

Kate used all the air in her smoke–filled lungs and it worked. Lordon broke away, just for an instant, but long enough to see Kate, standing on the window...long enough to understand what was going to happen.

Ripping the rope from her neck, she held the amulet in her fist, one last time. She opened her fingers and let it slip from her grasp. The necklace plummeted to the ground, where the fire would swallow it as it had everything else.

Kate turned her eyes to the heavens, arms out, feet together. The day had dawned crisp and clear and from the top of the attic, Kate could see the entire town. Brilliant blue sky surrounded the mountains and she saw the tail end of the storm disappearing over the horizon. And in the distance she heard sirens, frantic noises of reality racing up the mountain, but they would be too late. Too late.

She looked back at Lordon. He still watched her, a stricken man faced with the end of his own existence.

For Emily...

She raised her arms.

For Joey...

Her feet lifted her up and she felt herself begin to sway off balance.

For Will...

And then she was flying.

Epilogue

The scent of honeysuckle was fading, though it remained in her mind, a memory that needed only to be stumbled upon again. It was tucked away in its secret place now, as were so many other memories. Memories of laughter, of days spent running through the trees with only the wind to hold her back, but also of tears, shared in the comforting arms of another. All locked in a place that would be protected and cherished over the years and never, ever forgotten.

She turned toward Emily, the question still hanging between them and found she could not answer. Not here. Not at this place with so much death lying beneath their feet. But she couldn't leave. Not yet. There was something she needed to do, something she had waited weeks to do and finally...she was ready.

"Let's go," she said, taking Emily's hand.

Emily lowered her head and followed Kate through the cemetery, not looking at the gravestones, not wanting to see the names of people she too remembered. Kate led them in a wide circle toward the little hill by the creek. Emily's people were buried close by and Kate knew the girl wasn't ready to see those names yet.

Mrs. Whitmore had been found a week after the snow melted. In her madness, she'd wandered into the forest to get lost and eventually freeze to death. It was the fate of many Newclare residents, those that hadn't died in the fires and violence. Body upon body were found just lying on the ground, some as if they had simply fallen asleep in the snow, but others...

Again, the town was strangely quiet about the loss of so many of their own, but Kate had seen the trucks. The flatbeds that rolled through the streets with brown tarps thrown haphazardly over the back, but more than anything it was the faces of the men who volunteered to search the forest, that told her how it had been. Blank, defeated faces, that wanted only to forget.

Emily tripped over a twig, hidden in the grass and Kate helped her up, feeling the child's ribs through her dress. Emily had taken a long, long while to come back to her. She spent those first few weeks, not eating, not talking, not doing anything, but staring out the window and shaking. Trapped in a place where Kate couldn't reach her, Emily fought battles waged in her mind, in her dreams, torn between two worlds and edging away from Kate with each passing day. Then, on a night when the summer rain had pounded against the window, Kate woke to find Emily crying by her bed. Her tears were those of a child, waking from a long nightmare and Kate had gathered the little girl in her arms. By morning it seemed Emily had made her decision, but still she lingered, ever hesitant to embrace a life that had been so cruel.

The hill was close now and Kate's steps slowed. She would be changed when she came away from this place and part of her wanted to hold onto the blissful ignorance that had shielded until now. But it was time to move on, she knew that, time enough of holding onto something that had been gone for so long. And she would move on from here.

A white fence, no higher than her knee, surrounded the plot in a little square that separated it from the rest of the cemetery. Its stone rose out of the ground from a base of colorful flowers. Flowers it looked to Kate; that was placed here daily. Such careful maintenance which tried so hard to bring the illusion of beauty, but failed to do anything but bring attention to the fact that this was the last efforts of a family taking care of its own. The only way they could take care of him now.

Leaving Emily to pick at the dandelions in the grass, Kate entered the plot and stood at the foot of the grave, staring at the stone. She read the words, repeated them in her mind and forced them to connect with her heart. But they wouldn't. No matter how many times she tried, her heart rejected what her eyes told her.

Dark Legacy

William Dean Harrickson
Forever in Our Hearts

Kate glared at the blinding sun and wished the clouds she saw gathering at the peaks would hurry up and do their business. It should be storming. It should be blowing sleet and hail and be so cold, so incredibly cold, that she could shrivel up and die. Sunlight didn't belong here. Not here where only pain and bitterness resided.

She stood at the foot of the grave and felt the wind, cold against her heart...felt the skies darken and felt the pounding that would crush her eventually. Years and years stretched out in front of her, empty years, lonely years...no warmth to light her days, no laughter to guide her step... Where was there to go from here?

Sobbing, she fell to her knees and leaned her head against the cold stone. There was no place to go; nowhere she could go to escape the silence in her heart. With Will went her dreams, her hopes and now she was in limbo, just as lost as Emily and forever waiting for something that would never come.

And quietly, deep in the silence that surrounded her heart, came a voice. One she knew well and just as in the store on that day when the world was burning down around her, she heard it...and it guided her way.

It is worth looking for Katie; even a whole lifetime spent searching. And when you find it, you don't let go, not for anything...

She wiped the tears from her eyes and when she could see again, reached out to touch the chiseled words. She had come to say goodbye, but Will wasn't here. He was with her, as he always would be.

Rising slowly, she turned to leave, but at the fence she stopped. She looked up at the open sky and felt the warmth heat her skin.

I'll spend my life looking back, Will. But only to keep you close...only to keep you close...

The wind rose, rustling the newly sprouted leaves of the oak that watched from above and causing an outcry from its many feathered residents. Kate sighed, letting the breeze wash over her face. The clouds hadn't advanced from their position over the peaks but remained, nonetheless. That's how it was in the mountains, a steady darkness on the horizon, but if you were lucky, there would always be a strong wind to blow the worst of the storm away.

Giggling reached her ears, loud and free and Kate took a moment recognize its tinkling notes. Then, with a smile that stemmed from the contagious nature of the giggles, she turned.

The patch of dandelions had been whipped into a blizzard of fluffy white and dancing in the middle of the storm, was Emily. Dancing and giggling and spinning so fast her dress ballooned into a parasol around her legs. The seeds danced with her, twirling around in one direction, only to come soaring down to layer the ground with their cotton and then rush back up again to spin into the little girl's hair. Emily giggled louder to feel their tickle against her skin and Kate felt her eyes sting as she watched.

The wind shifted, blowing the storm away from the cemetery and Emily followed, skipping down the path and calling over her shoulder. "Come on Kaitlin."

Kate joined her by the bank of the creek, grasping Emily's small hand in hers and together, they watched the dandelion seeds dance across the water.

Lightning Source UK Ltd.
Milton Keynes UK
UKOW04f0917050615

252956UK00001B/60/P